Praise for *Midnight Rain*

"Chilling."
  —Lisa Jackson, *New York Times* bestselling author of
  The Morning After

"*Midnight Rain* is an engrossing read. It's every woman's dream—and every woman's nightmare."
  —Linda Howard, *New York Times* bestselling author of
  Kiss Me While I Sleep

midnight rain

Holly Lisle

AN ONYX BOOK

ONYX
Published by New American Library, a division of
Penguin Group (USA) Inc., 375 Hudson Street,
New York, New York 10014, USA
Penguin Group (Canada), 10 Alcorn Avenue, Toronto,
Ontario M4V 3B2, Canada (a division of Pearson Penguin Canada Inc.)
Penguin Books Ltd., 80 Strand, London WC2R 0RL, England
Penguin Ireland, 25 St. Stephen's Green, Dublin 2,
Ireland (a division of Penguin Books Ltd.)
Penguin Group (Australia), 250 Camberwell Road, Camberwell, Victoria 3124,
Australia (a division of Pearson Australia Group Pty. Ltd.)
Penguin Books India Pvt. Ltd., 11 Community Centre, Panchsheel Park,
New Delhi - 110 017, India
Penguin Group (NZ), Cnr Airborne and Rosedale Roads, Albany,
Auckland 1310, New Zealand (a division of Pearson New Zealand Ltd.)
Penguin Books (South Africa) (Pty.) Ltd., 24 Sturdee Avenue,
Rosebank, Johannesburg 2196, South Africa

Penguin Books Ltd., Registered Offices:
London WC2R 0RL, England

First published by Onyx, an imprint of New American Library,
a division of Penguin Group (USA) Inc.

First Printing, November 2004
10 9 8 7 6 5 4 3 2 1

Copyright © Holly Lisle, 2004
All rights reserved

PUBLISHER'S NOTE
This is a work of fiction. Names, characters, places, and incidents either are the
product of the author's imagination or are used fictitiously, and any resemblance to
actual persons, living or dead, business establishments, events, or locales is entirely
coincidental.

For Matthew

ACKNOWLEDGMENTS

Phoebe Rain and her story first woke me from a sound sleep in 1993, and I have been trying to get her on paper ever since. My deepest thanks to the folks without whom she would not be here yet:

Matthew, who kept believing in Phoebe—and in me— even when I lost faith, and who gave me the courage to hang in

Kerri Walters, who taught me to read tarot back in 1987

Sheila Kelly, who has cheered me on, thumped me soundly, and offered brilliant suggestions through the last four years of working on this

Kay House and Laura Kinsale, who dug into the first draft and came up with cogent commentary on what fit and what didn't, and why

Robin Rue, my amazing agent, who believed in the book and went to bat for it and won me the chance to make it everything it could be

David Highfill, for looking twice

Claire Zion and David Highfill, for helping me tunnel down and find the real story, and to both for an amazing willingness to keep fighting through a whole lot of layers to get there

Sheila Kelly, Rebecca Deaton, Jean Schara, Jim Woosley, and NymphDuPave, for the last-minute panic-crit

Billy W. Selph, owner of South Georgia Investigations, for technical assistance regarding wiretapping and telephone spy-tech (any mistakes that remain are mine)

And to Claire for winning Phoebe Rain her home at last

Thank you.

chapter 1

Phoebe Rain sat with her back to the bar that divided the kitchen from the dining room, watching the first traces of pink creeping across the Florida sky. She shuffled the tarot cards on the table in front of her and shifted on the kitchen chair. Her right knee was hurting again, but she didn't dare get up to stretch. Her call volume had been steady all night—she knew that as soon as she moved away from the table the phone would ring. Out west, where it was still dark and the insomniacs were pacing the floor, people were still looking for psychic comfort to get them through the night.

She smiled sadly at that. Sometimes she wished she, too, could have a little companionship, a little comfort, in the lonely hours before dawn. But she wouldn't consider paying Psychic Sisters Network prices for it.

So she straightened her right leg the way the physical therapist had taught her, concentrating on contracting the muscles as hard as she could, then relaxing them completely. Fire lanced out from the joint as she forced it to do what she wanted, burning down into the calf muscle and up into the thigh. She tightened the muscles again, gritting her teeth against the pain, and when it became too intense to tolerate, relaxed. One more time—then the phone rang, and she grabbed her pen, depressed the headset switch on the phone, and lowered her foot to the floor.

"Fifty-five . . . minute . . . YES . . . club," a recorded voice said as she wrote down the time: 5:57 a.m. She glanced at the flowchart again, noting the script she had to follow, and said, "Thank you for calling Psychic Sisters Network. My name is Ariel, and my extension number is 723884. May I have your name, please?"

A nervous-sounding woman said, "Clarise."

Phoebe wrote down the name. "Clarise, I need your date of birth." The woman sounded older than eighteen. The birth date she gave would have made her late thirty-something.

"Okay, Clarise," Phoebe said, scooping up the tarot cards. She shuffled the round deck and cut the cards with her left hand while she said, "I read tarot, and what I would like for you to do is focus on the question or questions that you wish to have answered. While you're doing that, I'm going to concentrate on you and begin a general reading for you. Is that all right?"

"Yes," that timid voice said.

"Fine." Phoebe put a card on the table. "The first card in the reading is the Significator, which tells us who you are right now. The card that comes up for you is the Hierophant at about one o'clock. This card says that you are under oppression in some way—that some person or some organization is telling you how you should think, how you should act, what you should believe . . ." Phoebe paused, then asked, "Does that sound about right?"

"I . . . yes." That soft, scared voice. "Yes. About right."

Phoebe put another card down. "The next card is the Three of Swords, straight up. This card refers to your Atmosphere—that is, to what's going on with you right now—and it indicates a disagreement. It can either be an argument you're having inside your mind, where part of you wants to do one thing and the other part wants to do something else, or it can be an actual physical argument with other people. Because it comes up in the upright position, I read this struggle as being very painful for you."

"Painful . . ." Clarise said thoughtfully. "Yes." And then,

under her breath, so that if the phone connection hadn't been so clear Phoebe wouldn't have heard the words at all, "You should see the bruises."

Phoebe's stomach knotted.

A picture flashed in front of her eyes then, as if she were looking at a movie screen. This call wasn't some cheerful girl wanting to know the sex of her unborn baby or whether she ought to take that new job offer. In Phoebe's mind Clarise became suddenly and terribly real: pale, about thirty pounds overweight, her lank brown hair pulled back into a ponytail, flyaway tendrils brushing the corners of her mouth. Hunched over her telephone, speaking in a soft voice not because it was her natural voice but because she had grown accustomed to listening for the sound of footsteps behind her. Something in the back of Phoebe's mind said that Clarise lived in a nice house, in a nice neighborhood. And that the people who knew her didn't know about the private hell that lay behind her go-to-Publix dress and her Taurus station wagon and her brief appearances at parent-teacher conferences and the Presbyterian church on holiday Sundays.

Clarise wanted comfort, wanted someone to talk to—and she sought it from a complete stranger at a four-dollar-a-minute psychic hotline because the only kindness that hadn't come back to haunt her had come from strangers.

Phoebe kept putting the cards on the table, reading their meanings by habit, while most of her attention focused on trying to come up with something genuinely useful to tell Clarise. She wanted to be able to say, "Everything in your life is going to turn out great," but the cards were falling ugly. In the Recent Past, the Ten of Swords reversed—wanting to die rather than have what had happened to her before happen to her again, and not being able to die, even though the horrors had returned.

Phoebe studied the cards for a moment, noticing that there were two Daughters and a Son in the layout.

"The problem is the kids, isn't it?" she said. "You can't

take them; *he* has money and power and position in your
town, and . . . you don't."

A soft gasp. "Yes."

"And you can't leave them; they're your children."

A sniffle. A muffled sob. "I have to do something. He's
good to them as long as he has . . . me . . . to take his anger
out on . . ."

But Clarise believed that if she left, he would hurt them.
And if she tried to take them, he'd hurt her. They were his
power over her. And he was killing her with them, with the
things he held over her, killing her with her own inescapable
love a little more every day.

Phoebe gave Clarise an 800 number for a national
women's resource center and suggested that she look
through her local phone directory for the addresses and
phone numbers of women's shelters. And she offered as
much sympathy as she could. She kept her voice upbeat and
tried to find something positive to tell Clarise, but Clarise already knew that she needed to get out of the house. She
knew she needed to take her kids and run to someplace safe,
but she couldn't imagine finding a place where he couldn't
find her.

And I am not the person to tell you that you're wrong for
being terrified, or for staying put.

Phoebe's knee throbbed, a painful reminder that sometimes when a woman ran, her abuser followed.

When Clarise finally hung up, Phoebe sagged. She didn't
want to take any more calls. Not for a while, anyway.

She picked up the other phone—her home phone, which
wasn't dedicated to the Psychic Sisters Network—and dialed the number that connected her to the system. She
wanted to log off before another call came in, and if she was
going to get off at all, she needed to do it fast.

"Welcome to the Psychic Network Center," the recorded
voice on the other end said. "You must have a touch-tone
phone to interact with this system. At this time, please enter
your ID number."

She punched in 7-2-3-8-8-4 and waited.

The system felt slow to her. Call volume might be high, or maybe a lot of other people were trying to log on or off at the same time.

"The number you have entered is 7-2-3-8-8-4. If this is correct—"

Phoebe punched 1, cutting a hundredth of a second off of her log-off time. Her other option would have been 2, had she entered her number incorrectly, as she sometimes did when she was really exhausted.

Don't ring, she told the Network phone. Don't ring. Don't ring. Just let me get off the system.

"Now enter your password."

9-4-7-7-5-2.

A long pause. Hurry, she thought. Come on. Hurry.

"The number you have entered is 9-4-7-7-5-2. If this is corr—"

She punched 1.

"To hear the daily message, press 1 now. Otherwise—"

She pressed 2. The computerized voice seemed suspended in molasses, dripping out one word at a time. Another Clarise was going to call, and Phoebe would have to take the call because she was technically still on the system. She wouldn't be able to finish her log-off, and she'd have to try again, and again. She didn't dare refuse calls—if she didn't answer each call by the second ring while she was logged on, she would lose her job.

And she had to have the job.

There was no way to cheat. Every call showed up in the computer log, as did the numbers clients called from, the length of time they stayed on the phone, and God only knew what else. Phoebe was supposed to capture addresses by requesting them and then writing them down, but she suspected that was only for legal purposes; the Network could probably have gotten home information on clients from any of a number of databases simply by backtracking the phone numbers. She figured the reason she was supposed to have the callers give her the information was that if the clients gave their addresses to her, the Network had implied consent to *use* them.

"The computer shows that you are currently logged on at 1-954-9—" and droned out her phone number.

I know where I am, she thought. Let me log off.

"To log on—" the final prompt started, and she slammed her finger against the 2.

"I'm off," she whispered and waited for the voice that would confirm this.

Before it could, the Psychic Sisters phone rang.

"You are now logged off the system, and will not be receiving any further calls until you log on again," the computer voice said. "If this is correct—"

She pressed 1 and hung up, and the Network phone rang a second time. "Shit," she whispered. She depressed the headset switch on the Network phone with a sense of resignation. "Fifty-five . . . minute . . . YES . . . club," the voice said.

She put the smile back on her face. It would be the last call, anyway. No more would come through. She said, "Thank you for calling the Psychic Sisters Network. My name is Ariel, and my extension number is 723884. May I have your name, please?"

She marked in the time the call started, then waited. "Hello? Are you still there?"

She heard a chuckle. "I thought you were psychic, Phoebe."

That voice. It couldn't be.

"I found you again," he said. "I found you, sweetheart. You would not believe how far I've had to come . . . but I found you, just as I promised I would. And now you're going to come back to me. Walking or crawling—you're going to come back."

She cut the call off and sat staring at the phone.

It couldn't be him. There was no way. None. But if it *was* him—

It can't be him.

Her first impulse, even all these years later, was to call home. To beg her father to come get her.

Her dad would have been there as fast as humanly possible. He would have stood between her and the nightmare. But her father, her mother, her younger sister, Nicki—a late-night drive through a wild storm, wet leaves on a winding Ohio back road, and bad brakes in an old car had taken the three of them away from her forever. Their passing had marked the beginning of Phoebe's hell.

But she did have another call she had to make.

With shaking hands, Phoebe dialed a number that she'd memorized a long time ago, a number she had always hoped she would one day forget.

The woman's voice on the other end of the phone was calm and no-nonsense. "Mercy Cove Total-Care Home, long-term-floor-can-I-help-you," she said.

Phoebe shuddered, the memory of all the times she'd heard those words suddenly sharp and ugly. She looked around her town house, at the triple-deadbolted front door, at the windows screened from the outside world, and she listened to the emptiness of the place. Just her. Just her—and that had seemed safest. Best. Only now it just felt vulnerable again.

"I'm just calling to check on the status of one of your patients. M-M-Michael Schaeffer."

"May I ask who's calling, please?"

"Phoebe Rain." A pause, then the reluctant, "Used to be Schaeffer."

"Phoebe . . . Schaeffer." The sound of a metal rack rotating, a heavy thud, a softly muttered imprecation she hadn't been intended to hear. "Okay. Just a moment, please." Phoebe waited some more, while pages were riffled, while two voices spoke, while—judging from the sudden silence—a hand went over the phone mouthpiece. Then the voice came back on the line, markedly cooler. "I'm sorry. We only give out information on our patients to family members."

"I'm his ex-wife."

"Yes, ma'am. Your name is not on the list the family approved."

Of course it wouldn't be. Her ex-in-laws would have seen to that.

"It's important," she said quietly. "I just need to know if his condition has . . . changed."

"I suggest you call his family, Mrs. Schaeffer."

"Rain. Ms. Rain." Either I'm Mrs. Schaeffer and you give me the information, or I'm Ms. Rain and you don't, she thought. You don't get to have it both ways. "He tried to kill me once. I have to know if he could try to kill me again," Phoebe said, fear adding a note of hysteria to her voice.

"Ms. Rain, then. Please call his family for information. No matter what the circumstances, I absolutely cannot give any information to you. I'm sorry," the woman said. But she didn't sound sorry.

Phoebe said, "I understand," when what she wanted to do was scream, "Bitch!" She hung up the phone.

Michael was still at Mercy Cove—otherwise the woman on the phone would have simply told her he was no longer a patient. But whether he could have called her—whether he might once again be a danger to her—that she couldn't tell. That secret lay in the nursing home in Ohio.

She couldn't find out about him as Phoebe Rain, or even as Phoebe Schaeffer. If she called again, she was likely to be told they couldn't give out information no matter what name she gave—she would guess, remembering her in-laws, that they would have requested notification if she called. They hated her for what she'd done to their son. They had never believed a word of what she said he'd done to her. She imagined that they would use any tool available to them to stand in her way. No way in hell would one of them tell her how he was doing.

If she had only thought to identify herself as Laine Schaeffer, Michael's sister, she could have gotten information. Laine and Michael had never been close, and with Laine all the way out in Oregon, they'd had almost no contact in all the years Phoebe and Michael had been together. But Laine and Michael hadn't been enemies. Phoebe guessed that Laine would be on the list to get information, even if it was a privilege she never chose to use.

Phoebe sat for a moment, staring at the little gray headset phone she used for the psychic line, thinking. The phone call had come through with a Network prompt. Which meant it had gone through the system.

Which meant the Network's computer had logged the originating phone number.

She smiled slowly. Which meant that whoever had called her, she had him.

She checked the Network's employee contact line number on her phone list—she'd only had to use it once before, when her priority rating had inexplicably slipped to 89,000-something. A man who called himself Therian answered.

Phoebe identified herself and said, "Can you do a check on the last call that came through for me? I need to take the phone number to the police. The caller used my real name, and . . . threatened me." Her throat tightened as the pictures flashed through her mind: blood on the chalkboards, terrified young faces, screaming. Blinding pain. She cleared her throat, got her voice back, said, "I can't afford to ignore this."

Therian sighed heavily. "It will take me a minute."

"I have all night . . . well, morning."

She heard him sigh again before he put her on hold. She found herself listening to bad, digitized New Age music; she blocked it out by trying to figure out how the caller had located her. No one except Ben Margolies in the Moonstruck New Age Shoppe, who'd recommended her, and the woman at PSN, Inc., who hired her and whose name she didn't even know—whom she had never even met except for a single phone interview—knew she worked as a psychic for the Network. Getting her extension number was simple—she gave that out at every call, hoping that her readings would be good enough that she would develop a clientele of regulars.

But knowing that she was the person on the other end of it—how could anyone have discovered that Ariel the psychic was Phoebe Rain? She'd been careful never to give out her real name. The caller had said he knew where to find her. Did he? He might. She didn't have any credit cards and all her mail went to a drop box, and both her home and Psychic Sisters phones were unpublished, unlisted. But her driver's license had her correct address on it—he might have managed to obtain her address from that. It still wouldn't explain how he'd reached her through the Psychic Sisters. They didn't have a directory—the only way a caller could get a specific reader was to have called her once before and to have copied down her number. The odds of the man with Michael's voice getting her and recognizing her had to be right up there with winning the big prize in the lottery.

But somebody won that, too, didn't they? Sooner or later, someone took it home.

With the feeling that her luck had run out, she stared at her phone and waited.

Therian came back on the line. "The last call I have for you is from Idaho. Our database lists the caller as Clarise. The phone number—"

Phoebe cut him off. "Clarise called at five fifty-seven a.m. I want the one that called at six twenty-eight a.m."

"The last call I show for you is at five fifty-seven a.m."

Phoebe shook her head. "This came through the system. Fifty-five-minute YES club prompt, I did the opening script, he didn't give me his name. He used my name, said . . . what he said, I hung up on him. It's got to be there."

"I'm checking. But I show you logged off at six twenty-seven, so any call that came through at six twenty-eight would have been dialed directly in to your number."

"I'm telling you, I got the system prompt. And the phone rang before I finished logging off," Phoebe said, but then she realized that it hadn't. She'd punched that final 2 that completed her log-off, and the phone started to ring the instant *after* that, though before she got confirmation from the system that she was off. Perhaps she really had already logged herself off, if only by nanoseconds.

"I'm sorry," Therian said, "but the last call that came through the system for you was the one from Idaho."

Phoebe sat there for a moment, eyes closed, fingers pressed against her temples.

"Okay, thanks," she said at last.

"Sorry I couldn't help. Why don't you call the phone company and see if they can look into this for you?"

"I'll do that." She hung up.

She sat staring out her window, wondering how the caller had managed to get a prompt from the Psychic Sisters Network on his call if he hadn't called through the 900 number.

It might really be Michael, though she couldn't imagine how that could be. The last she'd heard of him, he'd still been in a coma. Had been in a coma for more than a year. She'd stopped keeping track at that point—everyone she'd talked to and everything she'd researched insisted that anyone in a coma for more than a year wouldn't be waking up. Not that she slept any better at night for knowing that.

It almost had to be someone else, someone who could imitate Michael's voice and who had reason to hate her. To want to hurt her.

Maybe someone from the school. One of her fellow teachers. Or one of the parents.

Her skin crawled, and she tasted bitter fear. No matter who had found her, no matter why he had called her, he was the nightmare she'd been waiting for—the one that she'd known in her gut was coming. She looked at the four walls that surrounded her, at the big window with its drawn shades, with only the angled glass at the top open to the sky, at the sliding glass door pinned shut and also shaded. No one could see in, but suddenly she felt like a bird in a cage with the snake coiled just outside, studying her through the bars, looking for a way in.

She had to get out.

She rose, hurried, unthinking, and knives tore through her right knee, pain so white-hot she whimpered and fell back into her seat, tears flooding her eyes. She caught the table with both hands and pulled herself up, fighting the pain, trying to get on top of it; she clutched her cane with a sense of defeat. In the last few months she'd been making trips without it. But not this time. The damned leg felt like it might give out at any moment. Maybe that was just anxiety, which always made her pain worse, and maybe it wasn't.

She grabbed her backpack and her keys and threw open all three deadbolts, stopping on the other side only long enough to make sure all of them were locked again. Scared, shaking, unsure of what to do next, she hobbled down the walk.

chapter 2

Alan MacKerrie left the emergency room at the end of his shift feeling like he'd been kicked in the gut. His final patient of the night hadn't made it, and it felt like Fate slamming him in the face again—the fifth anniversary of his wife's and daughter's deaths, and once again he couldn't do a goddamned thing to save the life of the person depending on him.

He drove home with his head pounding. Logically, he knew it wasn't the same—he hadn't even been in the ER where they took Janet and Chick following the accident. No one had set out to destroy either of them—not even the wife-stealing bastard they'd been with. By contrast, his last patient of the night had died because of a drunken brawl with her husband, and her death left Alan sick with humanity. He couldn't understand the sort of heedless violence that kept pouring through the ER doors. He couldn't comprehend taking a life. To have something—to have some*one*—and to destroy that life instead of protecting it . . . he had never been able to get a handle on that.

He took a few deep, steadying breaths, determined to put his patient and her husband, the night, the anniversary—the whole hellish ordeal—out of his mind. At least for a while. He knew it wouldn't stay gone, but he could banish it for the drive home.

The morning traffic heading east on Commercial was brutal, but he was heading west. No sunlight in his eyes, almost no one else on the road with him, the brief but unquestionable pleasure of watching half a million poor shmucks coming the other way, enduring the dreadful commute to their cubicles when he was on his way home to sleep. That drive home was one of the few real benefits of having the night shift in the emergency room; Fort Lauderdale traffic rarely got better.

He drove through the nest of side streets that led to the development where he lived and pulled into his numbered slot in the communal parking lot. The neighborhood had headed downhill, but the place did look better in the long-shadowed light of dawn. The sun gave the peculiar flamingo pink of his town house—that shade so loved by Florida developers—a rosy glow and made the palm trees and the coarse grass look like they were made of emeralds. In a few hours the boom boxes and the stereos would start up, and the parking lots would fill with blank-eyed men with no apparent sources of income.

At the moment, though, the only people visible were the dog owners who spent their morning walks studiously not noticing their animals crapping beside the sidewalks, and carefully leaving the steaming messes behind. Aside from them, the place still looked deceptively middle class.

Alan took a deep breath as he got out of the car and consciously shook off the night and everything associated with it. He had a couple days off. And he had never been more grateful for those days. He walked around the corner of his privacy fence, rubbing his eyes and yawning, and ran right into the girl with the cane.

She went over backwards with a cry of pain, and his first ungallant thought was, Shit, my malpractice insurance. But he dropped to one knee beside her. "Christ, I'm sorry. I wasn't paying attention. Are you hurt?"

She closed her eyes and took a slow, deep breath, and with her eyes still closed said, "I'll be fine." She looked at him then, and he saw a flicker of recognition in her eyes—

and she managed a strained smile. "You're the guy next door. The doctor."

He nodded. "Alan MacKerrie. Sorry to meet you this way."

Her pained smile got a little broader, but he noticed that she did not offer her name.

"If you were going to get pasted on the sidewalk, I guess you got pasted by the right guy."

She was pretty in a delicate, underfed sort of way. Long, curly dark hair worn loose, large dark eyes, a pointed chin, the undeveloped build of a teenager who might one day fill out and be gorgeous—but this girl wasn't a teenager, he realized. If he looked at the first ghosts of smile lines in the corners of her eyes, he'd have to guess early thirties.

He'd only seen her in passing before and had never paid much attention—most too-thin women never showed up on his radar. "So where do you hurt?"

"My butt. My knee. The palms of my hands." She held them up and looked at them. Dirt embedded in the skin, a few scrapes and flecks of blood—nothing major.

"Any pain in your wrists?"

She wiggled them. "They're fine. My knee's the only thing that really hurts, and it already hurt."

"You feel a pop or a snap when you fell?"

"No. The pain just got worse, but it was already pretty bad."

"Let me take a look, okay?"

"I'd . . . rather you . . ." She sighed and shrugged. "Sure. Take a look. I don't think it's any worse than it was, but if it is I'd rather know now." She tugged up the leg of her jeans, and for an instant he thought she had really pretty legs, which made up for the flat chest, and then he saw the scar tissue and it was everything he could do to keep the shock from showing on his face.

He put his hands on either side of the knee and made a production of palpating and gently moving the joint to hide his reaction. Her right knee bore the branding of half a dozen surgeries; the square outlines of two grafts, one white and relatively old, the other pink and a bit puffy; a dozen black circles tattooed into the skin and grown over; a missing chunk that had healed hard and red and ugly.

"What happened?" he asked, keeping his voice neutral and not looking at her face.

"Shotgun." He looked into her eyes and saw a wall so solid no emotion leaked past. She said, "I've had a bit of work done on it."

"I see that," he said. "I don't see any new damage, but if you want, I'll take you to the ER and get it x-rayed for you. I'll cover the cost—I did knock you down."

She smiled and shook her head, and he marveled that her expression could convey absolutely nothing of what she was thinking. "I'll see if I can stand on it. It doesn't feel any different now than it did when I walked out the door. I think it just twisted a little when I fell."

"Twisting can be significant. Pins can slip loose, slice things up inside . . ." He stood and gave her his hand and said, "I'd feel better if you'd have it x-rayed."

He leaned back and pulled, and she rose to her feet without much difficulty. He guessed that she weighed less than a hundred pounds and that she was about five one or five two. But there'd been a sinewy strength to her grip that surprised him and a grace to her movements that changed his first impression of fragility. She was tougher than she looked at first glance.

"In the last two years I've seen more of the insides of hospitals than I ever wanted to; if I never have to go through the doors of one again, that will be just fine." She scooped up her cane and tested the leg, putting her full weight on it, then taking it off several times in a row. Testing. Her face remained impassive, but Alan caught the flicker of suppressed pain in her eyes. She wiped her palms on her jeans and slung her bag—a small canvas backpack that looked heavy to him—over her shoulder again.

"Good as new," she said, then with a shrug added, "or at least good as slightly used."

Definitely tougher than she looked. "Let me know if it gives you any trouble."

She smiled, already moving away from him. "I'll do that. Thanks. Thanks for being so nice." She headed towards the parking lot. He watched her for a moment, wondering about her, about the scars, about her polite but carefully maintained distance and the fact that she didn't offer her name. As she limped out of sight, he turned to his town house—a corner unit of the building, which had eight total units, four facing south, and four that mirrored them, facing north. Each had a little fenced patio to the front; each made an attempt to feel like a detached home from the inside. But all shared side and back walls. For just an instant he was conscious of those other people in those other units, with their separate lives kept apart from his by only a layer of studs and drywall—but the walls might as well have been acres thick. He didn't know any of his neighbors by name, only a couple of them by sight. They were neighbors only in the physical sense, in that they inhabited the same building.

We all keep our secrets, he thought.

He found himself wondering what hers were.

Phoebe went to Winn-Dixie and wandered up and down the aisles, getting a few cans of beans, three cantaloupes, and a bag of grapefruit. Her thoughts bounced between the doctor who had run into her, and Michael. She was surprised to discover that she wanted to like the doctor. She would never have noticed him, really. He was, well, plain. Sandy brown hair cut short, kept neat; light blue-gray eyes; straight white teeth in a face that had regular features that didn't quite add up to handsome.

She looked at him and thought, Reliable.

Not like Michael.

Nothing like Michael, who had been dark and handsome,

who'd had women swarming around him hoping for one of his electric smiles.

Michael.

Phoebe shivered and blamed it on being in the produce aisle. It probably hadn't been Michael on the phone, though she wished she could afford a quick trip to Cleveland to be sure. If she could see him curled in the bed, not responding to anything, she would feel better.

By the time she got home, her anxiety had passed; she felt certain she could figure out who was calling her and put an end to it somehow. She put the grocery bag down on her front stoop and started unlocking the deadbolts, but stopped as she realized she was being watched. She looked to her left and to her right. No one.

She felt the steady stare, though. The fine hairs on her arms and on the back of her neck rose, her heart began pounding, and her breathing got quicker. She unlocked the door, dragged her bags into the house, and locked each of the deadbolts behind her. Then she leaned against the cool, painted metal, shaking.

The sensation should have passed. But it didn't. Instead, it got worse. Her nerves and her gut insisted that even in her home, with the curtains drawn and the doors and windows *all* locked and securely barred, someone still watched her.

She left the groceries on the floor and grabbed the pistol—a Browning Mark III—from her backpack. She didn't have to fish around for it. When she got her Florida carry-concealed permit, she sewed a holster into the front section of the backpack so all she had to do was reach beneath the front flap, unsnap the holster, and pull the weapon out. Gun in hand, Phoebe leaned against the door and put most of her weight on her stronger leg, the left one. Then, safety thumbed to OFF, stance wide, and pistol gripped in both hands just the way the cop she'd trained with at the range had taught her, she surveyed the spaces before her. Stairs right in front of her leading up to a railed loft; most people, she supposed, used that loft as a TV room or a playroom.

She didn't use it at all—no furniture, no storage, nothing—so nothing blocked her view. No one up there. The second-floor bedroom door was closed, the way she'd left it. She hated the idea of fighting the steps to get up there. But she might have to, just to check things out.

To her right lay the open door to her bedroom. She could see her bed, the door into the connecting bathroom beyond, her closet door along the back wall. Bathroom door open, closet door closed. Had she left that closed? She couldn't remember. No one in the visible part of her bedroom, but there might be someone behind the partially open door to her right, up against the wall.

She scanned left. Impossible to tell about the kitchen, which lay all the way to the back of the open space, half hidden by the bar and shadows—because she'd turned the lights off back there before she left the house. Shit. Her gaze moved forward—her little dining room table, four chairs in their places, tarot stuff still spread all over. Underneath—nothing. Closer, the couch, which stuck out from the wall. Might be someone on hands and knees behind that. Dammit, she needed to rethink how she had her furniture arranged. She'd provided too many hiding places, when the place already offered too many.

She could put a few mirrors around, convex ones that would let her see into the blind spots. One of those would let her see the spot that concerned her most at the moment—the place just to her left, where the tiny coat closet jutted out from the wall and then, on the opposite side, dropped back, forming a little alcove where her television and a couple of bookshelves sat. Someone could be standing right there, just an arm's reach away from her, and she wouldn't know it until he burst out from around the corner.

So. How did she move so that she could check out the house? Possible danger to the left. To the right, behind the open door to her bedroom. In front of her, from both the couch and the kitchen. Did she trust her leg to get her safely out the door and back to her car?

Something moved. Back behind the table, in front of the bar, she saw someone take two steps forward and turn huge eyes on her. She aimed at the space between those eyes across the Browning's sights—then realized the person against the wall was a kid. A girl. Cute. Blonde hair. Maybe seven or eight.

"Oh, hell," Phoebe whispered and, shaking, lowered the gun. The kid took two more steps toward her, raised a hand, opened her mouth to say something. And vanished.

Phoebe's shaking got much worse.

The feeling that someone was watching her disappeared with the kid. Phoebe was once again alone in the house— she *knew* she was alone in the house, the way she could tell sometimes what the cards were going to be before she even turned them over. But being alone in the house had ceased to be the issue.

Hands trembling so badly she could barely hang on to the Browning, she managed to thumb the safety back into place and get the pistol back into its holster in her backpack. She let the backpack slide to the floor, let the door support most of her weight, wrapped her arms tight around herself.

Was she crazy? She'd thought she might have been the last time.

Shortly before Michael tracked her down two years earlier, she'd started hearing voices. Or, more precisely, a voice. Her favorite grandmother's. When Phoebe slept, Nana appeared in her dreams, shaking her head, telling Phoebe that disaster was coming. When she drove to work, Nana told her to keep going, to not look back. And when she stood in front of the classroom, it was Nana's voice whispering, "Run."

Phoebe wrapped her arms tighter around herself, fighting the wash of memories.

. . . screaming . . . the white-lightning flash of pain, the taste of iron . . . blood on the chalkboard . . .

Phoebe hadn't listened to the voice. Hadn't believed. Her grandmother had been dead for almost eight years at the time, and Phoebe had been sure she was suffering from stress and overwork, that hearing the voice was just imagination. She had not wanted to believe, had not wanted to throw away every bit of the life she had fought so hard to rebuild. She kept telling herself that she had earned her life, and the voice kept telling her she hadn't—that she had to run.

. . . blood on the floor . . . on the desks . . . on the display tables and the reports in careful cursive on lined three-hole notebook paper . . .

Phoebe couldn't breathe.

She shook, and closed her eyes tightly against the memory of the child standing there, looking at her, trying to tell her something. Maybe the child had been a hallucination. Maybe the phone call had not been real and the child's ghost had not been real, and Phoebe was simply losing her mind. That would be best—madness would be far preferable to the alternative. Because if she were going mad, she would still be safe inside her locked doors. He wouldn't be coming for her.

Again.

But could she hide behind the hope of insanity?

. . . blood on the walls . . . and small, broken bodies still beneath white sheets . . . and the anguished wails of bereaved parents . . .

Madness would be a comfort. But Phoebe hadn't listened before; she had instead sought comfort in excuses and a foolish faith in rationality, and the price of that had been more than she could bear.

Under different circumstances, she would tell herself that the constant grind of guilt and worry and the awful scramble to keep a roof over her head and the lights on and food on her table had taken its toll, and she would laugh a little and shake off what had just happened. Just as she'd done before.

Phoebe, however, didn't have different circumstances. She had *her* circumstances, and her circumstances included a man with Michael's voice calling her on a phone for which he should not have had the number, for which he could not have gotten her name. It included a phone call that had come through a closed system without leaving a trace. And it included the image of a dead child trying to tell her something before vanishing.

The phone call had been real. The man on the phone wasn't Michael. Couldn't be Michael. Couldn't be. But even if it wasn't Michael, it was someone who could imitate Michael's voice, someone who knew things about her that only Michael had known. It could be someone who hated her enough to try to turn himself into the man who had made her eight years of married life and three years of hiding a living, breathing hell. She ran lists through her head.

Who hated her that much? One of Michael's relatives? The father of one of the kids who died? Some psycho she'd picked up who wasn't related to her past at all?

Any of the above, or none of the above. Then who knew her that well? Who knew *them*—the couple that Phoebe and Michael had been, with all their terrible secrets?

Nobody.

The people at Sebastian Bright Experimental School knew some of the story, and the police knew most of it, but the real details—Michael's voice, his tone, the way he spoke to her and the words he used—were something only the two of them had known during the eight years of their marriage. Michael was a brilliant and dedicated criminal defense lawyer in front of his partners, his clients, the judges; an affable, intelligent, loving husband in front of her family, his family, the members of the country club, complete strangers.

She closed her eyes, hugging herself hard just to keep from feeling like she was going to fly apart, remembering the day she'd finally gathered up the nerve to tell someone the truth. Ran through the Yellow Pages, looking for women's shelters. Found several, dialed the first one on the list, waited for someone to pick up, and when at last a woman answered the phone, said, "I need help. My husband is . . . hurting me. Please. I need help."

"Where are you?" the woman had asked, skipping past all the unnecessary details and going straight to the heart of the matter.

And Phoebe had looked up to find Michael standing there, staring at her, smiling, his index finger pointed between her eyes, his thumb up. *Pow!* he mouthed, pulling the imaginary trigger.

Phoebe had hung up the phone without answering, staring at that unwavering smile, at the implied gun.

"Naughty girl," Michael had said. "Hope I heard all there was to hear of that, or whoever you called is going to have a terrible accident."

Terrified, her heart pounding, she'd dared to stand up to him. "I've had enough, Michael. You can't do this anymore. I'm not your prisoner, I'm not your slave, I'm not a toy for your sick games." She'd jammed her shoulders back straight and snarled, "And I'm not Eileen. I'm sorry she hurt you, I'm sorry she left you, but I'm not going to pay for what she did to you for the rest of my life."

And that smile had changed. Michael had watched her, so amused, so delighted. Murmured gently, "No one leaves me, Phoebe."

"Eileen did."

"Did she? Mmmmmmm. Lucky Eileen. And you want to follow in her footsteps."

His smile vanished then, and Michael stared into Phoebe's eyes, and she felt like she was falling down a well. His voice got softer. She knew in that instant what some part of her had suspected for years. No matter the sad story of betrayal he'd spun her when they were dating—his fiancée, Eileen Ganella, hadn't left him at the altar. She hadn't shown up for her own wedding because she was dead; he'd killed her. He'd successfully gotten away with murder once, and if Phoebe crossed him, he intended to do it again.

And he said, "You won't leave me, Phoebe. Not ever."

That was the moment she knew that if she stayed with
him she was going to die.

Hot tears burning down her cheeks—tears of shame that
she could be so much a coward, tears of fear that her life
could mean so little, could be crushed out so quickly—she'd
hung her head and said, "No, Michael. I'm ... sorry I tried
to tell someone. I'm so sorry. I won't do it again. And I
won't leave you." She had taken his punishment like an obe-
dient slave. Had endured the humiliation yet again, the careful, methodical torture.

And the next morning, when she knew he was in court
with a client, she ran. Aching and stiff, terrified for her
life—but not bruised, because he never allowed any evidence of his brutality to show—she withdrew five hundred
dollars cash from an ATM using two credit cards she'd
stolen from his wallet. She knew the PINs she wasn't supposed to know—she'd watched him when he didn't know
she was watching, and she got them one number at a time
over a period of weeks. He changed PINs fairly often. Just
not quite often enough.

She'd also used his platinum American Express card to
buy three bus tickets, all from different booths. She gave a
one-way ticket to Albuquerque, New Mexico, to a plump
young woman with wistful eyes who'd been staring at a
travel poster and a one-way ticket to Fort Lauderdale,
Florida, to a relatively clean homeless man who had seen
something of her terror in her eyes and had spoken kindly
to her. She kept the one-way ticket to San Francisco for
herself. When the bus got as far as Toledo, however, she
got off, gave her seat to a man who said he'd always
wanted to go to California, and purchased another ticket
for herself.

To Miami.

With her small supply of cash.

She diced both of Michael's credit cards into confetti with
a sharp pair of scissors, scattered the confetti in three differ-

ent full trash cans, and got on her new bus. From Miami, she headed back to Fort Lauderdale. She'd never been there, knew no one in the vicinity, had no reason to run there—and she'd made sure that anyone Michael sent to ask after her would be able to figure out that the person who had taken the Fort Lauderdale ticket that she'd purchased had not been her.

She'd hoped that when he eliminated Fort Lauderdale, Albuquerque, and eventually San Francisco, he would never consider those places again. That her careful deception would put him off her trail forever. Nonetheless, that finger had stayed pointed between her eyes for the three years she'd eluded him, and that smile had never left her nightmares, waking or sleeping.

"You won't leave me, Phoebe. Not ever."

In the end, he'd been wrong. And right. When he found her, she beat him. She won. But the price she'd paid in winning scarred her in ways she would never escape. She would never again walk without pain. Would never again trust. Would never again love. Would never escape the guilt or the nightmares that she'd earned for allowing other people to stand between her and Michael.

For just an instant she thought of her next-door neighbor—the doctor with the kind eyes. She remembered the gentleness of his touch as he checked her knee for damage, the way he tried to conceal his horror at her scars. He'd seemed—kind. Genuine. He hadn't been particularly tall or particularly handsome, but Michael had been both those things. The doctor—Alan—was someone that she'd wanted to like. She'd liked his hands on her knee, his wary smile, his wonderful, rich voice in the ordinary face.

But someone with Michael's voice had called her. The dead had come to visit. She wasn't safe. She would never be safe. She couldn't let her guard down for an instant. Could not chance having someone standing between her and Michael a second time if Michael returned.

Besides, her neighbor was simply another unknown. Another hazard. The men who seemed best on the outside—good families, good jobs, good looks—were sometimes the worst on the inside. And how could anyone tell until it was too late?

chapter 3

Alan stood over a stretcher in the ER, looking down at a dead woman whose unblinking eyes stared up at him. Janet, he thought, but Janet had been blonde and stunning, and this woman had dark hair and was . . . ordinary. Then she smiled, and her face changed—and she became his pretty next-door neighbor. Smiling. But still dead.

He woke and sat up and shook his head from side to side to clear the nightmare. "Hell," he whispered. Except for that first year after he lost Janet and Chick, he'd never been subject to nightmares—not the kind that came while he was asleep, anyway. He had always been a good sleeper. He brought his work home with him; no matter what anyone might say, doctors who gave a shit about their patients *did*. But he'd never carried his work into his sleep before.

"Hell *and* fuck that." He still breathed hard, and he realized he'd knotted the sheet in his hands. He was sweating. Middle of the day, hot as hell in the house—of course he was sweating. Which was probably what had caused the nightmare, too.

He considered going back to sleep, but he didn't want to sleep. If he was going to have dreams like that, he'd invest in coffee and never go back to sleep again.

He decided he might as well go work on his secret project for a while. He stretched and headed upstairs to his home office and the computer. Turned it on, brought up the document he'd been working on, and did a search for "aaa"—his place marker.

He wasn't too far into the book. He'd forgotten how much he'd deleted. Dammit. He settled into his chair and stared at the blinking yellow line of the cursor, at the deep blue background, at the smattering of white letters on the screen. He rested his hands on the keyboard, fingers on the home row, and he waited for the words to come.

The world stayed with him, though he needed it to fall away. The soft whir of the computer fan. From overhead, a small twin-engine plane circling for a landing at the Executive Airfield. The ticking of his watch, usually inaudible but now painfully loud. The oppressive air of waiting gave the town house a silence deeper than mere stillness.

The pretty woman next door.

From somewhere in the house, a soft thump that set his heart racing . . . and then the air conditioner kicked on. Alan sighed, the release from the tension almost painful, as if he'd been an overinflated balloon that had finally burst. Air conditioner. Outside, the temperature was in the high nineties. Without AC, indoors began to feel like the inside of an oven by ten a.m. And because he ran the damned air conditioner all the time, it wore out and broke down frequently. He had some sort of compressor problem, perhaps. Or maybe the ants had gotten into the outdoor circuitry again and eaten the plastic coating off the wiring. That had been $430 to fix last October, when it was still hotter than hell.

Hotter than hell. Heat. Heat and wetness.

Suddenly an image of his next-door neighbor was in front of him, with her clothes clinging to her, pert little breasts jutting out, hot and sweaty and with a look of utter, wanton passion in her dark eyes . . .

Alan frowned, stared at the blue screen. Where the *hell* had *that* come from?

Air-conditioning—he'd been thinking about air-conditioning and suddenly there was a woman he didn't know with little breasts and big eyes staring back at him, looking like the personification of wild sex.

He did not need to think about his next-door neighbor, sweaty or not. Unless she repaired air conditioners. He needed to think about air-conditioning, because the AC wasn't supposed to thump. If it did it again, he'd have to have someone come out and take a look. He had a contract with the service people. He could call them.

In a while. Later. Before the damned thing actually broke down again, stranding him with sweat-drenched sheets and ceiling fans that did nothing but circulate hot air.

But not right at that moment. Later. After he finished what he was doing.

He shook his head and resumed his writing stance: eyes fixed on the blue screen, hands resting on the gentle curves of his ergonomically correct keyboard, shoulders tense. He resumed his vigil for the words that wouldn't come. Words that were supposed to help him make sense of his loss, that were supposed to help him lay Janet and Chick to rest after five long, hard years, that were supposed to bring him through the pain and anger and despair to the place where his life would begin again.

Maybe he was asking too much of words. Maybe he was expecting too much of himself. But the endless stream of human misery that poured through the emergency room doors was becoming more than he could bear: In every child's face he saw his dead daughter; in every beautiful woman, his dead wife. His bitterness towards beautiful women, his anguish in dealing with children—they were getting in his way. If he couldn't deal more productively with his loss, he was going to have to find another line of work.

"Healer, heal thyself," he muttered, and glared at the blue screen.

MacKerrie/ WILD ANGELS/ Version 6/ page 1

Chapter One

I fell in love with Janet Terrell the first time I saw her. I was thirteen and she was eleven, and I was carrying home bread and milk for my mother, and I pedaled around the corner of the sidewalk too fast and almost ran into her. She was hanging upside down from the lowest limb of a maple tree that grew between the sidewalk and the street. Her hair was honey gold, tangled, and so long the tips of it brushed the grass beneath her. Her bare knees were skinned and scabbed, and her eyes were the same blue as the sky that day—the autumn Kentucky sky, which is the bluest and most perfect of blues.

Her parents were directing the movers, who were carrying furniture into the big old house next to ours—the Victorian monstrosity that had been empty for eight years, ever since the last of the Hardings died. I'd watched the work crews repairing it all summer. I'd been mightily interested, hoping that the people who moved in would have kids, and that the kids would be boys, and that the boys would be about my age, and especially that they wouldn't be dorks. I wanted a kid on the street besides Kenny Unger, who was pudgy and pimpled and whiny and whose mother hovered over him and made him keep his hands clean and wouldn't let him ride a bike because she said he was too uncoordinated and fragile.

"Hi," I said to the upside-down girl. "My name's Alan. I live next door."

She grinned at me: a lopsided, broad, fiendish grin. She said, "Go to hell, penis-breath." Then she laughed like a hyena and launched herself into the uppermost branches of the maple tree like a cat chased by wolves.

Both her parents heard her laughter and looked over, squinting at the tree, then at me, then finally directing their gazes upward until they located their wild offspring, who was swaying in the topmost branches where only a few yellow leaves still clung. They studied her for an instant.

Then, to my amazement, they both went back to directing
the movers. Neither one yelled at her for being on thin
branches forty feet in the air. Evidently her parents weren't
worried about her being uncoordinated or fragile. I thought
right then that she looked a lot more interesting than
Kenny Unger.

That was the sum total of what he'd written yesterday.
The day before he'd deleted the fifty-seven pages he'd done
on version five. He decided that the last sentence needed to
be a paragraph on its own instead of the concluding sentence
of the previous paragraph, moved it, and looked at his
watch. He'd been sitting there for an hour.

He swore softly and closed his eyes. He shouldn't have
dumped version five, but he'd lost everything about Janet
that had been good in a haze of anger. Fifty-seven pages of
rage. He had to let go—had to move past the fury and the
hatred and the feelings of betrayal at her infidelities, or he
was never going to be able to live again. And he wanted to
live. He didn't want to give Janet any more of his life than
she'd already stolen.

And he'd been making her the only villain—but he wasn't
writing fiction. If he'd been writing fiction, he would have
come up with a better ending for himself. For Janet. For Chick.

He typed:

> Let her go.
> Let her go.
> Let her go.
> Let her go, let her go, let her go.

He stared at the words on the screen, and at the yellow
cursor that blinked behind the last period while it waited for
him to continue.

"And with her and all the bad, Chick and all the good," he
muttered. If it hadn't been for Chick, he would have moved
past Janet and all her poison the day of the wreck.

He highlighted the new material and deleted it.

Chick, he thought, and started a new chapter. The words were there—for Chick, he thought, he would always be able to find the words.

Chapter Two

Chick was both our triumph and our downfall. We didn't really name her Chick, of course. Her name was Emily Helen, after Janet's mother and mine—the name picked out even before her conception. She would have been Bryant William, after my father and Janet's—in that order—had she been a boy. But Janet had an amnio, so we knew early on that this child, our one child, planned, yearned for, and finally gifted to us, would be Emily Helen. We thought we knew what to expect. Saw our futures with our daughter-to-be spreading out before us like a comfortable road, well marked by signs and well appointed with all of life's necessities and a plentiful share of its luxuries.

But the surprises started early. Emily was born with a head full of scruffy blonde hair, and when the nurse dried her off and handed her to us there in the birthing room, that hair stood up in all directions like the down on a chick. We had planned to call our daughter Em, but that plan never made it off the ground. Chick she was, ever after. She didn't go along with our other neat plans, either—she neither slept during the night nor during the day. She talked early, walked early, and graduated immediately from crawling to mountain climbing up the front of the refrigerator and caving in the cabinets. She figured out the childproof locks, the childproof bottles, the childproof plug guards. Things childproof were not Chick-proof, and we learned early and well that the only guarantee that our feral offspring would survive from one day to the next came from our constant, unblinking supervision.

"She's just like you," Janet's mother told her one after-

noon when she was visiting us, and I'll never forget either
the smugness in her smile or the inescapable gleam of
vindication in her eye.

We were infatuated with Chick. She became the center
of our universe, our gravity and the air we breathed. Her
laughter pealed like bells, her face was the sunshine, her

He stopped typing. Glare from the brilliant sun outside
found its way through his window to the bottom left-hand
corner of his monitor, making a few of his words and part of
his page disappear into the yellow haze. Alan reached up
and to his left without looking, pulled the cord that closed
the vertical blinds, and then the chain that rotated them. For
the next few hours, he could work in relative gloom.

The air conditioner kicked off, and Alan became conscious of the sound of his own breathing, the hum of the
computer fan, the low drone of someone cutting hedges outside. The dry fronds of the palm tree that grew up against his
window rattled on the window glass. He leaned back in his
chair and shoved the nearest panels of the verticals back so
that he could look outside. The sky was pale and clear, with
the hard tropical brightness that still surprised him—the
brownish greens of winter had given way to the jungle
greens of Fort Lauderdale's summer, but the intensity of the
sun still made the sky look almost white. The palm fronds
twitched beneath a light breeze, but the breeze didn't look
like it was strong enough to offer any reprieve from the heat.

He turned away from the window, which was entirely too
seductive; he'd never get through the book if he didn't force
himself to write it. He found that the distraction had cost
him the end of his sentence—he didn't remember what he'd
planned to write next. He tapped on the space bar. Then the
backspace key. Then the space bar again. Then the backspace key. The cursor slid right, then left, then right, then
left, over and over.

Downstairs, he heard the thump again. He waited for the
air conditioner to come back to life, but it didn't. Instead

something tickled across the nape of his neck, as light and gentle as the brush of a cat's whisker. He reached back with one hand to see if a thread had worked loose from his collar, and his fingers caught in a fold of thin, crisp cloth that blew against his skin. He felt a breeze, and smelled rain and wet earth and the peculiar heavy smell of ozone and dust washed out of the air. The impossible scents and textures flashed into his brain in a fraction of a second.

He yelled and jumped, moving so quickly the chair he'd been sitting in toppled backwards to the floor. He grabbed for the baseball bat that leaned against the corner of his desk and spun to face the intruders with it gripped firmly in both hands.

No one else was in the room. What he found, however, was worse. The window he had just looked out of was changed. The vertical cloth blinds were gone, replaced by pale, translucent yellow curtains that billowed in the breeze. A steady, heavy rain streaked down the glass and blew in through the open lower half of the window, wetting the carpet, and the dull roar of the water and the scents of dust and greenery tickled at his memory. Something about the smell . . . about the rain itself . . .

Who had opened the window? He needed to shut it; something inside of him said if he could shut it, he could shut down whatever was happening. He could make it go away, make it not happen. Gut instinct assured him the open window was the culprit. Closed, nothing could come through it to threaten him. He edged towards it, brandishing the baseball bat against any intruders who might materialize. But nothing entered through the round-bellied curtains except for the alien, sweet-scented breeze. *Spring* breeze. Jesus, it was a *spring* breeze. Spring scents in the air—but spring up north. Kentucky spring.

He rested a hand on the windowsill to shove the window shut, and realized it was wood instead of metal, and that his office window slid from side to side instead of up and down as this window did. And then he looked outside, at a girl who stood in the rain, soaked to the skin, staring up at the window and at him, and for a moment she looked like a stranger, and then she didn't. Then he realized that she was Chick—Chick who had died, Chick who had vanished from his life in a hell of twisted metal and shattered glass and who had not been able to emerge—until this very moment. He would have known his daughter if he had been blind and deaf and underwater. And the child standing in the rain watching him was undeniably, inescapably Chick.

She didn't look like a ghost—he couldn't see through her. She looked solid. Completely real.

He tried to breathe. Said, "Oh, Christ, oh, Jesus." Screamed, "Chick, sweetheart, stay right there! I'll be right down!" And said, "Jesus,, please, please, please don't go anywhere please." And he thought for one insane moment about climbing out the second-story window and jumping to the ground so that Chick wouldn't have time to go back to wherever she'd been.

She smiled at him, and he could see her yell, "Daddy!" but for some strange reason he couldn't hear her.

He started to back away from the window, wanting to run down the stairs, out into the rain beside her, but afraid to let her out of his sight. But that single step backwards broke the spell. The curtains disappeared, and suddenly the window was covered by the thick cloth vertical blinds that were supposed to be there, blinds that blocked his view of his daughter. The sweet wet-earth-scented air became once again dry and air-conditioned.

Alan screamed a second time, just "NO!" and clawed through the blinds and blinked at the harsh sunlight outside and fumbled with the lock on the window.

But she was gone, of course. No sign of her remained, and no sign of the rain that had brought her to him. Heat shimmered off the bone-dry walk and the cloudless sky offered no hint of moisture, and after staring into the midday sun with tear-blurred eyes, he finally let the blinds fall back into place.

Causes of hallucinations, he thought: mourning and stress, sensory deprivation, sleep deprivation, epilepsy, brain tumors, central-parietal foci. Tumors, if he remembered his *DSM-IV,* gave the best hallucinations—full scenes, the presence of voices, complete sensory input while they lasted.

He forced himself to breathe slower and deeper. That had been a very . . . complete . . . hallucination.

He sagged against the wall and slid down to the floor in one long, slow movement, weeping for his loss and for the pain from that single moment of hope.

And the rainwater in the carpet beneath the window soaked into the knees of his pants.

He ran the palm of his hand over the spot and pushed his face down to smell it. Sweet—the scent of rainwater, ozone, and spring.

Alan shuddered.

chapter 4

Phoebe slept on the couch facing the town house's front door through the heat of the long afternoon, with her handgun within easy reach on the little coffee table in front of her. Her dreams—dark and restless and filled with shadowy shapes that danced just out of her line of sight, mocking her—left her tired and tormented. She woke several times, certain that she had heard something moving through the town house, and each time she got up and walked from room to room, searching, and found nothing disturbed, nothing wrong.

At last, at nine o'clock, she admitted defeat. She wasn't going to get any more sleep, she wasn't going to feel any better than she felt at that moment. She might as well get up and get to work.

With a sigh, she got out both decks of tarot cards—the round Motherpeace deck that she used for reading women and the rectangular Universal Waite that she used for reading men—and shuffled them with practiced hands. She put her headset on, dialed her log-on number, and waited.

Phone traffic was heavy, which was a blessing, and in the early-evening hours not so grim as it sometimes got. A lot of men called that night with relatively simple questions: Will my promotion come through? Is this very young woman I like interested in me? Has my wife been seeing someone else? Does my wife know I've been cheating on her? Fewer women called—a reversal of the usual run of things—and their calls, too, were mostly simple. Does he love me? Will I ever get pregnant? Should I wait for him to get out of prison? Can you give me a number to play in the lottery?

Phoebe talked, listened, read the cards, and started to relax. She was keeping her times up—her call volume, and thus her paycheck, was completely at the mercy of her call-length average. She made twenty-five cents a minute, and those minutes were hard to hold on to, especially since she insisted on being ethical and giving people good value for their money. She never put anyone on hold, as some readers did; she never dawdled or pretended to need to light a new candle or to meditate for a few moments while her caller's clock ran. She had to be bright and cheerful and entertaining in spite of the fact that she felt anything but; she had to give good readings, she had to give her callers a reason to want to hang on. That night she was lucky not to get too many clock watchers who wanted their free three minutes or their free five minutes and who then hung up, cutting her off in midsentence.

"Thank you for calling Psychic Sisters Network. My name is Ariel, and my extension number is 723884. May I have your name, please?"

"This is Louisa." Her dog had run off, could Phoebe tell her what had happened to him?

"This is Bob." Bob just wanted to be amazed. He was. Fifty minutes later, after one marriage proposal and several attempts to get her home phone number or at least the state she lived in, Bob hung up, satisfied that he'd gotten his money's worth, anyway.

"This is Danny." His girlfriend was pregnant, and he wanted to know if the baby was his. The cards said it was. He was okay with that.

And then a caller who said nothing.

Phoebe didn't like pauses. "Are you there?" she asked.

"Closer than you can imagine, Phoebe."

She hit the switch-hook button, her hands shaking, and

shouted at the phone, "Don't you ever call me again, you son of a bitch. Not ever!"

The calls were coming faster. She wasn't going to be able to log off. She couldn't afford to take the night off. She tried *69 on her work phone, hoping no calls would come in while she was trying to get information, because if they did, they would count as hang-ups and drag down her minute average. She'd end up farther down the priority list, get fewer calls, and make less money. She was barely hanging on already.

The last number that had called her was the psychic hotline—exactly what she would find if the call had come through the system. No help there until she logged off, then. She marked the time the call came through on her log sheet and wrote "prank caller" in the place where the name should have gone. She would call the service once she logged off to see if she could find out where the call came from.

"My name's Charlene. I'm psychic, and I'm looking for a job. How can I get on the network?" Phoebe told her. Phoebe got a little kickback for any referrals that PSN actually hired. But if Charlene had been much of a psychic at all, she would have picked up Phoebe's panic, her terror at being tied to the phone in a room with windows in it, with doors. *He* was watching her, whoever he was. Phoebe could feel him watching. In the cramping of her belly, in the cold sweat on her skin, in the white fire in her knee, she could feel his presence. His slow, patient hatred.

She could feel Michael.

Not a stranger playing with her, not a father of one of the kids who had died out for vengeance against the only target left, not one of Michael's brothers distraught at what she'd done.

Michael.

Phoebe could almost feel his finger trailing down the back of her neck. She shivered. One way or the other, she was going to have to get information out of the nursing home people. Any means necessary, she told herself.

Logging off took her a dozen tries.

When she finally succeeded, she worked herself into a tearful state and called the nursing home. It didn't take much; she was already right at the edge of panic. "This is Laine Schaeffer," she said between hiccuping sobs. "I just got a call from someone who said that Michael was dead, and I can't get anybody back home to pick up the phone. I don't know who called, I can't trace the number. Is it true?"

Perhaps it was the genuine fear in her voice; perhaps it was the fact that at three thirty in the morning the on-duty nurse was less inclined to be suspicious; perhaps the nurse was simply sloppy. She said, "Oh, Ms. Schaeffer, I'm so sorry about whoever told you that. I was in there not fifteen minutes ago changing his tube feeding and turning him, and he's the same as he has been for the past few days."

"You're sure?"

"I'm sure. The ventilator is breathing for him now, and he's running a bad fever, but we're working on it."

"Any sign that he's waking up?"

A soft sigh. "I'm going to sound so mean saying this, but he isn't going to wake up, Ms. Schaeffer. It's been too long. He doesn't respond to painful stimuli, he doesn't follow with his eyes, he doesn't move. People always hope for miracles, and I know you will, too, no matter what I say. But I've never seen a miracle after this long. I don't think anybody has." She paused and sighed deeply. "And he isn't doing well. I know he's pulled through before, but I really think you should prepare yourself for the worst."

"Well. Then. Well . . . thank you," Phoebe said and hung up.

The call ought to have reassured her. She should be relieved. Michael was still in a coma, still in a nursing home bed all the way up in Cleveland, Ohio. Not doing well. She was safe from him. He would never hurt her again.

But in the back of her mind she could hear Michael laughing.

Then, from the corner of her eye, movement again. The

little girl. The ghost, or the hallucination, or the physical manifestation of her guilt. The child stood staring at Phoebe for the longest time, while the room got colder and colder, until Phoebe's skin felt like ice and she wanted to scream to the apparition just to go away. But Phoebe couldn't scream. She couldn't move. She sat there frozen, with her heart pounding in her throat and her hands clenched into fists, and she couldn't do anything but blink.

Go see my daddy, the child's voice whispered inside Phoebe's head. An image flashed through Phoebe's thoughts—the doctor next door. Alan Mac-something. That was the little girl's daddy? Oh, Christ.

And then the kid vanished.

At three in the morning, Phoebe couldn't imagine Dr. Alan Mac-whatever being happy to see her on his doorstep—assuming he was home—but she didn't want to spend another minute alone in her house with that telephone, either. With Michael's voice inside her head, with that feeling of knowing her that had always oozed from Michael. She didn't know how he could be in a coma in the nursing home in Ohio and on the phone with her. At that moment she wasn't going to try to figure it out. The child had come to her and had told her what she needed to do. Just like Nana had. This time, she was going to listen.

Phoebe got her cane and her backpack and hobbled to her front door. She had no idea what she was going to say to her neighbor when he opened his door. If he opened it. She knew she had to look like a crazy woman, and she knew when she opened her mouth she was going to sound like a crazy woman. But she hadn't listened to the voice that had tried to warn her when she'd had the chance before. She hadn't trusted whatever it had been—whether it was her grandmother or simply her own instincts manifesting in an unexpected form—and people had died. People she could have saved if she had just believed.

Go see my daddy.

Phoebe stepped out into the muggy, jasmine-laden Florida

night air, hobbled the few steps between her front door and the doctor's, and before she could think about what she was doing—about how completely crazy her actions were—she rang his doorbell.

It took him only a second to open the door, and he looked wide awake. So he'd already been up. She didn't remember him being quite so tall, or quite so . . . solid. He looked like hell—unshaven, with swollen red eyes and a red nose, and Phoebe thought, Oh, shit, he's drunk.

But he didn't look drunk. He didn't smell drunk.

Honestly, he looked like he'd been crying.

What the hell?

He said, "You."

"Me," she agreed.

"The knee?"

"No."

They stared at each other for a long moment, and then he said, "I hate to be blunt, then, but what in God's name do you want at this hour?"

"I wish I knew," she said. "Things have been—strange—at my house."

He narrowed his eyes. Studied her warily, and came to a decision. "Look, I was up anyway, and I could use some company right now. Turns out being alone in this place tonight hasn't worked out too well for me. If you tell me your name, I'll let you come in."

Which seemed reasonable. Phoebe looked through the door behind him, eyes scanning for chains, body parts, animals nailed to walls—if the child she'd seen and heard had been real, and not an omen of impending madness, then Phoebe didn't know how the little girl had died. And there was a big difference between *Go see my daddy* (because he needs to know I'm all right) and *Go see my daddy* (and see that he goes to jail for what he did to me).

But the unit had a surprising amount of very nice furniture, tastefully arranged. No heads on spikes. No naked women in dog collars or black leather straps.

"Phoebe. Phoebe Rain," she told him. "Bad day for me, too. Worse night." She took a deep breath and stepped inside. Looked around. "Pretty."

"A colleague—friend—of mine dropped by about a year ago, saw the place, and told me that sleeping on the floor in a sleeping bag and eating off an unpacked cardboard box four years after I bought the place did not look good and if I didn't get some furniture, he was going to take pictures and pin them to the wall in the doctors' overnight room. Morrie's the kind of guy who would do that. And he was right. So I paid a decorator." He looked around at the place, shrugged, and turned back to Phoebe.

"I don't have the talent or the money to decorate," Phoebe said, and laughed just a little. "What furniture I have is the kind that comes in a box that you put together yourself, with dowels and glue and parts labeled *A, B,* and *C.*"

Alan pulled an ottoman up to one of the armchairs for her and said, "Have a seat, put your leg up. Want some coffee?"

"Just water," Phoebe said. "I'm a bit sensitive to caffeine."

"I live on it," Alan told her. "Though today I'm wondering what I *am* sensitive to." He went over to the kitchen that was a flipped image of hers and poured coffee from a pot. Then rummaged around in his cabinets and found a nice, heavy glass, filled it with ice and filtered water. Carried both drinks back. Cleared away a couple of cartons of Chinese takeout and put the glass in front of her. He glanced at her. "Want some? Or some cookies?"

"I mostly eat raw," Phoebe said. "Lots of cantaloupe, lots of carrot juice. Tofu. Steamed stuff occasionally."

"Vegetarian?"

She nodded. "Vegan. Keeps me healthy and keeps my weight down. With the leg pain, not carrying any extra weight has become critical for me."

"I imagine." Alan looked thoughtful. She saw him start to say something, then stop himself, shake his head, and sigh. "Who shot you?"

She arched an eyebrow. Direct, wasn't he? "My ex-husband."

Alan winced and stared at her. "I'm . . . Fuck. Is he in jail, at least?"

"In a coma," Phoebe said. She didn't add anything about that being better than jail. Because Michael had called her twice in one day. Had talked to her. Had threatened her. She couldn't rejoice over his coma anymore, over the fact that she'd beat him, stopped him from killing anyone else, including her—she couldn't rejoice in anything again until she knew how he'd called her.

"Good," Alan said. He watched her.

And she watched him. "I thought it was. He's in a coma because of me."

"Want to talk about it?"

"Maybe if I do, I'll be able to make sense of what's happening with me today." Phoebe settled into the chair. It was wonderfully comfortable, and just sitting in it soothed her frazzled nerves.

"Your family not being much help?"

She exhaled slowly. "They're all dead."

He looked stricken. "God. I'm so sorry."

She nodded. "They were driving home from visiting me in college, my last year there. My dad, my mom, my sister. They had a bad, wet, hilly road, bad brakes, old car. And an eighteen-wheeler coming the other way."

He closed his eyes. "How did you get through it?"

"Badly," she told him. "I fell to pieces. I turned to the first comfort offered. And I married the biggest mistake of my life."

"Your ex."

"Yes."

Alan rose and walked around the small front room. For a while he didn't say anything at all. Then, with his back to her, he said, "What about your friends? Whatever support system you have?"

"I have me," Phoebe said. She shrugged. "I see myself as

a woman who has someone who wants to kill me. I'm not willing to put friends in the line of fire. So I don't have any."

"Line of fire. I thought you said your ex was in a coma."

"He's been in a coma for almost two years," Phoebe said. "But my . . . gut, intuition . . . nightmares . . . whatever . . . insisted that even though he was in a coma, he wasn't going to stay that way. That he was going to come after me again someday. And that he would be perfectly happy to have an excuse to hurt anyone I cared about on the way to me."

"If he's been in a coma for two years, the odds of him coming out of it now are almost astronomically bad."

"So I've been told. But I have very good reason to never want to take any chances where he's concerned."

Alan settled back into his chair and took a sip of his coffee, clearly waiting for her to go on.

Phoebe took a little drink of water. "We'd been married for eight years when I finally got up the nerve to run. It took Michael three years to find me; just long enough that I was finally pretty sure I'd successfully gotten away from him. He came into the school where I was teaching. Had a shotgun with him, and a pistol, and a lot of ammunition, and I don't know how he got into the school with it. No one does." Phoebe closed her eyes, trying to blank out the pain that came from talking about it. She'd been over the story so many times—with police, with counselors, with nurses and physical therapists—that she thought she'd gotten numb to the whole nightmare.

But she was discovering that all the numbness wore off the second the danger came back.

"He walked into the classroom, smiled at me, and said, 'Hello again, Phoebe. I told you you'd never leave me. Time to go home,'" Phoebe said. "Then he pulled out the pistol and shot one of my students through the head. Twelve years old . . ." Phoebe couldn't speak for a moment.

Alan's lips thinned, and his body tensed. She could see his hands knot into fists, could see the knuckles go white.

"I saw him aim at another one of my students and I

charged him. He pulled the trigger, hit the boy, and had the shotgun in his other hand part of the way up to shoot me when I landed on him."

"You jumped a man who was trying to shoot you?" Alan asked, studying her.

"Yeah."

"Shit. Little guy?"

"He *was* six four and about two hundred thirty pounds. I've been told that now he's rolled into a fetal ball with a gastric tube through a port in his stomach, and last I heard he was down about a hundred pounds."

"You attacked a guy that size?" Alan looked like he didn't quite believe her.

"At that moment I would have jumped King Kong. What were my other options? Stand there and die? Watch him kill all my students in front of me, then kill me—which was, I think, his plan?"

"Run, maybe?" Alan suggested.

"That option didn't even occur to me. My students were in there with him; all I could think was that I had to stop him. Something inside me snapped when he brought up the gun. I was scared, but just too furious to think."

Alan nodded. "Adrenaline rush. It hits people different ways. We get some strange things through the ER—people who have done impossible things."

"That was me," Phoebe said. "All adrenaline. I hit him, the shotgun went off and took most of my knee with it, but I went for his eyes with my thumbs and his throat with my teeth and his groin with my good knee. We fell. I jammed an elbow into his throat. I remember hearing the crunch. That took him out of the fight—he was too busy trying to breathe."

"Could have killed him right there, actually."

"I wish I had," she whispered. "But I didn't hit the cartilage hard enough to completely crush it." She stared down at the glass of water in her hands, realizing that it was shaking. She tightened her grip on it. "I grabbed his hair with both hands," she continued, "and started smashing his head up and down on the floor. He couldn't fight me off. I'd crushed his windpipe. I just kept thinking of all the times he'd hurt me, tortured me, and I kept thinking if I'd had the guts to fight back just once *then,* two kids wouldn't be on the floor dying . . ."

Her voice flattened and her pulse galloped. She was back in the nightmare again, back in the endless recitations to police about what had happened, and all of a sudden her voice sounded tinny and far away to her, as if she were listening to someone else talking. "I remember my hands clutching his hair and the sound of his head hitting the industrial carpet and, under it, the concrete floor—the sound it made. And how the sound changed."

Phoebe looked up to see Alan staring away, a look of sick horror on his face.

It was horrible. The whole ordeal was still with her on the bad days, and though she hadn't suffered from so many of those of late, the events of the day had just made it all sharp and clear and brand-new again.

"In the back of my mind, I could hear the screaming, and I could see blood," she said, barely able to force out the words. "Lots of blood. And I realized that my right leg hurt a lot. But I was inside a dark tunnel and the only people in it were Michael and me. And Michael's head slamming and slamming and slamming. Then that tunnel narrowed down to a pinpoint, and then to nothing. I woke up in the hospital. He never woke up at all. At least that's what the hospital says."

"The kids?"

"Both died."

He reached over and took her hand and held it, not saying anything. That single human touch undid her. Tears filled her eyes, and she closed them tightly, swallowing hard until she knew she could keep going without crying. She didn't let herself cry anymore.

"You don't have anybody?"

"I learned something from my last meeting with Michael—keep innocents out of the line of fire. You don't know what it's like, having people murdered because of you."

Alan was quiet for a moment. "You're right. I don't. But I know what it's like to feel guilty." He didn't look at her when he said it. "Still." He took a long sip of coffee. "Two years. You could surely at least risk a phone call to a friend after two years."

"A friend who would come running to help me? And then what if Michael showed up?" Phoebe considered her next words carefully. "Which of the people that you love would you intentionally put between you and a bullet, if you only had to do one simple thing to prevent any of them from being there?"

Alan didn't say anything.

"It's not a rhetorical question. Which of them?"

"None of them, of course."

"Me either," Phoebe said. "And I only have to do one simple thing to keep them out of harm's way. I have to stay away from everyone I've ever known."

Alan nodded. "I truly understand that." He put his coffee on the table and leaned forward, elbows on knees, hands clasped together. "But if I can offer an opinion as a doctor, if he's been in a coma for two years, you can probably stop worrying."

Phoebe shook her head.

"No?"

Phoebe's mouth went dry. She didn't want to say anything, but she didn't see how she could avoid it, either. "Michael called me today."

The color drained out of Alan's face. "He's out of the coma?"

"The nursing home says no. That he's very close to dying, in fact."

"Then . . ."

Phoebe looked into his eyes and tried to look like someone sane. Because as bad as this confession was, everything else she had to say was worse. "I can't explain it. I know Michael's voice. I would bet anything that it was him on the phone." She took a deep breath and added, "But that's not why I'm here."

"I was wondering about that." He smiled a little. "Though I am grateful for the company."

"You may not be. Do you believe in ghosts?"

She could see him forming the word "no"—could see the flat, automatic denial already on his face and then something . . . something . . . It was like watching a man get hit in the face by a bucket of ice water. He froze and his eyes went wide, and for just an instant she could see fear and denial and the strangest little flash of what might have been hope. And then it was all gone. He was under control again. He's really good at that, she thought. And he said, "I try to maintain a healthy skepticism about the paranormal."

Phoebe nodded. "I taught science and math—could have taught at the high school level, but I enjoyed working with younger kids." Her voice didn't break there. She could almost have been proud of herself, had the circumstances been different. "I understand about skepticism. It's a lot more useful than, say, dogmatic denial."

"Why do you ask?"

Phoebe let herself look at Alan—really look at him. His was a pleasant face worn not so much by age as by pain. She could see the pain in his eyes. No one would ever mistake Alan for a movie star; no woman would ever stop in her tracks to stare at him as he walked by. But Phoebe had a sense of underlying solidity to him. Of something genuine. Something good. And she could hear the little voice in the back of her head.

Go see my daddy.

She already had some idea of what had happened to him. He had been someone's daddy, though in his home she could see no signs of anyone else in his life at all. If she'd brought her cards with her, she might have had a clearer picture of what she was stepping into—but she hadn't been ready to show that part of herself to anyone, and especially not to the neighbor who had politely invited her into his house at three in the morning.

"Because I saw a ghost today."

He hadn't changed position, but she noticed that his knuckles had gone white. "This happen to you a lot?"

"Second time in my life," Phoebe said.

"When was the first time?"

"Also today."

He took a deep breath. "I see. Spooky white sheet sort of thing?" he asked, and he was trying to be casual about it, but Phoebe could hear in Alan's voice that the casualness was an act. All of a sudden he wasn't so good at keeping his emotions in the box.

And this was where it got hard. Because Phoebe hadn't seen something vague. She'd seen some*one.* Someone very specific. Someone who had mattered a whole hell of a lot to somebody—probably to this man, unless Phoebe had misunderstood.

She said, "My visitor was a little blonde girl, blue jeans and a pink blouse with a big red heart on the front. Short, curly hair. Sweet smile. Sort of . . . pixie-ish."

Alan shuddered and swallowed. Closed his eyes and turned his head to one side, and then abruptly stood up.

Turned his back to her.

Beneath his shirt she could see muscles in his back knotting and flexing.

"You teach science," he said.

"Not anymore."

"Doesn't matter. You must still remember some of it." His voice had gone hoarse, scratchy. "You have any explanation for what you saw?"

"No."

"Where . . . where was this little girl?"

"In my living room."

"Not . . . outside a window?"

"No." Phoebe was trying to figure out where his questions were coming from. They weren't the sort of questions she would have asked had she been on the receiving end of this conversation. "She told me to come see you."

He turned to stare at her. To glare at her. "She *talked* to you."

"She told me, 'Go see my daddy.' She showed me . . . you."

Alan's body went rigid, and the bones stood out under the skin of his face. Phoebe realized again that he was a big guy. Not as big as Michael—but a hell of a lot bigger than her.

"My daughter. Talked. To *you*."

"I told you what she said. It wasn't much. Just to come see you."

She saw something heartbreaking in his eyes. He'd loved his little girl. Phoebe didn't know how or when the child had died, but she could see in every line of Alan's body that it might as well have been five minutes ago. That he hadn't found any peace. Hadn't come to terms. He was still raw and bleeding inside.

"And your husband who is in a coma called you today, too." Another statement, not a question.

Phoebe nodded.

"Right." Alan stood there, staring down at her, wearing an unreadable expression. "What do you do for a living now?" he asked.

Phoebe's heart sank.

"Why do you ask?"

"I'm curious. You have some . . . interesting things going on next door. Ghosts and mysterious phone calls. You aren't teaching anymore. These places cost money. Unless you own yours outright—and I'm guessing that you don't—you have bills to pay. So . . . what do you do? How do you make a living?"

Phoebe had never sought out the paranormal. It wasn't an area of special interest for her, it wasn't something she loved. It was, most times, an embarrassment. Her mother had taught her to read cards when she was little, so Phoebe had thought it was normal—that everyone did it. She'd proven to be good at it. But the world had quickly disabused her of the notion that anyone else thought reading cards was normal. She'd learned not to mention it at all in most circles and, when she did, to never suggest that it might be more than an amusing parlor game. Because if she did, she was suddenly a threat. Or a crazy person.

She'd learned to shut up about the cards. About the world she could sometimes sense just on the other side of conventional reality. She had learned never to suggest that she got information from anywhere except television, radio, or something she'd read. Except with people she knew very well, she covered her few slips with the stock line "I must have read it somewhere," along with a smile and a shrug.

Which wasn't going to work here, because he'd asked her a direct question.

Phoebe stood up. Grabbed her cane. "My job isn't a part of this."

"Humor me."

"I'm all out of humor. It's been a very bad day for me," Phoebe said evenly, "because I received a call I can't explain from someone I hoped I'd never hear from again. And I saw a ghost. Twice. And while I can understand that you don't want to believe me—or maybe just that you *don't* believe me—I only came over here to give you a message. It wasn't easy for me to come, and frankly, I'm not sure why I'm here. The little girl—your daughter—told me to come see you, but she didn't tell me why. So. I'm here. I've told you what she told me. But now I think I'm done."

Phoebe discovered that she didn't want to know what Alan would think of her when he discovered her current line of work. She didn't want to know any more than she already knew from the look on his face—that he thought she was a scammer. A charlatan.

As she limped to the door, he was still demanding answers, sounding angrier and angrier. "Who sent you here?

Really? Who told you about my daughter? What sort of game are you playing? Answer me, dammit. You come here and say something like this, tell me you saw my daughter—"

His voice broke, and Phoebe's heart broke with it. But she wasn't going to tell him any more about herself. Wasn't going to let herself be the target for all of his pain.

She'd spent too much time as a target already.

"You owe me the truth!" he was shouting as she stepped out of his door.

"I *gave* you the truth," she said as she slammed the door behind her.

She wanted to cry. Why couldn't she have still been a nice, normal science teacher when this happened? Then she could have admitted to her job without instantly destroying whatever credibility she might have had.

I read tarot for a psychic hotline. Yeah. That would really add to the poor man's peace of mind.

Alan stood behind the heavy vertical blinds over the front window and watched Phoebe leave. She'd claimed that Chick had come to her, that Chick had appeared to her on the anniversary of Chick's death and told Phoebe to come see him.

Alan wanted to think that someone had put his neighbor up to it. That this visit had been some disgusting, heartless trick, or maybe the opening move of some bizarre money-grubbing scheme, something foul. Because that would make sense.

But after Phoebe closed her door and moved out of Alan's sight, he shut his eyes and saw Chick standing in the rain, staring up at him, trying to tell him something that he couldn't hear, and he felt the tears burning paths down his cheeks again.

chapter 5

Phoebe curled up on the couch, wrapped in an afghan, cold and shaking in spite of the heat.

Bad. That could have been so bad. She'd gone into a stranger's house in the middle of the night on the advice of something even she couldn't quite believe. The doctor could have gone psycho on her, and people would have been picking pieces of her out of neighborhood Dumpsters the next day.

She pressed her cheek against the rough weave of the couch and closed her eyes. He could have done anything. He'd been angry, he'd been demanding, but it could have been a lot worse. He could have reacted the way Michael had reacted when he caught her reading cards at a party Halloween night and realized that she hadn't thrown her cards away. Three months after they got married.

That Halloween incident had been such a stupid thing. Dr. Luckreed found out from his wife—who taught sixth-grade social studies at the school where Phoebe was in her first year of teaching—that Phoebe read tarot, something she had kept from the attention of the principal and the school board. Up to that time, she'd just read occasionally for her friends—she'd never charged for a reading and had never gone public with her odd talent. But Sherry had been having problems, and Phoebe had offered to read for her, and the reading had helped. Phoebe thought nothing more about it until a month later, when the Luckreeds wanted a tarot reader as entertainment for a Halloween party and Sherry had asked Phoebe if she would come and throw cards. Phoebe had been delighted.

They set her up in a little heated gazebo outside the main house, with the pathway lit by pumpkins and with ghosts, bats, and spiderwebs fluttering from the bare-branched maples that arched overhead.

Phoebe's evening had started slowly—she'd thrown cards for one woman and had been really on. Then she'd sat for a while, sipping a cup of hot chocolate from the big electric pot Sherry had supplied. She'd had time to finish almost a full cup before she heard a laughing couple come up the walk. She'd quickly nailed both the fact that they'd been trying to get pregnant for ages and that the woman had finally succeeded—something she hadn't yet dared tell her husband, fearing that it wouldn't last. The cards said it would.

Phoebe had had time for a few sips of hot chocolate after those two—but then she'd looked up to find a line of people stretching all the way back to the big old Victorian house. Word had gotten out, and she didn't have time for another sip of chocolate all night.

She'd had a ball, and she'd been hot with the cards, too, steadily digging out hidden issues, helping people get a different perspective on problems that had been stymieing them, and simply letting the querents know how things were going in their lives. The whole tone of the evening had been pure, unadulterated fun.

And then she'd looked up to find Michael next in line, his patrician features twisted with fury, his green eyes glowing. Michael, who had been working late on a case and who'd said he wouldn't be able to make the party and couldn't really stand the Luckreeds anyway and suggested that she really should just decline the invitation. She looked into his eyes as he stood in the gazebo archway, and she saw murder. Her hands had stilled on the cards, and he'd said in a voice too low to cause a scene but poisonous nonetheless, "Forgot to tell me a few things, didn't you, Phoebe? How dare you make a spectacle of yourself like this? I told you never to do this—this *witch* crap of yours—again. Don't you know who I am? Don't you know how this reflects on me?"

"I'm having fun at a party. The people here are also having fun. I don't see how it reflects on you at all."

"You will," he said. He'd insisted that she leave right then. Claiming a family emergency, he'd dragged her past disappointed guests waiting in a line that had only gotten longer. He had hunted up Dr. Luckreed and made excuses, and then had hauled Phoebe home, telling the Luckreeds he would have someone pick up Phoebe's car the next day.

He'd hurt her in ways she would never have been able to imagine, and he hadn't even laid a finger on her. He never raised his voice, never lost control—but he started in with her trailer-park childhood and the way her lower-class manners, speech, and actions were constantly making her look like a fool and humiliating him by association. He'd mocked her career as something fit only for the talentless and unambitious, utterly ridiculed her use of the tarot deck, and called her both gullible and scheming. And then he'd accused her of being like the girl who'd left him—of being cheap and tawdry and a charlatan, of letting him down, of making him so angry that he'd said those terrible things to her when he never wanted to hurt her. When he loved her so much. And when he'd been a fool, because he'd fallen again for the same sort of woman who had hurt him before.

They'd only been married three months. She'd been young. She'd been stupid. She'd believed that she was partly at fault—that at the very least she'd humiliated him and perhaps caused him potential problems with his work. And she had let the pity that brought them together and that kept them together overshadow the stirrings of self-preservation that told her to walk away. She'd held honor in high regard back then—had believed that when she gave her word she had to keep it no matter what. No matter whether the person to whom she'd given her word was upholding his end of the bargain or not.

Young and dumb.

Over the next few months, to appease his various hurts and humiliations, she'd resigned her teaching position, had almost vanished from the lives of people who knew her, and had cut off almost all communication with her friends. Michael's associates started being the only people that she saw.

And then, when she'd voluntarily cut herself off from everyone who might help her, the real horrors had started. And she was too ashamed at having been played the way he'd played her, and too afraid of what he would do to her, to run for help.

Young and dumb.

Eight years and the dumb had worn off, as had any illusions she might have had about honor, either his or hers. She'd run. And five years after *that*, she wasn't all that young anymore, and the smarts had apparently stuck. She could see trouble and stay out of its way.

She took a deep breath, uncurled herself from the couch, and cautiously stood up. She had daylight, and errands to run.

The leg felt better. Some days were like that, and she was sure that with enough exercise and care, she would eventually be able to get rid of most of the pain and regain most of her mobility. She yearned to be able to run again; she'd loved running.

She decided to go without the cane—just tough it out. She grabbed her backpack, swung open the door, and there stood her next-door neighbor, just coming out his own door.

"Four years I managed to live here without running into you," he said, "and now you're everywhere." Then he noticed she wasn't using the cane. "Miracle worker, too, I see. Very nice." He looked disgusted. He stared at her the way people used to when she was a kid. They'd find out she was from whichever trailer park her family was living in at the time, and they'd act like she had something contagious that would rub off.

"Like I have nothing better to do with my life than hoax some shallow, money-obsessed snob like you," she said. "Your kid came to me at that ridiculous hour of the morning because she wanted to tell you something. No skin off my nose if that doesn't matter to you," Phoebe snapped and headed down the sidewalk, taking her time and going easy on her knee.

And then he was right beside her, glaring down at her. "I want to know what your game is. You think you can—what—blackmail me? Get me to pay you to tell me some story you made up about her? You figure I have a lot of money because I'm a doctor?" He looked like he'd be willing to strangle her if she just gave him that little extra nudge. "What's your angle?"

"You're the conspiracy theorist. You tell me." Phoebe reached her car, grateful that her parking space was close to her front door. "But not now. I have things I need to take care of." She gave him a cold, haughty smile—the one she'd perfected as a kid living in a one-bedroom single-wide trailer in an endless succession of dreary trailer parks, sharing a foldout couch in the wall-less den with her sister and wearing homemade clothes and hand-me-downs from relatives who were better off.

She got into her car wanting to hate Alan, slammed the door, and drove off.

But she couldn't hate him. If she put herself in his place and tried to imagine someone coming to her in the middle of the night, claiming that he'd had a visit from her dead child, she would have been skeptical, and probably hostile. She would have been looking for the angle, too, had some lunatic claimed what she had claimed.

Phoebe could tell herself that Alan was like Michael—but her gut said he wasn't. That the two men were about as far apart on the spectrum as two members of the same species could be.

Her gut said more about Alan, but she didn't intend to listen to that. She'd given up on men. Living the life of a nun suited her—no one hitting her, no one hurting her, no one threatening to kill her.

Not until yesterday, anyway.

Phoebe spent an hour at the shooting range, plugging targets in tight clusters with the Browning, something she did twice a week every week, because she was never going to be unarmed and helpless again.

Then she drove down University to the Moonstruck New Age Shoppe, parked, and eased herself out of the car, careful of the knee but pleased at how it was holding up. Ben Margolies saw her crossing the parking lot and had the door open for her by the time she reached it.

Ben was, Phoebe guessed, in his late thirties or early forties. But from a few feet away he could have passed for ten years younger. He worked at his looks; his pale hair fell over his forehead in a boyish, clearly expensive style that she suspected included coloring. His eyes were the startling blue that Phoebe attributed to tinted contact lenses. He dressed in Banana Republic and Gap, and kept his body lean and supple with yoga classes he took in the gym next door. Classes he'd invited her to take with him more than once and which she had, more than once, declined.

The irritating young witch wannabes who hung out in the shop gushed about how cute he was. Phoebe thought Ben was trying too hard—but he *was* nice-looking.

"Hi, beautiful," he said. "You couldn't have picked a better day to come in. How's the knee?"

"Hurts . . . But see? No cane." She held out her hands and demonstrated cane-free locomotion for him. "I had something I wanted to ask you, but first tell me what's great about today."

"Ummm . . . I'm going to ask you out and you're going to tell me yes?"

"Clearly you fail the psychic test," Phoebe said. She smiled when she said it, but her stomach gave that queasy little flip she got every time he joked about asking her out. If he hadn't recommended her for the job with the psychic

hotline, she probably would have found another place to re-
stock, just because he was endlessly persistent, even if he
kept his persistence low-key and friendly.

He had helped her get the job, though, and she felt like
she owed him. And even though she didn't know him very
well, he was a familiar face, and was someone who actually
knew her name. She didn't have many people like that left
in her life.

Ben laughed. "Actually, I knew you were going to say
that. No, today is your lucky day because I got in a new
batch of incenses and some fascinating new decks. You're
going to love them."

Phoebe smiled at him and sighed. "I'll take a look, but
you know what I like."

"Plain white candles and Nag Champa are fine, but you
could have a little zazz in your life. You *deserve* a little
zazz." He held out his arms and gave her a showman's
smile.

She made a face. "Last couple of days, I've had more
goddamned zazz than the Boston Pops."

Ben looked at her sidelong, and an odd smile crawled
across his face. "Have you been cheating on me behind my
back, beautiful?"

Ben laughed then, but in the instant before he did, her
mind reframed everything. Ice slid down her spine and into
her bloodstream, and she thought, He knows my real phone
number, he could probably get my work number under some
pretense, and the fact that he's always been nice enough
doesn't mean that there isn't something seriously wrong
with him.

If he could do voices—if he'd ever heard Michael
speak—

He patted her shoulder in a fashion probably meant to be
friendly but that made her heart leap into her throat, and
strolled across the store to pick up a big box of her favorite
Nag Champa incense for her, and a dozen white pedestal
candles.

"How's business?" she asked. Her mouth was dry.

He had his back to her, putting the candles she got every time she came in into a box. "Steady. Lot of new clients—enough that I may be able to afford a full-time reader to work with me. The offer is still open."

Chills skittered down Phoebe's spine. "Too public for me," she said. "Working in the shop would involve a lot of standing, and you have way too much glass in the front window."

"You're still doing the phone readings?" He turned, the box with the candles and the incense in his arms.

She nodded.

"That's shit money. You could make so much more reading in here, Phoebe, and you'd develop a regular clientele in no time."

"Reading is a stopgap for me," Phoebe said.

"You've been saying that for a year."

"I know."

He shook his head, put the box on the counter, and added the purchases up on a receipt pad. "Thirty-four fifty-nine. That's my cost—I'll let you buy wholesale today."

Phoebe reached into her backpack and brought out her wallet. She counted out bills and change with hands that were shaking and quickly put the money on the counter.

"Thanks," she said.

Ben reached for the box, but Phoebe picked it up first and hobbled out of the store as fast as she could.

She didn't think Ben had ever met Michael. What were the odds? She couldn't imagine how Ben might be able to imitate Michael's voice, either, or how he might have said the things Michael would say.

But he knew who she was. And where she was. And how to reach her. And as far as she knew, he was the only one who did.

chapter 6

"What the hell are you doing in here on your day off?" Morrison Beacham-Smith, one of the rotating ER physicians and Alan's friend, looked like he'd been strapped to the undercarriage of a train and dragged for five hundred miles.

"I heard you were having fun?"

"Can't have heard that. It's been hell on wheels today."

Alan feigned casual amusement. "Saturdays. Whatcha gonna do?"

"So . . . you here to help out?"

Alan laughed, and this time the amusement was real. "On my day off? No—but my suspicion that you've been into the narcotics cabinet just got a lot stronger." Alan looked around. The ER actually looked pretty sedate at the moment. The nurses were walking, not running—always a good sign—he couldn't hear anything beeping, and he didn't smell blood. "Morrie—can you come for a walk with me? Ten, fifteen minutes tops?"

Morrie said, "Your timing is good. This is the first sane stretch we've had all day. And I *so* need some munchies." He caught the attention of a blue-scrub-suited nurse propped against the nurses' station, working on a chart. "Sheila, I'll be in the cafeteria. Page me if things go boom."

The nurse nodded and gave him a wave.

As they headed down the hall, Morrie was still on ER wires. "Back-to-back crashes, one blunt amputation, a guy with an ice pick in his skull all the way to, but not through, the fornix, who fucking *walked* in. Then we get three cardiacs, one of which coded before arrival and one after. The third we shipped upstairs with standard orders, but he's been tearing downhill ever since. We've filled ICU and taken about half of the overflow up on Med-Surg. And at the moment, over in X-ray, we have this guy with a G.I. Joe doll stuck in—"

"Morrie," Alan interrupted.

Morrie stopped.

"I'll have to get the war stories later. I need to ask you something."

They'd reached the cafeteria. Morrie went straight to the row of vending machines and bought a couple of candy bars, a can of soda, and three packs of peanut butter crackers. Then he led the way to a table in the corner.

"Okay, shoot."

"I won't have to. You keep eating like that, you're going to keel over on your own."

Morrie just grinned.

Alan shook his head and smiled. But the smile vanished as he said, "I had a visitor last night."

Morrie nodded, popped the top on the soda, and took a drink.

"I was inclined to think she was a charlatan, or some sort of gold-digger out for money, but I spent a lot of time thinking about this after I, ah, chased her out of my living room. A couple of things don't add up."

Morrie grinned. "You discovered that her hair really is that shade of blonde, that her tits are real, and that she and her little brother *are* orphans."

"Not that sort of gold-digger," Alan said. He didn't allow himself to express his impatience; Morrie was *always* trying, but underneath the pain-in-the-ass exterior he was an intelligent, curious man. Excellent diagnostician. Explorer of things a bit beyond the pale.

"Too bad," Morrie said.

"I'll cut this short. She came to me last night to tell me that she'd talked with my daughter. That my daughter told her to come see me."

Morrie put the candy bar on the table and sat up straight. "Your kid died in . . . Kentucky, was it?"

"Right."

"This woman came from Kentucky to talk to you?"

"No. She lives next door to me, and has for most of the time I've lived in the place."

Morrie nodded and rested his chin in his hands. "She hasn't asked you for anything before now?"

"Never so much as said hello. I bumped into her getting home from work yesterday. First time we had any contact at all."

"And what makes you think she might be legit?"

"Two things," Alan said, wishing he had some way of not mentioning the second. "First, she exactly described what Chick was wearing the day she died."

"Any place she could have found that information elsewhere?"

"No."

"Okay. That's pretty compelling, then. What's the second thing?"

Alan took a deep breath. "I saw Chick yesterday, too."

Morrie looked at him like he'd grown a second head and said, "Fuck me. You're kidding."

"I'm not kidding. I don't intend to tell anyone else, but I'm absolutely serious."

Alan described Chick's visitation and the events surrounding it, from the brush of the curtain on the back of his neck while he was working clear through to the spring-scented rainwater on the carpet that was the last thing to vanish.

When he finished, Morrie sat there for a minute, then gave a low whistle. "Duuuude. Dude, dude—you must bring in a couple of guys with meters and cameras to see if they can validate this for you. No? What no? This is potentially huge." Morrie, in moments of excitement, fell back into the persona of Surfer Dude, which had kept the expectations surrounding him low through high school, college, and the first couple of years of medical school, while permitting him to pursue a slew of outside interests. Beaches. Babes. And, somewhat off the beaten track, ghosts.

Alan said, "This isn't about science, Morrie. This is about my kid."

"Well, of course, but . . . man, if you could do the science, too . . ."

"No. I knew you were into this sort of thing, though, and I wanted to know if you were aware of any instances where . . . ghosts . . . appeared to people away from the place where they were killed."

"Oh, shit yes," Morrie said. He evidently felt himself on solid ground again, for he ripped open one of the packs of crackers and started munching. "Happens a lot. People get a visit from a son stationed across the ocean fighting for his country and find out later that he appeared to them the moment that he died, just to let them know he loved them. Or a parent in the hospital with something terminal shows up in the house of the one kid no one has been able to reach to let the kid know he needs to call home. Or ghosts will show up to tell the people they loved when they were alive not to go someplace or do something, and that bit of advice turns out to save the people who get it."

"So Chick coming to me now . . ."

"She didn't appear to you when she died. That would have been a bit more common. The message for that is usually just 'I love you, I'm going to be okay.' She's come a long way, both from the time of her death and from the place of it. So odds are she's trying to tell you something. Something fairly fucking important. Assuming you don't have a tumor. We should schedule you for a CAT scan immediately to rule that out."

Alan studied him sidelong and saw the grin. "Thanks, Morrie. You're always reassuring."

"That's what friends are for." Morrie offered Alan one of his plastic crackers, and Alan waved it off. Morrie shrugged, crunched his cracker and said, "But you couldn't hear anything when you saw her, right?"

"Right."

"And it was after she appeared to you that she appeared to the next-door neighbor."

"I'm not sure of the time sequence. Could have been before, could have been after. My neighbor and I didn't actually, um, discuss this. But, yes, I think so."

"And the next-door neighbor could hear what she said."

"She *said* she could."

Morrie shrugged broadly. "Then, my man, this is easy. You go over, you make nice to the neighbor, and you try to find out why the hell your kid has come a very long way to talk to you."

"You don't think a . . . séance . . . or something like that would be better?"

"No," Morrie said. "If your little girl can talk through the neighbor and is willing to do that, don't screw around trying some other method that probably won't work. Use the method you know will work." He was watching Alan's face, and suddenly he grinned. "Oh, I get it. The neighbor looks like Magilla Gorilla, and you're afraid if you go over and make nice, she's going to want you."

"Not exactly," Alan said, "but I'd rather not deal with her again if I can figure out an alternative."

Morrie sat there for a moment, studying Alan, an expression of frank suspicion on his face. Then his eyes lit up. "Oh, sweet jumping Jesus, she's a babe, isn't she? She's *ripe,* and suddenly my man's little soldier has remembered he can do something besides piss."

"She's cute, in a short, starved, waiflike sort of way. But she's not my type. And I don't need that sort of complication in my life anyway."

"Duuuude, you *so* need that sort of complication. I have never in my life known a man more in need of getting fucked through the floor than you. You are so *rigidly* uptight the nurses finally gave up on you and moved your name to the Not Running section of the Pussy Pool. You're down there with Milton Stanback." Milton Stanback was seventy-eight, the oldest physician on staff. "The best odds on you right now are under what circumstances your testicles will explode from lack of use."

This diverted Alan for a moment. "The nurses have a ... Pussy Pool?"

"Not that you heard about from me," Morrie said. "They run little side bets about when various doctors get some, with payoffs based on mood when called at three in the morning, gender, age, and sex appeal of the voice answering the phone, and traitors like me who feed them details for a piece of the action." Morrie waggled his eyebrows. "They should just call it the Get-Laid Pool, since about a third of the doctors on the list are women and only a couple of those are actively chasing other women. But a couple of the nurses liked the alliteration too much to give up the name." He grinned and took a swig of his soda. "I'll have to tell them to put you back in as a dark-horse candidate."

Alan shook his head. "Do *not* do that to me."

"Hey, it's better than your only get-laid odds now, which are for 'Sympathy fuck on the X-ray table' and which are running an outrageous two hundred to one against. Shit, I have ten bucks on that one just because it's almost impossible to get the nurses to handicap that high." His eyes narrowed. "You wouldn't feel like ... um ... waiting a day or two and then hitting up, say, Denise in Respiratory Therapy for ..."

"No," Alan said. "I wouldn't."

Morrie considered that for a moment, then, apropos of nothing, said, "Odds on your nuts exploding during a code are three to one."

"Thanks, Morrie," Alan said, standing. "That's always nice to know."

Morrie shoved extra crackers and candy bars into the pockets of his lab coat, tugged the drawstring a little tighter on his scrub pants, and said, "Denise. X-ray table. Three minutes, dude, and you'd make me a happy man."

"The nurses are a whole lot scarier than I thought they were," Alan said, walking back toward the ER.

"Believe it," Morrie said, grimacing. "You have no idea. They tell me things . . ." His voice trailed off, and he shuddered. Then his mood changed, and he rested a hand on Alan's shoulder. "Let me know how this thing with Chick and the neighbor turns out. Let me know that you get through it okay, at least."

"Thanks," Alan said. "I will."

Morrie gave him an evil little grin and said, "And if by chance you and your luscious next-door neighbor get nekkid, pleeeease let me know. Fortunes will be made and lost, and empires rise or tumble, on such information."

"No," Alan said as they stepped through the double doors from the crowded hallway in front of the ER into the department itself. He was, however, grinning just a little as he headed for the door that led to the staff parking lot. And he could only shake his head as, behind him, he heard Morrie saying in a low, urgent voice, "I have a great tip on a returning player. Break out the Hot Sheet."

Phoebe saw Alan sitting on the front step of her town house as soon as she came around the corner from the parking lot and started up the walk. For just a second her heart started to race.

Then she remembered that Alan had decided she was some sort of fraud with an angle, and she pulled her shoulders straighter and lifted her chin, staring through him.

She started to step carefully around him, but he stood up as she reached him and put a hand on her arm. "I'm sorry," he said. "You . . . I wasn't ready for what you had to tell me last night."

Phoebe stopped and looked up at him. He looked sincere enough. Anxiety drew deep lines on his forehead and at the corners of his mouth, but then, last night she'd told him his dead daughter had dropped in to visit her. That would give almost anyone reason to be anxious.

"That's all right," she said. "You're not the only person who ever reacted that way." She even managed a smile, though she suspected it wasn't a convincing one.

"I'd . . . really like to hear what you wanted to tell me about my daughter." Wary eyes, nervous twitch of a smile, first two fingers and thumb of the right hand rubbing nervously against each other. Alan didn't look like a man who'd ever asked a psychic anything. He didn't look like he wanted his world to have dark corners or unexplained nooks. Phoebe felt for him—he'd probably spent a life lived in hard light without shadows, and now the shadows were there and they were moving.

"I'll tell you what I can. There really isn't much. She just told me I was supposed to come see you—and she gave me a quick image of who you were."

"But you could hear her."

"Oh, yes. Quite clearly."

"And you could see her."

"I could. I've never actually seen a gho— . . . ah, an . . . apparition . . ." She fumbled to a stop. There was no socially acceptable way to refer to the spirit of someone's dead child, was there? Nothing gentle, nothing soothing, nothing vague and kind. If there was, Phoebe couldn't find it. "I'm not a spiritualist or anything like that. I . . . I read cards. Tarot cards. Sometimes I get impressions. Usually of the person I'm reading, sometimes of someone important to them. Voices, pictures. But not physical manifestations. It's an inexact thing, usually." She looked away, past the palms and the bougainvillea and the long spikes of the bird-of-paradise plants lining the privacy fences. The little girl's visit hadn't been fuzzy or vague at three in the morning. Phoebe, feeling again the chill in the room, shivered in the Florida heat, and Alan gave her an odd, searching look.

"But, yes—I saw her."

"I saw her yesterday, too," Alan told her. "In my office. It scared the shit out of me, and it was the weirdest thing that has ever happened to me."

She caught the shaking in Alan's voice, the fear and confusion and disbelief—and the trembling hope—that lay just beneath the surface of the man standing before her, and the sound of it almost broke her heart.

Phoebe knew the sounds of loss. She heard those same sounds more often than she could bear in the voices of the men and women calling her in the dark hours, asking without words for some proof of a world beyond the stark, harsh reality of their lives. They were searching for immortality at $3.99 a minute, looking for the face of God in the fall of painted cardboard circles and rectangles, listening for magic and compassion in the voice of a stranger. They wanted a touch of grace. They wanted hope. They had a thousand different questions, but at base, those questions were all the same: Is there more than this? Am *I* more than this?

And sometimes Phoebe could reach beyond painted cardboard; sometimes she could transcend telephone lines and the carnival Psychic Sisters schlock and her own tired desperation and worn-at-the-elbows despair and find for those waiting, broken strangers a single small flash of magic. A candle's worth of light from somewhere neither she nor they had ever been. Sometimes she could give them a whiff of something outside of their workaday lives that would let them hang on. Let them believe.

Sometimes she could find hope for them.

And when she found it, when she connected with something real and true for them and heard the wonder in their voices—across a hundred miles of wire or across two thousand—sometimes for a moment she could catch a little of that wonder for herself. Sometimes the light shone for her, too, and she could believe that she was more than her despair, her shame and fear and loss and pain.

Sometimes.

Phoebe looked back at Alan, stared deep into his eyes, and the chill inside her deepened.

It was the same question once more: Is there more than this? Is my daughter still out there somewhere, not lost forever but simply somewhere else?

"Tell me what happened," she said.

They stood on the walk in front of her door, with the never-ending heat cooking both of them. Yet the cold lay bone-deep in Phoebe as Alan told her about sitting in his office and having a window to another place and time open beside him. He could easily enough be a madman, a kind man shattered by his life and fallen off the edge of reason. It would have been easy for her if he were. But he finished by saying, "Then I took a step away from the window and almost everything disappeared," and against her will and against her wishes, Phoebe believed him.

"Almost?" she asked, shivering, with the oppressive Florida sun too weak to melt away the cold inside her and burn through her fear; no sun, she thought, could burn hot enough for that.

Phoebe's dread sprang from a simple enough equation: If Alan's daughter could step beyond death into her father's life, then Phoebe's murderous, comatose ex-husband could step beyond whatever ties bound him to flesh and bone to reach into *her* world. The possibility of one meant the possibility of both.

Hope for Alan meant deeper terror for Phoebe.

She wanted to run. To hide. But where would she hide from a man who could reach from a place as near to death as any living human could dwell to find her?

Alan said, "For a few minutes after . . . she disappeared . . . the carpet was still wet where the rain blew in through the window. It soaked into the knees of my pants before it was gone, too."

And all Phoebe could think was, Oh, my God.

She said, "Where's your office?"

"In my town house. Upstairs."

Phoebe blew out a short breath, feeling the pain in her

knee from just standing still with her weight half on it. "Of *course* it is. How did I know?"

"Because you're psychic?" Alan's faint smile suggested that this was intended as a joke.

Phoebe laughed politely. She'd heard that one before. "No. Because Murphy's Law has a corollary that says if you have a blown knee, everything you desperately need to reach will be at the top of stairs."

"You need to see the office?" Alan shook his head. "It wouldn't be worth your effort now. The carpet is dry. There's nothing left."

But Phoebe gestured that Alan should wait for her; she walked to her front door, unlocked and opened it, tossed her few purchases on the couch—she'd gotten nothing that would be destroyed by a few hours outside of the fridge—and scooped her Universal Waite and her Motherpeace deck from her work space on the table. She rejoined Alan on her front stoop and closed the door again, stopping to lock all three deadbolts. "Not a waste of time," she told him. "The room might hold some sort of residue of what happened there. Maybe I can read it for you and give you something useful."

Alan nodded, though his arms crossed over his chest and his lips pressed together in a small, tight line. "How much do you charge for this, by the way?" he asked, and the question, and the faint tone of suspicion that underlay it, lit quick-burning rage inside her that she had to fight to quench.

Chin lifted, jaw tight, she said, "I don't."

"Oh." Alan had the conscience to look embarrassed.

As they walked the few steps to his front door, she regained control of her temper and told him, "I'm not an expert on spiritualist things. I've read on the subject, but it isn't my area. The event you describe—where your daughter actually created a physical contact from you to her into this whole other realm—sounds like the spirit-world equivalent of jogging to the top of Mount Everest. If it happened, that amount of energy should leave traces even *I* could pick up. Reading physical manifestations is not my talent. I read cards. Still, there had to have been a huge reason for your daughter to make that degree of contact. Maybe if I go up there, I'll be able to figure out why she went to so much trouble. I'll sit up there and throw some cards and see if I can draw out what's going on for you." She shrugged. "No sense in me not using what *does* work for me."

"*If it happened?*" He glared at her.

As he unlocked the door to his home, she repeated, "*If* it happened. I tend to believe you, but you must realize that there are other, much more logical explanations for what you describe. From my perspective, I have no way of knowing if you did drugs in your youth—or last night, for that matter. You might have fallen asleep at your desk and dreamed the whole thing. I've read that brain tumors can cause very complete, realistic hallucinations."

"I don't have a tumor," he growled. "And how would any of those things explain what *you* saw and heard?"

"I might have a brain tumor, too," she said evenly. "In which case we have the beginnings of a very nice class-action suit against the property management company. Have you seen how they spray around here?"

He didn't laugh. He didn't say anything at all.

Phoebe sighed. "I already told you that I tend to believe you. But I do think you need to consider all the possibilities."

He shoved the door open. "I'm relieved that you *tend* to believe me. To reassure you, then—I never did drugs. I was wide awake—I'm quite certain of that. And my colleague Morrie asked me this morning if I wanted a CAT scan, and if necessary I can look into that later, but I haven't had any other incidents of this sort, I don't have headaches or sensory alterations, and I'm willing to take my chances on the brain tumor angle for just a bit."

Phoebe did not permit herself to laugh out loud at his clear annoyance. He didn't enjoy being doubted any more than she had, but she didn't see any benefit in pointing out the parallels. She just said, "Why don't we go upstairs and I'll throw cards and see what I get."

"You don't think she'll just come back?" Alan stood at the foot of the stairs, frowning. "She looked so real, and I thought if I could just get out to her before she left, I could be with her again. She didn't look anything like a ghost. She wasn't any older . . . she looked just the way she did the day I lost her. But I couldn't see through her or anything. I should have climbed through the window while it was open."

That last comment slithered down Phoebe's spine, and she shook her head vehemently. "No. Definitely no. If any more of these windows open, *don't* go through them. A window like the one you describe might just throw you out your second-story window to the ground below, which would be bad enough. But if it led to where your daughter is . . ." She faltered to a stop and shrugged up at him, palms wide. "Where is she, Alan? Wherever she is, it isn't someplace where you belong right now."

"I don't care. If I could have my kid back, do you think I'd care where I had to be to get her?"

"I don't suppose you would. But I doubt that she went to all this trouble to reach you just so that you could kill yourself. They're usually trying to save the people they love, you know." Phoebe stood beside him, eyes closed, listening and smelling. The too-dry stale scent of air-conditioned air; the drip-drip of a leak in the faucet in the downstairs bathroom; the hum of the fluorescent light over the washer and dryer behind their louvered doors in the kitchen; coffee and the faintest memory of sizzled steak.

No false scents—potpourri, carpet freshener, lemon cleaner. No off scents—spring or autumn, rainstorm or smoke from burning leaves. No off sounds—voices, bells, music.

She could feel nothing uncomfortable.

"You okay?" he asked her, and she opened her eyes to see

him, very close and concerned, looking at her with eyes both beautiful and kind, and his clear concern shook her. She thought, No, I'm not all right. I'm getting myself in trouble, and I already have enough of that. If I were smart, I'd turn my ass around and go home. But she smiled. "I'm fine. Just trying to get a feel for anything . . . supernatural. Hokey as I know that sounds."

He smiled—a real smile this time. Like he was on her side. White teeth, slightly crooked. Crinkles at the corners of his eyes. He had a wonderful smile.

"Upstairs, then," she said, and swallowed hard.

He started up the stairs at a jog, and she reminded herself that she was alone by choice and that she was never going to let a man into her life again and she tried hard not to notice his butt in the tight jeans.

I'm hopeless.

She followed him, stepping up with the good left leg, bringing the weak right one up second. She climbed stairs the way three-year-olds climbed stairs, and she hated it.

She had her head down, focusing on the next tread, grimacing from the pain. She expanded on objects of her hatred—she hated climbing stairs, but she also simply hated stairs. She hit the third one wrong, and her right knee twisted just a little, and in spite of her usual control, she hissed breathing in.

And Alan was right beside her.

"There's no sense in this. You're light. I'll just carry you."

He scooped her into his arms before she had a chance to protest, and he was careful of her knee, and he was strong and his hands were sure and she damned near stopped breathing. He started up the stairs holding her close, cradled against his chest.

His right arm brushed against her right arm and their skin touched.

Phoebe closed her eyes, fought off her hunger for that touch. She'd taught science, for God's sake. She *knew* that at the moment of contact between two people, the skin transmitted electrical signals and pheromones and other chemicals; she knew that the instant chemistry some people felt toward each other truly was *chemistry*—a compatibility of the chemicals their bodies were excreting. She knew. But knowing was not experiencing—and until that instant she'd never collided with chemistry.

Alan's touch went straight to her brain. Her heart raced, her mouth went dry, her breasts tingled, and her skin ached for more.

"Oh, you don't need to carry me," she murmured. "I'll get there." But that protestation would have earned a big fat zero on a sincerity meter. For the first time in her life, a man was holding her in his arms like that, and she lost anything he might have said in response to the sheer wonder of his touch, and the feel of his arms around her, and the brush of his warm breath against her cheek. She couldn't say that it had been a long time since a man had touched her like that. It had been a long time since a man had touched her—but until exactly that moment, she'd thought that was a good thing. Because in her entire life, a man had never touched her *like that*.

Her body hummed with an electricity she had never known before.

In her mind Phoebe ripped Alan's clothes off of him, ran her hands over his warm skin, buried her face against his chest and . . .

Damn.

Thank God *he* wasn't psychic.

chapter 7

Alan realized halfway up the stairs that he'd made a mistake. Phoebe smelled sweet—like new-mown hay and sunshine. She felt soft and solid and warm in his arms. The surprising weight of her hair spilled like a curling waterfall over his right arm, and she moved her head and his lips brushed her ear, and it took all his control not to pursue that fleeting touch. Her small, tight muscles would feel so good beneath the palm of his hand. Her full lips were designed to be kissed. She had curves that fit against him in a way that just meant sex.

She was saying something about how she could make it by herself—that he didn't have to do this—but he couldn't hear the words too well over the sound of his blood rushing in his ears. His heart pounding in his throat made breathing so much of an effort that he didn't dare speak. And his body was reacting to having her in his arms in ways he was pretty sure a psychic would notice—ways that, if he let her slide down another half inch while he was carrying her, she wouldn't *have* to be psychic to notice.

And how the hell was he going to put her down without embarrassing himself?

Okay. He'd been neglecting his physical needs and desires—well, actually, until he ran over her on the sidewalk, he hadn't been *having* any physical needs and desires, but five years plus change of being celibate were bound to take their toll. He could surely have done something to prevent what was going to become an awkward situation in just two more steps.

I should have gone for the sympathy fuck on the X-ray table and made Morrie a little bit richer, he thought. Because then Phoebe wouldn't end up looking at me like I was a pervert or a molester, and that's where we're going to go with this the second I put her down.

He reached the landing, winced a little at the discomfort of jeans that were suddenly far too tight, and leaned over a bit while putting her down, contrary to all principles of good body mechanics. But he didn't betray his arousal, and the sudden sharp pain in his lower back gave him a much-needed distraction. He lunged past her to the door, hurried into the office, and switched on the light.

"In here," he called, and by the time she made it into the room, he was sitting at his desk. Not smooth, but it worked. He wasn't sure why he cared so much that she didn't think he was some lecher who'd dragged her up the stairs just so he could grope her on the way up. But he did care. A lot.

She came through the archway, the limp not too pronounced, and glanced at him. Then she turned her attention to the window.

She moved toward it slowly, eyes half closed, with a sort of out-of-focus expression on her face, and she looked like a Botticelli angel in the sunlight that angled through the glass; she wore sparkling dust motes for a halo. And he thought, Yes. Simply, yes. To whatever place she might have in his future, his life, this room—yes.

She stopped a few feet away, her eyes went all the way shut, and he saw her shiver.

Suddenly the room felt cold to him. Not air-conditioner cold. Sweating-ice cold, like someone had poured water on him and shoved him into a meat freezer. He stood up, his other issues erased by the shocking temperature change, and by the fact that he could hear whispering all around him, though he couldn't make out a word. The hair on his arms and the back of his neck stood up, and his testicles felt so tight they seemed to be trying to climb into his abdomen.

That's one way to get breathing room in the blue jeans, he thought.

Phoebe took another step toward the window, and Alan wondered if the window was going to change, and if he was going to see Chick again. No matter what Phoebe said, he would jump through that window if he ever got a second shot at it. What was a broken leg if he got to be with his kid again—no matter where she was?

But the verticals stayed the same. Everything stayed the same, except that the temperature kept getting colder and colder and colder. Phoebe shivered again, took another step forward, and cocked her head. She opened her eyes and looked at him, then walked the rest of the way to the window and put her hands on the sill.

"I can't find anything here," she said. "I mean, it's obvious to me that something happened here. And from the sudden cold I felt when I moved towards the window, this seems to be a contact point. But your daughter didn't leave any tracks that I can read—not where she was, not how she opened the doorway between there and here."

"I still feel the cold," Alan said. "I've never felt anything like it before. Is she here now?" he asked.

"The cold is related to her, but it isn't . . . her. It's just . . ." Phoebe sighed. "It's like—the contrail of a jet."

"She's been here, but she's gone?"

"She's close, and this is blowback," Phoebe said. "If I can sit at your desk for a few minutes, I can throw a few cards . . . maybe see if I can shake something loose. Maybe I can help her bridge the gap."

Alan nodded and cleared a space on the desk where Phoebe could work. The computer was easy enough to pick up and move. Notes and other things he just gathered up and deposited on the floor.

Phoebe sat, closed her eyes for a moment, then pulled cards out of a dark blue drawstring bag and began shuffling them. These weren't the round ones he'd seen her scoop up from her table and drop into a silk-and-wool card bag. These were big and rectangular and had tiny gold stars on a navy blue background. She shuffled them competently, her hands flashing. When she stopped, she cut the deck into three piles with her left hand, picked one of the piles, and started laying the cards out on the desk, placing them in an odd pattern that made no sense to him. She didn't do any oohing or ahhing, nor did she suddenly look up at him, stab a card with one finger, and say, "This portends financial ruin unless you pay me to put a spell on your enemies." Some still-wary part of him had been expecting both responses.

Instead, she sat looking at the spread for a moment, counted the cards on the table, said, "Ick. Five majors," and went back to looking at the spread again.

Finally she looked up at him. "This first reading tells me about you," she said. "I always use the Universal Waite when I read men." He tried to concentrate on what she was saying, but logically, he couldn't see where the cards could have any real relevance to his life, and illogically, he kept imagining Phoebe naked and in interesting positions on the desk, and the chair, and the floor. She pointed to the card in the center of the spread and said, "The reversed Page of Swords represents you. You're facing a challenge right now where your instinct is to approach with all your analytical skills front and center, but that's truly not a good idea. You're going to have to close your eyes and trust your gut to find your way through the current problems."

This comment caught his attention, since it told him both what he'd been thinking and why he shouldn't think that way. Damn.

Phoebe continued, "Your atmosphere—basically what's going on right now—is Strength, a major. It represents courage, compassion, patience, and strength—all of which you have, all of which you'll need. Your obstacle is that what you face may be too much for you—the Ten of Wands upright." She turned to him. "I have some unpleasant feelings related to this card, too, but I'd like to do my second layout over the top of this one before I say anything specific."

He shrugged. "Sure. Fine." Like he had any opinions on this bizarre process.

"Beneath your feet," she said, "is your Ground—the Hierophant—a major arcana card that indicates a tendency to conformity, strong personal beliefs, and occasionally an unwillingness to bend. It isn't a bad Ground card when you're in trouble, though. Over your head hangs the Nine of Swords. Nightmares. If you open your eyes and face them, you can deal with them, but so far the reversal of this card indicates that you have been letting the nightmares control you."

He stopped her. "This is really strange. What you're saying makes sense, but is it making sense because you know a little bit about me and the situation I face, or is it making sense because this thing you're doing works—and if it works, how does it work, because, really, I only had the one nightmare?"

Phoebe looked bewildered for all of half a second as she parsed that tangle of a sentence. Then she laughed, and he discovered that he loved her laugh. It was warm and rich and throaty, and he found himself right back with the Phoebe-naked-on-a-desk images, and revisited, as well, by too-tight jeans.

"It works. As for why it works, I can tell you what *I* think, but you're welcome to your own interpretation. I think we're all linked. That we are beings of light that wear these mortal forms for some reason we can only guess at while we wear them. That beneath these shells of flesh, we're part of a . . . a river of energy that fills the universe and moves through us and binds everything."

He raised an eyebrow. "That's either religion or quantum physics."

"I'm not convinced that religion and quantum physics aren't both aspects of the same thing."

"Actually, I'm not, either," he said. "I'm just at a place in my life where neither one of them seems to make sense."

Phoebe laughed a little and nodded. "Both seem to defy logic at the best of times. But that doesn't make them irrelevant. They both speak to how we affect each other. We touch each other, all of us, for good or bad. We never know what we do that matters, or whose life we change with a simple, unthinking action—but our touch spreads out infinitely far, altering and mutating and affecting even more people as it goes. I know you've heard this before, but all of existence is so closely bound that when a butterfly flaps its wings in China, it rains in Iowa."

"I've heard that," he agreed.

"I think that's why tarot works. I think the energy that is us and that moves through us responds to our will—whether we call that prayer or magic or simple action. And that because we are all connected pieces of the animating force of the universe as a whole—holograms or fractals, maybe—the fall of a piece of painted cardboard on a table echoes the movement of intelligence through the galaxy."

Alan laughed, then caught the expression of hurt on her face. "I'm not laughing at you. It's simply—well—the last person I would have expected to blow me away with quantum physics was a woman who reads tarot cards for a living."

"People are never just one thing," she said, and her smile was almost devilish.

"No, we aren't." He shook his head again. "But why did you put so much thought into this?"

Phoebe shook her head. "It's the science teacher in me. I've always preferred to understand the 'why' of things. Tarot gave me results that I couldn't explain. So I tried to figure out why."

"Not happy with the 'it's magic' explanation?"

"I don't believe in magic," she said.

Neither did I, he thought. Until I touched you.

She returned her attention to the cards.

"In your recent past I see hiding away from opportunities, refusing to explore new horizons: the Three of Wands reversed."

And he thought, That pretty much defines my last five years.

"In your near future, the Wheel of Fortune. Another of the major arcana cards. Chance, the roll of the dice, opportunities for a big win or an equally big loss."

"Major arcana cards. What are those, and why do you keep mentioning them?"

Phoebe said, "The tarot deck is divided into major and minor arcana—'arcana' means secrets. So think of them as big secrets and little secrets, more or less. We read minor arcana differently than major arcana. Minors are transient, changeable cards—you get them and you say 'Okay, those are things I have to work on and then they won't *be* an issue.' Majors . . ." She shook her head. "Major arcana tell of—well—the movement of the finger of God, or a shift in the energy of the River of Life. However you want to think of it. The majors depict events and qualities that are fixed—that you cannot change. That you can only deal with."

"And I got five of those."

"Yes."

"Five is . . . a lot?"

"Yes."

"Is that bad?"

"It's neither good nor bad. It suggests, however, that you have stepped into a place in your life where events you cannot control will move you in ways you do not expect, cannot escape, and may not welcome, and that for a while your challenge will simply be to get through them."

Alan didn't care for the sound of that.

Phoebe rested her chin on one hand and said, "Death, also a major, sits in your House, which is someone or something that is not you but that is related to you closely—and though in most cases I would give the card the traditional interpretation and say that someone who matters to you faces change and letting go of the painful past to move into the new future, I think in this instance Death has to do with your daughter. I'm not sure. This one feels muddled to me, as if other things are also suggested, but I'll find out more about the connection when I lay out your daughter's cards in a minute." Phoebe glanced up at him. "Some of these cards are trivial, simply noting the woman who is currently in your life and your wishes to have both financial stability and some sort of freedom very different than what your current work permits. You want to do something wild and irresponsible, which is interesting, considering your Ground."

I don't have a woman in my life, Alan thought, and looked at Phoebe and knew as the words were forming in his mind that they were a lie, and that at least from his perspective, he suddenly did.

Alan was getting tangled up in the cards, where everything seemed to make sense, but always in a vague way. That comment about doing something wild, though, cut straight to the bone.

He wanted to write. He'd always wanted to write. But he'd made a deal with God that he would give up writing and trying to be the next Jack Kerouac to become a doctor if his father would survive the heart attack Alan witnessed but couldn't stop. God had seemed to listen. Alan's father had lived, and in gratitude—mixed with a bit of resignation— Alan had become a doctor. And then God, the bastard, had let Alan's kid die alongside his wife, and Alan was left with ashes, and a career he'd never wanted.

Phoebe was still reading. ". . . but the core of the reading, and the part that I find most interesting, comes in the outcome. It's quite fascinating, really."

She pointed to three cards descending from the left side of the circular layout at a forty-five-degree angle. Alan looked over her shoulder at the cards; they looked like all the rest of the cards to him. Colorful, weird, alien.

"Tell me the first thing you notice about these two," she said, pointing to the two cards closest to the circle.

"They're upside down," Alan said. When she didn't say anything in response to that, he looked closer and noticed an odd mirroring of the body positions of the lone figures on each of the first two cards. "They're both sitting in the same position, with their knees and feet out and their arms crossed."

Phoebe nodded. "The Two of Swords and the Nine of Cups. In a way they're polar opposites, too. She's cut off from everything, guarding herself with swords, blindfolded only to bring her other senses to sharper awareness. She sits small and alone in the center of a vast world, in the dark, outdoors, beneath a moon, before a sea. She is uncertain and afraid, wary and armed. But, because the card is reversed, no matter how hard she tries to prepare herself, she's not ready for the challenge she faces. He, on the other hand, has his eyes wide open, but is also cut off from events happening before his eyes—both by comforts and wealth and by the fact that he sits in a sheltered location indoors, where everything seems bright and safe. His confidence that all will be well with him is his blindness. The reversal of the card lets us know that he, too, is unprepared for the challenge he faces."

"Who are they?" Alan asked, intrigued in spite of himself.

"Good question. They could be two facets of you. They could be you and your girlfriend."

"I don't have a girlfriend," Alan finally said.

"Some woman you know or are attracted to, then," Phoebe told him, and Alan felt his heart thud in his chest and did not let himself look at Phoebe or think of Phoebe, and said, "Oh. Her."

"And the final card is big. It's the World, a major, which,

along with the presence of the other four majors in this reading, indicates that Fate is playing fast and loose with your life right now. What's the first thing you think when you look at it?"

"That my World is upside down."

"Since this is an outcome, it isn't yet," Phoebe said quietly, "but it sure looks like it's gonna be."

chapter 8

Phoebe got ready to do the second layout—the one for Alan's daughter—over the top of the reading she'd done on Alan.

But Alan put a hand over hers before she could shuffle or deal the cards, and her nerves gave a little skitter.

"No more cards," he said. "I don't think I can stand to find out the rest of this. I thought I could, but she's my kid, and . . ." He shook his head, and Phoebe saw that he had grown pale.

"We can do it another time if you want," she said, and started to scoop the cards into a pile.

Ice air slammed into Phoebe like a gut punch and drove right through her, straight into her bones and her blood, so hard and fierce that for just a second she couldn't breathe. Her skin crawled, and a voice whispered in her ear, close and urgent. A child's voice.

Phoebe swallowed hard and gripped the edge of the desk.

Alan shivered, staring into her eyes. "What is it?"

And Phoebe found the breath to say, "She's here."

"My daughter?"

"She says you call her Chick. She can't stay long. She says she's tired from yesterday—that just getting here is hard for her, and making me hear her is almost impossible."

Phoebe stood, unsteady, heart racing, hanging on to the desk for support. "She says this can't wait. That you can't not listen to her. If you don't listen, one of us will be dead before a birthday. Either yours or mine—either I'm having a hard time hearing her or she's being intentionally vague."

Alan leaned against the desk, and Phoebe could see sweat beading on his upper lip. "I never told you her nickname," he said.

"*She* did," Phoebe said. "She's showing me pictures now—those are easier for her, I think." Phoebe relaxed and let the words and the images she was getting tumble out without censorship. "A tall, golden blonde woman. Green dress. A silver sports car. Convertible. The top down. Camaro? No. More expensive. I suck at identifying cars. Foreign, though, I think. Smarmy young man, good-looking, has that sort of tennis-pro country-club ooze about him. Alcohol—a lot of it. And your little girl, in the backseat, no seat belt. She says she's sorry she sneaked out."

"Chick sneaked out?"

Phoebe sat still for a moment, trying to read the images and catch the words and impressions that flowed over her. "She didn't want her mother to leave. She saw the suitcase and thought if she hid in the back of the car, she could find a way to make her mother stay—to make her come home and be a good mommy."

Alan had tears running down his cheeks; his eyes were tightly closed. "That sounds just like her," he said, and his voice was tight. "All this time, I thought Janet was just being irresponsible again for not having anything packed for Chick. That she was stealing her . . . but not because she wanted her. Just because she . . . knew . . . I . . . wanted her."

Phoebe touched his arm and said, "I'm sorry. I cannot imagine what it would be like to lose a child."

She didn't say anything about losing a spouse—especially not a spouse who had turned out to be a nightmare. She didn't offer any sympathies for the loss of Janet, either. She had the powerful impression that, at the end, the loss of his wife had not been a loss Alan regretted much.

Alan's body was rigid, his arms tight at his sides, his fists clenched. "This isn't happening," he said.

Phoebe looked at him and said, "Your daughter says she had her lucky stone in her pocket at the time of the accident. That you have it in your wallet now."

"She told you about her lucky stone?" He shook his head. "She can't have told you that."

"She says it's in your pocket. That you have to believe, so she told me. Because you're in danger. We're both in danger, and you have to believe."

Alan pulled his wallet out of his back pocket. It had a lump in one side where the leather had stretched and worn over a long period of time. He hooked a finger into the bill-fold and came out with a flat white stone about the size of an old silver half-dollar. On one side Phoebe saw a flower in bright blue with a yellow center, done in paint—lopsided, smeared, and worn away by time and much handling. "Forget-me-not, she said," Alan whispered. "She made it when she was four."

He stared at the stone lying in the palm of his hand, frozen. Then he slid bonelessly to the floor, to his knees, and his shoulders started shaking, and he began to sob. His fingers wrapped tighter and tighter around the stone until his knuckles went bone white and the veins at his wrist popped up. His head dropped to the carpet.

Chick was gone. The cold drained away, and Phoebe cautiously knelt beside Alan on the floor and put an arm around his shoulder. "Hey," she whispered, and stroked his hair. "Hey. She showed you she's okay. She showed you that she still loves you. She's watching out for you."

Phoebe sagged a little from the relief of being alone in her own head again. Her relief didn't last long, though. Alan's grief bled over to her, inescapable and overwhelming. He clutched that little rock like a drowning man hanging on to floating wreckage. "I . . . she was really here."

"I know," Phoebe said. "She wants you to be all right, and she says you haven't been."

He raised his head, closed his eyes tightly, and took a deep breath. It took him a few moments, but when he had himself under control, he said, "I buried myself the day I buried Chick. I've never believed in anything beyond this life—and Chick *was* my life. Especially once her mother . . ." He shook his head. "Her mother was wild. I don't know that Janet was faithful a single day of our marriage. I do know that Chick was mine, but only because when we had to draw blood on her once, I had a friend check for me. It wouldn't have changed the way I felt about Chick if she hadn't been mine," he said, turning to look at Phoebe. "But knowing that I had a legal claim to her that her mother couldn't refute gave me options, I thought. There at the end, I'd started looking for options."

Phoebe nodded and slid her hand into his, and squeezed, offering what comfort she could. "I know all about hunting for options," she said.

Alan met her gaze and took a slow, shaky breath. And squeezed back, and Phoebe realized how warm his hand was, and how strong. How big. How good it felt touching hers. He said, "I know more about avoiding them. I didn't want anything to change. I wanted Janet to love me. I'd loved her since we were both kids, and for a long time I thought she would eventually see how much I loved her and that would win her over." He laughed a little, sounding bitter. "It didn't. She might have been capable of loving *someone,* but not me. And not Chick."

And Phoebe heard what he was saying, but her focus was on their hands touching, on the feel of his skin against hers. Simple touch, and it undid her, and she ached for something she'd never had, something she never would have. The caring touch of a man.

She looked away from him, afraid that he would see her need and think that she was after him, that everything she had done had been an attempt to seduce him—as insane as that sounded even to her with her fogged thoughts and her galloping pulse. She started to get back to her feet, easing her bad leg straight underneath her, preparing herself for a quick exit.

Alan stood with an easy, smooth grace that Phoebe, struggling to get to her own feet, envied. Then he gave her an odd, intense little smile and bent down to slide an arm around her waist. "That has to be hell," he said.

She shrugged as he lifted her to her feet. "I'm not dead. Under the circumstances, I'm inclined to treat the knee as no big deal."

He left his arm around her waist, and she felt her mouth go dry and her pulse tear faster through her arteries. Alan stared into her eyes, and she saw a hunger there unlike anything she'd ever experienced. Naked desire. Real desire. For her. He licked his upper lip—just the quickest nervous darting of the tip of his tongue. In that instant he no longer looked so ordinary. To her, he looked exciting. Wild. Beautiful.

She had time only to notice that his breathing was as quick and uneven as hers; then he tightened his arm around her and stepped in to pull her against the length of his body, and he leaned down to kiss her.

In the back of her mind, the nervous voice of reason said, *Put a stop to this right now. Get out of here. Go home.* But Phoebe answered that sensible little voice with an irritated *Shut up.*

She slid her hands up over his shoulders. Thrilled by the unexpected power and the incredible flood of desire she felt, she pulled him closer. His lips moved across hers, hard and hungry, demanding instead of asking. She gave as good as she got, tangling her fingers in his hair, darting her tongue with desperate stabs against his, and sliding her right thigh up the outside of his leg to his hip. He groaned as she arched against the length of his erection and he lifted her off the ground, his hands under her skirt, hot on the soft cotton of her panties. She wrapped her strong left leg around him and stared straight into his eyes, which were suddenly level with hers.

"Oh, my God . . . you have to go now or I'm going to go crazy," he said, his voice lower, rough, as if he was having a hard time forcing the words out.

The sensible little voice—the same one that had told her to marry Michael because she'd promised to, the same one that had told her that nice girls didn't have sex before marriage, the same one that had said if her fiancé didn't touch her before the wedding it was because he respected her and not because something was wrong, the same one that had told her after the wedding that if Michael hurt her it was because she was doing something wrong—that voice said, *You are not going to lower yourself to doing anything vile and degrading with this complete stranger because you aren't that sort of woman.* And Phoebe knew that, just once, she could find out what it was like to be touched by someone who wanted her. Who desired her. Just once.

More than anything, at that moment she wanted to know. So she countered that worried little voice by taking a deep breath and pressing her lips softly against Alan's ear and saying words she had never in her life even dared to think before: "You're not going to go crazy. You're going to lay me down on the floor and pull my panties off and have your way with me."

And then she bit his ear.

Alan growled and his eyes went black with passion, and he tightened his grip on her and carried her out of the office to the soft, plush decorator rug on the carpeted floor of the loft. He knelt quickly, gently lowering her to the floor, still holding her, and—staring into her eyes—pulled up her skirt and grabbed her panties. He didn't pull them down, though. He slid them down fast, his hands burning a line along her bare skin, and she kicked free of the panties and watched as he tossed them and they went sailing over the balcony. He moved in, shoved her thighs apart with his. He leaned over her, and she could feel his hardness through his jeans. She reached for his zipper, but he shook his head. "My job," he said, and kissed her again, so perfectly that she thought she'd gladly give up breathing if he just wouldn't quit, and he caught her wrists in one hand and pulled them over her head. With his other hand, he grabbed the hem of her blouse and pulled it over her head.

She shuddered and lifted her hips and tightened her thighs against his hips, shoving herself upward against him. The denim of his jeans separated his skin from hers, but the teasing closeness just made her hungrier to pull him inside her. She hooked her left leg over the small of his back and whispered, "I want you."

He smiled just a little and shook his head. "Not just yet." He undid the front hook on her bra and tugged the bra under her back and up. Blouse and bra tangled around her wrists; she squirmed out of them and started to touch Alan.

He kissed her and caught both of her hands in one of his and held them over her head. "Not yet. You'll distract me," he said. Then he stretched out over her and lowered his body onto hers.

She whispered, "Yes." He remained fully dressed while she lay, captive to his touch and nearly naked, with her skirt pooled around her waist and her sandals still on.

She should have felt helpless. But Phoebe had never felt more powerful in her life. She nuzzled the soft skin at the juncture of his shoulder and neck, licking and nipping, then slid her lips to the hollow of his throat and kissed him, and when she heard him gasp, caught the smooth skin of his throat in her teeth. He trembled at her touch, and she heard the sharp intake of his breath.

"Give me," she said without letting go.

He lifted himself off of her and broke away from the grip of her legs around him. He gently lowered her right leg, and let her fend for the left one herself. He sat looking down at her, lips parted, breathing hard, pupils huge. He placed one hand flat on her belly, just above the soft nest of curled hair, and she thought he would slide it down between her legs, to the desperate, yearning, aching nub hidden there. "Yes," she whispered. But he moved upward instead, his hand tracing a line from belly to ribs to tingling breasts and tight, erect nipples.

He caught one nipple between finger and thumb, tugging and teasing, and she moaned and dug her fingers into the carpet. He pressed his thumb hard into the lower curve of her breast, circled it around the outside of the nipple, and she closed her eyes and bit her lower lip to keep from crying out at the pleasure of it.

Then he was stroking both her breasts, kneading and tugging her nipples, and she squirmed beneath him, excited by his hunger, by the fierce yearning in his touch, by her own raging desire. He suddenly dropped his mouth to one breast and started sucking and licking, and while he did, he held himself above her with one hand and moved the other between her legs, stroking the inside of her thighs, still withholding the contact she craved, the penetration of him into her.

"Don't tease me," she groaned, her eyes tightly shut, her body arching against his hand, trying to force him where she wanted him.

She reached for his buttons, and he caught her hands and pushed them over her head again. "*Leave* them there."

His shirt against her bare skin drove her crazy. "Take your clothes off," she begged him. "I want to feel your skin on mine. I want you in me."

He lifted his mouth from her breast and grinned at her. "Hush," he said. "You're in too big a hurry. It's been . . . a while for me. I want this to last. So you have to go first."

He lowered his head again and began licking and nibbling down the center of her chest, down her belly, and then between her legs. His thumbs separated the folds that hid her clitoris, and she whimpered and hung on to the leg of the coffee table as he licked and sucked, bit and teased.

"Oh God." The intensity of the pleasure was too much—in her whole life she'd never felt anything like it. She shuddered and her body trembled at his every touch. Heat flooded her, spreading upward, and waves of little explosions from deep inside her rocked her, and she cried out, wordless, eyes closed, thrashing to get away from pleasure so fierce she didn't think she could take any more. She pushed against the table, felt it slide, squirmed upward, pushed again.

Alan grabbed her hips and dragged her back down to him, laughing at her response, and started in with his tongue again—but this time he slid two fingers deep inside her, moving them while he caught her clitoris lightly between his teeth and flicked it with his tongue. Phoebe lost her breath and her entire body went rigid, and inside she exploded. She couldn't think, she couldn't speak, she couldn't do anything but moan and tremble, while the thrill of his touch drove her to the brink of passing out.

He stopped, and pulled his shirt off, and then his jeans. She watched him undress through eyes heavy-lidded with lust—but her eyes opened wide as he slid out of his Jockeys.

He moved over her, a satyr's wicked smile on his lips, his gaze fierce and ravenous, and he lowered himself until the soft furring of his chest brushed her breasts and the heavy head of his cock pushed against her.

She lifted her hips up to him, crazy with desire.

He stilled himself, his body over hers, his muscles bunching beneath her hands, and closed his eyes, and let out a long, slow breath.

"Phoebe . . . ?"

"I'm ready," she whispered.

And he groaned. "Oh, Phoebe, so am I."

She dragged her nails lightly down his back and over his buttocks. "Don't tease me."

A soft, strangled sound at the back of his throat. "I wish I were teasing you."

She stroked his shoulders, willing him to get back to touching her, to making love to her. "What's wrong?"

"I am trying to remember the last time I saw a condom anywhere nearby."

Condom. Oh, hell. Phoebe had forgotten about condoms. "And that was . . . ?"

"In the hospital restroom." He grimaced. "I don't suppose you're in the habit of carrying condoms in that backpack of yours?"

She dropped her head back on the carpet, but she still couldn't stop touching him. "Not a chance. I gave up on sex a lifetime ago. You?"

"Haven't had one in six years. Maybe even a little longer. I decided I was going to be a monk." He looked down at her. "It seemed like a good idea at the time." He kissed her gently, and with evident regret. "Not so much, now."

Her hands stroked circles on the small of his back. "I could cast a vote for complete irresponsibility right now," Phoebe said.

Alan said, "I could, too. You have no idea." He looked wistful. "Well, maybe you do." He kissed her forehead, the tip of her nose, her chin, and then he moved gracefully away from her, turning to kneel beside her with his back to her. And he started gathering up his clothes.

No, she thought. "There are things I can do instead," she whispered, sitting up. She ran a finger up his spine, slowly.

"These days, all those things require a condom, too."

He turned towards her and ran one hand gently over her shoulder, her breast, along her rib cage, over her hip. "You are so beautiful." She could see the resolve in his eyes as he moved away, stood, and pulled on his blue jeans.

Phoebe's skin pebbled with a sudden chill, and for a moment she could almost believe Chick was returning—and wouldn't *that* be embarrassing? But then she realized the air conditioner had kicked on and she was right under the vent.

She couldn't stand that he had stopped touching her. She wanted to feel his hands on her, to feel his skin beneath her palms. She wanted him inside her.

But he wasn't going to give in to temptation. With a pang of regret, she stood and looked around the loft. Her bra and blouse were under the coffee table. She fished them out and put them on. The panties were caught high on Alan's dining room chandelier, she discovered when she looked over the balcony railing for them. They were reachable neither from the loft nor, without a ladder, from downstairs. But the skirt was long enough she could just forget about her panties for the short trip home.

As dressed as she could get, Phoebe stood there looking at Alan for a moment, wanting him even more than she had just moments earlier, when she'd thought she was going to have him.

"You do naked better than anyone I've ever seen," she said. The look he gave her turned his ordinary face beautiful, and the lines of his body, in jeans and nothing else, made her ache to touch him.

"Thank you for the very best time I ever almost had," he said, and walked over to her and kissed her lightly on the lips. She started to move in, to let her hands explore him, but he pulled away with a soft laugh and a shake of his head. "If we go there again, we aren't stopping for anything short of the end of the world," he said. "And if you touch me, we're going there."

She laughed a little, amazed at how shaky her voice sounded. "Well. Thank you for the very best time I *ever* had," she said.

Neither of them said, "Let's do this again." Neither of them suggested a quick trip to the drugstore, or a date for the next day. This had been a one-time thing, Phoebe knew— Alan had been emotionally shattered. Phoebe had let herself take advantage of that. She'd matched him challenge for challenge and pushed his buttons and let her passion stand in the way of her good sense. And it had been worth it, and she wasn't the slightest bit sorry. In her entire life, no one had ever touched her with such passion, or looked at her with such hunger, or made her feel so good. She would have paid a thousand dollars for a single condom right then, because she wanted to finish what they'd started before Alan came to his senses.

But she didn't have a thousand dollars, and no one had a condom, and this moment had passed. It wouldn't come again.

Alan was, in fact, looking at her strangely. Of course. He was already having second thoughts, wondering what the hell he'd been thinking. Time, she thought, to make a graceful exit, before he realized she was evidently every bit the sex-crazed slut Michael had accused her of being for most of their relationship.

Pity it hadn't been true at the time, she thought, caught up in a wave of rebelliousness. She'd never imagined how delicious it was to be a slut.

She gathered up her tarot cards. He gave her his home and work numbers in case Chick left her any messages. She wrote her home number on the back of an envelope for him in case Chick tried to reach him. They said polite good-byes, all very proper and distant, and she made her way carefully down the stairs, just a little thrilled by the breezes that blew up her skirt as she descended and the wicked depravity of walking home wearing no underwear.

chapter 9

Alan shut the door behind Phoebe and leaned against it, eyes closed, wanting more than anything to run after her and shout, "Wait, wait, come back!"

He knew why he'd backed away. He could look at his list of reasons and tell himself he'd done the right thing. The strong thing. He *didn't* know what kind of woman Phoebe Rain was. He *couldn't* be so heedless as to risk conceiving a child with her when he no longer had the courage to face any of the consequences of such a conception—that Phoebe might abort their child; that she might leave without letting him know that she was pregnant, thus preventing him from having a part in his child's life; that she might turn out to be as wonderful as she seemed, that the two of them might fall in love, that they might become the family he'd always dreamed he would have, giving him a second chance to have his whole world destroyed.

God.

And what about Chick's warning? That he and Phoebe were in danger? That one of them might soon be dead? This was no time to risk a pregnancy.

What about Chick? Say that everything worked out perfectly—that he became a husband and a father again and it didn't end horribly. Would he forget his first child? Wouldn't having another child be consigning Chick to some sort of oblivion? In his memory, she still lived. Another child might erase her.

Yes, he'd been strong. He'd done the right thing.

But he hated himself for it. He'd turned away from something magical.

He'd never experienced anything like those moments with Phoebe. Janet had been wild in her personal life, but distant in bed. She'd wanted to be admired—and the more men who admired her and chased after her, the happier she'd been. But she'd considered the act itself a messy duty and had refused anything but missionary sex.

He'd been faithful to Janet during their marriage, but it had been faithfulness born of his own sense of honor and the fact that he had taken an oath he intended to keep. Sex with her had always left him vaguely dissatisfied—he wanted to excite her, and the only thing that really made her happy was when he finished.

Since his wife's death, he hadn't been able to look at a woman without thinking of Janet and thinking, too, of the years of unhappiness the two of them had given each other. Women wanted to marry doctors. They wanted the prestige, the country-club lifestyle, and they were willing to lie on their backs and give doctors dutiful sex in exchange for charge cards at Neiman Marcus and a shot at the Junior League.

He started up the stairs. He should write. He needed to work on the book.

And then he looked over at the chandelier, with Phoebe's panties still hanging on it, and his underwear on one side of the loft and his shirt on the other. He remembered Phoebe, her dark eyes gleaming with excitement, her skin warm beneath his fingers, her cries of pleasure as he touched her, and he started to get hard again. He could feel her teeth on his neck, her fingers in his hair, her sleek-muscled body naked beneath him. He could see her tossing and moaning as he teased her, and hear her screams as he brought her over the edge again and again.

God damn.

When he reached the loft, he looked at the expensive designer rug, now askew; at the upstairs coffee table cockeyed and with one corner shoved all the way up against the couch because he'd been chasing Phoebe across the floor with his tongue.

God damn.

He could close his eyes and see her in his bed for the rest of his life. And on the kitchen table. And up against a wall. And on the washing machine. And with that sweet round ass bent over the back of the couch. And out on the balcony, in clear view of God and everybody. He could see an entire lifetime of deliciously depraved sex in wild places with Phoebe.

Except, of course, that everything else stood in the way.

Tea. Hot green tea, poured through loose leaves in the strainer, with just enough honey to take the edge off the bitterness. Phoebe, underwear replaced and wearing jeans because the skirt had become an unbearable reminder of what she'd missed out on, stood in the kitchen. She heated the water, went through the ritual of making the tea, and poured it into her favorite cup—a big, heavy clear-glass mug from Target, not some delicate china thing from an expensive department store—and breathed in the aroma and tried to convince her heart to slow down. She took her seat at the kitchen table, and propped her bad leg on the footstool she kept beneath it, and closed her eyes.

And sipped.

Some woman had cheated on that man. Some shallow, brain-dead bitch had broken his heart, and all Phoebe could think was that death had been too easy for the worthless slut. Phoebe would have given anything to have someone like that to love her and touch her and want her, and instead she'd gotten Michael the monster, with whom she had experienced something that she had mistaken for sex a total of three times in their eight years of marriage, because Michael didn't like the mess, or her body's responses to even his awkward caresses—responses that disgusted him—and as much as that, Phoebe suspected he didn't like his own body's loss of control.

Michael had liked inflicting pain, though, both physical and mental, and so instead of sex he had introduced Phoebe to shame and degradation and fear and agony.

On the third and final time that he had experimented with actual sex, she'd gotten pregnant.

Phoebe had been ecstatic, imagining a baby as someone she could love who would love her back. Michael had been livid, and had accused her of sleeping around on him, and had taken her—the day after she told him—to a hunting cabin in the woods far from any help, claiming to his friends that the two of them were having problems with their marriage and that he was doing everything he could to save it. In that awful plywood shack he had beaten her within an inch of her life. Repeatedly. He'd kicked her, he'd hurt her, and in the end she'd lost the pregnancy.

She'd thought she was going to die, the bleeding had been so bad; he'd told her that because she'd been sleeping around on him, she was getting nothing less than she deserved. If she'd died, he would have told everyone that in spite of his best efforts she had left him. And almost everyone would have believed him. And no one would have known the truth.

Phoebe sipped her tea and pretended that living in a rented town house with three deadbolts and almost no furniture was normal, that reading cards for a phone psychic line was reasonable employment, that she had earned the life she was living and that she deserved nothing better.

But the touch of a stranger who had—if only for a moment—truly wanted her had undone her, and all the lies she'd told herself just to keep going lay revealed for what they were.

She'd been a kid from a poor family, the child of parents who'd moved from one end of the country to the other, dragging their little trailer and their two daughters from place to place in search of better work. The Rain girls were perpetual outsiders, forever the new kids, always rail-thin and dressed in homemade clothes; they clung to each other as best they could in a series of school systems that split them apart—different buses, different buildings, different playgrounds—but mostly they were alone. Phoebe's mother kept Phoebe and Nicki clean, kept after their vocabularies with a bar of soap and their manners with the fastest yardstick in fifty states, and made sure they went to church Sundays, kept their grades up, and were respectful of their teachers, so that they wouldn't earn the epithet "trailer-park trash." But they got it anyway.

Both girls believed that their family was special and meant for greater things, because both their father and mother told them it was so.

Phoebe, the first child, had graduated from high school with honors and worked her way through college on scholarships, student loans, and work-study programs, and had been the first person in her family to graduate from college, staying in school even after her parents' and sister's deaths destroyed her world. She'd gotten a job as a teacher because teachers, to her, symbolized a sort of stability that she could only imagine.

She'd been a good girl. Had waited until she graduated and had a job lined up to get married, had waited until she was married to have sex, had married a handsome boy from a good family, had shaken off the trailer-park dust and the endless wandering, had sworn to put down roots and build a strong home and a strong family in one place. She had promised herself that she would belong somewhere and that she would make her life good. That she would stick, because that was what her parents had wanted for her.

She'd stuck. When, even before she married Michael, things started to feel wrong, she'd stuck. For her vision of roots, a stable life, security. She'd stuck through bad, and through worse, and then through her own little slice of hell itself, and—finally, finally, finally—when some sliver of sanity made its way through her bullheaded promise to her-

self and showed her that she had to run or die, running had
still felt like defeat. Like she'd failed.

And when she'd found the courage to start over, to rebuild
her life, to claim a place for herself as a teacher and to try
once more to put down roots and to belong, that had twisted
into a deeper hell.

And now she stayed not because she had roots but because she was afraid to move. She was afraid to live. She'd
become a ghost in her own life, moving in rote patterns,
changing nothing, invisible to almost everyone. She had let
cowardice and self-pity absorb her—had *chosen* solitude
and fear.

And then, for just an instant, she'd had a taste of what
really living might be like.

Phoebe sipped her tea and pictured the life she'd planned
for herself. A piece of ground she owned, a house without
cinder blocks beneath it or wheels hidden away under alu-
minum skirting, a big brood of kids who would all have
friends they knew from earliest childhood and with whom
they would grow up and share memories. And a man who
came through the door each day from whatever sort of day
he'd had, but whose face lit up when he saw her. A man
whose hands touched her with longing and hunger, who
made her laugh, who brought not chaos but stability into her
life. A man who would cherish her. A man who would love
her.

She might have been a fool to think that she could have
all that—that if she were just good enough, she could whee-
dle such a future out of the Fates. She might have been a
fool to dream.

But Alan's touch had shaken that damned dream off its
dusty shelf and brought it roaring back to life, leaving her
feeling hungry and passionate and wistful. And foolish.

Because Michael was calling. A child's ghost was warning her of disaster yet to come. Any dreams Phoebe had ever
dared dream were dead and burned to ashes and scattered to
the four winds.

The phone rang. Not the psychic hotline phone, just the regular one. But the hair stood up on Phoebe's arms.

What if it were Michael? She didn't want to pick up the phone. But she wanted to know why he was calling.

She stared at the receiver. Caller ID wasn't showing anything. Not PRIVATE NAME. Not UNKNOWN NAME, UNKNOWN NUMBER. Just nothing.

Hand shaking, she reached over and lifted the receiver. "Hello." Her angry voice cut, knife-edged, through the silence in the room.

And on the other end, a voice sounded nervous and not like Michael. "Phoebe? Is this Phoebe?"

Ben Margolies.

The shaking in her hand got worse, and she pinned the phone to her ear with her shoulder to keep from dropping it and pressed both her hands flat on the table in front of her.

"This is Phoebe."

"It took me a while to find your number," Ben said, and she thought he must be lying. This call confirmed her suspicions. Ben had given her number to Michael; that was how Michael had it. Ben had told Michael how to connect with her employer, how to use the system, how to find her. He'd done a good job of hiding his complicity when she was in the shop, but he was involved in whatever was going on. "It seemed like something was really wrong when you were in the shop today. I wanted to check on you—just make sure you were all right. Maybe take you out for . . . coffee or dinner."

Phoebe closed her eyes, swallowing against rising nausea. If she went out with him, then what? Would he kidnap her? Or kill her? Was he working for Michael?

Michael was in a coma in a nursing home in Ohio. Michael was in a coma.

None of this made any sense, because Michael was in a coma, and Michael couldn't be calling, and Ben couldn't know Michael.

But Phoebe couldn't go out with Ben. Couldn't trust Ben,

because Ben knew everything Michael had needed to know, and now Michael had found her.

Phoebe hung up the phone without saying anything else, and almost instantly it rang again.

She wasn't going to pick it up. She wasn't. Caller ID still showed nothing on the screen.

Phoebe listened to it ring three times, then picked it up.

"Slut," Michael snarled in her ear. "Two of them in one day, you bitch. You cunt. You fucking whore."

She slammed the phone down in its cradle and hobbled into the bathroom as fast as she could and barely made it to the toilet in time. She vomited. Out on the kitchen table, the phone was ringing. And ringing. And ringing. In the bathroom, kneeling on the tile with her knee in screaming agony, puking her way to dry heaves, clinging to cold porcelain, Phoebe willed it all to stop, prayed that it would stop.

Eventually the phone stopped ringing.

Eventually her stomach exhausted itself.

Eventually she wobbled upright, and brushed her teeth, and showered, and shrugged into her bathrobe. She couldn't stay like this, with Michael calling her, with Ben calling her, with her fear and the insane impossibility of it all.

Tea. She needed a soothing cup of green tea to settle her stomach. Maybe a few soda crackers.

Phoebe left the bathroom, went around the corner, and her tea mug wasn't on the table.

She'd left it on the table.

She looked underneath—maybe in her run for the bathroom, she'd knocked it off. But, no, it wasn't there either.

She straightened and frowned. She'd been sitting at the table drinking tea. The phone had rung. She'd answered it against her better judgment and had hung up, and it had rung again, and the second time it had been Michael, and from there she had fled to the bathroom. So the mug should have still been on the table, or perhaps under it. She checked the floor all around the table, but she didn't have much furniture, and no clutter, so there wasn't anyplace where it could have fallen that she wouldn't have seen it.

It wasn't there.

She walked around the raised counter where she kept her fruit in bowls, and into the tiny galley kitchen.

And there was the tea mug, sitting beside the sink where she left it when she was going to wash it. Empty, except for some leaves in the bottom, dried in place.

They couldn't be dried—she would have had to leave it sitting out all night for them to be dry, and she'd just had tea.

Her teakettle was full of water and cold. Her box of loose-leaf green tea was not on the counter where she was sure she'd left it; instead it was up in the cupboard.

She'd had a cup of tea. She *knew* she had.

Hadn't she?

She leaned against the counter, feeling panic rising.

Carefully, she made her way back out to the kitchen table, picked up the phone, and dialed *69.

It rang, and on the second ring Ben picked up and said, "Moonstruck New Age Shoppe—readings, supplies, and more. This is Ben Margolies. May I help you?"

Phoebe hung up the phone. It hadn't connected her to Michael.

The phone never connected her to Michael. Never gave her any proof that he'd called her. And Michael was in a coma in a nursing home in Ohio.

She walked back into the kitchen and stared at the tea mug on the counter with its crust of dried leaves in the bottom.

There was another explanation for everything that was happening to her, one she hadn't sufficiently addressed.

The phantom phone calls from the comatose ex-husband, the visitations by the ghost child, and the tea that she seemed not to have made all had a simple explanation.

She was losing her mind.

Too much time alone, too much stress, too much guilt— she remembered the term from her abnormal psychology course. "Psychotic break." That was a sort of mental snap

that changed someone from a normal person to a crazy
one—maybe dangerously crazy. Maybe Phoebe was experiencing a psychotic break. What if there had been no phone
calls from Michael? What if every bit of it had been in her
head? She could really hurt someone. What if she thought
she saw Michael standing in a crowd, pulled out her handgun, and shot him, and it wasn't Michael after all but just
some tall man with dark hair and a good smile?

Phoebe really needed to know that Michael was in a
coma. That the nurse hadn't lied to her. If she knew that, she
would know that she was safe from him, and she would . . .
see a psychiatrist, maybe. Or put herself in voluntary lockup
at whatever facility Broward County had for the dangerously insane.

But she had to know.

She stood there for a long moment, considering, and decided the FBI was her best bet. Michael had crossed state
lines to murder people once before. He had escaped prose-
cution by virtue of being in a coma, but his family had a lot
of money, and they weren't the most ethical people in the
world.

They'd seemed like nice enough people when Michael
took her home to meet them. Hardworking folks who'd
come up from nothing to become pillars of their community.
Michael's father bought houses, fixed them up, and rented
them, and from the money he made doing that, he bought
businesses. Michael's mother had been born well-off and,
for reasons known only to her, had married beneath herself.
She had then shaped Michael's father to fit into the society
that was her home. She played hostess to increasingly important partners and clients and considered it her job to keep
the best face on everything her husband did. When her children started growing up, it was her job to keep the best face
on everything they did, too. No matter what they did.

And she was good at her job.

Phoebe had needed a while to discover that neither Mr.
Schaeffer, nor Michael, nor any of Michael's siblings, had

ever faced the consequences of their actions. And that people who were protected from the consequences of their actions turned into monsters, to the precise degree that they were protected.

Phoebe wondered if somehow Michael's mother had figured out a way to protect him from the murder he'd committed. If Michael was still in a coma. If the man in the nursing home bed was really Michael.

It sounded paranoid as hell, but this was Michael she was dealing with, and Michael had called her.

She found her phone book, located the number for the local branch office of the FBI, and explained her situation to the agent who took her call. He was a patient man, and she was completely straight with him, telling him what she had experienced and what she suspected, but also explaining that she had been unable to track the calls from Michael and that a nurse at the nursing home had insisted that Michael was still in a coma.

The agent suggested that she contact her local police department to see about getting a tap put on her phone, but he also said that because of the seriousness of the crimes that Michael had committed, he would pass on the information that she had given him to the appropriate people in Ohio and that he would let her know what they found out. He said it might take a few days for her to hear back; he didn't know how their workload was.

She returned to the kitchen, washed out her cup, emptied her kettle and rinsed it, refilled it, put the water on to heat, and then sat down at her table to wait.

She considered her situation as objectively as she could. She might be crazy—that would be the simplest explanation. But the simplest explanation wasn't *always* the right one, Occam be damned, and if she wasn't losing her mind, she also wasn't going to let Michael win without a fight.

After what seemed like an inordinately long time, the kettle whistled, and she returned to the kitchen and made herself more tea.

She would consider calling the police, but that depended on what the FBI found out.

The Fort Lauderdale detective assigned to her case following the shooting had despised her—had told her bluntly that if she had been a decent wife and had honored her vows, two dead children would still be alive. He'd been cold and harsh, but he'd also been right, and although the couple of uniformed cops who had checked on her while she was recuperating had been kind to her, it didn't change the fact that her actions had led directly to those two students' deaths.

By the time she was out of the hospital, the thing she'd wanted most was to move away. To run away from her shame and guilt the way her parents had run from their problems. She hadn't had the money to flee following her hospitalization; she hadn't been teaching long enough to be making decent money, or to have become vested in the system, or to have put aside a nest egg.

And her financial situation had only gotten worse. She couldn't run. But she also couldn't bear to face the Fort Lauderdale police again unless she had absolutely no other choice.

Phoebe took her tea over to her couch, sat down, and drank it in silence. She had to get to work pretty soon, but she was still too shaky. She was not ready to deal with strangers and their problems—not by a long shot.

The tea proved surprisingly soothing. Phoebe leaned back and put her feet up, snuggling into the couch cushions, sipping slowly. She smiled as she finished the cup, as wonderful calm stole over her. She felt heavy. Soft. And incredibly tired.

She put the empty cup on the end table beside her and told herself, Just a little nap. Five, maybe ten minutes. Then work.

The room swirled around her, and just as she would get her eyes fixed on something, it would slide sideways or turn liquid and dissolve.

She still lay on the couch, but the room wasn't the same. She couldn't pinpoint the differences; this was one of those dreams where she couldn't get a firm grasp on anything.

Except that Michael was with her. Standing over her, smiling at her. Looking perfectly healthy, nothing like a man in a coma. Nothing like the man she'd done her best to kill with her bare hands.

He shifted in and out of focus, too, and slid sideways in the melting room. But his voice in her ears was clear. "Hello, Phoebe," he said. "Do you want to play with me?"

She tried to scream, or to speak, but she couldn't. She couldn't move. She couldn't do anything but lie there as he undid the belt of her bathrobe and pulled the terry cloth out of the way, leaving her naked and helpless. She couldn't even whimper as he started touching her. Started doing things to her, poking and pinching and twisting and invading with his hands—just his hands. Lights exploded silently around her at odd intervals, blinding her. And when they did, the room would slide and dissolve and re-form—and then Michael would reappear, doing something else, somewhere else. She could only watch him as he took hold of her injured knee with both hands and twisted it—and she couldn't actually feel it twisting, but she knew he was hurting her.

More explosions. Lightning? She was trying to make sense of what was going on outside her nightmare, but she couldn't make the pieces fit. Maybe outside her dream there was a storm.

And then from somewhere Michael produced a knife and smiled at her and said, "Are we ready for this yet, my faithless whore of a wife?" and ran the blade across her breasts and down her belly and between her legs, laughing softly all the while, and finally she found her voice.

chapter 10

It was the cold that woke him, but it was Chick's face—glowing softly in the dark room and hovering inches above his own—that launched Alan from the bed with heart pounding and skin prickling. Chick looked terrified.

She was pointing towards the west wall.

And then Alan heard the screaming. From next door.

Phoebe.

He didn't bother with robe, shoes, shirt, pants. In bare feet and a pair of thin cotton pajama bottoms, he raced out of his room, out his front door, and across the few steps to her place, scattering half a dozen Muscovy ducks that had been sleeping on his stoop and the sidewalk in the process.

He hit Phoebe's door hard and damn near killed his shoulder. "Phoebe!" he shouted.

Inside, she still screamed. At least he knew she was alive.

But how the hell could he get to her? Three deadbolts and God only knew what else stood in his way; the door hadn't budged when he hit it. Dammit—he could break a shoulder or a foot trying to batter down that door and even if he eventually got through, he was losing time. He might not arrive until he was too late to do any good. Frustrated, he hammered on the door with his fists and bellowed, "PHOEBE!"

Then he realized that if she was being attacked, whoever was in there with her had to have gotten in somehow—and since the front door was still locked, maybe her attacker had gotten in some other way. Phoebe's town house had a tiny fenced patio with sliding glass doors leading onto it from the living room and the downstairs bedroom; perhaps her attacker had gone in through one of those. Alan looked up—Phoebe didn't have a balcony like the one he had outside his office. He could see her ground-level front window from where he stood. It was closed. He tried it. Locked.

He ran in and tried the sliding glass doors. Locked.

He remembered something about being able to lift sliding doors out of their tracks, even if they were locked, and get in that way—but if that was possible in some cases, it didn't work this time.

He hit the glass with his shoulder, but like the doors at his place, it was tempered thermal glass, and it didn't break. Phoebe had nothing on her patio that Alan could use to smash into it—no furniture, no flowerpots, no tools or toys. For just a millisecond he considered running to his place to get a hammer, but he didn't think Phoebe had time for that. She sounded desperate. He didn't dare waste a second.

He swore and went back to the front door and started pounding on it again and yelling her name.

Across the quad, lights started coming on.

And then he realized that the screaming had stopped.

He closed his eyes, scared and defeated.

Heard the locks' tumblers turning over.

The door opened and a pale, but very much alive Phoebe stood in front of him.

"Help me," she whispered, and grabbed his wrist and dragged him through the door, and closed it behind him, fast, and locked all the locks again. And then, for good measure, she jammed a bar under the doorknob.

"What the hell was going on?" he asked her.

"Michael," she said. "Nightmare."

He stared at her. "It can't have been. Chick woke me up and sent me over here—she was hovering over my bed, pointing, and then I heard you screaming. She wouldn't have woken me up for you having nightmares."

"Michael was killing me." Phoebe's skin was ash gray, sheened with sweat. Her eyes looked glassy, her pupils were huge, and she was weaving from side to side as she stood there. She licked dry lips.

"You have to lie down," he said. "Put your feet higher than your head, or you're going to pass out. C'mon—" He scooped her up, looked at the couch, and bypassed it for the un-slept-in bed in the next room.

"I can't go to sleep," she said. She had her arms wrapped around herself, and she was shaking and staring around wildly. "He's waiting."

"Nobody is here," Alan told her. "Well, nobody but you and me. I'm going to go get you something warm to drink and cover you up. And then you can tell me about these nightmares."

She wasn't all the way out of whatever she'd been through—she thrashed as he tried to arrange pillows under her legs, though he wouldn't have quite classified her as combative, had he had her in the ER. Restless, though, definitely restless. "I'm thirsty. And I feel like I'm going to throw up," she said. He grabbed the wastebasket from the next-door bathroom and put it beside her bed. "In there if you do. I'll be right back. I'm going to get you something to sip on, and we're going to see what's going on."

She nodded and managed to lie still while he covered her. He didn't like her color, her quick respirations, or her *bounding* pulse, and he *really* didn't like the way her pupils stayed huge even when he turned on the light in her room.

It looked something like shock to him, but it looked a bit like a drug overdose, too. Phoebe had that bad knee; she probably had some pretty potent pain meds in the house. He decided to do a quick inventory to see if he could turn up anything.

He found her glasses, filled one with ice cubes, and yelled to her that he was going to make her some ice chips if he could find something to crush the ice. It made as good an excuse for rummaging as anything.

And it turned up nothing. She had four cheap stoneware place settings of plates, saucers, and cups, four sets of stainless-steel flatware, a couple of good knives, one large and one small cooking pan, a wok. Tylenol, aspirin, and generic ibuprofen. Frozen peeled bananas and fruit in bags, a lot of vegetables, tofu, raw nut butters, and very dense, hard, dark breads in her fridge, and in her tiny pantry, a few bags of corn chips and a couple of different types of hot salsa. Fresh fruit on the counter. One opened and several unopened boxes of caffeine-free loose-leaf green tea, and a good supply of clover honey. Paranoia pushed him to open the green tea box and check the contents, but the contents were nothing but tea leaves.

Under the sink, cleaning stuff.

He detoured through the bathroom to check out her medicine cabinet and found the usual bathroom things. Combs, brushes. A blow-dryer. A lot of rubber bands for her hair. Cheap shampoo, cheap conditioner. In the toilet tank, nothing but water.

He carried the glass of ice into the bedroom and said, "Couldn't find anything I could use to crush these."

"I don't have much stuff," she told him, which he thought was a huge understatement. She owned almost nothing. Her bedroom was as bare as the rest of the place—mattress and box spring on a metal frame with wheels, plain sheets, plain blanket. Half of her north wall was bathroom, the other half was closet, just like his.

The closet was a walk-in, longer than it was wide, with a bare lightbulb overhead, shelves and racks on the left and the right, and a blank wall in the back. Janet would have had that closet filled to the brim and would have been looking for ways to claim whatever space he had for his clothes. Even in his place he'd mostly filled the space; he'd stacked a lot of boxes that he'd never unpacked against the back wall to act as soundproofing, because his north-wall neighbors had a loud stereo that played at all hours. Evidently her north-wall neighbors were quiet.

Phoebe, on the other hand, owned so little that the single closet rack on the left that she was using was mostly bare, even with her clothes spread out. She'd hung up a few pairs of jeans, a couple of dressy-looking skirts a few years out of fashion, sweatshirts, T-shirts, and a handful of dressy blouses, also from a few years back. Folded underwear on the top shelf—not much of that, either.

Everything was clean, everything was neat, and everything was well maintained.

Whatever was wrong with Phoebe, it didn't look like it stemmed from a drug problem.

Alan sat beside her on the bed. "Tell me about your nightmare." Phoebe seemed a little more with it, but her pupils were still large and she was still breathing too fast.

"I'd rather not."

"I'm here. You don't want to go to sleep. I don't *want* you to go to sleep until your color is better and your pulse settles down and I'm sure you're going to be all right. And obviously anything that is causing you this sort of distress is something that you need to let someone know about."

Phoebe turned her face away from him again. "Michael was standing over me. I was on the couch in the dream, wearing the bathrobe. He opened it. Touched me. Did things to me."

He waited, and after a long, uncomfortable silence, he realized that was all she was going to say. He sighed. "That's a start. More detail would help."

With her face turned toward the sliding glass doors that led out onto the patio, she said, "He was hurting me. Twisting my nipples. My knee. He had a knife. He was . . . it seemed like he was cutting me open, only I couldn't see that he was making any cuts." The tonelessness of her voice, her flat affect, her pallor, and the way she wouldn't look at him while she spoke all created shadows in Alan's mind—lurking monsters that dragged their claws through the rooms of his thoughts, always just out of sight. He didn't like the feeling.

"I couldn't wake up," she continued. "I tried, but I couldn't. Michael was right there, but in that sort of hazy way people are in dreams, where they keep changing around, or sliding, or dissolving . . . I told myself if I could just open my eyes, or scream, or move, I could make the dream end and he would be gone. But I couldn't. I couldn't do anything but lie there watching him while he—" Her voice broke.

"Rape?" Alan whispered.

"Not Michael's thing," Phoebe said. "He detested anything sexual—Rape would be too messy and grotesque for him. He liked inflicting pain, though. And that was what he was doing. Humiliating me. Hurting me. And then, with the knife . . ." She closed her eyes and shuddered.

"That was when you screamed?"

"Yes."

"And what happened?"

"He ran away, vanished. Dissolved. I don't know. I kept screaming, and I heard you at the door in my dream, but I still couldn't wake up. And then, at last, I came out of it. Woke up, got to my feet, got the door before the neighbors called the police. And here we are."

"Here we are," he said, and took her hand, and the sleeve of her bathrobe slid upward and he looked for needle tracks. But her arms were perfect. "I'm going to check your knee," Alan told her. "It seems pretty swollen."

"It hurts a lot."

It was red-hot, swollen, bruised. Heavy bruising. He would have thought it was from her fall, but she hadn't fallen on her knee. She shouldn't have such heavy bruising.

Fear skittered down the back of his neck, but he pushed past it. She had to have been dreaming. He'd been in all the rooms. (*Not the upstairs ones,* a little voice whispered in the back of his mind.) No one had come in or gone out of the house. Alan had been in a position to see all the possible exits. Everything had been locked, everything was still locked.

"What do you take for the pain?" he asked.

"Mostly nothing. When it gets bad, some Tylenol or, for the worst of it, Tylenol and either aspirin or Motrin at the same time. But I don't like taking aspirin-related drugs if I can help it. I bruise easily anyway, and they increase bleeding times."

"They do," he agreed, trying to imagine getting through every day with that knee and nothing stronger than Tylenol or nonsteroidal anti-inflammatories for the pain. Not even a bit of booze to dull it, he thought, realizing that Phoebe hadn't had any alcohol in the place, either.

She was a woman with no visible bad habits.

But she might be suffering hallucinations or psychotic episodes. She showed no signs of multiple personality. But the dream she'd described, and her lasting physical reactions, suggested to him that it was more than a simple nightmare.

"I'm going to do a quick run-through of your place," he said. "Just to make sure it really was a nightmare."

She smiled weakly. "It was a nightmare. What else could it be?"

He didn't know. But he started by checking under her bed and in her closet. She had nothing odd under her bed. Nothing odd in her closet.

He went through the rest of the town house at a near run, charging up the stairs, to her loft—devoid of all furniture; to her furnace closet—empty; to her upstairs bedroom suite—nothing. Bathroom, empty. Closets, empty. Bedroom, empty. She had a window rather than sliding glass doors and a balcony at the front of the upstairs bedroom, and the window had been painted shut ages ago. No one had gone out that way.

Except for the skylight there were no other windows.

No one had used the top floor for anything. The two of them were alone in her town house.

He hurried back down the stairs, not liking to leave her alone for too long when she seemed so unstable.

"Have you had anything like this before?" he asked.

"No. Nightmares, yes. For years. But not—not like tonight. Even with the recent ones, I never saw Michael. I heard his voice. Sometimes I dreamed I could feel him touching me. He would say terrible things. But, no."

"Something was different with the recent ones?"

She nodded, pretty and fragile, and he wanted—God help him—to save her from all her monsters, even as he was beginning to believe that her monsters were living inside her where he wouldn't be able to slay them.

"The last two, or maybe three weeks, I've dreamed about Michael almost every night."

"And then two days ago the phone calls started."

"Three days now."

"And no one can find any proof that these phone calls have been made?"

She looked at him sidelong. "If you're trying to figure out if I'm going insane, don't think that you're alone."

"You're wondering the same thing?"

She managed a weak smile. "I could make a pretty good case for it. I'm still giving myself the benefit of the doubt, though. I called the FBI to let them know about the calls and about Michael. Because of his record, they said they would make sure that the person in the hospital bed was really him."

Alan studied her. Generally schizophrenics and psychotics didn't have the self-awareness to realize that they were acting bizarrely; they were usually quite confident that they were perfectly normal—or even better than normal. Phoebe was full of doubt. And knew where she was and who she was. Though she still seemed foggy, and definitely paranoid about her ex, he couldn't make a case for insanity.

So what about the nightmares? Might she just be someone who suffered from some sort of sleep anomaly?

"You haven't tried to treat these nightmares yourself? Never gone to a psychiatrist, or someone who could give you some sleeping pills, or . . . anything?" His voice sounded hoarse and shocked in his own ears, a far cry from the detached, calm professional he was supposed to be. "A sleep researcher? There has to be something that could help this."

A tiny flicker of a smile across her lips, gone as quickly as it had appeared. "I'm . . . please forgive me . . . not a huge fan of the medical establishment, or of medical treatments in general. The whole medical establishment is enslaved to corporations that look at drug development as a profit center. And I don't feel like being someone's guinea pig for profit."

And that was true, he thought. He hugged her gently. "There's something charming about your cynicism." He swallowed hard, envisioning her in his loft, naked. Seeing her at her own front door, lost and bewildered and fragile. "You don't have to be alone in this, Phoebe. I could help you."

"You don't want to be involved in my life. Horrible things happen to people who get involved with me."

"I'm *already* involved," he said. "My daughter . . . Chick . . . she woke me from a sound sleep and aimed me over here as fast as my body could bring me because this is something that concerns both of us. You and me. Whatever is going on with you has dragged both of us in. You know this. It's connected in some way that we can't see. The cards said so—the man and the woman at the end. Chick implied as much. Maybe I'm the one who's supposed to help you end it, whatever it is."

"You don't want to be involved with me." She opened her eyes and studied him. "Michael knows about you."

"Michael is in a coma a long way from here."

"Whoever is calling me sounds just like him and knows things only he knew, so until I have some proof to the contrary, I'm going to act on the assumption that somehow Michael has found a way to reach me. Anyway"—she shook her head—"Michael called me today and said awful things about me. And he mentioned you."

Alan sat on the edge of the bed, trying to get his mind around the insanity that Phoebe had just presented to him as reality. *Someone* might be watching her. But her comatose ex-husband?

Still, he could not let himself forget that he *already* stood firmly within the realm of the impossible—with Chick's presence and Phoebe's strange talents, he had moved into his own personal Twilight Zone, and he wasn't sure he would willingly leave if given the opportunity. He had some small vestige of Chick back, and if nothing else, he now believed that she had not ceased to exist with her death. And he had this new and tenuous connection with Phoebe.

He didn't know if he dared think of that connection as a relationship. He wasn't sure he was ready for a relationship, and the idea of choosing to be with a woman who made her living reading tarot cards and who, by all appearances, was a magnet for every awful possibility that life had to offer unnerved him.

But there he sat, on the side of her bed, looking at her lying with her eyes closed, her long black hair fanned out across the pillows in wild curls. She was still too pale, still breathing a little faster than she should have been. He couldn't forget how strong she had been in facing a man who had tried to kill her, and how hard she had fought for her life, and how hard she was still fighting against *something*. He knew that she mattered to him. Chick had brought her to him, and that, too, had to mean something. He tried not to see her lying beneath him on the soft, deep rug up in his loft; the hunger that image stirred deep in him, no matter how eager it was to come to mind, could only confuse this issue. Love was a thing that built slowly over years, that started with friendship and grew into something more, and this—this had happened too quickly, and it didn't make sense, and he couldn't look at Phoebe and think about having loved her since he was just a boy. He couldn't even pretend that he knew her. But his heart and his gut both insisted that she belonged in his life.

Platonically. That would be best for both of them. Certainly until the two of them figured out what was going on with her. With Chick. With the phone calls and the nightmares and her terrible dread—yes, he needed to keep things platonic.

He would take the role of brother, perhaps. He would watch over her and he wouldn't let anyone hurt her and when she got through whatever she was going through and when he'd made sense of Chick's appearance, maybe they could see if they might have something else.

"I'm staying the rest of the night," he said.

She looked up at him, shook her head, and he could see concern on her face. "No. I'll be fine. I'm feeling much better. And I'm serious. You need to get away from me and stay away."

"I can't," he said, discovering the truth of that only as the words came out of his mouth. And then, with his mind asking him what the hell he thought he was doing, he leaned over and kissed her firmly on the lips. He felt her start to pull away and then fall into the kiss. She twined an arm around his neck and pulled him down, and suddenly she didn't seem helpless or fragile. The kiss deepened, and his protective urges slipped aside, to let the hunger she brought out in him come to the front. "I'm not going anywhere," he told her, and heard his voice go husky.

chapter 11

Phoebe woke to gentle warmth and surprising weight behind her, to an arm thrown over her, and to vague memories of horrors—but this time, horrors banished.

She lay with the light slanting across her face, and for the first time since that devastating night when she lost her family, she felt warmer on the inside than on the outside. Safe. She smiled a little, and closed her eyes, and drifted down into a wonderful, soothing sleep.

"Have to get to work," Alan said, kissing the side of her cheek. "Before I go, I want to make sure you're really awake. No more of those nightmares, okay?"

He was leaning over her, dressed in drab green scrubs, beat-up white leather cross-trainers, and a white lab coat. His stethoscope, draped around his neck, bumped its cold little metal heads against her neck. She disliked lab coats, scrub suits, and stethoscopes. All of her associations with them involved terrible pain.

But she liked Alan.

She stretched and shook off the last of the sleep. "What time is it?"

"Just a little before six."

She looked at him and frowned and sat up. "In the afternoon?"

"You slept for a long time. I borrowed your keys and did

a little shopping," he said. "Didn't want to wake you, but didn't want to leave the door unlocked. My cell phone number is on the table—in case you woke up and needed me."

"You *shopped*?"

"Your fridge was awfully empty." He grinned at her. "Sweet dreams?"

"No dreams at all. That's better—trust me."

He ruffled her hair with his hand and said, "Then get out of bed, sleepyhead, and don't go back to sleep until I'm here."

Phoebe smiled. She remembered her mother doing that when she was little—that same gesture, almost the same words. Nice. It made her feel cared for, and if that was just a fantasy, it was a good one.

She followed him out of the bedroom and locked the front door behind him. After Alan left, she got up, showered, got dressed, and decided while pulling on jeans that her knee hurt enough to justify Tylenol but not aspirin or ibuprofen.

She headed out to the kitchen. She found a note taped to the door of the fridge—"Got you a couple of veggie subs, vinegar and oil, no mayo, no cheese. Figured you could eat those." The handwriting was both atrocious and endearing.

She stared at the note and blinked back the tears that started to well up in her eyes. He'd gotten her sandwiches?

Just enjoy it now, and don't think too much, she told herself, and pulled out one of the subs, turned to get the Tylenol out of the cabinet—

Her tea mug was sitting beside the sink, waiting to be washed. Dirty. Dried tea leaves in the bottom of the cup.

She'd had tea the night before, sitting on the couch. She'd put the mug on the end table and had fallen asleep on the couch, and that was when she had the nightmare. Alan had come to her rescue, she'd spent the rest of the night in her own bed. She'd never moved the mug to the sink.

She studied it more closely. It seemed to her that it was in exactly the same spot it had been in the day before, when she hadn't been able to find it on the table. Exactly the same spot.

She shook her head. That *was* paranoid. Alan had no doubt seen the mug on the end table and picked it up and put it by the sink for her. Because he was being thoughtful.

She washed the mug out, rinsed it, put it in the dish drainer, and then got herself a glass of water and took her Tylenol.

And then she sat down at the table and went to work. Six in the evening was not prime phone time, but she hadn't been too regular with the work the last few days, and she needed to log some call time or her priority number was going to drop into the basement and she wouldn't be able to make rent.

She spread out the cards and started doing readings while she waited for the phone to ring.

She didn't like the way the cards were falling. Lots of Towers, lots of Deaths, way too many majors and none of them in good configurations.

She was just being sloppy, she decided. She hadn't paid proper respect to the process. She got up and gathered candles and incense, and took a few deep breaths to clear her mind. She lit the candles. Put a little classical music on her CD player and looped it—Vivaldi for once. Light, happy stuff.

With her space set up, she sat down again. The phone still hadn't rung. She hoped she hadn't lost too much of her ranking in the network by taking a few days off. Rank was supposed to be determined by call length, not by volume handled—but she didn't believe that. She knew short calls counted against her, but she suspected not taking a lot of calls in a day counted against her, too.

She settled into her chair, exercised her knee. Shuffled. *Relax. Relax. Empty mind. Breathe in . . . two . . . three . . . four . . . and hold . . . two . . . three . . . four . . . and*

The phone rang.

She took the call on the first ring. A girl named Marti listened while Phoebe uncovered an awful childhood. When Phoebe noted a violence-filled past that still haunted her,

Marti admitted that her father had murdered her mother in front of her. Marti talked about a life of hell in foster homes and losing track of all of her brothers and sisters, and finally got to the meat of what she wanted to know, which was if she was going to be able to find any of them again. The five other kids were all scattered, and Marti hadn't been able to locate any of them since she was old enough to get out of foster care.

Phoebe tossed cards on the table, but she wasn't looking at what fell so much as just taking impressions. She described rolling hills and monuments and a little book chained to a stand, and it turned out that one of the last things Marti and her family did together before everything went to hell was go to a Civil War battlefield. Marti remembered a guest book kept there.

She and Phoebe talked, Phoebe tossing cards and making suggestions based on what she saw, and at last Marti decided to go to the battlefield, leave her name and address in the guest book, and see if any of her siblings had done the same. It wasn't much, but it was a start, and she sounded a little more hopeful when she hung up.

Phoebe found herself wondering about Marti and whether she would ever succeed in finding her brothers and sisters again. That was another thing about the psychic hotline job that really got to Phoebe. She never did find out what happened next, how it all came out.

She spent a moment wishing Marti well, then flexed her leg, stood, and stretched. That had been a long call—good for her averages.

She had another long wait, this time only to get one of the Three-Minute Clock Watchers. That *wouldn't* help her average, dammit.

Then the pace started to pick up, and the next time she got a breather and really noticed the clock on her wall, it read 10:40 p.m.

She logged off on the first try, deciding that she needed a tea break, and walked around the counter to make some tea.

Her mug, dirty, with dried tea leaves in the bottom, sat next to the sink, in the precise location where she had found it before. Heart fluttering, breath quick, blood chilled to ice, she crept across the kitchen as if it were a snake coiled on the countertop.

She studied the leaves dried in the bottom of the cup. Previously, she'd half noticed that the dried leaves had clumped in a sort of rough triangle. They were still clumped that way. She couldn't be certain, but they looked very similar, if not identical.

Phoebe picked up the cup and studied it. Poked a finger down into the leaves. They were completely dry.

But she had washed the cup. She knew she had. She'd washed it and rinsed it and left it in her dish drainer to dry, and now it was back where she'd found it. But it couldn't be.

All her brief happiness and tenuous security bled out of her.

"The hell with this," she muttered, and from under her sink she took out one of the brown paper bags she saved from grocery shopping. She put the mug in the bag and smashed the bag to the floor again and again until she heard the glass shatter.

She opened the bag and looked—just to be sure. Yes. The mug was in a million pieces. She closed the bag, dropped it in her trash, and considered taking the extra step of taking the trash out to the community Dumpster. But it was late, and she wasn't crazy about limping across the parking lot in the darkness. She felt far too vulnerable.

She'd solved the problem, though. She could get back to work.

She logged in, and waited, and while she was waiting her regular phone rang. The damned caller ID still wasn't showing anything. She was going to have to call the phone company and tell them something was wrong. She let it ring twice more while she hesitated, but at last she answered it.

Alan said, "We got a break. I'm just checking to make sure you're all right."

She bit her lip. She wasn't going to mention the cup. "I'm okay. Thank you for the sandwiches. They were wonderful. I'm getting a little work done now, but it's been slow tonight." She made herself smile when she answered him, because if she smiled she would sound more relaxed over the phone. She didn't want him picking up on her anxiety. He didn't need to be worrying about her.

"Good. I've been thinking about you—" And then he swore. "I'm going to have to run—something big just blew through the doors. Be careful," he said. And was gone.

Careful. Yes. She should be careful. But of what? She heard voices no one else could hear, got phone calls no one could trace, and had two sightings of a ghost that hadn't even helped her credibility with the girl's own father until he was willing to admit that he'd seen his child, too. The only solid, tangible, real thing Phoebe could point to that anyone else could actually see or prove existed was a dirty tea mug. Was she supposed to take that to police and tell them, "I had a cup that wouldn't stay clean, so I put it in a paper bag and smashed it, and I want you to open an investigation because of it"?

No. She didn't think so.

And then her Network phone rang, and Phoebe got back to work.

Alan got home on time for once—he'd dashed out the ER doors the instant he handed off to Morrie, getting suspicious looks but ignoring them.

He stopped at his place long enough to pick up a tooth-brush and a change of clothes, and then walked next door and knocked.

Phoebe opened it, and for a moment Alan forgot to breathe. Botticelli angel, he thought again—black hair and black eyes and an English rose complexion, made more wonderful by a smile that radiated pure delight at seeing him. She said, "I wasn't sure you'd stop by, but I'm glad you did."

And he stepped through the door and wrapped his arms around her and kicked the door shut behind him. "I told you I wasn't going to let you have any more of those nightmares alone. If you don't mind, I'll stay." He paused. "I can sleep on the couch—"

She put a finger to his lips and grinned a little. "We've moved a bit past that. If you don't kick, I'll share the bed with you."

He showered, pulled on a pair of pajama bottoms, and headed into the bedroom to find her already asleep, far to one side of the bed. He went into the living room to make sure the door was locked. It was triple-locked and had a bar jammed under the doorknob. The rest of the place was tight, too. He found a note she'd left on his side of the bed. *Right half of the closet is yours if you have anything you need to hang up.* He smiled. He didn't. But he'd make sure that he did tomorrow. He slid into bed beside her. Put an arm around her and felt her nestle against him.

And dropped into exhausted, dreamless sleep.

The sound of a phone woke him.

Phoebe wasn't really awake when she reached over and picked up the receiver, but the first words she heard woke her up fast.

"Ms. Rain, this is Special Agent Toeller from the FBI."

She stared at the phone. "Yes, Agent Toeller. Have you found out something already?"

"My colleague in Ohio was both prompt and very thorough. He went in to see your ex-husband in the nursing home yesterday. Due to the critical nature of Mr. Schaeffer's condition and the fact that the family wanted all measures taken to preserve his life, the doctor refused to permit any blood to be drawn. Apparently even small amounts would jeopardize his life at this stage."

"What a pity," Phoebe muttered.

Agent Toeller either didn't hear her or pretended not to. He said, "However, the agent did take fingerprints, which matched those which we have on file for your ex-husband. He reviewed the patient's record, and the blood type on the charts matched the known blood type for your ex-husband. The agent also took a hair sample and epithelial cell scrapings from the inside of the cheek, and sent these off to the lab for DNA matching. I won't have final results on the DNA samples for several days—maybe more, depending on how backed up the lab is. But I can tell you that the fingerprints were a match. I'd be willing to suggest that when the tests come back, they're going to match, too. The man in the nursing home *is* Michael Schaeffer."

Phoebe flopped back on her pillow and realized that Alan was watching her, puzzled. "F-B-I," she mouthed.

He shrugged a silent question. She raised her index finger and said into the phone, "Well, I see, Agent Toeller. I'd appreciate a call from you with the DNA results if you could—whenever they come in—but thank you for your help on this and for looking into it for me."

When she hung up, she turned to Alan and said, "The FBI says the fingerprints of the man in the coma in Ohio match Michael's. They say he's Michael."

"Then he's Michael."

"The DNA results won't be back for a few days."

"Sweetheart, if the fingerprints match, the DNA results are just a formality. They probably won't even bother to process them—why should they? No two people have the same fingerprints."

"I know. But . . ." She knew in her mind that if the FBI said the man in the coma was really Michael, he had to be Michael. But her gut said Michael—not some impostor—was calling her on the phone.

"I'm going to the bathroom," she told Alan. "To get a drink. My mouth is kind of dry. And then I'll come back to bed."

They'd only been asleep for a couple of hours. She was so exhausted, she felt like she should be able to sleep for a week. And having Alan beside her felt better. Safer. She hadn't let herself think before about how tired she was of being alone.

She didn't want to think about how tired she was going to be of being alone once Alan was gone again.

"Don't be long," he said, and smiled at her, and she thought that she could happily look at that smile every day for the rest of her life.

Stupid. Stupid. She needed to remind herself that this was temporary. That the good things never lasted. Or weren't what they seemed.

Alan lay back when she was gone, bothered not by what the FBI agent had told her but by her reaction. They'd actually gone in and checked the bastard's fingerprints, and the prints matched. He was surprised the FBI had gone to the trouble, but he supposed they would double-check in situations where people like Michael might be pulling a fast one. So, fine. They checked, the prints matched.

And Phoebe was not convinced. She wanted the DNA results, too. She was hanging on to her theory that her dying ex-husband was coming after her even though she'd had it proven to her that her theory was wrong.

He was trying to see her situation from her point of view, from the fact that the man she feared so much *had* tracked her down once before and had killed two kids on his way to her. That was big. And she was getting threatening phone calls. That was big, too.

He remembered a line from a mystery he'd read long ago: Once you eliminate the impossible, whatever remains, however improbable, must be the truth.

So. The impossible was that the man after Phoebe was her comatose ex-husband.

What were the improbable options, then?

That some other man was stalking her, and that he sounded enough like her ex to fool her, and knew enough private details of their life together to convince her utterly that he *was* her ex.

Pretty fucking improbable, that one. But it wasn't Alan's only option.

Option two was that she could be a lot crazy, and imagining the phone calls. That wasn't particularly probable, either. He'd had plenty of dealings with the genuinely crazy, and he was having a hard time fitting Phoebe into that group.

She could just be a little crazy—she might be getting calls from someone who sounded nothing like her ex, but because she was already primed to be terrified of him, she *thought* the second man sounded like her ex.

Alan didn't give that option particularly good odds, either.

That left the possibility that she might be scamming him. He didn't want to consider that as his best option, because for reasons he couldn't explain, as well as a handful of fairly obvious ones, he was hugely attracted to Phoebe.

But look at the supporting evidence for the scam theory. It was all circumstantial so far, but there was a lot of it. He'd done a pretty thorough inventory of the contents of her town house. She had nothing. She lived in an adequate neighborhood, but he would bet that the little town house took just about everything she made and that every month was an adventure that ended with her wondering if she'd still have a place to live or food to eat the next. She owned a Salvation-Army-reject rabbit-eared television from the seventies, no computer, and so far as he could tell, no radio. She had a handful of dog-eared books stacked in one furniture-less corner; she didn't have any friends; she didn't have a real job. That knee of hers constituted a significant medical problem, one that was going to require ongoing—and expensive—care. And sooner or later, whatever coverage she'd had through the school (if she'd ever worked as a teacher at all) was going to run out.

Alan supposed a single doctor might look pretty good to Phoebe. He imagined that living as she did, she would be vastly relieved to have someone provide for her, watch out for her, take care of things for her.

Running counter to the scam theory was Chick's presence

and involvement with Phoebe. Alan still couldn't quite figure out Chick's place in all of this. He couldn't put together the connection between Phoebe and Chick. But whatever was going on there, it didn't completely rule out the fact that Phoebe might be playing a few angles of her own.

Alan heard the toilet flush, heard water run in the sink, heard Phoebe rattling the towel rack. The door on the other side of the bathroom, the one that led directly into the kitchen, opened with a click and a little creak.

He didn't want all this to be a scam. He wanted to believe in Phoebe; he wanted her to be as real as she'd felt up in his office and on the floor of his loft.

But he had to admit that the case for the situation being anything but a scam wasn't looking too good.

Out in the kitchen, Phoebe screamed.

That scream cut straight through thought to nerves and muscles, and Alan launched himself out of bed and through the door and across the main room to her before he could even think. He was ready to kill something or someone, or ready to pull her to safety.

But he couldn't see anything wrong. Phoebe was standing in the kitchen, her skin ashen and her hands over her mouth, looking like she was going to faint and staring at her sink.

Alan couldn't see anything wrong with the sink. It had a dirty glass mug on the side of it and a couple of clean dishes in the dish drainer to the left, but it wasn't full of cobras or tigers or the sawed-off head of a horse or anything. It was just a sink.

"What happened?" he asked her.

And her phone rang.

He went around the counter to her table and looked at the display. No caller ID. He shook his head and picked it up. "Yah."

"She's coming back to me. Of her own free will. Because she's *mine*." Alan recognized a bit of a Midwestern accent in the cold, deep voice. "And when she does, the two of us are going to watch you die."

"Don't count on it," Alan said and depressed the switch hook. He stood there for an instant, as blindly enraged as if a stranger had walked up to him and punched him in the nose. And scared, too. He walked into Phoebe's bedroom without another word, picked up his wallet, and went back out to the kitchen and dining room.

"That was Michael, wasn't it?" Phoebe said. She looked like hell. Terrified. Sick.

"It was a man. I don't know which man, but he threatened to kill me." Alan wasn't in the mood to be particularly comforting. The scream had been convincing, but the timing had been awfully good—he ran out, saw her all shaken up, and the phone rang, only she was too distraught to answer it, so he picked up. And got the putative dying husband, who made sure to stake his claim to Phoebe while threatening to kill Alan.

It was a bit too pat.

Alan found the card he'd been looking for in his wallet, picked up the phone, and dialed the number.

"Detective Hafferty, Homicide."

"Brig. This is Alan MacKerrie. I just took a phone call in which someone threatened to kill me."

"Why?"

Alan looked at Phoebe, who still looked scared. "It's complicated. *Very* complicated. Any chance you could come over here? I need your professional opinion on something."

"Can't talk about it right now?"

"No."

"Not even yes-or-no type answers?"

Alan considered the phone and the possibility that if this were a complicated scam, Phoebe and an ally might have bugged it, and said, "No."

"Do you think you're in immediate danger?"

"I honest-to-God don't know."

"You at home?"

"I'm next door to home."

A pause. Then, "Reeeeallly? I'll be right there."

Phoebe waited until he hung up and then asked him, "Who did you call?"

"Friend of mine on the local police force. A detective."

"Named Brig?"

"Brig Hafferty. I suspect Brig isn't his full name, but even when he came in through the ER after being attacked, it was the only one he used."

"So you met him as a patient?"

"I sewed him back together after a pretty nasty knifing. He thought he was going to die, and for a bit I was afraid he might be right." Alan shrugged. "It all worked out."

He walked back into the kitchen. "The phone call distracted me. You were going to tell me why you screamed."

Phoebe's face flushed red, and she shook her head. "It wasn't anything important. You told your friend that Michael had threatened to kill you."

"No, I didn't."

She looked puzzled.

"I told him that *someone* had threatened to kill me. The FBI agent told you that Michael is the guy in the nursing home bed, and you said that he was near death. In a coma. So whoever the man on the phone was, he wasn't Michael." Alan paused, looking at her, feeling like he was being played. "I really want to know why you screamed."

She swallowed, looked away, and then turned to stare fixedly at the dirty glass mug on her counter. "I broke that mug last night," she said. "But it's back on the counter. Unbroken."

He studied the mug. "You broke it?"

"On purpose. I put it in a heavy paper grocery bag, and then I slammed it against the floor until it shattered. Last night."

Alan was going to ask her why, but "why" could lead him off-track. "Why" around Phoebe was looking like a pretty wobbly thing. He was better off sticking to the strictly physical. "After you broke it, did you take the pieces out to the Dumpster?"

She shook her head. "I dropped the bag into my trash can."

"This one?" Alan pointed to the one that sat beside the counter.

Phoebe nodded.

"And you haven't emptied this since you did that?"

"No."

He opened the trash can lid with his foot and leaned over to look closely at the contents of her trash.

Fruit peels, some paper. No crumpled grocery bag, either empty or full.

"It isn't there?" she asked. He shook his head.

And she leaned against the counter, trembling visibly.

She was either crazy or a very talented scam artist. Or maybe there was something seriously wrong in her life—something in which she had no hand and for which she had no explanation—but Alan was having a harder time believing that every minute. It simply wasn't what was most probable.

She walked past him without a word, looking haunted and tiny and fragile and terribly vulnerable, and in spite of his doubts, he wanted to pull her into his arms and hold her close until the fear he saw in her eyes melted away. But before he leapt all the way into the frying pan this time, he thought it would be a good idea to hear what Brig had to say.

"Where are you going?" he asked.

"Bedroom. To get dressed. For the detective," she said. She sounded like she was about to cry. Alan couldn't understand her reaction—unless she was afraid she and a scamming buddy were going to get caught.

Alan turned away. He wanted to believe her. He wanted to believe *in* her, because she held the key to Chick, and he wanted to—

He paused, staring at nothing in the middle of Phoebe's front room. What did he think he wanted to do where Chick was concerned? He'd been about to think that he wanted to get Chick back. But Chick wasn't coming back.

That was what he wanted, though, wasn't it? He was hoping that he'd get another chance to go through that window in his office, that he was going to be able to reach Chick, wherever she was.

Because she couldn't come to him.

Phoebe had told Alan not to go through any supernatural windows. But if one opened, he was going to go through it. He knew that. Because he couldn't get Chick back in this world, but if he got the chance he was going to try his best to reach her in the next one.

He walked over and settled on Phoebe's couch, trying to decide if that made *him* obsessed. Or crazy. Or just a father. Even if Phoebe was on the level, though, it didn't make him a good bet for any long-term commitments, did it?

Phoebe still looked shaky when she came out a few minutes later; she was wearing a plain white button-down shirt with the sleeves rolled up and a pair of jeans. She'd pulled her hair back in a ponytail and had put on a pair of those plain white tennis shoes that women had been wearing since the fifties. She looked sweet, and young, and very scared.

Alan swallowed hard, suddenly seeing her beneath him on the floor of his loft, feeling her responding to his touches, hearing her excitement as he teased and caressed her toward climax, and suddenly he was grateful to be sitting down.

He took a long, slow breath, wondering if he'd been born to fall for women who wanted to use him. But he didn't *know* that Phoebe was trying to use him. He might suspect it, but that didn't change the fact that her knee injuries were real. He wasn't an idiot for being sympathetic about that. He wasn't foolish for being attracted to her; she was pretty and kind and her first kiss had turned his knees to jelly, and there might be some other explanation for everything that was going on with her in which she was completely innocent and in real trouble and in which he could protect her.

He wanted to be the one to protect her. But he couldn't understand why she wasn't doing a better job of protecting herself.

"Why didn't you call the police when you got the first call?" he asked her.

"I don't like the local police."

He raised an eyebrow and waited.

She sighed. "The detective working on my case after Michael shot me blamed me for the whole thing. I wasn't blamed officially, of course. Officially, everyone said he was a murderous freak and that he got what he deserved. Unofficially, however, the detective assigned to my case told me that if I had been a good wife and a decent human being I would have stayed with my husband and those two children would still have been alive." She looked away from Alan and added, "It doesn't help a bit knowing that he was right."

Alan leaned back on the armrest and stared at her. "A shit-bag who would say that to a woman who had just been through what you had been through was *right*?"

Phoebe looked grim. "If I had stayed with Michael, those two children wouldn't be dead."

"But you would be."

She stared fixedly at something on the far wall, and he saw her swallow hard. "That's right."

"You ran from that bastard to save your own life. You couldn't know what your lunatic ex-husband was going to do."

"I couldn't know, but I should have been able to guess. If I had it to do over again, if I knew those two children were going to die because of me, I wouldn't leave him." She made a little brushing gesture with her hands and pressed her lips together. "It doesn't matter now. The past can't be fixed. I'm not even sure the present can be."

"Those two kids didn't die because of you," Alan said. "They died because of your ex-husband. It wasn't your fault." Hearing himself saying that to her, Alan faced again his own guilt about Chick's death—that he hadn't seen what Janet was before it was too late, that he hadn't given up on his marriage and just fought to keep his kid.

No one had managed to convince him that Chick's death hadn't been his fault.

He wasn't going to be able to convince Phoebe of anything just by saying words at her, either.

"The heart knows what it knows," his mother had told him more than once. When she'd said it, he, being young and stupid, thought she was conceding that he knew better than she did what was right for his life—not, as he later discovered—that she saw a train wreck coming but had discovered that nothing she could do would stop it.

The heart knows what it knows. She'd meant, "If you used your brain, you'd see the huge mistake you're making, but you disconnected your brain where Janet is concerned back when you were nine." But she stepped out of his way to let him make the mistakes he was going to make without becoming his enemy. And she was there to pick up the pieces as best she could when the disaster she could not avert happened.

Now he and Phoebe were both making decisions based on what their hearts knew—Phoebe's about her ex-husband, and Alan's about Chick. Which was a recipe for disaster that probably made both of them fools.

And yet, sitting there hearing another train coming, he found himself unwilling to get off the tracks.

He rose at the sound of someone knocking on the door. "Brig, I imagine," he said, and saw Phoebe wince. "You want the three of us to go over to my place to talk? We'll still have to come back here, because Brig's going to need to look around the place."

She looked at him with mute appeal.

"Someone threatened to *kill* you," Alan said. "That same someone threatened to kill me, and he clearly knows where you are and what you're doing almost all the time. To protect both of us, we need to know how he knows that, Phoebe. I'm not crediting the supernatural with this. That's just too much. Everything that's going on is already unbelievable—but that your dying ex-husband can call you on some sort of ghost phone? No. That may be what the caller *wants* you to believe. But do you think that means you should believe it?"

She closed her eyes in defeat. "The three of us might as well all stay here. Your friend isn't going to find anything, but . . ."

"Brig isn't the kind of man who would tell a woman whose husband had just tried to kill her that she should have stayed with him. Trust me."

Phoebe nodded.

chapter 12

Alan's friend Brig landed in her front room like a brick through a window; solid, rumpled, in a white shirt with the sleeves rolled up, with his tie already loosened around his neck, wearing blue jeans and black running shoes. He didn't look like anything would disturb him. He had his badge clipped to his belt and a shoulder holster on, and with his weathered face and his mussed hair he could have been a misplaced cowboy.

He didn't look anything like the other one.

That other detective had looked at Phoebe with eyes that would have been at home in a golden retriever—big, sweet brown eyes at odds with the hawkish features, the military haircut, the anal-retentive wrinkle-free clothing.

And when he got the details of her case, he had been coldly and hatefully terrifying. She'd never understood why. She'd only known that he loathed her and that he sympathized with Michael. Phoebe could never understand that.

Alan and Brig shook hands and clapped each other on the shoulders, and then Alan turned and said, "This is Phoebe Rain." He paused a little, his face odd, and added, "A friend of mine."

Brig said, "Ma'am," in a long, slow drawl, and Phoebe could almost hear the horses whinnying in the background.

She rose carefully, took her time walking over to him to hide the limp as best she could, and shook his hand.

The corner of Brig's mouth quirked in a smile, but that quickly vanished. "You having trouble?" he asked Alan.

"All sorts of trouble," Alan agreed. "Culminating today in a man claiming to be Phoebe's ex-husband calling here and threatening to kill me."

"This the sort of thing your ex might actually carry out?" Brig asked, turning to Phoebe.

Which was, of course, the part of the conversation she would gladly have skipped. "You remember the shooting at the Sebastian Bright Experimental School a couple of years ago?"

He thought for a moment, and she saw the instant when the case clicked. "Nutcase went after his wife with a shotgun, killed two kids on the way to her. She took him out with her bare hands."

"That was me."

"Are you kidding?" Brig said. "You were our fuckin' hero." He winced. "Pardon my French."

He turned to Alan. "She saved the lives of twenty-seven kids and a couple of teaching assistants and God only knows who else. The motherf——pardon me, ma'am—the *bastard* who broke into the school was seven feet tall and weighed three hundred pounds."

"Six four," Phoebe corrected. "And about two-thirty."

Brig grinned a little and looked over at Alan and raised an eyebrow. That glance said, *Doesn't change a thing, does it?* "And he was carrying a twelve-gauge shotgun, along with a rifle, and enough ammo to take San Juan Hill on his own. And she took him out. Bare-handed and shot, a hundred pounds soaking wet, she took him out. It was beautiful. There was some talk among the guys of making her the patron saint of abused wives and women with stalkers. Some of us were much in favor." He turned to Phoebe and said, "I never got to meet you. And I regret the circumstances, which I take it are not good. But I am honored."

Phoebe, stunned, said, "Patron saint? That isn't at all what I heard from Jakelowitz."

Brig made a rude noise and said, "Him. Well. He had your case?"

"Yes."

"What did he tell you?"

"That if I'd stayed with my husband like a good wife, those kids wouldn't have died."

Brig turned to stare at her. "Jakelowitz is a horse's ass who gets his wives mail-order from Russia and the Philippines and China because no woman who has actually talked to the shitbag—pardon my language, ma'am—will give him the time of day. His wives leave him, he blames all womankind, and then goes on the Internet and buys himself another innocent kid to mistreat for a few months or a year." He raised an eyebrow and studied her. "You didn't think any sane person felt that way, did you?" And leaning down a little, looking into her eyes, he said, "Christ. You did. You went through all of that, and you thought . . ." He swore under his breath. "Brotherhood of blue and all that, but I swear someone needs to peg Jakelowitz."

"What that detective told you was the reason you didn't call the police when this started, isn't it?" Alan said.

Phoebe shook her head. "The fact that what he said was true stopped me. The fact that I didn't want anybody else between Michael and me. Nobody's father. Or mother. Nobody's husband or wife."

"And the man calling is your ex? Coming after you again? And you didn't call us about him because of—oh, FUCK!"

"It's not that simple," Phoebe said. "I did call the FBI. They checked on Michael—because of the state-lines issue and the possibility that he might be active again, they looked into it for me. According to them, he's still in a coma, and apparently now he's critical. Not expected to live much longer." She sighed. "They matched fingerprints, so they're certain the man in the nursing home bed really is him." She wished she could tell Brig that no matter what the FBI said, the man on the phone was Michael. But she couldn't. He

would think she was crazy, and that would make one too
many people in the room who already thought that.

Brig said, "You mind if I sit down?"

Phoebe indicated a chair and returned to her place on the
couch. Alan, after a moment's hesitation, sat beside her.

"All right," Brig said. "Tell me what's going on."

So she told him about the phone calls, about her attempts
to backtrack them and how she never could, about the psychic line and how that worked, about why she was reading
tarot for a telephone hotline instead of teaching school or
working at some other more respectable job. He listened, he
never got that tight look of disbelief on his face. He was, she
thought, a patient man.

"Sounds . . . off. Not a typical crank caller by a long shot.
I'm inclined to think that you might have picked up some
sort of copycat—though like you, I can't explain how he's
getting through to you. But that's something we should be
able to figure out pretty quickly. I'll look around here and
see if I can find anything out of the ordinary."

Phoebe nodded and Brig rose. Then Brig's cell phone
went off. He took the call, and she saw his whole body pos-
ture change, and she thought, Whatever is on the other end
is bad.

"I'm going to have to go now," he told them both. "I'll do
my best to make it back later today, but . . ." He shook his
head. "I'm off tomorrow. You'll be better off expecting me
then."

Alan followed Brig to the door and said, "I'll walk you
out." He turned to Phoebe and added, "Be right back."

Out at the car he said, "I want to believe her, Brig. I want
to believe she's exactly what she looks like."

"A sweet little kook?"

Alan sighed. "There are some things I haven't told you—
they involve me as well as her, and they're what make me
think she isn't a kook. But I have to consider the possibility
that she's scamming me."

Brig looked startled. "She's a nice kid. Nice *lady*, I guess. She went through hell a couple years back. That was all real, Alan. I didn't have her case, but I sure as hell heard about it."

"I wasn't sure about that. It seemed kind of dramatic. But I'm relieved to know that part of it is true. Still, though . . . I want to believe her, but she's done a couple of things that make me suspicious."

"Care to give me the details?"

"I'd rather not unless I know she's faking all of this." He rubbed his forehead and stared down at his shoes.

"Considered hiring a detective?"

"No. I feel slimy enough doubting her. God help me if I paid someone to investigate her and she came back innocent." He frowned. "I hate to ask, but could you run a background check on her? Nothing official. Just a little peek to see if she might be trying to bag a doctor for a husband."

Brig sighed. "I like her. I admired the hell out of her for what she managed to do. I don't want to think she's just another bitch with an angle, Alan. We all need a few things to believe in."

Alan knew how much Brig was suffering at the moment at the hands of one such bitch with an angle and her lawyer. "I know. If it makes you feel any better, I feel like a scumbag for even asking you to look."

Brig reached his white Crown Vic and opened the door. "I'll check. I promise. And if I find anything that gives me cause for alarm, I'll let you know."

"I hope you don't find anything."

"Me, too." Brig swung into the car and stuck the key in the ignition. "We have a fucking mess over in the Hilldale Apartments. Sounds like a big, sloppy murder-suicide. That's the rest of my day. It's probably going to be tomorrow before I can look into the situation over here. I'll bring some guys over in the morning to look at her phones and dig around a little—see if we can shake the caller loose. Meantime, any more threatening calls come in, you need to call the station and get someone out here right away."

"Right." Alan watched Brig drive off and turned back to the town house with mixed feelings.

While she was waiting for Alan to get back, Phoebe's phone rang. No caller ID. Dammit, where was her caller ID?

Then she remembered that she'd only paid part of her phone bill the month before because she didn't have enough money to cover the whole thing.

BellSouth might have dropped her caller ID. Her voice mail. She had to call and find out.

She got up, hobbled over to the table, and answered the phone, trying to stay calm.

"Agent Toeller here. I just received notice that Michael Schaeffer died a few minutes ago. This is to let you know that we're closing his case."

Phoebe froze. "What about the DNA evidence? You're still checking that, aren't you?"

"Your ex-husband is dead, and the case is closed, Ms. Rain. You have to accept that."

Phoebe leaned against the table, fighting back tears. Michael was dead—the FBI had checked and the body of the dead man was really Michael's. But Michael was still calling her. It *was* Michael. Wasn't it? "I understand."

"You've talked to the local police, haven't you?"

"I have," she said. "The detective left just before you called, in fact."

"Good. Work with them. Let them help you find the person who's really after you."

Phoebe thanked him again.

After they hung up, she realized that she had tears running down her cheeks. She wasn't sad. She wasn't relieved. She was, instead, scared almost witless. What Toeller had told her left her feeling like she was in a tiny boat that had been moored to the dock by one frayed little rope, and now that rope had been cut. She was adrift, alone, with a storm building. And no one was going to save her.

Her phone rang again.

She picked it up.

And Michael said, "Time for you to join me. You and your doctor and that cop. 'Til death do us part."

And then he was gone, and Alan walked through the door looking thoughtful and saw her standing there with the phone still in her hand.

"The FBI called. The agent said Michael is dead. They're closing his case." Her voice was shaking when she said it.

Alan felt like a complete shit for asking Brig to investigate her. She wasn't a con artist. He could look at her and see that. "We'll figure this out, Phoebe," he said. "Brig is a good guy. He'll get to the truth of this if anyone can."

She wrapped her arms around herself and turned her back on him. "Michael called me right after Agent Toeller did," she said, ignoring his attempted comfort. "He says it's time for us to join him. You and me and Brig. He said . . . 'til death do us part.'"

Alan stared at her. "The guy who called you mentioned Brig? By name?"

"No. He called him 'that cop.' But he knew Brig was here." She tightened her grip on herself. She felt like she was going to fly apart if she didn't hang on harder, but no matter how hard she tried, she couldn't hang on hard enough. "It was Michael who called," she whispered. "It was Michael. It was really him. Michael is dead, but Michael called."

Michael, dead Michael, had threatened Alan again. Only no one had heard but her. No one was there but her. The phone would say that only the FBI had called. There were no records of Michael, no tracks, he was dead and the mug kept moving and in her dreams Michael came to her and he touched her and when she picked up the phone Michael was there but no one else would know it was him only she knew his voice only she heard him in her nightmares and felt him watching her when she was alone.

And Michael was going to kill her. This time he was going to do it. But first he was going to kill Alan's friend Brig. And then he was going to kill Alan.

Alan, who in an impossibly short time had come to seem to her like the only solid ground in the midst of a tempest.

Michael was going to kill Alan. Or perhaps nothing was the matter, no one was calling, the mug was exactly where she left it, the phone wasn't really ringing, and she was losing her mind. Hearing voices. Seeing shadows. Living in a nightmare of her guilty mind's own making, because she was the reason two kids were dead and the guilt was going to devour her.

But no. Michael had called *Alan*. That had been real.

Alan needed to get away from her. Phoebe had already known that Alan had to be temporary in her life. Even if Alan wanted to be with her, the poison from Michael was going to keep coming, and it was going to destroy anyone who stood between Michael and her. She hated the idea of letting Alan slip away from her, or of pushing him away, which was what she probably needed to do. But she couldn't know that Michael had threatened Alan and not take every possible step to protect him.

Phoebe turned to face him, determined to save him from Michael, or from herself if she was the danger. "I don't understand what's going on, but I know you need to get out of town. To get as far away from me as possible. You need to just leave from work and . . . go on vacation or something. I don't want—anyone—coming after you."

Alan said, "I'm not leaving town. Brig's good; he'll figure out what's going on with your crank caller and take care of it."

"What about Chick?"

"What about her?"

"She came to you to tell you that you were in danger."

"I haven't figured out what's going on with Chick yet, Phoebe. I just don't know. I don't know about anything right now." He sighed. "I'm about eight hours behind on charting—I'm going to have to get caught up. I won't be able to finish before I go on shift, but I should be able to make a big dent in the paperwork."

"When does your shift start?"

"Seven p.m. I'm on until seven tomorrow morning. Maybe it'll be slow and I'll be able to sleep once I go on duty."

He yawned and rubbed his eyes with his knuckles, a gesture that Phoebe found endearing. Boyish.

"You're vulnerable. Michael wants to hurt you. He wants to kill you. You don't know him. You don't understand what he's capable of. If you're at work, he'll know how to find you."

Alan shook his head and rested both hands on her shoulders. "Phoebe, sweetheart, the Michael you knew is dead. I don't know who's after you—but whoever he is, this guy isn't a god. He isn't a ghost. He's a man, and while he may have some tricks up his sleeve, he isn't invulnerable, and he can't just appear out of nowhere and get you or me if we're watching out for him. Don't worry. I'll be careful. That'll have to be good enough, because I have to go in to the hospital today. People's lives depend on me being there. And you'll be okay, too. The police are looking into this mess. They'll find the guy who's calling you. In the meantime, keep your doors locked, check before you answer, and don't let anyone in but me, or Brig if he comes back today. Okay?"

Phoebe thought, You're too busy saving other people to save yourself. But she didn't say that. Instead, she said, "You think horrible things never happen to people once the police start looking into it? You think that all those women with restraining orders who end up slaughtered on their kitchen floors were saved by the fact that the police knew who wanted to hurt them?" She leaned forward. "We have to save ourselves, Alan. We're the only people who can watch out for ourselves twenty-four hours a day. If Michael—or whoever—comes after you, the police will end up picking up what's left after the fact and trying to figure out who did it, and how. They can't be everywhere that he might be all the time to protect you."

But Alan just gave her a hug and said, "You're afraid, and I really understand that. The call I took was frightening. I'd think that knowing your ex-husband is dead and can't hurt you anymore would help. Knowing the police are involved should help. Knowing that I'm here for you—that should count for something, too. You aren't alone, Phoebe. Not anymore."

And then he kissed her and headed out the front door to go to work.

And she was alone.

Well, she was used to being alone, and unlike Alan, she didn't have any illusions about how much help the police would be or how safe she was. She locked all the locks and jammed the bar under the front door.

Called the phone company. Her problem with caller ID was, in fact, that she hadn't paid the full bill. The customer service representative told her BellSouth would be happy to reinstate full service as soon as she was caught up on her bill.

It didn't matter, Phoebe decided. Even if she could look at the phone and know it was Michael on the other end, she would still answer it. What else could she do? She had to know what he wanted. What he was planning.

Phoebe stood in the main room, looking back at the dining room table, the raised counter and her bowls of fresh fruit, the tiny kitchen behind that. All one room, really, and to the right the open door into her bedroom. She could see almost everything on the ground floor, plus the steps set just back of her bedroom door, and the loft above those—empty. The door into the furnace at the top of the steps. Right of that, the door into the upstairs bathroom/bedroom combination.

She needed to go upstairs, just to make sure everything up there was the way it was supposed to be.

The trip up the stairs hurt like hell and proved to be a waste of time. The upstairs bedroom was empty and dusty. The upstairs bathroom, the same. Her pins locking the bedroom window shut were in place, dust-covered, untouched. The window was still painted shut. The big walk-in closet with its sliding mirror doors stood open so that she could see in, the light worked, the closet had its own layer of dust. Dust and tan carpet.

It hadn't been worth the trip up, but now she knew.

She sat on her butt and scooted down the stairs, keeping her bad knee straight. It was just easier that way.

If Alan wouldn't leave town, perhaps she should—but if she left, Michael would still know where to find Alan, and he might decide to go after him just because he could, before he picked up her trail and tracked her down.

No leaving, then.

Should she warn Brig that Michael had threatened him, too? She decided against it. He'd be coming by tomorrow morning; she could tell him then.

She did a careful tour of the downstairs—bedroom, bedroom closet, bathroom, laundry closet, kitchen-dining-living room. Everything was in place, everything looked just the same. The tea mug sat where she'd found it. She decided to leave it where it was.

Tea, though—she could definitely use a good cup of tea. She heated the water in the kettle, made green tea and skipped the honey, and drank it standing at the counter. The tea made her feel better. She knew it was only a quirk of habit—that she associated green tea with good feelings— but that single cup of tea was as soothing as an hour in a hot bubble bath.

The town house was warm in spite of the air-conditioning, and Phoebe realized she was exhausted. She'd only had a couple of hours of sleep, and while that had been good sleep, there hadn't been enough of it. She looked at the couch. She could keep her backpack with her, have the handgun close by, just close her eyes for a few minutes and rest. She needed the rest.

Just a few minutes.

She lugged her backpack over to the couch, put it on the

floor, and stretched out in the single block of sunlight pouring in through the angled top window.

She sank into blissful comfort. It was a cheap, lumpy, secondhand couch, but she didn't care. It was the middle of the day, everything was locked and tight, for a little while at least she could stop worrying. She felt so much better.

And then she was dreaming. Alan, at first. Kissing her; pulling her close, wrapping his arms around her, telling her she was not alone. But somewhere along the way, the dream changed. Because suddenly Michael was there, whispering, "You're all alone, Phoebe. No one can save you. No one. I brought you a flower for your funeral. The first flower."

And suddenly Phoebe was as cold as if she'd been drenched in ice water. She was freezing, drowning, she was sinking into an icy lake and she had to wake up. Wake up. *Wake up, wake up.*

Wake up.

Phoebe woke into darkness, the air around her freezing, her skin prickling from the chill, with the child's voice in her head screaming, *Wake up! Wake up!*

She tried to sit up, while the room spun around her, and as she did something dry and rough poked her neck. Wobbly, confused, dry-mouthed, and terrified, Phoebe reached over her head and managed to fumble her reading lamp on.

In the warm yellow glow she saw something long and thin and dark lying angled across her chest, snagged on the cotton of her blouse. She tried to pick it up, and it stabbed her fingertips. She couldn't get her eyes to focus—she was having trouble waking up, and her chattering teeth and shaking hands from the cold were slowing her down, and Chick—who was inside Phoebe's head panicking and screaming, *He was here! I chased him away*—prevented her from thinking straight.

What was going on?

Phoebe finally managed to sit up, and the cold vanished, and so did the screaming inside her head. She pulled the dry thing off her chest with two fingers, managing not to hurt herself on it anymore, and she stared at it until her eyes co-operated by bringing it into focus.

It was a single rose. Dead. Dried. The stem covered with needle-sharp thorns.

Oh, God.

She'd slept the day away, and somehow Michael had reached out of her dreams into reality and given her the flower from her nightmares. The one for her funeral.

She made her way to her feet and wobbled into the kitchen. The clock on the stove said 11:50 p.m.

All day. She'd slept all day.

She was queasy, and shaky, and she needed to get out of the house. If Michael could reach her behind her locked doors, he could reach Alan, too. And as long as she and Alan were apart they were vulnerable.

The phone rang. She didn't answer it. She couldn't stand to hear Michael's voice again. She was too near throwing up. She couldn't listen to his threats again. She wouldn't.

She closed her eyes and clenched her fists while the phone rang, and rang, and rang, and with every ring she got angrier. How dare he? How dare Michael threaten people around her again? How dare he use other people as disposable playing pieces in his game to get to her? She wasn't as afraid for herself anymore—she had her gun, she'd taken precautions with her home, she lived watchfully, and she'd had a lot of practice doing it. She would find a way to keep him outside her doors. She knew she had beaten Michael once before, which had to count for something. Even if this wasn't truly Michael—*but it is,* the little voice in her head whispered, *it is*—he'd made himself close enough to the original to be indistinguishable to the person in the world who knew Michael best, and hated him most. Her.

So until she found proof that *she* considered satisfactory that Michael was dead, she would keep thinking of the man coming after her as Michael. Because so long as she was dealing with Michael, she would never let herself cut corners or make assumptions.

She would take on whatever he threw at her. She might not survive it, but if she went down she was sure she wouldn't go down alone.

Phoebe didn't feel confident at all about Alan, though. He'd never lived under siege. He had no idea how tight his focus would have to stay to keep himself ahead of someone who wanted to kill him. He would have had dozens of opportunities already to make a fatal mistake—to go down empty hallways, walk across parking lots past blind spots and traps, speak to people he didn't know in situations where no one else was around to back him up. He didn't know about checking every step he took five steps ahead of time to make sure he never went around a corner he couldn't see. He just didn't know how to keep a constant watch, because he'd never done it. And he didn't understand Michael—that Michael would just keep coming and coming and coming until Alan was totally destroyed.

And the time for Alan to learn how to save his own life was not during and after a twelve-hour night shift in an emergency room. His mind would be on other things all the time.

He needed a guardian angel.

He needed her.

chapter 13

Just past midnight. Not, traditionally, the best time for ER docs, and Alan, looking over the unit, wanted to be anywhere but where he was. He'd tried to call Phoebe half a dozen times in the last few hours—at first just to check up on her, but then because he started being scared. He'd been pretty sure when he left her house for the hospital that he was fine where Phoebe was concerned—that he could take her or leave her and that if Brig found proof that she was conning him, he could go on without missing a beat. But not being able to reach her had left his heart thudding like a jackhammer, and he couldn't get her beautiful smile out of his mind or stop thinking about the way she'd looked at him as he left. Alan was sure Phoebe was all right, but he couldn't leave the ER to go check on her, and as a result he was having a hell of a time staying focused on his work.

The late-night pediatric clinic had cleared out, as had the felt-bad-after-the-doctor's-office-closed crowd. There wasn't as much busywork as a result, but the people remaining to be seen had bigger problems than "head cold for last month" or "wrenched ankle last week."

Three patients were on beds, with another three or four going through the triage process out in the waiting room. The first of the full stretchers held a knife wound to the shoulder that was deep and about six inches long and covered with a tight pressure dressing—and that would get about sixty stitches as soon as the combative drunk attached to it stopped threatening to kill the staff. The second held a fifty-four-year-old white male with chest pain radiating down the left arm for the last four hours, growing increasingly more severe, with current complaints of nausea, vomiting, and severe shortness of breath. He was in the middle of his first heart attack and getting everything in the book tossed at him while Alan waited for Admitting and the nurses in the cardiac unit to ready a bed upstairs. The third was a stressed-out man in his early thirties complaining of migraines and blinding lights behind his eyes.

The thing all three of them had in common was endless puking. The drunk had brought up his Mad Dog 20/20 dinner about an hour earlier and was now trying to rid himself of the turpentine dessert—and the whole ER reeked of it. The heart attack threw up in incessant tight, short little bursts, and apologized to the nurses after every round. And the migraine—oh, the migraine. The migraine made more noise than a twelve-cat fight; he sounded like he was trying to turn himself inside out every time.

Alan hadn't been so close to throwing up himself since his first cadaver.

Even the nurses—as tough a bunch as had ever run an ER—looked a little green around the gills.

"I say we TOBASH Knife-Boy and ship the other two now," said Helena, the night ER charge nurse. "TOBASH" was an acronym for Take Out Back And Shoot in Head; dealing with people who had just spent hours trying to kill themselves or others, and then when they almost succeeded, who arrived in the ER demanding care while simultaneously threatening to kill the people waiting to give it had given birth to that acronym. Helena smiled when she said it, but her eyes were grim. Twenty-three years as an emergency RN had ground a few sharp edges onto her personality.

This wasn't what Alan had thought medicine would be— and worse, this was as good as it got. ER was still the place where doctors got closest to actually practicing medicine.

Every other specialty ended up so tangled in paperwork, insurance, government-mandated categorization, and corporate bullshit that the doctors and nurses couldn't do much patient care. The field had lost something essential when insurers started calling the shots on what they would cover, and it lost a lot more when hospitals went from being private community-funded services to the next big corporate profit-centered acquisition. Alan didn't know if medicine would ever regain the ground it had lost.

It had lost its humanity.

He turned and found one of the nurses leading in a slender young black man who'd fallen down stairs at home—at least that was his story. A badly healed break in one arm and bruises in all stages of healing suggested that the truth was a long way from a simple accident. And the boyfriend, a trim, older copper-skinned man in pressed slacks, wearing a neat white shirt and tie not even loosened at the collar at this god-awful hour, acted suspicious as hell.

At least this newest patient wasn't barfing.

Alan closed his eyes against the coming lies and thought of Phoebe. He wanted to talk to her—to reassure himself that she was safe and then to bitch to her about the night he was having, to hear her laugh at his description of the puke-fest. Better, he wanted to curl up in bed with her again and hold her, and then he wanted to make love to her. On his balcony. On the rug. In her bed. In his bed. On the kitchen table at his place. On hers . . . no, not on hers. She had one of those spindly, feminine tables made strictly for dining, and even that only if you ate with little forks and elbows down.

Furniture ought to be multipurpose, he thought, and bolstered by the obvious truth of this, he took a deep breath. Phoebe was all right. She was just taking calls on the psychic line and was too busy to answer his calls. Or afraid to answer, for fear it might be the freak. Maybe he should pick up an answering machine for her so she could screen her calls. She should have one. Why didn't she? In any case, though, he was sure she was fine. He promised himself that

he would try her again as soon as he finished the new as-
sessment. Then he headed behind the curtain to listen to lies
for a while.

Twelve fifteen a.m., and Phoebe had gotten over the
shakes. She took out her Browning, stripped it, and spread
the pieces on an old towel in the center of her bed. She sat,
bad leg positioned off the side and aligned to cause her the
least possible pain, and carefully cleaned the weapon and
put it back together. She checked the mechanism to make
sure it worked smoothly, then slid the shell cartridge in with
a satisfying click. When she was finished, the oddly sweet
smell of the cleaning oil filled her bedroom, and she felt
confident that the handgun would operate correctly if she
needed it.

She slid the Browning into its holster, secured the holster
within her backpack, and stared at the ceiling. She tried to
find the woman she had been at the moment that she managed to stop Michael. She had only been that woman for a
short time—a few minutes, less than half an hour at the
most. But that woman had moved beyond fear into a cold
place where sound fell hollow and pain washed out like the
blue in a South Florida sky and colors faded away to black
and white and blood red. When she had been that woman,
and in that cold place, she had been able to stand against
Michael and win.

It was the first time. The only time.

And now she had to do it again.

She thought of Alan, and what Michael would do to him
if he got him in a shotgun's sights or within reach of his
knife. Phoebe frowned. She didn't know that she could find
the woman she had been for those few critical moments—
but even if she could, the effort would be useless if she
wasn't in the right place to make a difference. And the right
place at that moment had to be the emergency room.

She looked at her knee. "You hurt," she told the damaged
joint. "A lot." It didn't—or at least it didn't hurt any worse

than its baseline level. But the nice thing about her knee was that it always *looked* like it hurt. Anything that could make medical professionals flinch and stare fixedly at other things while they corralled their shocked reactions had to be pretty bad. Her knee was.

She looked at the clock. Already twelve forty—she had taken far longer than she should have to clean her gun. Pushing one a.m. was a ludicrous hour to be out in her neighborhood. The neighborhood scared her even without having to think about Michael. But she thought of Alan, and how a death he wouldn't see coming hovered over his head like a dark angel.

She had to get moving. "Right. Out the door. Don't think. Just do." She swung her backpack over her shoulder, grabbed her cane as she headed for the door. She kept her free hand under the backpack's front pouch flap, resting on the grip of the Browning, and she tried not to let herself think about Michael and whether he was flesh and blood or a ghost bent on vengeance or some stranger coming after her for reasons she didn't know—or if he might be someone she knew. Like Ben.

The weight of the gun had grown in the backpack. Phoebe could find no beauty in the thing, no grace. Nothing but efficiency and a tight, tense freedom—the freedom to stand between death and those she . . . loved?

She could not think of love. Not yet. Probably not ever. Love was an emotion reserved for those whose lives were not lived under a deathwatch. She could not afford the messiness of love, or the hope.

Phoebe could only afford a dark, ferocious intent to survive.

Outside was typical South Florida summer—the air filled with the perfume of night-blooming jasmine, voices from one of the enclosed patios nearby speaking softly in Spanish, dogs barking. The night, still too warm and humid to be genuinely comfortable, nonetheless felt better than morning would in a few hours when the sun came up again.

Palm fronds rattled in a faint breeze. Phoebe's skin

crawled. She thumbed the safety off, but nothing and no one came after her. She reached her car, checked it for intruders before getting in, locked it as soon as she was seated, and managed to start the thing on the first try.

She drove to Alan's ER, parked in a location that gave her a clear view of the entrance doors while still letting her see around her, and tried to spot Alan's car. She didn't see it—perhaps the doctors had a parking lot away from the general traffic. Alan had a fairly nondescript car—a four- or five-year-old well-maintained green Toyota Corolla with M.D. plates—but she was certain she would recognize it if it were in view.

That late at night, the parking lot was almost empty. She waited with the car doors locked and her heart in her throat until she saw a security guard making outdoor rounds—then she flashed her headlights and got out, grabbed her cane, and shouted for help.

He turned.

"Wheelchair, please!" she yelled, and he grabbed one from just inside the doors and hurried to help her.

"What's wrong?"

"Can't walk." She slid her pant leg up to the knee, showed him, and watched him wince. "Dr. MacKerrie is expecting me."

He looked down at her leg, and his gaze focused, then slid away. "You call ahead?"

She nodded. "We're next-door neighbors."

He waited while she levered herself into the wheelchair, carefully not bending her supposed-to-be-injured leg. He adjusted the footrest to let her keep the leg straight—she kept the pant leg pulled up for the shock value. The knee did look swollen, actually. It didn't hurt any worse than usual, but maybe she should have let Alan take her in to have it x-rayed after they crashed into each other.

"How did you do that, miss?" the guard asked.

She shrugged, not wanting to go into the sordid details. "Accident. Long story, and not very interesting."

"He going to admit you?"

"I certainly hope not."

The guard nodded and came to a decision. He took her in through a side entrance, skipping the admission office and triage. Alan saw her as they came through the double doors. He looked at her, and Phoebe saw an expression of relief wash over his face, and then he looked down at her leg and said, "Room one's open. I'll be right in."

The guard offered to help her onto the stretcher.

"I'd rather stay in the chair—I don't want to move it any more than I have to. I'm afraid the pins might be loose again."

Alan came in as the guard was leaving. He waited until the guard was gone, then closed the door and said, "I've been trying to call you for hours. You scared the shit out of me, Phoebe. What *happened*?"

"That was you on the phone?" She cringed. "I'm sorry. I thought it was . . . Michael. I fell asleep on the couch, and slept for hours, and then—" She considered telling him that Chick had woken her, but decided not to. "In my nightmare Michael was giving me a flower for my funeral, and when I woke, I found this on my chest." She'd wrapped the dead rose in plastic. She pulled it out of her backpack and showed it to him. "I was afraid to answer the phone."

He stared at the rose, and she thought he paled a little, but it was hard to tell under the fluorescent lights. "Oh, God, Phoebe. I thought you were just busy taking calls."

She shook her head. "I didn't wake up until just before midnight. My call average is going to plummet if I don't get some time in." She grinned a little. "Not that I don't have bigger things to worry about."

He took a deep breath, reached down, and gently palpated her knee. "You have some new swelling here and some heat over the joint. What happened?"

"Nothing. I wanted an excuse to come in here that wouldn't draw too much attention to me."

"Walking in would have worked."

Phoebe shook her head. "I meant, that wouldn't draw too much attention from Mi— . . . from the stalker. If he was watching me, I wanted to have a seemingly legitimate reason to be here."

"It looks like you have some fresh damage. More bruising and swelling since the last time I looked at it. Nothing huge, but I'm not happy about it."

Phoebe shrugged. "It's the same as usual. I don't know that I'd go so far as to say it's all right, but I don't really want to do anything with it. I can't afford the X-ray and the ER fees and everything else right now." *And I don't dare let you out of my sight when Michael may be coming,* she thought.

Alan nodded. "An X-ray wouldn't hurt, I don't think, but if you're sure you haven't done anything new to it, we can let it go with Ace, ice, and elevate. You and I can do that as a private visit so we don't have to do a chart on you. I'll cover any costs." He crouched beside the wheelchair. "You sound like you've finally decided the guy coming after you isn't your ex."

"Why do you say that?"

"Because just now was the first time I heard you call him anything but Michael." He smiled. "That's good, Phoebe."

"Actually, I'm pretty sure the person coming after me *is* Michael. I called him my stalker for your benefit, but not because that's what I believe."

Alan's smile died. "Oh." He sighed deeply. "He can't be Michael."

Phoebe held up a hand. "How does Chick come to you?"

"I don't know."

"But she does—right? I mean, you know it's her."

"Of course I know it's her. She's my daughter."

"He was my husband. He was my stalker. He was nearly my killer. I know him better than I know anyone on the planet except myself. I don't know how he's coming after me any more than you know how Chick has come back to you." Phoebe leaned forward in the chair. "But I think the two things are related—Chick and Michael. I don't know what form he's in, but I think Chick knows about him. What I don't know is why she got you involved with me. You would have been a million times better off if you'd never met me."

He stood utterly still for a long moment. Then he just shook his head. "No. That isn't true."

"You would have. Your life is in danger now, and that's because of me. Anyway, I'm just saying that these contacts with Michael aren't necessarily taking place on the physical plane."

"Michael's spirit is bringing you dead flowers?"

"And moving my tea mug around. And, I don't know . . . watching me all the time."

"How is that possible?"

"I don't know how he's doing it. But I know it's him, the same way that you know Chick is really Chick." She closed her eyes. "It *feels* like him."

"I thought knowing he was dead would be a comfort to you."

She smiled up at him. "I know. But right now it would be false comfort. That's . . . no. We don't want false comfort. We don't want any sense of security that's based on a lie, because that could get us killed. *This* is real comfort. The two of us in here—just being with you, knowing you're safe." She reached over and took his hand. "I know I don't know you very well, Alan—"

"You almost knew me a lot better." He smiled at her, and she couldn't help but laugh a little.

"True. And I don't want to make any assumptions and I don't want to crowd you. But I feel better being here. Knowing that you're safe, at least right this minute."

"You can make a few assumptions." His sudden grin flashed wickedly, and his eyes lit with an unholy come-hither glow.

"I can't. *We* can't. We don't dare. We're in a tight spot right now—shared fear, shared strangeness—and that's going to create a sense of false intimacy. We're going to have to ignore it, because it isn't real. You know this. You know how people act in traumatic situations."

Alan looked startled. Head cocked at an angle, he studied her. And smiled a warm, winning smile. "You mean like survivor sex?"

Phoebe felt her cheeks get hot. "Yeah. Like that."

"And you think that *we* would be a bad idea? Us? You're trying to talk me out of us?"

Phoebe wanted nothing in the world less than that, but she said, "I just don't want . . . um . . . either of us mistaking this for something it isn't. Something more permanent."

She looked away from him. She didn't want him to say something he didn't mean. Something that he would regret when sanity returned and it was time to move on.

Something like *I love you.*

She wasn't going to let herself say those three words, either.

"When we get through this, things are going to look different. And I don't want either one of us getting hurt."

Alan took two steps towards her, so that he was close enough that she could feel the heat of his body and smell the lingering whisper of aftershave. "You can't know what the future holds," he said. "And in the meantime, I'm all in favor of survivor sex."

She got all warm and tingly, and a wicked little voice inside of her said, *I'm all in favor of survivor sex, too.* But she smiled a shaky smile and said, "Well, it's not anything we have to worry about right now."

"Who's worrying?" Alan asked and took the step that closed the gap between them. He wrapped his arms around her and lifted her up. "You're sure the knee is okay?"

"Um—" Phoebe said, but didn't get a chance to say anything else, because he was kissing her, his big hands cradling her buttocks, and she wrapped her legs around him, being very careful with the knee because there were some things she simply did not wish to explain to anyone—ever—

and explaining how she'd dislocated her knee while jumping the bones of an on-duty ER doctor (in a trauma room, no less) while pretending to be a patient certainly ranked high on that list.

Their lips crushed together, their tongues stabbed and thrust, their bodies tried to push through clothing to reach each other. The kiss—the kiss tossed Phoebe into a place of pure red unthinking haze, into boiling blood and howling images of him naked her naked them rising and falling, heaving, thrusting, and she wrapped hands around the back of his head and pulled him tighter, closer, wild with a desire so consuming that she would willingly have stripped him bare and thrown him to the cold linoleum floor and impaled herself on him and ridden him to screaming, shrieking climax right then and there.

He broke free, looking dazed, and slid her onto the Stryker stretcher that filled the center of the room. He stepped back, and she felt suddenly like the sacrifice on a pagan altar.

"Where have you been all my life?" he said, and his voice broke.

"Where are we going to be ten minutes from now—that's what I want to know," she replied.

"I'm here until seven a.m. We have two other doctors in the ER for this shift, but leaving early—no. It's just not done."

"Time now?"

"Almost three. Wow, time drags when you want to get moving."

"I'm going to explode before then."

Alan looked down at the tented fabric of his scrub pants and muttered, "Shit. Look—I'm going to put an Ace wrap on your knee, put you back in the wheelchair, and put you in the doctors' lounge—we have a couple of bunk beds in there, and you can rest—"

For a moment that sounded eminently reasonable to Phoebe. Then the whole reason she'd come to the ER in the ridiculous hours of the morning fought its way through the fog in her brain, and she said, "Could I just sit at the nurses' station, out of the way? I promise to keep my hands to myself and not say anything that would embarrass you."

"Not going to do any tarot readings for the nurses, huh?"

"I was a teacher," Phoebe said. "I'm certified to teach math, chemistry, biology, anatomy, and honors science all the way through twelfth grade. I can pretend to be normal." She smiled a little. "I had lots of practice passing for normal as a kid."

"You could never pass for normal," Alan told her. "Only for extraordinary." He took an Ace bandage off a huge metal storage shelf and started wrapping her knee with it. His timing couldn't have been better. A nurse knocked and popped her head in the door. "We have a two-car collision on the way in. CPR in progress on one that's already tubed, two dead at the scene, two with big trauma, one baby in a car seat that sounds unscathed but is going to have to be checked out. You need me to finish up in here?"

Alan said, "I've got this wrapped. She'll need an ice pack. And let her wait at the nurses' station; she shouldn't have driven here with this, and she definitely doesn't need to drive home on it."

"You want me to call a ride for you?" the nurse asked. Her tone was professional, but Phoebe could see curiosity in her eyes.

"I'm going to drive her home," Alan said.

"My car . . ."

"Morrie owes me a favor. He'll bring it for you."

Phoebe smiled at the nurse and tried hard to look like someone who hadn't just been kissed to within an inch of her sanity. She had the feeling the nurse wasn't buying any of it, that behind that polite, curious face lay a mind saying, "Yeah, sure, I've got eyes, honey."

So Phoebe sat tucked away in a corner of the nurses' station, her backpack on her lap, her hand on top of the flap, watching the doctors and the nurses hurrying between patients, and watching cops and paramedics and EMTs pouring into the open spaces bringing patients on stretchers, and watching techs running in and out of the department. And all the darkness of the past two years filled her again. She had been in places like this, surrounded by doctors and nurses and cops like these, and her scars were still fresh and she was not yet free. She watched Alan, listened to him taking charge, making things better, saving people's lives, and everything he did just pounded home to her the reality that all she was doing for him was bringing him trouble and danger and the threat of his own death.

And for what? On her part, she didn't know. On his, though—for a psychic connection with his dead daughter? He could replace her with someone else who could do the same thing better, by a real medium, not a sideline tarot reader. Someone who wouldn't risk his life simply by being there. For a passing sexual attraction born of shared fear and danger and strangeness? Phoebe could see the female members of the ER staff all around her—nurses, a doctor, lab and X-ray techs. Most of them were young, all of them were strong and healthy, and many of them were very pretty. They had everything in the world in common with Alan—shared goals and shared careers, a common philosophy, understandings that came of fighting together for something worthwhile. And futures.

She could see the dead rose lying on her chest, as clearly as if it had been branded there.

She didn't have a future.

So she and Alan shared a transient connection to his dead child's ghost and to her reportedly dead psychopath of an ex. Well, that and a sexual chemistry so explosive it hurt. It was going to be agony when Alan moved on with his life, leaving her with memories of the best thing she'd ever experienced—and the knowledge that it hadn't even been real. That was . . .

That was pathetic.

Once she'd found a way to protect Alan from Michael,

she could just get in her car and drive away. Save face, protect her feelings. Until then, she could avoid any more kisses, or touches, or curling up in bed together.

She watched him, and thought, Yeah, I could protect myself and my feelings later, and miss out on everything now. But I've never had great sex. Hell, I've never even had great chemistry. All I need is once. Just one time with him, in bed or anywhere, all the way, just to know what it's like. What it could have been for me with someone better than Michael. Then I'll step gracefully out of his way and live with reality. At least that way I'll have an amazing memory—for however long I have left. And if I'm out of time, I haven't thrown away my last opportunity for something wonderful because I was afraid to take a chance.

She stared at her right leg. She figured she could take hurt feelings—or even a broken heart—standing on her head. She'd been through a lot worse.

Here and now, he wants me. It doesn't have to be forever, it doesn't have to be real. I'm an adult. I just have to make sure I don't let myself fall in love with him. That I remember who I am and who he is.

That I remember that no one gets to keep every wonderful thing that moves through her life, and I'm no exception.

chapter 14

Alan had always been good at keeping his mind on his work, even when his personal life was a shambles. And he didn't make any fatal errors or get sidetracked from what he was doing. But he couldn't make himself forget that Phoebe was in the ER, just a few feet away, watching him. He couldn't make himself forget the taste of her lips, the scent of her hair, or the feel of her tight, lean body wrapped around his.

The way she'd tried to talk him out of the two of them. No way she would have done that if she were trying to con him. The heightened emotions surrounding the bizarreness they were both dealing with would have been like the . . . the golden ticket to a con artist.

Which meant she was on the level.

Which meant he could allow himself to feel what he was feeling for her. She wasn't Janet. He could let himself trust her—at least enough to pursue the real stirrings between them, to see where those emotions led.

Alan got through the trauma code, got the patient stabilized and shipped upstairs—but the whole time he was working, he was feeling his hands on Phoebe's skin and seeing her smile, and imagining the look he would see in her eyes when he plunged into her for the first time.

He did his charting standing up, leaning against the counter, not daring to move. The hard-on was persistent,

obvious, and annoying. Annoying only because he and
Phoebe weren't someplace where they could put it to good
use.

She looked sad and tense sitting over there, he thought—
like she'd lost her best friend, or maybe like he had and she
was the one who was going to have to tell him about it.
Pretty—God, she was beautiful. His parents would love her.
And his brothers. When he introduced her to his brothers,
he'd have to club them once, just to make sure they knew
not to try poaching.

He wanted to see her smile. Wanted to hear her laugh
again—she had a wonderful, rich, throaty laugh, but he had
the feeling she only took it out of mothballs on blue moons.
And that just wasn't right. She deserved to be the happiest
woman on the planet. She deserved to be free of all the horrors haunting her, all the pain that chased after her, and definitely free of that psychopath who was scaring her,
whoever he was.

Brig would be by later and would start straightening
things out for her. Meanwhile, she was where Alan could see
her and make sure that the phone freak didn't turn into an in-
person freak.

She'd been scared to be by herself. It should have been
obvious to him before that whatever was going on with her
was real—at least to her. Jesus, look at her. She was truly
afraid. She couldn't see him watching her—he was catching
glimpses in the convex mirror at the nurses' station. As long
as she thought his attention was elsewhere, she looked like
a violin string stretched too tight, like at any minute she was
going to snap in two and go whipping around the room in
two different directions. Every time he'd been with her before, he'd only felt her strength, her quiet belief that she
could protect herself. And when she realized he was looking
at her, she did the same thing. Drew courage from someplace and projected calm.

But it was the hint of weakness, of fragility, that gave him
a sudden rush of "Me Tarzan, you Jane" machismo. Under-

neath everything, she was afraid, and even if she didn't want him to know how much, she'd sought *him* out for protection. He discovered that he liked the feeling.

He smiled at her, a smile that he just meant to be reassuring and comforting and maybe a little heroic, but somewhere between his brain and his mouth, he all of a sudden wanted to kiss her again, and the expression on his face must have done something bizarre, because she looked at him exactly the way the one deer he'd almost run over had looked at him.

Big deep brown eyes. A man could get lost in those eyes and never find his way out again. And, Alan thought, a man could like being that lost.

Every time he looked at Phoebe, he kept seeing those two narrow, lonely bunk beds in the overnight room, and her naked on one of them, turning that room into something magical.

He was supposed to be an adult, for chrissake. Yet he felt like he was fourteen again, accidentally brushing against girls in the crowded hallways at school, flooded by insane teenage hormones and imagining every pretty girl he passed undressed.

He looked at the nurses.

No. They still had all their clothes on.

He looked back at Phoebe.

Naked, on the bed in the doctors' overnight room.

Well—this was better than when he was fourteen, anyway. At least now it was a selective phenomenon.

Alan finished the chart. Looked at the clock, then over at Phoebe. "Time to go home," he said, and she was amazed that he didn't look tired. She heard a tension in his voice that made her skin tingle.

Desperate yearning filled her.

"Ready?" he asked her.

She nodded, not daring to say anything. Her mouth was dry.

"I have to stop in the overnight room and pick up my stuff on the way out."

"That's fine. I'm . . ." She swallowed hard and lied. "I'm not in any hurry."

She watched him, feeling the air between them crackle. He might be willing to amble along, but if she didn't touch him soon—and a lot—she was going to explode.

He said, "I'll wheel you out."

"I'd rather walk." She smiled at him. "The knee is not so bad now."

He took her hand, helped her to her feet—and the way her hand fit into his and the heat of her smooth skin bypassed rational thought entirely and made her belly knot and her nipples tighten and her heart race.

"You okay?" she asked him, frowning a little. Up close, he looked violin-string tight.

"It's been a long night," he said.

She nodded fervently. "It has. I'll be so glad to get in bed." And touch you, she thought.

She heard his breath catch. Then, hoarsely, he said, "C'mon. Let's get out of here."

He steered the two of them past the watchful eyes of the rest of the ER staff and led her into a room that would have made fleabag hotels look good. It was clean—the two-high metal bunk beds against the walls to left and right were made, the carpet had been swept, the two metal desks on either side of the door held a few reference books. But Phoebe had a first impression of grayness that went deeper than the industrial carpet, the burlap walls, the fluorescent lighting, the gray desks, the gray bed frames, the dismal gray-blue bedcovers, the beige lockers against the back wall. This was a lonely, sad, tired place.

"This is the best they can do for you guys?" she asked.

He nodded. "I think Administration figures, 'God forbid any of them should actually want to be in there.'" Alan stood studying the lockers. "Jane is already gone, we passed Farris making tracks out the door on our way in, and Morrie and the other day-shift guys have already been here and locked up." He gave her a smile that offered delicious wickedness.

She returned the smile, hoping he was thinking what she was thinking. "Anyone ever . . . ah . . . you know . . . in here?"

Alan shoved the door shut and locked it without turning away from her. "If they haven't, it's their loss." He walked over to her and pulled her into his arms.

"We won't get caught in here?"

"Well, we won't get walked in on without warning. I locked the door."

Phoebe ran a finger from the hollow of his throat down his chest and belly. "That's not quite the same thing."

Alan kissed her, and Phoebe felt the world and all its problems fall away into irrelevance. "No," he whispered, "it isn't."

Abruptly she pulled away. "Shit."

"What?"

"Condoms."

He dug into the pocket of the lab coat he hadn't yet taken off and pulled out a handful—all promising NEW, BRIGHT COLORS! and RIBBED FOR HER PLEASURE. "Restroom earlier," he said. "After you got here."

She laughed, soft and low, and stared into his eyes. "I hope that'll be enough." She undid the drawstring of his scrub pants and tugged them down. Slid her hands down his back, under the waistband of his underwear, and dragged her fingernails lightly over his buttocks. And felt him shudder.

"You have too many clothes on," he murmured right before her hands pulled his underwear down and moved around to the front and he groaned.

She pulled the front of his scrub shirt up and started licking and nibbling her way down the center line of his chest, and suddenly he said, "Not yet. You first."

Her pulse skittered and her breath picked up as Alan slipped her shirt over her head.

"We're not going to have a lot of time," she murmured. "Someone is sure to interrupt us."

"This is just to tide us over until we get home," he said. "Sort of an appetizer."

He undid her bra with one hand, pushed her back against the burlap-textured wall, and leaned into her, the length of his body hot and hard against hers. He slid down slowly, his mouth grazing her lips, her throat, her clavicles one at a time, embracing each breast in turn, sucking hard, moving away as she started to cry out. He grabbed a rocklike little hospital pillow from the freshly made bunk nearest them, handed it to her. "Bite this. No noise." He grinned, but his eyes were hungry, the grin predatory. Her heart pounded in her throat and her skin tingled. His mouth resumed its downward journey, and now his fingers slid between her legs, flicking lightly, applying gentle pressure. The pleasure of it made her dizzy—she shoved an edge of the pillow into her mouth, bit it hard, screamed as his tongue found her clit and his fingers slid inside her. He moved both, and she rocked into him, her muscles tightening, her body locking into an orgasmic spasm. His tongue moved faster, his fingers plunged harder, and she bucked and screamed into the pillow, and as the pleasure became more than she could take, tried to climb the wall behind her.

"You're fun," he said. "You do more than just breathe. And you're ready already."

"I've been ready all night," she muttered and lost her grip on the pillow. It fell, bounced off his head and onto the floor. He picked it up and stood up, swept a *PDR* and a couple of emergency medicine reference books off the little desk beside them. He put on one of the condoms.

"Purple. Think it's my color?"

"Anything would be your color," she said.

"I'm glad you approve." He put the pillow on top of the desk, picked her up, turned her around, bent her over it. "God, you have a gorgeous ass."

Some part of her realized that this position put no pres-

sure on her bad knee—she only had an instant to wonder if
he'd thought of that, and then he thrust against her, and slid
in slowly. And in, and in, and she got the sharp pain of having not had sex or anything like it in almost thirteen years,
and with it the incredible pleasure of the two of them. She
only barely remembered to scream into the pillow. He felt
huge, and hard, and hot inside her, and his hands grabbed
her hips and she could feel the rough furring of his hard-
muscled thighs pressing out against the insides of her thighs.
It was so much—too much—nothing had ever felt so good,
and she thought she was going to pass out.

He stilled inside her, stroked a finger down her spine. She
shuddered.

"So beautiful . . . all of you," he whispered.

"Don't stop," she told him.

"I don't want it to be over too soon," he said and dragged
his fingers down her back. "It's been a long time."

She moaned. He filled her, overwhelmed her. Remember
this, she told herself. Remember every second of it. Don't
let it get away—his voice, his touch, the feel of the wall on
my back before, this cold desk now. Just hang on to it all . . .

He stirred inside her and slowly, slowly, began to move in
and out, not thrusting, just sliding, pushing, one slow inch at
a time. He tightened his grip on her hips and thrust once,
harder, and an "Oh, God!" escaped her before she bit into
the pillow.

He picked up his pace, moved harder, and she went over
the edge again, her entire body locking into tight, hard shud-
ders as she came. He lay his upper body atop hers and whispered in her ear, "I didn't know women came with a
'vibrate' option."

If she could have laughed at that moment, she would
have. But he lifted up again and came crashing into her, hard
and fast, powerful, hungry. She pushed against him, tightened around him, arching and shuddering, lost, lost, lost.
The desk thumped against the wall, faster and louder.
Phoebe and Alan melded, merged, collided, faster, faster,

harder, and the pillow muffled but did not silence her screams, her ecstasy, and nothing stopped his own sudden cry as he exploded into her and her body notched tighter, bucked harder at this last best crash in their tempest. He held her tight, shuddering against her in a moment of forever—and then he dropped forward, still inside her, catching his weight on his forearms, his body lying lightly along her back, and he kissed her and whispered in her ear, "Good God, you're amazing. I'm going to die now, I think."

"Me, too."

"Housekeeping's in for a hell of a shock." Alan laughed softly, and his breath tickled the back of her neck.

"Perhaps we shouldn't die just yet, then."

"When I get my legs back, I'll get us out of here and drive us home." They lay that way for a while, and she thought he was the best blanket she'd ever had.

Finally, though, a hand rattled the doorknob, and out in the corridor someone said, "Dammit, Littman, you could do that in the restroom, and we're getting busy anyway. Hurry the hell up."

Alan whispered in Phoebe's ear, "I have just been accused of being 'Left-Hand' Littman, one of our residents who sexually has not moved past the age of self-discovery."

Phoebe giggled.

"Littman? You have a *girl* in there?" Out in the hall the voice took on a tone of wonder.

"Not Littman," Alan said.

"Oh, shit." A long pause as the person on the other side of the door sorted things out. "Sorry, MacKerrie. I was looking for Littman."

"Try the restroom."

"Yeah. I'll do that."

When he was gone, Alan sighed and slid out of Phoebe, and a little sob of loss escaped her throat. He kissed the back of her neck. "Hey, that was just an appetizer. I want to look in your eyes when I enter you; I want to see you sitting on top of me, riding up and down on me. I want—oh, hell, a lot of things. That was just a promise of what's to . . . come . . . so to speak. But we need to get out of here before Bahoudi finds Littman and gets back to the ER. Because Bahoudi is going to mention this to Morrie. And Morrie . . ." Alan sighed heavily. "We need to hurry."

He stood up, and Phoebe pushed herself to a standing position and discovered that she could only stand by hanging on to the corners of the desk. "I have no legs," she said. "I'm Jell-O below the waist."

He wrapped an arm around her, turned her to face him, and gave her a light kiss on the forehead. "If I didn't want to get us out of here and back home before we get more company, I'd offer to take a few bites right now."

Phoebe closed her eyes, imagining, and sighed a happy little sigh.

"Hold that thought, whatever it was," Alan said. He leaned her against the desk and grabbed her clothes off the floor for her, and she realized she didn't even remember most of them coming off. How the hell had he *done* that?

They drove home without hurry, and Phoebe—comfortable in the passenger seat, filled with afterglow and the promise of more wonders to come, thought, If I could just freeze time—have this moment forever, at this point of total contentment between perfection and expectation—I would ask for nothing else.

Clouds were building toward what would become a wonderful thunderstorm later in the day. The sunlight slanted across the road, and traffic moving in their direction was so light it was almost nonexistent. Alan, beside her, was humming something vaguely Bach-ish, though Phoebe was at a loss to figure out exactly what it might be.

Yes. This moment.

They pulled into their subdivision, and suddenly Phoebe wanted nothing more than to beg Alan to turn the car around and go back to the hospital. Or maybe to a hotel. Or . . . something.

Alan's friend Brig was standing beside a big white Crown

Vic looking grim, and with him were two young men in jeans and pullovers who, despite their clothing, gave off an air of official business. Phoebe looked at Alan, aware that the perfect moment was gone. Something waited for them that was going to change everything.

chapter 15

Alan saw Brig in the parking lot and his stomach dropped.
He glanced over at Phoebe, and her face wore his feelings.
"Don't worry," he told her. "This will be all right."

She nodded, clutching that backpack of hers like it held
the Holy Grail, and the two of them got out of the car. She
grabbed her cane and made her way carefully toward Brig
and the two strangers. Alan stayed right by her side.

Brig didn't waste any time giving them the bad news. "I
got here a little while ago—figured I'd catch you as soon as
you got home from work. Alan, Ms. Rain, these two are
Steve Beams and Hooter Duffy, who do various forms of
tech work for the department. Hooter already found something."

"What?" they both asked at the same time.

"A very small, very expensive, high-tech camera-listening
device. It's on the outside of the angled window that Ms.
Rain doesn't have covered, and I suspect it gives whoever is
watching her a very clear view of everything she does in the
main room of the town house, the stairs, the loft, and even
the bedroom if she leaves the door open."

Phoebe said, "A bug?"

Brig nodded. He said, "It's one of the best I've seen—
very small, quite well hidden. Hooter told me this particular
variety isn't available on the open market and sells for *several* thousand dollars on the black market."

"I've started seeing them, but they're pretty fresh from the government black box," Hooter Duffy said.

Alan frowned. "So the person after Phoebe has some money."

"Or is involved in government, if there's some sort of legitimate investigation under way. I did some calling around after Duffy found it to make sure I wouldn't be stepping on any toes, though, and I've cleared Ms. Rain with every agency I know of."

Phoebe said, "If money is all it takes to get hold of one of those, it wouldn't be an issue. Michael's parents have enough. And they are very proud of the fact, too. Plus, Michael was a tremendously successful criminal defense attorney, and I know he had both offshore accounts and Swiss accounts when we were married. He also kept in touch with all sorts of clients on a friendly basis after he won their cases for them."

"You think the family might be coming after you?" Brig shrugged. "Could be. In which case, I'll need names, contact information you might have—his family, friends, colleagues, all of it. This is definitely something that we'll look into. Between the phone calls and the clear evidence of bugging, we can count this as a verifiable threat to both of you."

Alan said, "Tell him about the rose."

Phoebe reached into her bag and pulled it out. "I woke up on my couch late last night and found this on my chest."

Alan noticed that she didn't tell him about the dream. She didn't mention hearing her dead ex-husband tell her that the flower was for her funeral. He supposed she didn't want to end up sounding crazy.

Brig took the plastic-wrapped flower and said, "Did it come in the plastic?"

"No. I got it off of me as quickly as I could, but I wrapped it so little pieces of it wouldn't fall off or anything. I didn't know whether you would be able to use it for evidence, but I tried not to handle it. Once I woke up, that is. I speared my fingers on the thorns a few times before I really came around and understood what was going on, so any blood on there is most likely mine."

Brig nodded. "All right. Can you unlock your place for me? I'd like to have our specialists go in and dust for fingerprints and check out your phones and see what else they can find."

"Of course." Phoebe reached into her backpack without actually digging around inside it and immediately came out with her keys, something Alan could never remember seeing a woman do. Mostly they fished, and fished, and had some big brick their keys were attached to that they were supposed to be able to find by feel but that seemed to do nothing in actual practice. He said, "That was pretty quick, Phoebe."

She glanced over at him, puzzled. "What was?"

"How you found your keys there."

"I have them clipped to the inside of the backpack. I don't take any chance of not being able to find them when I'm in the parking lot or unlocking my door. It's a safety measure. The faster I can get behind the door and lock it—whichever door it might be—the better off I am."

"I ran a check on you," Brig said as they were walking to her front door. "I found out you have a carry-concealed permit."

Alan was startled. Phoebe nodded.

"You have a gun with you right now?"

"Yes, I do."

"Where is it?"

"In here." She opened the front flap of that backpack— the flap her hand had rested on all night while she was sitting in the ER in her wheelchair—and Alan saw a flash of wood and dark metal. "Also my permit if you need to see it."

"Browning," Brig said, glancing in.

"Mark III. It's a good gun."

"It is. You keep up with practice?"

"Twice a week at the shooting range since I was able to stand up. I have a problem with stability because of the bad leg, so I don't dare let myself get rusty."

"This was because of your ex."

"Yes."

Alan said, "But you put him into a coma. You did this knowing that he was in a coma? You went to all this trouble?"

Phoebe glanced at him. "I did it because no one could promise me that he wouldn't come out of the coma."

"But even so."

"I knew that if he ever came out of the coma and was able to get around, he would come after me again. I knew it. And now it looks like even without coming out of the coma, he's still coming after me."

Alan sighed. "Phoebe, the FBI called you yesterday and told you he's dead. That they've closed his case."

"And yet someone with a tremendous amount of money to spend on spying on me is calling me threatening to kill me, and he sounds exactly like Michael, and he knows things that only Michael knew, and you and . . ." She paused, and Alan realized that she'd almost mentioned Chick, whose presence was something that Alan wasn't ready to confess to Brig just yet. "You've been threatened, too—and warned," she said, and that was about as careful as Alan guessed she could be.

Brig looked from one of them to the other. "You received notice that your ex is dead?"

Phoebe unlocked her door, opened it, and let Brig go in first. "I did. And just after the FBI called to tell me that Michael was dead, Michael called to tell me it was time for me, and you, and Alan, to join him."

"Join him . . . in being dead?"

"That was the feeling I got from the call."

"So. He threatened me in this phone call as well?"

"Yes."

Brig turned to Alan. "You were there for this call?"

"No."

He turned back to Phoebe. "You have no other witnesses, then."

"No," Phoebe said.

"And these calls aren't traceable by *69."

"No. Not so far."

"And your answering machine hasn't caught any of them?"

Phoebe sighed. "I *had* voice mail and caller ID. Yesterday I discovered that I haven't had either since . . . well, probably a bit before this started. A . . . I have a bit of a problem with my bill." She shook her head. Alan could see her struggling to decide whether she ought to say something or not. "At the moment, I have seventy-one dollars and change in my bank account. A check due from Psychic Sisters hasn't gotten here yet, but it's going to be smaller than usual. And two more weeks to make rent and cover the electric bill and water. I have no room in the budget for frills. None at all."

Alan leaned over and whispered in her ear, "Why didn't you *say* something? I could have helped you out with that."

And she stared into his eyes and murmured, "I didn't want you to think of me as a gold-digger."

Brig, oblivious to that last interchange, sighed. "We're going to set up an answering machine and caller ID for you. We'll be recording calls. Besides, you need to have some idea when the stalker is calling. Give yourself a chance to prepare for the call." He looked down at her and smiled a little. "Threatening me would be a different crime we could pin on this bastard whenever we find him. Something else to pile onto the charges. But I think he's already got enough to put him away for a while."

Phoebe was staring at her dining room table, Alan realized. Staring at it like it was poison.

He moved past Brig to see what she was looking at. And saw the mug that had so upset her the day before. And dead roses scattered all around it.

"I'm guessing this was not here when you left, Ms. Rain," Brig said.

"It wasn't. And please call me Phoebe." Alan heard a tremor in her voice.

"Dead roses."

"He told me they were flowers for my funeral," Phoebe said.

Brig turned to look at her. "During the phone call, he mentioned the flowers?"

"No. That was . . . I fell asleep on the couch yesterday while it was still sunny out. Maybe one o'clock, maybe a little later than that. And I slept until almost midnight, when I had a nightmare that woke me up. I dreamed that Michael was here and that he was telling me that he was coming to kill me and that he was giving me flowers for my funeral. And I had a hard time waking up, and when I did, the rose was there."

Brig frowned. "You often have nightmares?"

"Recently I've had some bad ones. I sometimes had nightmares about the shooting at school—a lot after it happened, and less over the last year. But the nightmares about Michael have only been in the last few weeks."

"I saw the aftereffects of one," Alan said. "I thought she'd been doing drugs—she had a very sluggish pupillary response, dry mouth, some paranoia, rapid bounding pulse, rapid respirations. But there wasn't anything in the house, and she didn't have the opportunity to hide anything."

"You checked me for *drugs*?" Phoebe said, and she looked at him like he'd just kicked her. Maybe in her bad knee.

"I thought you might have taken too much pain medicine for your knee. So I looked for pain meds. I didn't find out until later that you didn't have anything in the house but aspirin and Tylenol." It embarrassed the hell out of him that he'd thought she might be a druggie, and now it doubly embarrassed him that she knew he'd thought it. "When I came over, you looked very unstable. I was afraid I might have to take you to the emergency room, and I wanted to see if I could figure out what was causing your symptoms."

"You figure her response was just the nightmares?" Brig asked him.

"I couldn't find any other explanation. But I've never in my life seen anyone react so badly to nightmares. I couldn't have sworn, in those first few minutes after I got there, that you weren't going to pass out," he said, turning back to Phoebe.

"Did she call you?" Brig asked him, and Alan shook his head.

"I heard her screaming. I tried to break her door down or find some other way into her place. It sounded like someone was killing her." He didn't mention Chick's warning. He should, he thought; he should let Brig know that Phoebe wasn't the only potentially crazy person in this scenario. But he just couldn't. Telling about Chick would somehow make her less real. He couldn't do that.

"And how did you get in?"

"Eventually she came to the door and opened it. By then, I thought she was dead, but when I saw her—" He remembered again how panicked Phoebe had looked, and at the same time how completely out of it.

"We're going to do a substance check, too, Ms. Rain," Brig said.

"I don't do drugs."

"I understand that. But you're describing strange sleep patterns and nightmares and other things that don't make sense. Have you considered the possibility that someone might be drugging you?"

"No."

Alan hadn't considered that either.

"Do you have anything you drink out of regularly?"

"The mug with the roses around it," she said. "My teakettle. That's about it." She frowned. "I have loose-leaf green tea. I suppose someone might mix something in that, but—" She stood, head tilted, looking around her room as strangers crawled over it, taking her phones apart, bagging the roses and the mug and taking samples of the water in her teakettle, and she frowned. "It didn't happen every time I drank my tea, but there have been a few times when I drank it and felt very soothed afterward. And then fell asleep even though I didn't mean to. I didn't really think anything of it."

Brig said, "We'll look into it." He sighed. "Now I need to ask you—who aside from your ex-husband would have reason to want to hurt or kill you? Who would want to take such elaborate measures rather than just finding you away from your home and killing you? Because the method here is odd. Much of what is being done here is geared to frighten you without actually harming you."

"I suppose Michael's family would have reason to want to hurt me. He has brothers. And one sister. I know that Ben Margolies at Moonstruck has my phone numbers and knows that I work at the psychic service. He got me the job, actually. And—I *think* he likes me, but . . ." She shrugged. "I've made mistakes about people before."

"Margolies. Moonstruck," Brig wrote. "That the New Age store on University in Tamarac?"

Phoebe nodded.

"Margolies the owner or an employee?"

"Owner."

"Right. I'll get to him today. Anyone else?"

"Maybe the parents of the two children who were killed in the shooting." She looked bewildered, completely at sea, and Alan ached for her. He couldn't think of anyone who had reason to want him dead. He couldn't imagine anyone wanting to kill a person as gentle and kind as Phoebe.

But people were strange. This was something that years in the ER had ground into him. They did weird, horrible things to each other, things that not even they could explain rationally when they were questioned later.

Brig settled Phoebe on the couch and started asking her a lot of questions—where people she had named might be, how she'd come to know them, why she was so sure that Michael was still behind what was happening.

Alan tuned out. He walked back to where one of the techs was checking for fingerprints and the other one had both of the phones apart and the pieces spread out on the table, and he tried to figure out why Chick had involved him in this. She'd told him—through Phoebe—that if they didn't help each other, one of them was going to die.

But if she had not appeared to either of them, he would never have gotten to know Phoebe.

And he would have come home from work some morning and found crime scene tape around her front door and guys taking pictures of a blood-spattered corpse in the front room. And he would never have known what he missed. He would never have suspected the thrill her body offered, her passionate responses and sheer exuberance at his touches. He would never have known how strongly he could want to be with a woman he didn't even really know. He would never have dared to hope that somewhere his daughter still existed—that she still thought about him, that he still mattered to her.

He would have lost so much.

But he wouldn't have been in any danger.

Why was this happening to him, then?

And why was it happening to Phoebe? Which lunatic in her life was bent on destroying her? How was he doing what he was doing to her? And *why* was he doing it?

chapter 16

"Yo. Brig. Her phones aren't bugged, but both of them are tapped."

Phoebe turned to look over the back of the couch, and there was Hooter Duffy, holding up a little monitor with a light that actually glowed green. "They're tapped?" she asked.

Hooter nodded. "I'd guess your stalker has a listening post close to here that lets him hear everything you say on the phones. And, for that matter, if he's technically proficient, he could set up a way to make your phone ring before he talked to you on either line so that you would think you were answering real calls. Calls made through a tap from a listening post wouldn't show up in a *69 search, either."

Brig was on his feet and across the room in just a couple of steps, looking at what Hooter was showing him.

"That's how he's doing it?" Phoebe gasped. "That's the way he's been reaching me? Oh, my God." And then she felt herself get light-headed. "Oh, my *God*. Then that means that he's been inside my house. Touched my phones. Was actually *in the house* when he left the rose on me."

She realized Brig was staring at her with a strange expression on his face. "What exactly did you think was happening?"

"I thought . . . I don't know. That Michael's spirit was

doing it." She felt her face go hot, and her hands flew over her mouth. "I know it's stupid. Or gullible. But I didn't want to believe that he had actually been in here. Because as bad as a ghost would be, a real live person is worse."

"Yeah, I can see that," Brig said. "We're going to have to have someone watch your place, Phoebe. And have a couple of detectives go door-to-door and see if they can find out where your stalker has his watch post. Someone has to have seen something."

Phoebe closed her eyes.

The techs were moving into the downstairs bedroom to see if they could find any evidence of the stalker in there. Brig headed for the door.

Phoebe just stood there, while the truth that someone had been in her house—with her there—settled in.

She overheard Brig tell Alan, "You two look beat. Why don't you take her over to your place for a couple of days— if you wouldn't mind having her there. Looking at the two of you, I'm guessing you wouldn't. Just until we have a chance to get this all sorted out. The guys are likely to be here all night, and if you're here you're going to be in the way."

Alan said, "Sounds like a good idea. I'll help her pack up a bag and get going."

"I have to go, too, but they'll call me if they find anything more," Brig said. "And I'll call you."

Phoebe started to protest that she wasn't really ready to be pulled out of her house, and then she thought of Michael standing over her while she slept and putting a rose on her chest—and she thought of the nightmare in which he was touching her and she couldn't wake up. And she shuddered. "I'll go pack right now," she said.

She hurried into her room and shoved a couple of pairs of jeans, shirts, and underwear into a brown paper bag. Gathered her toothbrush from the bathroom, along with a hair-brush and some shampoo. Packing took her about three minutes.

"I'm ready," she said, and Brig and the techs and Alan all turned to stare at her.

Brig said, "You're kidding."

"I live light."

She grabbed her tarot decks in their silk-and-wool bags and dropped them into the brown paper bag.

"What are those?" Brig asked her.

"Tarot decks."

He raised an eyebrow.

"I don't want to leave them behind. I don't want Michael touching them."

And Brig said, as gently as a man could who was showing clear signs of annoyance, "Michael Schaeffer is dead, Phoebe. Dead. We don't know *who* is doing this to you, but we know who isn't."

"I'm sorry," Phoebe said. "The man who calls just sounds like Michael." She let it drop, but she was still sure that somehow, somehow, it really was Michael coming after her.

Alan and Brig exchanged glances, and Phoebe felt a little twinge of uneasiness. They thought she was crazy. Or unbalanced. Or something.

But Alan came over to her and put an arm around her and said, "The techs have all the stuff they need right now, and you have a little stuff. We can just head over to my place for a while. A couple of days, probably, and they'll find out where this lunatic is hiding, and they'll put him in a cell, and then you can get your life back."

Phoebe couldn't keep the bitterness out of her laugh.

He didn't say anything as they walked from her place to his. He just held her hand.

At Alan's she started to put her things in his guest bedroom. "I don't want to crowd you," she said, but he smiled at her.

"You aren't crowding me. You're the best thing that has happened in my life in longer than I can remember."

He sat on the edge of the bed and closed his eyes. For an instant he looked like he was hurting. Phoebe suspected that he was remembering his lost daughter.

"Hey," she said, "think good thoughts."

He smiled at her. "Better thoughts, anyway." Then he sighed and shoved his hair back from his forehead in a worried gesture. "Could you let me talk to Chick again? Find out some more details about what she's been trying to tell us, maybe?"

Phoebe shook her head slowly. "I'm not a medium. I have only heard spirits, I guess twice in my life. Once was when I heard my grandmother telling me to run, in the few days before Michael caught up with me. And I didn't listen then. The second time has been with Chick, who has gone to a lot more effort to force me to pay attention. I can't call her, though, Alan. Mediums say that they can see the spirits of the dead surrounding the living. I can't do that. I look at you and all I see is you. I read cards. I'm pretty good at that, and sometimes I get very specific answers by reading cards. I could do a reading about Chick if you want. But I can't bring her here. I can't even promise I'll hear her the next time she talks to me. I don't know how she does what she's doing, and if she doesn't do it again, we won't hear from her again."

He looked down at his feet, then away from her. "I figured it was something like that."

"I'll read for you," Phoebe said. "Maybe I can get something useful about Chick that way—"

"Don't," he said. "I was serious when I told you up in my office that I don't think I could stand to hear any more about Chick, or my future. It's too strange." And then he said, "But since you have your cards, could you do a reading about Brig? He's—should I tell you what's going on with him?"

"Why don't you let me tell you?" Phoebe suggested. "And maybe when you watch his reading, you'll decide that you want to take another look at one about Chick, or about you. It's not a spooky thing. Really."

As she picked up her card bags, he stood and gave her a quick hug. "Not to you. But honestly, I'd love to see you do a cold reading of Brig. I know him pretty well, so I can tell if you're on with him or not. And if it's about him, it won't be spooky for me." He grinned a little. "In some regards, I'm a big chicken." He headed out toward his kitchen table, then looked back over his shoulder. "And this way I can pass on anything cool that you get to him and see what he has to say."

That impish grin took her breath away. "I can do that," she said, thinking there were other things she'd really rather be doing.

She sat at his very sturdy dining room table and shuffled her Universal Waite cards. Seven times—always seven. Closed her eyes, feeling the cool cardboard slide against her skin, familiar as the air she breathed after so many years.

She put the deck on the table facedown, cut the cards into three decks, and with her left hand chose the deck from which she would read.

She started putting down the cards, looking at them as they fell.

"He's alone right now, afraid to take chances, afraid to be made a fool of. Fool, reversed—Significator. Ick. He has some very hard feelings about that. His life at the moment is all about turmoil and change—the Tower, upright—stuff just crashing all around him so that he doesn't know which way is up, where the ground is under his feet, or what is going to fall on his head next." She put down the next card—Queen of Diamonds, reversed. "His obstacle is a woman. I'm going to go out on a limb and say that she's young, pretty, confident, and money-grubbing. Has he been through a divorce recently?"

"Shit," Alan said. "His wife walked out on him a couple of months ago and currently is trying to take him for all he's worth. How the *hell* did you get that from the cards?"

Phoebe shrugged. She kept reading, but suddenly the tenor of the reading changed.

"I'm not reading for Brig anymore," she said, feeling a

chill run down her spine. "But this is something that is going to mean something to him." She looked at the cards and started to feel scared.

"Alan—this is really bad. Write this down for me as I tell you what I'm getting here, will you?"

He said, "Hold on. I'll get paper and pen."

When he came back she started right in. "In his recent past, there is someone that Brig knows or is looking for. A pretty girl. Dark hair. Teenager, I think—definitely a young woman not yet in bloom. I think she's . . . dead. Murdered."

She was putting out cards, staring at them as they dropped into place. "Her father is responsible. He was . . ." She dragged out the round Motherpeace deck, because she'd been using the Universal Waite for Brig. "Hang on."

Alan said, "I'm writing, I'm writing."

The Ten of Swords popped up, and Phoebe felt her stomach flip. The image was one of her least favorite in the entire deck. Women holding swords and jumping off a cliff—committing mass suicide. Men behind pursuing, intent on— "He was raping her," Phoebe whispered.

"What?"

She tried again, managed to say it a little louder. "He was raping her."

"The father?"

"Yes."

Then the image of the father, the Patriarch, the one in charge. In control. "He's done a very good job of pretending he had nothing to do with this, and Brig may even like him. May think highly of him. Think he's respectable, upstanding." All the signs were there.

And in the back of Phoebe's mind, two pictures, one after the other. A diary, hidden away. And a shiny silver locker.

She closed her eyes, trying to bring the images closer, to get more detail, but nothing was coming. "There's a diary or a journal or a notebook involved in this—probably the girl's, probably with incriminating evidence in it. It's hidden, not destroyed. And I think . . . I think lockers are involved. Shiny. Silver. Like school lockers, except—this sounds silly—except *chrome*. They're essential. Brig has to know about the lockers."

She looked up to see Alan frowning at her. "Lockers?"

"I don't know why. That was the image I got. Sometimes when I'm reading cards, I get pictures, too. Not often, usually not very clear. But when I get them, I've learned to make note of them. I saw two pictures—one of a diary with a lock hidden in a dark place. And the second, one big locker in a row of shiny silver lockers."

"And you don't know what the locker picture could be about?"

"No. But it's important."

Alan sighed. "The reading you had on him was dead-on. But you know the odds are that Brig is going to look at this and shake his head and think you're nuts."

"I know that. But it might mean something to him, and I don't want to not tell him. I have a high tolerance for scorn—and if I'm right on this, it's something important to him. So I'll take my chances."

He shrugged. "We'll give this to him the next time we see him, then." He looked around the town house. "Do you want to stay here? Or go out to eat or something?"

"I want to sleep. Could we do that?"

"I don't know that I can. I'm sort of wound up from everything today." He reached over and took her hand and held it in his. "Some of it has been absolutely amazing."

Amazing. Yes. That would pretty much sum up the doctors' lounge. Everything before that—tense and frightening. Just about everything after that—tense and frightening. But that short time with Alan had been miraculous. And all Phoebe could think was that she wanted more.

"You wouldn't by any chance still have a few of those condoms with you, would you?"

She loved the expression of hope mixed with lust that

crossed his face. He replied by pulling several out of his pocket and spreading them across the table.

"Red this time?" she asked, pointing to one.

"I've always thought red was a fun color," he told her. He kissed her, scooped her into his arms, and carried her into his bedroom.

chapter 17

Alan woke feeling remarkably good and wonderfully sated. His muscles were sore in interesting places, and he had a lovely woman dressed in nothing but one of his T-shirts curled tightly against his chest. When he closed his eyes, he could see her again—sitting astride him, wearing that enormous blue T-shirt, her dark hair curling and tumbling forward, brown eyes gleaming, white teeth flashing as she laughed. Then, of course, the T-shirt had come off for a while, and that was good, too.

He glanced over at his bedside table and saw that the message light on the phone was blinking. He'd turned off the ringer. He had remembered to set his alarm, but he was awake a good hour before that was due to go off. He was happy.

Holy hell, he was happy.

He would have thought he could never feel so good again.

He got up, brushed his teeth, and then, so he wouldn't wake Phoebe, went out and took the message from the phone by the couch.

It was Brig, tense and frustrated, saying, "Call me the second you get this."

Alan tried the station, and the switchboard put him through to Brig, who was less than enthusiastic to hear from him. "Where have you *been*?"

"Sleeping."

"You're a doctor. People are supposed to be able to reach you."

"I'm an *ER* doctor. I work regular hours and get to turn off my phone when I'm not on duty or on call."

"Must be nice," Brig snarled.

"It is," Alan said. "What's the matter, Brig?"

"Phoebe with you?"

"No, but I can get her."

"Don't. I don't want you anywhere near her right now. I want you to sit down, and listen, and don't move until we've gone over everything. All right?"

Alan said, "I don't—"

"Friend to friend, Alan—just do this. All right?"

Alan sat, staring through the front window at clouds scudding by too quickly, at palms bending toward the west, and at the occasional bit of paper soaring past the window from the Dumpster east of his place. "Fine. I'm sitting."

"The guys found something in Phoebe's town house that changes the situation. It explains what's going on over there. They called me as soon as they found it, and I've spent the last God-only-knows-how-many hours double-checking everything. This is . . . bad."

"What did you find?"

Alan heard Brig take a deep, slow breath. "I'm sorry that I have to tell you this, Alan."

"What did you find?"

"A detective's report, stashed in an envelope in a blue shoe box at the back of her closet. It's all about you. Phoebe obtained it a few days ago—it's very complete. Has details about your wife and daughter, your position at the hospital, your financial status, credit history, current friendships, lack of sexual involvement with anyone. Just about anything a woman looking for a sugar daddy would want to know."

"No," Alan said.

"That's not all."

"No," Alan said again. "She's for real, Brig. I know she is."

"Just hear me out," Brig said. "And don't move. Don't confront her with this. Don't do anything stupid."

Alan had no words. He sat there, fists clenched, eyes tightly closed, breathing around the lump in his throat. And Brig said, "I've been calling and pulling records all night. What I have is still sketchy, but Phoebe was arrested in Ohio when she was nineteen years old. Some sort of confidence game charges, contributing to the delinquency of a minor, attempted fraud—I don't have all the details yet. The case was eventually dismissed, but not before she got herself a lawyer. A young guy named Michael Schaeffer, who already had a reputation for being pretty slick."

Alan said, "It's some sort of mistake." A chill spread through him. This was going to end with a fucking Scooby-Doo moment, when Chick was revealed to be nothing but a projected image on his wall, when the cops were going to pull the mask off Phoebe's "stalker" and he was going to be her husband or her brother or some very close friend of hers who was good with electronics and who was helping her for a cut of whatever Alan had socked away. When Phoebe in handcuffs turned to him and said, "We would have gotten away with it, too, if it hadn't been for you and your friend Brig."

"I double-checked this before I called you because I didn't want to find out that Phoebe was named after her mother and her mother was the one arrested. I didn't want to screw up."

Alan sat, not moving, while the old hell became the new hell. While the tendrils of new life inside him—tendrils that sprang from the hope that Chick was safe somewhere and from dreams of a woman who might love him for himself—withered and blackened.

"Alan? Are you still there?"

He swallowed hard. "Yeah."

"Has she taken you for any money, Alan?"

"No."

"Any chance you got her pregnant?"

Condoms, he thought. He'd trusted condoms. Idiot. "Always a chance, isn't there?"

"Don't worry about it. You're going to walk away from this, Alan, and you're going to be fine. She isn't going to get anything out of you."

She already had, he thought. She stole my heart. She let me think she was special. She let me be happy. "I . . . let myself trust her," he said at last. "I guess I shouldn't have."

"Definitely not. Every single thing that has gone on over there can be easily explained if she's involved. The dead rose on her chest when she wakes up, the roses on the table, the mug that moves. None of it happens, but she says it does, and for some reason that I cannot for the life of me figure out, you buy into it hook, line, and sinker. To the best of my knowledge, you've never been a big believer in the supernatural. Or if you have been, you've sure as hell hidden it from me."

Alan said, "There are some things I didn't tell you."

"You mentioned that this morning."

"I saw my daughter."

The silence on the other end of the phone stretched out for what seemed like forever. "Your little girl who was killed in a car crash?"

"Yes."

"When? And how?"

"I was sitting at my desk and suddenly the window in my office seemed to lead to someplace else. I stood up and it was open, but I hadn't opened it, and it was raining outside, and my daughter was standing in our backyard in Kentucky looking up at me. I almost went out the window after her." He stopped, feeling again the breathless impossible wonder of seeing Chick alive, whole, and the frantic urge to get her back. "And then she was gone."

"Okay—think hard about this now. By any chance did Ms. Rain give you anything to eat or drink before you saw this hallucination?"

"I'd just run into Phoebe for the first time at that point,"

Alan said. "I didn't even know her name. In fact, it was *after*
I saw Chick that Phoebe came over to the house and told me
that my daughter had told her to come meet me."

"Really?" Another long pause. "What the fuck . . . that
doesn't make any sense, unless . . ." And a sigh. "We're
going to have to come over and do a sweep of your place,
too. See if your drinks have been drugged, too, or if her partner in this has access to your place."

"Drugged *too*?"

"The lab found enough scopolamine in Ms. Rain's tea
water to knock over an ox."

It was like being hit on the forehead by a solid steel door.
"Scopolamine? Shit! Dry mouth, hallucinations, bounding
pulse, enlarged pupils slow to respond, rapid breathing, nausea. Dammit, that's what was wrong with her."

"Alan, you're not making a lot of sense."

"When I heard Phoebe screaming and ran over to her
house, she was in bad shape. I told you about that. I checked
her and the house for drugs, couldn't find any. She didn't
have any track marks or other signs of addiction, and she insisted that she didn't do drugs."

"You really think that she *took* this scopolamine? We'd
figured it was in there to make us think that someone was
drugging her."

"She must have taken it. Too much of it, at that. Some of
her symptoms couldn't be faked."

"Why would she do that?"

"Maybe for the hallucinations. Maybe it makes reading
the cards easier." Alan closed his eyes. "I don't know.
Maybe to make her story that much more real. But I do
know that I didn't have any of it. And . . . Chick . . ."

"It was some sort of trick, Alan. But we'll go over your
place with a microscope, and whatever she did to you, we'll
find it." He said, "I talked to her ex's parents. They're pretty
distraught right now, of course, since their son just died and
they have the funeral to get through yet. But they had plenty
to say about Phoebe Rain. They said she had her hooks in

Michael Schaeffer from the moment he took her case. That she was charged with doing phony tarot readings and had pulled some little kid into her con game to help her as a shill. That she was guilty as hell. That their son felt sorry for her because she was young and pretty and she did a very good impression of innocence. They said their son had moved on, finally, but that Phoebe used her family's deaths to reconnect with him, and once she had him back in her life, they suspect that she pulled the old 'I'm pregnant' trick on him to get him to marry her."

And Alan could see Phoebe on the loft floor, saying, "I could vote for complete irresponsibility right now," knowing already that a baby would be an almost certain way to control him. And suddenly Alan wanted to throw up.

Brig was saying, "They said that she used him for everything she could get out of him, and when he finally mentioned divorce, she stole his credit cards and ran with them and told a lot of people a lot of horrible things about him in an attempt to ruin his reputation."

But Alan still didn't want to believe Phoebe could lie to him. Use him. Use *Chick*. Maybe even plot to use a new baby against him. "This is still the same monster who burst into a classroom and murdered two kids and shot Phoebe?"

Brig sighed. "I know his parents have a biased point of view. I know Schaeffer was a shit-weasel. Look, to me this feels like finding out that Mother Teresa ran a crack house on the side. But what the Schaeffers say about Phoebe Rain adds up, too. Her ex might have been the typical big-shot criminal defense scumbag, and he was definitely a psychotic killer, and the fucker deserved what he got. But that doesn't mean that Phoebe Rain hadn't figured out a way to take him for a ride first. Think, Alan. She claims her dead husband is stalking her, she has some guy who's in on this with her who is going to help her make you believe that she can talk to your dead kid, and no one can verify a single goddamned thing she's said. The only things anyone can verify right now are that she did a real good job of checking you out and

that she's out of her piss-poor little town house and sound
asleep in your nice one."

Alan wanted to cry. He'd believed in Phoebe—not as a
psychic but as a woman. As someone special. He'd let himself believe. "You want a laugh?" he said instead.

"If you have one right now, I could use it."

"I had her do a card reading on you. She was dead-on—
your business with Kathie, the way you were reacting to it,
Kathie's personality. Guess that detective of hers has been
really busy. Anyway, in the middle of the reading, she gets
all mysterious. Says she isn't reading for you anymore.
And—hang on. I wrote this down. She insisted."

He got up, got the notes he'd made on Phoebe's reading,
and read them off to Brig. "In his recent past, there is someone that Brig knows or is looking for. A pretty girl. Dark
hair. Teenager, I think—definitely a young woman not yet in
bloom. I think she's dead. Murdered. He was raping her—
the father. He's done a very good job of pretending he had
nothing to do with this. Brig may like him. May think highly
of him. Think he's respectable, upstanding. There's a diary
or a journal or a notebook involved in this—probably the
girl's, probably with incriminating evidence in it. It's hidden, not destroyed. And shiny silver lockers of some sort are
involved—they're like the ones in schools, but chrome.
They're essential. Brig has to know about the lockers."

A long silence. Then, "Shiny *silver* lockers?"

"That's what she said."

"I'll want those notes," Brig said.

"Sure. Come by the ER and pick them up. I'll bring them
with me. But they're in my handwriting—she had me write
things down while she read the cards."

"No one is going to think you're a conspirator in this,
Alan," Brig said. "Don't worry about it."

Alan clenched his fists and took a deep breath. "I'm going
to go wake Madame Believeme from her cozy sleep and
send her back home. Unless you think there's any danger to
her."

"I think there may be a danger to you. I think Ms. Rain, however, will be just fine until we arrest her. Please do not mention to her that we are pursuing that outcome. I'd rather not have to chase her across the state." He said something to someone with him—for a moment his voice got muffled as he covered the receiver with one hand.

Alan waited.

"Anyway," Brig said after a moment, "you going in to work tonight?"

"Yes."

"I'll come by for those notes. Now, are you calm enough to deal with her?"

"I'll be fine."

"Don't touch her. Don't threaten her in any way. Don't damage anything that belongs to her. Just tell her to leave, watch her to make sure she doesn't leave anything behind or steal anything, and when you get her out of the house, do not have any contact with her again. You understand?"

"Yeah."

"I'll see you later. I've got to catch a couple hours of sleep first. I've been up straight through since yesterday on this."

Alan stood in the dining room for a long moment after he hung up the phone. Janet had seen him as a surefire social ticket, a way to pay her way through life without her having to work at it—a conveniently busy husband whose job would give her plenty of free time for her extracurricular activities.

Phoebe evidently had an angle, too. She'd married the lawyer first and was going for the doctor second. The scumbag that Janet had driven off with was a stockbroker.

It was all about the money. Sooner or later, it always came down to that. To some women—to the women he seemed to fall for—men were nothing but credit cards with dicks.

And it didn't matter whether you'd known them all your life or for just a few days. Brig's jaundiced view of women as a whole was looking truer and truer by the minute.

chapter 18

Phoebe woke to Alan tapping her on the shoulder, saying, "Okay. You did a good job on me, but now it's time for you to go home."

She opened her eyes to see him staring down at her, anger and hatred twisting his features.

"What?"

"I heard the news, con girl. Brig's good—he checks all the angles. And he found out about the report. And about how you got your first husband."

"How I—"

"You and I aren't talking. You aren't saying another god-damned word. Not one. And I'm standing here watching you just to make sure you don't steal anything on your way out the door. You're gathering up your things, and then you are going home, and I never want to see you again."

He leaned against the wall and stared at her.

Phoebe sat up, dazed. What had Brig told him that had made him *hate* her? How could he hate her? She had just experienced the most magical, wonderful few hours of her life, and they had been with Alan, and now he was looking at her like he hoped she would catch fire and burn to ashes before his eyes.

What could Brig have said that would have caused him to look at her that way?

How she'd got her husband? Michael? How she'd got

him? There hadn't been any chicanery in that. Not on her end, anyway. Michael had lied through his teeth.

"Talk to me, Alan. I haven't done anything wrong—honestly. What did Brig tell you?"

"I'm not telling you anything."

The last thing she remembered, as she was drifting off to sleep, he'd been holding her. Touching her. They had been wrapped in the comfort of each other, and she had let herself relax. Trust.

Surely there had to be some way to get back to where they'd been. Brig was mistaken. He'd gathered information on the wrong person. Alan would see that if he would just tell her what Brig had told him and give her the chance to explain.

"Alan—just tell me what he told you."

"No chance. You gold-digging fraud. You charlatan. Just get out of here. Now."

Gold-digging fraud. Charlatan. Anger boiled through Phoebe's blood. She could have forgiven Alan's unjust accusations if he had at least been willing to tell her what had gone wrong, what he had been told. But he wasn't even willing to consider doing that. Brig had told him something, and Alan had decided that Brig had it right, and he wasn't even willing to think there might be a mistake somewhere. Was not even willing to give Phoebe a chance to defend herself.

Her temper snapped.

She rose. "Con girl? Charlatan? Who the hell do you think you are? I'll let you in on a little secret here, doctor-boy. Not every woman on the planet is aching to climb into your bed and be *Mrs.* Doctor and live in some pathetic cage of other people's expectations while you go off to be Marcus-goddamned-Welby." She looked him up and down, hurt and betrayed and detesting him and detesting herself for having fallen for him. "You don't have anything I want. If your kid hadn't come to me—"

"My kid *didn't* come to you, and I cannot believe that you're caught and you're still trying to use Chick. We're going to find out how you did your tricks with my daughter. How you *used* her. We're going to find out, Phoebe."

She stared at him. "Your heart knows she's real. But you're willing to deny her out of your own fear. You're a fool, Alan MacKerrie. And you *deserve* the life you've had. The life you're going to keep on having."

"Get out. And be grateful your little pregnancy plot didn't work. Because I would have gotten my child away from you, and you wouldn't have gotten a penny."

Phoebe couldn't believe what she'd just heard. "You're insane," she whispered. She pulled off Alan's T-shirt, dropped it on the bed, got her little bag of clothes, pulled on clean ones, watching him the whole while. He'd averted his eyes while she was dressing, but the second she was done, he was staring at her again, with that look that told her he wished she was dead.

She felt tears building behind her eyes, running down the back of her throat. But she didn't let herself cry. She'd known all along that the magic she'd felt with Alan was just a tease—some temporary thing to let her know how much better her life could have been.

Now at least she knew she was lucky not to be involved with Alan MacKerrie. She grabbed her cane and, with the bag holding her few belongings tucked under her arm, headed for the door.

Phoebe wasn't happy about going home. Home, to whatever Michael had planned for her. But she didn't really have a choice, did she? She couldn't afford a single night at the cheapest hotel. Had no credit cards. No place to run. No one to run to.

So she went home, fighting to keep her feet against the gusts of wind that kept catching her from behind. The palm fronds made a sort of wet-sheet-snapping noise that she couldn't remember ever having heard before, but she didn't give it much thought. She had bigger problems than a bit of wind.

Home was exactly the same as she'd left it. Or at least it was exactly the same as the police technicians had left it.

Phoebe threw her backpack on the floor, dropped onto the couch, and cried. She sobbed until she couldn't breathe, until she was hiccuping and gasping. She felt foolish, but she just couldn't stop herself. Even though she'd known she was going to get hurt when Alan decided to move on, she'd been hoping somehow that he wouldn't ever go. That he might come to love her. She'd never thought that he would turn on her.

It wasn't as though she loved him, she told herself. She wasn't losing anything real. She didn't even really know him.

Someone had told him lies about her. Someone had made them believable enough that he had turned away from everything he had seen of her to believe those lies. Because he didn't know her. Because some lies seemed safer and less crazy than the truth.

She could look at him rationally, and see that he was a good man who had been hurt. The two of them had only had a few hours together, really, and those hours had been strange. Wonderful in many ways, but not something that any sane person would look at and say, "Yes, you have a future there. Yes, this is a solid rock on which to build your life."

Logically, she could tell herself that. But illogically, she felt like her whole world had collapsed on top of her. Her mind knew she didn't love him, but her stupid heart seemed to think it did. She kept crying, feeling like the world's biggest fool.

She closed her eyes, rolled into a tight ball on the couch, and gradually her sobbing stopped. Gradually exhaustion overcame her, and she dozed.

And the phone rang.

Phoebe pushed her head into the couch cushion and closed her eyes tightly and clenched both fists. She didn't want to answer it. But it might be the FBI with news about Michael. It might be Alan wanting to say he was sorry. It might be Brig with information about the phone calls or the rose or . . . It might be important.

It wasn't important. Everyone who mattered, who could

have helped her, had turned away from her. Everyone had
decided she was a con artist. A fraud. Everyone.

But still she hoped.

She got up, hobbled to the phone, and picked it up.

"Fucking the doctor didn't turn out too well, did it?"

Michael's voice. Michael's amusement. She slammed
down the phone.

It rang again immediately.

She snarled, but picked up. "Get out of my life."

"Hey! Don't hang up on me, babe. You're trying to go get
yourself a new husband, I'm trying to help you. As long as
we've been planning this, as much work as we've put into
it, you can't think I'd drop out on you when things got bad."

"What?" Phoebe said. The voice was Michael's, but the
words belonged to a complete stranger.

"They found out about us, honey—but don't worry. I
think we can still get the doctor for you. We drug him again,
you hypnotize him and convince him that his kid says he's
going to have to marry you because that's what she wants.
It'll still work. He still wants you, even if he and his friend
are on to you."

She held the receiver, staring at it, bewildered—and then
she realized what it was. "You know the police found your
phone taps. You think they may be recording what you say.
So you're trying to implicate me in whatever you're doing."

"Amazing," Michael said. "When I was his client,
Michael told me you were treacherous, but I really didn't
think you'd try to sell *me* out. No, I didn't know the police
were listening in on our line, but I guess I do now. I'm outta
here. Deal with the mess you've made by yourself."

And he hung up, leaving Phoebe staring at the phone and
wondering if the police had heard that conversation, and if
they had, what they made of it. Did they think she was working with the man who was threatening to kill her?

No. They didn't think anyone was threatening to kill her
at all. They'd found the bug on her window, and they'd
found the taps on her phone line, and Brig had found out

something about her past that made him think that she was responsible for these things—or at least in on them.

But there *wasn't* anything in her past that would make anyone believe that. She'd been a nice kid with poor parents who had grown up poor but with ethics, who had worked hard and made herself into the woman she wanted to be, who had then married the man she'd promised to marry and who had lived to regret it. That was her life story. Where in any of that did Brig get con artist?

It was working for the psychic hotline. That had to be it. Phoebe knew some of the lines had been investigated for fraud and other illegal activities. She knew the Psychic Sisters line wasn't the best line out there. But it was the best she could do at the moment, and she was scrupulously honest in her dealings with clients, even though she suspected she would have made more money if she'd cheated a bit.

God, when Alan had chased her out of his house, she'd seen such loathing on his face. He'd *hated* her. And he looked like he thought she'd betrayed him, too. That he was certain she'd been out to trick him or trap him or use him or take him for his money? What *did* he think of her? How could he think she would ever do anything to hurt him, when she loved him?

She froze. No, that couldn't be right. She didn't love him. She was never going to love anyone. It didn't work out for her. She hadn't known him long enough. She wouldn't consider falling in love with another professional man, anyway. Look how things had turned out with the last one. Lawyers, doctors, probably scientists and professors, too—all trouble.

But as Phoebe scrambled for excuses and reasons why she couldn't love Alan, why she *didn't* love Alan, she had to face the fact that no matter what her head insisted, her heart still thought she had fallen in love with him. Her heart loved his rare smiles and the amazing way he touched her. Her heart loved his calm, deep voice, and the muscular, heavy lines of his thighs, and the way he felt when he entered her. Loved his belief in doing what he could to make life better in his little corner of the world. Loved his passion. Loved his shoulders and the way they felt beneath her fingers, and the way he breathed when he was asleep.

She loved going to bed with him, exhausted, and waking up feeling as if the world was a wonderful place after all.

She loved the fact that he'd actually thought to bring her vegan subs.

She loved the way he loved his daughter and the way he'd kept his word to a woman who hadn't deserved him—who hadn't been good enough for him. Phoebe would have done anything for Alan, and she would never, never have betrayed him or hurt him.

But he hated her. She'd seen it in his eyes. He hated her the way he must have hated Janet after she'd been the cause of Chick's death. And all the hatred Alan hadn't been able to take out on Janet had come through his voice at Phoebe in those venomous few minutes when he'd made sure she didn't steal anything while he got her out of his bed and out of his home.

Oh, God.

How could he have believed whatever Brig had told him about her? Couldn't he tell from just being with her that she was honest? That she was a good person? *Why* couldn't he tell? She could tell everything that she needed to know about him.

But if he couldn't tell, if he couldn't have faith in her, then he *couldn't* be the right person for her, could he?

As if that mattered.

Michael, dead Michael, was coming for her, using high-tech spying devices and phone taps and God only knew what else. Michael had found her, just the way he'd sworn he would before she found the courage to run, and he was going to kill her, just the way he'd threatened to. And no one was going to believe her until she was dead. No one was even going to care.

Because the one person who might have cared now hated her.

But Michael was going to kill Alan first. And now Alan thought he was safe. Brig thought so, too. They both believed this whole business was a con game of Phoebe's, and Alan wouldn't know that because he had touched her—because he had dared to make love to her—Michael would kill him no matter whether Alan was still in her life or not.

How was she supposed to save Alan? He wasn't going to believe anything she had to say. He wasn't going to have anything to do with her. The police thought she was a fraud, the FBI had declared Michael dead and closed the case, Alan thought Phoebe had used Chick as some sort of trap to lure him into falling in love with her—or getting her pregnant, apparently, and meanwhile Michael could reach Phoebe when she was asleep. Could move things around in her house, leave flowers lying on her. Watch her. Call her without getting caught.

Bastard.

Phoebe found her phone book and called the first locksmith listed. "I need to have you come and change the locks on my house immediately," she said. "Just the front door, but I'm going to need three deadbolts with different keys." She listened while the locksmith expressed disbelief. "Yes," she said. "I'm sure. And while you're here, I'm going to want to have you check two sliding glass doors and make sure they can't be penetrated from the outside. And two windows."

The locksmith quoted a price to her that sounded outrageous. Phoebe didn't have that much money. She was going to have to float a check, overdraft her account, and then work twice as hard on the phone line to make enough money to cover all the bank charges that overdrafting would generate.

But a spotless bank record and no debts would be meaningless if she were dead.

Because Michael was calling her by telephone tap, he was probably also doing his little magic tricks with her mug and the flowers by means of being able to come through one of her doors or windows. The idea that he had been physically inside her house—that he might even have touched her—horrified her, but she was going to put an end to it.

And if Michael *was* really dead and some bit of insanity or obsession on her part was making her think that her caller sounded like Michael, and if her caller really was some other psycho—well, new locks would work on him, too, wouldn't they? Once she could be sure that she was safe inside her own home, she could figure out how she could keep Alan safe.

Brig would be fine without any action on her part. He'd made Alan believe Phoebe was a fraud, and had gotten him away from her. Which gave Michael a clear shot at both of them. Brig had done exactly what Michael had wanted him to do.

chapter 19

The locks were in, including new ones on the windows. New bars on the sliding glass doors. They couldn't be lifted out of their tracks, they couldn't be opened from the outside. The front door required two keys—the locksmith had convinced her that having three would be a danger to her if she were caught outside with someone pursuing her, and he wasn't happy that she would need two keys to open the doors. She was determined on that score, though. And she still had three locks.

She'd marked her keys, put caps on them so she could tell them apart even in the dark, and stood on her front stoop in the worsening wind and practiced grabbing the keys out of her backpack, opening the door without looking at keys or locks—simulating night conditions, because she could never know what might happen and she had to prepare for the worst—and she could get in her door in six seconds.

Three locks, six seconds. Good as it was going to get, she thought.

She stripped and cleaned the Browning again, put the loaded magazine in, checked the safety. Put two more loaded magazines in the elastic pockets on either side of the holster.

She went through the whole town house from top to bottom one more time, to make sure she was alone. She did her walk-through with the Browning in her hands. She checked

closets, she checked under her bed, she checked behind the
shower curtain, she checked in cabinets. And in the end, she
was convinced that she was alone in the house.

From this point on, if she was ever not alone in the house,
the intruder would have to have left clear signs of entry. A
broken window. A broken door.

Inside the house she was safe.

And the phone rang.

All right, you bastard, she thought. You may know it, or
maybe you don't, but the games you were playing with me
are over.

Except the caller wasn't Michael. The caller was Ben.

And she shivered a little.

"Phoebe, you sounded so funny on the phone the last time
I talked to you, I've been worried about you ever since. And
I got the feeling that you didn't want me to call you, but I
just wanted to make sure you're okay."

"I'm better," she said, and she meant it. She figured she
sounded like she meant it, too, because she heard a relieved
sigh on the other end. She was suspicious of Ben, though.
He might have sold her information to Michael, he might
have given it to him accidentally.

A thought occurred to her. He might have actually seen
Michael.

She told Ben, "I have to run some errands today—groceries,
a few things like that. Why don't I come by and say hello?"

Ben sounded elated when he hung up.

Phoebe needed to decide where Ben actually stood in this
mess of hers. She had to know whether he was involved, or
entangled in it innocently. Or if he was truly clear of and
apart from the whole thing. That last she wouldn't really
ever know, she supposed; it was damned near impossible to
prove a negative. But she did have a picture of Michael still,
tucked away against future need. Paranoia on her part, perhaps, but she'd hung on to it even after the shooting, because
she'd been so afraid he was going to come out of the coma
and hunt her down again. And she wanted to be able to give

the picture to the police so that they could put it on WANTED posters or something. She hadn't thought through her rationale for keeping the picture—but she'd always been dead certain she needed to have it. And then, when Michael didn't come out of the coma, she'd sort of forgotten that she had it.

It was in a blue shoe box on the left shelf of her bedroom closet, toward the middle.

She went to get it. But the shoe box wasn't in the middle anymore. It was all the way to the back.

Had she moved it?

The techs, she thought.

She looked in her closet, frowning. A number of things in there were not where they were supposed to be, now that she was actually looking. She'd kept a few boxes of work that students had done for her, and she had some old clothes that were too big now but that were nice, which she had intended to cut down so she could wear them. Not a lot of stuff—not clutter by any means. She knew where everything was. Or where it was supposed to be.

But the techs had moved things, or maybe when he was in the house, Michael had gotten into her closet and had gone through her things. And had put them back neatly, but not where she'd had them.

Which meant she wasn't going to find the photo of him in the shoe box.

She checked anyway.

It was right there. Right on top. And she didn't know what to make of that.

She took the photo, puzzled. Had Michael gone through her boxes? Had he not considered a clear photograph of himself important? Had he missed it? She couldn't believe that.

Perhaps he just figured no one would believe her. Or maybe the photo *wasn't* important anymore. Maybe he'd had plastic surgery and no one would recognize him.

She decided she would show it to Ben anyway to see his reaction.

*   *   *

Phoebe watched the clouds. They were *unnerving*. Long, narrow bands that fled overhead so quickly their shadows made the ground seem like it was flowing. The wind had stopped gusting and gotten down to serious blowing. She could feel it against the car as she drove.

The humidity made the air nearly unbreathable, but humidity defined South Florida in the summer. This was worse, but even average days were awful. And the sun overhead was still painfully bright. The fleeing clouds offered almost no shade.

Moonstruck was swamped. Apparently Ben had found himself someone who would read tarot in the store and teach classes in the back room, too, and Phoebe got there just as a class let out. She found herself surrounded by a wild assortment of people—mostly women, of all ages and dressed in everything from faux gypsy garb to business suits to tees and jeans. She saw only a handful of men, and while some had short hair and some had long, they all wore jeans or shorts—no visible business types in that lot. One girl with hair dyed black at the roots and purple at the ends was dressed entirely in black leather; she wore black lipstick, black eyeliner, and white face powder, and enough silver jewelry that she jangled as she walked. Her "Look at me—I'm baaaaad" attitude was so overwhelming that Phoebe had a hard time not laughing. And an equally hard time seeing anyone else until Bad Girl left. A lot of the other students hung around and studied the merchandise and debated which decks they liked best and discussed books and candles and incenses. The place sounded to Phoebe like a cage full of parakeets.

Ben came over to her, smiling. "You made it."

"I did."

"I have some great new decks," he told her. "And this spectacular new Thai restaurant I found that I'd love to take you to."

He looked like such a nice guy. He really did. Phoebe couldn't imagine him wanting to hurt her. But she *could* imagine him wanting to help her and giving her info to

Michael because Michael managed to convince Ben that he was someone who was trying to help her.

She pulled the picture out of her backpack and showed it to Ben. "Have you ever seen this man? In here, maybe, or near your home?"

He studied the picture. "This guy the source of all that worry you've been vibrating with?"

"I think so."

Ben looked closer, frowned, covered half the face with his thumb, then the other half. "I'm sorry, honey. I'd love to tell you that I'd seen him, that I know where he is, and that you could send the cops after him right now, but he looks like someone you'd remember, and I've never seen that face."

She sighed.

"He a little guy? A big guy?"

"Big," she said. "Last time I saw him, he was six four, and around two hundred thirty pounds."

"Okay, I'll tell you what. If I see him, I'll find out whatever I can about him and then call you."

"Don't mess with him, don't talk to him. He's dangerous," she said. "He's my ex-husband."

"The one in the coma?"

"The one who killed two of my students while he was coming after me. I think maybe he isn't in a coma anymore. Be careful, okay?"

Ben nodded. "So. About dinner?"

Phoebe sighed. Ben seemed nice. She didn't get any feeling from him that he was hiding some murderous psychosis beneath his friendliness. And maybe she wasn't the best judge of men, but it would at least be reassuring to know that there was a man out there who would know where she was and be concerned if she didn't show up from time to time. That had to matter, didn't it?

"I have things going on right now that you really don't want to get caught up in," she told him. "But once I get through this, maybe we can go to that Thai place you found. Just as friends."

He grinned a little. "Hey, that's better than 'No, not no way, not nohow.' If you go out with me, maybe you'll see what a sterling guy I am. So I have your word on this?"

She thought of Alan. Of Alan, whom she loved. Alan, who hated her.

"Yeah," she said. "Sure. You have my word."

Ben gave her a quick squeeze and a kiss on the forehead that was a little friendlier than what she'd had in mind. "Fantastic!" he said.

He heard someone calling his name and turned. Phoebe realized that he had people waiting to buy things.

"I'll go," she said. "You're busy."

"Come back again soon," he said. "Let me know how things are going. Let me know if I can do anything to help you. Anything."

She smiled at him. "Thanks. I really appreciate that."

Ben watched her leave, smiling at the tight, delectable curve of her ass. And his customer, a slouching seventies reject with a beard and ponytail, watched him watching her and raised an eyebrow.

Ben said, "Cute, huh?"

"Attractive," the guy said, passing Ben a book on ghosts and one on black magic.

"You buy two, you get any third book that sells for same price or less for half price," Ben said, but the guy wasn't interested. He *was* interested in Phoebe.

"She your girlfriend?"

Ben shrugged. "I'm not really a girlfriend kind of guy. I like women, you know? You start calling one your girlfriend, it limits your action."

The guy looked interested. "You get a lot of action?"

Ben dropped his voice. There were, after all, still a couple of hot girls from the tarot class hanging around. "If you don't mind flaky chicks, these New Age places are Babe Central. I owned a gift shop before this, but you don't get many opportunities to meet the customers. Here, I'm Mr.

Sensitive because if I own the place, I must believe all the crap, right? I give classes, I offer some of the real lookers jobs. It's sweet. I talk the talk, they all come flocking."

"I would never have guessed."

"Take Phoebe—"

"Phoebe?"

"The one who just left."

"Of course."

"I've been working on her for ages. She comes in here because I got her a job—she's the classic hard-luck chick. Absolute shitty life, and I come along, give her work, stay in touch, give her a price break on the supplies she buys. All along I've been nice, I've been patient. And now she's ready." He closed his eyes, smiling, and sighed, then glanced at his listener. "Friends. Riiiiight. A day or two, my hands are all over that sweet little ass."

The guy paid cash with exact change, took the bag with the books in it, and said, "A little warning. You'd be wise to watch where you put your hands where she's concerned. Some women are strictly"—he grinned—"strictly hands off."

He left, and Ben watched him walk across the parking lot and get into a boring little beige Ford and drive away. And he thought, What the hell was the matter with that guy?

chapter 20

Alan felt like his world had ended all over again. He didn't have a single patient in the ER, but he wished every bed would fill so that he would have something to keep him from thinking about himself. Or Phoebe.

He'd been such a fool. He'd let himself believe again. He'd gone out on a limb with a woman that any sane person could have told him was trouble, and he'd let himself care for her, and he had been well and truly hooked. Sucked all the way in.

He'd fallen because Phoebe had been a great lay, he told himself. That was all. She'd been willing to really put some effort into her scheme, whatever her scheme might have been. To get his money? To get him to marry her? Whatever—it didn't matter anymore, did it? Brig had saved him from himself, saved him from being taken by yet another woman who wanted to use him.

And he had never been less happy to know the truth in his life.

He kept seeing Phoebe smiling at him. Kept hearing that brief, startled laugh of hers when he said something she thought was funny, like she had forgotten that anything in the world could still be funny and was delighted to rediscover this whole misplaced part of her universe. He could still feel her pressed against his chest, asleep, warm and solid and sweetly and delicately curved. Nothing flashy about her, no supermodel features and no oh-my-God curves—but she had radiated. She had shone. She had been like a ray of sunlight sparkling through clouds for just an instant before disappearing again, and he'd found himself holding his breath and hoping that he would catch another glimpse of her light.

And all the while, he'd been courting Janet the Second.

Sucker. Sucker. He was such a sucker. He should just stay the hell away from women. Maybe find some amenable lab tech who'd give him quickies in a closet or something, just to keep himself from getting so sex-starved that he got stupid. That he lost his vision and started fumbling blindly after anyone who touched him and made him feel good and who had been born with a face that could pretend innocence while plotting betrayal.

From now on, he decided, he would avoid relationships that had any potential strings. He would avoid illusions. He would embrace Brig's philosophy, that women were fun for the first five days and hell in descending layers thereafter.

He came out of his funk with the feeling that something was wrong and turned toward the ambulance doors to find Brig charging through them, looking like a shot of Death with a Hell chaser.

Alan started toward him. "What's the matter with you?"

"I called the FBI," Brig said, "to see if they'd done any background checks on Phoebe Rain either recently or before, when they were investigating her husband and the shooting. And I got Toeller, the agent she called the other day. And this FBI agent was about to jump out of his skin because he's been trying to call Phoebe for the last couple of hours and he can't reach her. Any chance she's here?"

"After what I said to her?" Alan shook his head. "What do you think?"

Brig said, "The DNA samples didn't match."

"What?"

"The DNA samples didn't match on the guy who died.

They weren't Michael Schaeffer's DNA. The guy who is dead isn't her husband."

Everything that had happened since Alan had talked on the phone to Brig rewound in an instant. Phoebe the scheming bitch dissolved like the Wicked Witch of the West hit by water, and Phoebe with the angel's smile stepped out of the smoke. "How the hell—what—they had *fingerprints*."

"The Schaeffer family has been covering up a big lie. Somehow, someone used the same laser skin resurfacing technique that plastic surgeons use to remove wrinkles and . . . some sort of lesions from faces . . ."

"Precancerous lesions."

"That sounds right. Toeller—the FBI agent—managed to get a forensics guy to the funeral home to stop the family from cremating the body, though it was a close fucking call. The forensics guy took a look and was able to piece together what had happened. Best guess is that Michael Schaeffer started coming out of his coma early on, and one member of the family or someone close to the family didn't want to see him charged with the murders he'd committed. So the accomplice found some indigent in a coma and offered to cover his hospitalization. The FBI hasn't managed to identify the body yet or figure out who Michael's accomplice was. However, the person on the inside hired someone talented to remove the impostor's original fingerprints and then, with templates from Michael's fingers, to burn on new ones. The results aren't perfect; the forensics guy could tell what had been done by looking at the fingers with a magnifying glass. But those prints were good enough to fool the FBI's computer."

Alan was staring at Brig, but seeing Phoebe abandoned by everyone she should have been able to count on, alone in her house, with her murderous ex-husband given a clear shot to walk right in and kill her.

"The FBI thinks the family may have been considering this possibility early on—that they probably made preparations almost immediately. When they started seeing Michael coming out of his coma, they complained of incompetence at the hospital where he was receiving care and arranged for a private ambulance to take him to a private institution. Somewhere. At that one point, there was a complete break in continuity—all new doctors, new nurses, new techs. There was literally no outsider left who could point out that the man who left in the ambulance was not the one who arrived at the new facility. And apparently those records that went with Michael suffered some tampering en route. New sets of X-rays, new sets of lab work. Everything that arrived with the John Doe fit what the new doctors were supposed to be seeing."

Alan transferred patients all the time. "It would be difficult to do," he said. "But only from a logistics standpoint. Not in fooling anyone. If the chart is there and all the signatures are on it, we treat the damned thing as gospel. The patient is almost secondary."

Brig growled, "The whole thing had to cost the family a fortune. The FBI is hoping to track down the forgers, the attendants and ambulance drivers, the money. But the bastard had connections."

"Criminal defense lawyer."

"Right. Had a few friends among his clients."

"So the FBI thinks he rehabbed at home."

"Or in Europe somewhere, or South America, or God only knows where. He was a *successful* criminal defense lawyer."

Alan shuddered. "And the Schaeffers were going for cremation of the stand-in to cover their tracks. Get the ashes, scatter them, and Michael is good and gone forever."

"Looks that way."

"So Michael Schaeffer is likely in Fort Lauderdale right now. And everything Phoebe has been saying is true."

"I don't know. There's the detective report she had on you. There's her arrest record. I don't know what's true."

"I do. We abandoned her. *That's* what's true."

"Yeah. That's true."

Alan turned and slammed his fist into the nurses' station wall. And pain enveloped his hand, his wrist, and his forearm. Waves of nausea doubled him over, and without warning he lost everything he'd eaten all day into the nearest trash can.

"Alan?" Brig said. "Thanks for not putting that fist into my nose."

Alan grabbed a paper towel and wiped his mouth. "Was my first thought, actually. Should have gone with it." Alan took the Ace wrap that a nurse silently offered him, and the water and Motrin another held out. "Wouldn't have done as much damage to the hand." He started wrapping the palm and back of his hand, and the pain hazed his vision. "I'm a fucking idiot. I knew she wasn't conning me."

"We're trying to find the truth right now," Brig said. "Our guys are door-to-door in the neighborhood, asking about her. I have an APB out on her car. We haven't turned anything up yet. Can you think of anyplace she might be?"

Alan leaned against the nurses' station, closing his eyes against another wave of nausea. "No clue. I can't think of a thing. You think he has her?"

"I don't know," Brig said. "He might."

"I'm calling Morrie. He'll cover for me. I have to get out of here. I'll help you find her."

chapter 21

After she left Moonstruck, Phoebe didn't want to go home. She felt safer with the locks changed, but going home meant walking past Alan's place, and that was going to hurt. She wasn't ready.

She thought about going to the range and shooting for an hour, but she wasn't in the mood. The clouds still ripped by overhead with terrifying speed, but now they were bunching up like cows in a tight corral getting ready to stampede. The wind ripped and tore at the palm trees. Phoebe saw branches down all over. The weather was giving her the creeps; her knee hurt too much to make anything that required standing or walking seem appealing. She decided driving around for a while would be a better idea than getting out of the car.

That turned out not to be her best idea.

She made it down to the beach, just because traffic headed in that direction was surprisingly light. And then she saw the line of blackness lying offshore, and her stomach clenched. Red-and-black hurricane flags whipped and snapped, and undertow and riptide warnings and NO SWIM-MING signs shimmied against the building gale. Highway A-1-A swarmed with tourists and residents fleeing the coast, getting to higher ground. Caught in the traffic, moving at a snail's pace, all Phoebe could do was creep forward and wish she'd thought of someplace besides the beach to drive.

She turned on the radio. Tropical Storm Helene was

aimed straight at Fort Lauderdale, stalled not far offshore, building strength and organization. There was some concern that if she stayed stalled, she was going to roll over the city as a full-fledged hurricane instead of at her current tropical storm level.

Phoebe didn't want to think about dangerous weather, but she was going to have to. She had almost no emergency supplies in the house. Nobody to get them for her. No friends to ride out the storm with.

She looked at the line of dark haze offshore, black against the deepening blue of twilight, and at the heavy breakers already threatening to come over the retaining wall and across the road. Storm surge. It could be bad.

And somewhere along the way she realized that a red Porsche had been beside her in the left lane for a long time. She looked over and saw that the dark-tinted passenger-side window was down. And that she was staring at Michael. Michael, smiling at her.

Phoebe almost wrecked. She was trapped in traffic, trapped in her car with no way to get away from him. Cars jammed together like sardines. She wasn't going anywhere. At the next light, Michael could get out of his car, walk over to her, shoot her in front of everyone, then run away on foot and make better time than the traffic.

Her hands locked around the steering wheel, she started praying—and when she glanced over again, this time in an intersection, the tinted window was rolled up, and the Porsche was making a left turn away from her.

She couldn't believe it. He had her trapped and he was driving away?

She had to run before he changed his mind. Before he came after her.

But—

The inside of that Porsche had been dark. She'd only had the one glance at the man in it. He'd smiled at her, and the smile had looked like Michael's smile. But could she have been seeing things?

She kept her eyes open for a red Porsche, but she didn't see one. It couldn't have been Michael, because Michael wouldn't have let her get away. Still, she wasn't taking any chances. She got off A-1-A at the first opportunity. Just to lose anyone who might be following her, she meandered, making risky turns at the last minute, causing horns behind her to blare. Fifteen minutes of execrable driving and she was sure any tail she had was three bad turns behind, swearing.

She tried to figure out where she should go next.

Home?

The storm wasn't going to give a shit whether she was scared or not.

She had to get some groceries. Had to float another check and pray that the last few days hadn't killed her priority level so badly that she wouldn't be able to make rent and cover the bills that were going to smash her.

A couple of gallons of bottled water, she thought. Some batteries. Some bread—or maybe soda crackers. Some canned vegetables. Nothing big, nothing expensive.

Phoebe turned into the Winn-Dixie parking lot, still watching for the red Porsche, just in case. It wasn't there. Of course it wasn't there.

In the store, she grabbed the next-to-last empty cart and leaned heavily on the handle, babying her knee, watching out for people who didn't see her who might run into her or trip her.

Shoppers jammed the aisles, grim-faced. The shelves already looked like they'd been hit by a plague of locusts, and Phoebe realized that she wasn't going to get anywhere near bottled water or batteries. She'd be lucky to grab a couple of cans of beans.

She needed to get home. Fill the bathtub upstairs with water—which meant climbing the damned stairs—

And suddenly she got the feeling that someone was watching her. She looked down toward the other end of the frozen foods aisle, and Michael was standing there.

Smiling.

She had good light this time. It was Michael. She let go of the cart, turned away, and walked as quickly as she could back towards the doors.

She looked behind her, but he was gone.

Coming down another aisle to cut her off?

Her throat constricted, and her hand patted the flap of her backpack. All those people—if she missed Michael, they were going to backstop the stray bullets. And if she hit him, the bullets might go through him and into them anyway.

She had to get out of the store. She couldn't pull the trigger knowing that she might kill innocents.

Which was what he'd planned, wasn't it?

But he wasn't at the end of the aisle. Or by the front door. Or out in the parking lot.

Where was he? What was he doing?

In the parking lot, hurrying towards her car, she tried to spot the Porsche. It wasn't there.

She had to get home, she thought. Behind closed doors. Where she was as safe as she could hope to be.

She had the gun. It was loaded. She had new door locks, her windows were secure. She would get through this. Wouldn't she? Wouldn't she?

She had to. She couldn't let Michael win.

She pulled into one of the two entryways to the neighborhood, and there was a roadblock, and cops. And her first thought was, Oh, God, Michael's killed Alan.

But the cop came to her window and said, "License and registration." She handed them to him. He looked at them and walked away from her car, but she could still hear what he said into his walkie-talkie. "I've got her. East entrance. She's alone." And a furious voice demanding, "Keep her there."

"Pull off to the side right here and don't move."

Her mind ran scenarios. Michael had framed her for Alan's murder. Or his attempted murder. Maybe Alan was at least still alive. Or Michael had framed her for a whole lot of murders. She laid her head against the headrest and closed her eyes. Maybe jail would be a safe enough place to spend the night. Or the next ten years. She would have to specify no visitors. Couldn't chance Michael getting through to her. Being alone was better than being dead. She'd been getting good at being alone before Alan came along.

And she tried not to see Alan lying on the floor of his town house, shot or stabbed. She tried not to think of him dead, because the world without him in it would be hollow.

He'd hated her at the end, but it wasn't his fault. Someone had told him something about her that wasn't true, and it had sounded true enough that he'd believed it.

"Phoebe! Oh, God, Phoebe, you're okay!"

Her eyes flew open and Alan, alive and unscathed, was pulling open the door of her car, and he didn't seem to hate her at all. In fact, he pulled her into his arms and hugged her and buried his face in her hair and sobbed, "I thought you were dead. Oh, Phoebe, I thought he'd gotten to you."

She gave Alan a hard hug, not understanding what had changed. "When I saw the roadblocks, I thought he'd killed *you*," she said.

She pulled away after a moment and saw Brig standing there looking like warmed-over hell, and behind him a man in a dark suit and white shirt and gray-striped tie who had to be FBI.

"You found out he's alive, didn't you?"

Brig said, "We don't have any solid proof yet that he's alive, but the man who was in the coma and died wasn't him."

"I've seen Michael twice today; once in traffic driving a red Porsche, and once in the grocery store when I was going to pick up some storm supplies."

All any of them seemed to hear was "red Porsche."

"Did you get his plate number?" Brig asked. "Or even a partial? Anything that would help us sort it out from the ten thousand other red Porsches in Broward County?"

She could have gotten that. Michael had been in the turn

lane. Ahead of her. He'd been stuck there for long enough that if she'd been thinking, if she had just been *thinking* instead of panicking like a bird watching a snake coming for it—IDIOT! She closed her eyes, seeing the two of them in traffic again, seeing him in the left turn lane and her about a car length behind him, feeling her heart racing, feeling her blood pounding through her veins, and she could see the place where the tag was, and there was one there, and it was . . .

"Not a thing," she said. "I cannot remember a thing. I can't even tell you if it was a Florida tag or out of state. I know it was there, but what it was—nothing." She hung her head. "I'm sorry. I should have been able to get that."

And then the hair went up on her arms and on the back of her neck, as she realized that there had been a red Porsche parked in the reserved space to the left of hers in the parking lot of the development for the last month or so. She closed her eyes and imagined the parking lot layout. Alan's car sat to her right. Her car. The red Porsche to her left. Then the white Sunbird that belonged to the widow who owned the unit on the other end.

"Is there a red Porsche parked in space four fifty-four right now?" she asked.

Brig spoke into his walkie-talkie and got the reply that the space was empty. "But there's been one there before?"

Phoebe nodded. "It would belong to the town house to the left of mine. I've never seen anyone going in or out of there, but that's not unusual. I've spent almost all my time in my own place with the curtains drawn for the last two years. My neighbors are all quiet all the time. Either that, or the walls between these places are very well insulated."

"They're *pretty* well insulated," Alan said. "Not perfect. The family who lives behind me has teenagers, and I know they play their stereos all the time, and loudly, because I get the bass through my closet wall. I keep the door closed, though, and mostly don't hear it."

Phoebe nodded. "The builders made sure that there were

closets and bathrooms and public spaces along the shared walls, as much as possible, anyway. That was one of the features the real estate agent pointed out to me when I looked at the place. She said they did that to keep the bedrooms quiet. It seems to work."

Brig nodded. "Okay—so your ex might have been living in the town house right beside yours without you knowing it. That would be the perfect place for a watch post. And if we can figure out how he got into your place the first time, it would explain how he was able to drug your tea water and move things around."

Phoebe froze. "Drug my tea water?"

"The samples we got were laced with scopolamine," Brig said.

"You knew that he'd . . . that he'd drugged my tea water? And you *didn't believe me?*"

Brig said, "We need to go sit down and talk."

"I just need to go sit down," Phoebe said, feeling sick.

chapter 22

Phoebe and Alan and Brig and Special Agent Toeller went to Alan's town house for the time being, because the FBI wanted to search Phoebe's place for any further evidence of Michael, as did the police.

Alan kept his front curtains open, so Phoebe could tell that outside was like a fire-ant hill someone had stirred with a stick. She saw men and women in uniforms, in suits, in lab coats swarming everywhere.

She felt bad for them. Tropical Storm Helene finally made landfall, and the weather, which had been weirdly bright and windy all day, turned to shit.

Inside, dry and secure, the four of them sat in comfortable chairs around Alan's elegant coffee table, and Brig said, "First, let me tell you how sorry I am, Phoebe. I talked to Michael's family about how you and Michael ended up getting married, and one of our guys found a detective's report about Alan in a blue shoe box in your closet. It covered his credit, his income, his behavior and habits, his past including some details about his wife and daughter, and an estimate of his financial net worth."

"I never had him investigated. I couldn't *afford* to hire a detective."

"We're checking into the origin of the report right now." Brig looked down and shook his head. "I know that good people sometimes make mistakes; I'm not used to dealing with good people, though. And the detective's report combined with your current form of employment and your arrest record made me think I knew more than I did."

Phoebe sat there staring at him. "Brig—I don't have an arrest record."

"Yeah, you do," he said. "Up in Ohio when you were nineteen years old. You were charged with fraud, contributing to the delinquency of a minor—"

She interrupted him. "Those charges were dropped and the case was dismissed."

"You were still arrested. And the charges were dropped only after you got yourself an expensive criminal defense attorney—whom you later married."

Phoebe rested her face in her hands. "Good Lord." She looked up. "If you're here, I guess you're at least open to hearing my side of this."

"Yes."

She folded her hands together and leaned forward in her chair. "I was in college at the time—had just finished my first year. I'd earned a full four-year scholarship to Muskingum College and was pursuing my bachelor's degree in science. But while the scholarship covered room and board and tuition and books, it wasn't enough to cover things like clothes. Or transportation. I had a Vega station wagon that I could barely keep running, and even though I kept my needs simple, I had to have gas, car insurance, and the occasional new pair of shoes or jeans.

"While I was home over the summer, my sister, who was seventeen at the time, reminded me of how we'd made our own spending money with lemonade stands and by selling homemade pot holders door-to-door in the various trailer parks where we'd lived. I told her I didn't think I'd be able to cover the Vega's expenses with homemade pot holders, and she told me she had a better idea. We could set up a little fortune-telling stand under this awful striped awning that my parents had tacked onto our trailer, and we could stick a classified ad in the local paper and charge a few bucks per reading. I read tarot, and she had a real knack with psychometry—holding things that belonged to other people and telling them about the owners of the objects." Phoebe shrugged. "It seemed like a good idea at the time."

She saw Brig and Alan exchanging glances. Agent Toeller sat quietly, looking at his hands, not saying anything.

So Phoebe continued. "We started slowly, but our prices were low—I think we were charging five dollars for a reading, and we were both pretty good. We got busy, and then we got very busy, and then one of the neighbors called the police and complained because our summer business customers were blocking her driveway. And the police came and discovered that we were running a business without a license, which neither of us had the faintest idea that we needed, and that we were engaged in a business that the State of Ohio at that time looked upon as criminal, or at least questionable. Nicki was underage, so she basically just got yelled at. I was nineteen, almost twenty. So I got booked and charged—and would have had a public defender, except that Michael Schaeffer happened to walk through and see me during the booking phase. He told me and my defender that he'd take my case pro bono."

Her hands locked tightly together, she looked from one man to the next, trying to see what they were thinking and getting . . . nothing. No expressions, no emotion. Nothing. They were hearing her out. But she couldn't tell whether they believed her or not.

"Michael flirted with me. And took everything he could find out about me before the judge—my grades, my public service in high school and at college, and the story about how my sister and I were poor and just trying to earn enough money to further our educations, and how I was going to be a teacher and how she wanted to be a nurse. His details were all true, but he made the two of us sound like saints. And, worse, he'd put together this little photo presentation of our crappy trailer and how clean and bare the inside was, and how my sister and I shared a foldout couch in an eight-by-eight sunroom. The judge wasn't thrilled about our interest in psychic readings, but he was very, very generous. He told me to research the law surrounding any further businesses I might pursue and to pass this suggestion on to my sister as well. He made us return the money to any of our customers who requested it and forbade us to do anything further along psychic lines. And then he dismissed the whole thing. And as soon as we were out of the courthouse, Michael asked me out. I turned him down, explaining that I didn't intend to date until after I got my degree. And a job. I was determined to keep my grades up and my scholarship intact. I couldn't afford distractions." She turned to Brig. "I'm surprised that you found the case."

"Your ex-in-laws told me about it," Brig said. "And it was easy enough to confirm the broadest facts, and easy to fill in the missing ones with a lot of things that weren't true."

"The Schaeffers were not happy with Michael choosing me," Phoebe said. "They had this rich blonde country-club debutante who'd graduated from Vassar picked out for Michael. I didn't fit their plans. But the deb didn't fit Michael's. So he married me instead—lucky me. I was a sucker who thought he was a nice guy who'd had bad luck with women before and just needed more love."

"It wasn't your fault," Toeller said suddenly. "I've been going through Michael's file. Schaeffer was trouble before you met him. He'd had a long history of serious behavior problems that his parents covered up with money. He's one of the bad guys."

Brig nodded.

Alan said, "You don't have to worry anymore, Phoebe. Everyone who matters is on your side now. We're all watching out for you. Michael isn't going to get anywhere near you again."

Phoebe leaned back in the chair, her leg propped on an ottoman, with thunder roaring outside and lightning crashing, with rain slamming into the windows, and she thought, It's over. I can't believe it, but it's over, and I'm still alive.

She would have thought she'd feel better. She didn't.

Alan was watching her. "What's wrong?"

"He isn't in jail yet, I guess," she said. "I need to know that he's locked up. That he isn't going to ooze up through the floor or something and grab me."

She smiled at Alan, and he said, "We'll take care of you. We'll keep you safe. I promise."

A knock on the door. Brig went to answer it.

"Next door *was* our guy," a woman in uniform said.

Brig pulled her in out of the rain.

"He has a huge setup in there. Has recording devices attached to the phone taps, a psychic-line prompt taped so that he could play it before speaking to her, TV monitors—one that must have been for the bug you found on the front window and three others that we located only by checking the angles. One was in her bedroom and one in the bathroom. And there was a third that covered the whole parking lot plus the street leading up to it."

"The . . . bathroom?" Phoebe said.

"Yes, ma'am," the officer told her.

"How did we miss them?" Brig wanted to know.

"These are microcameras. Each about the size of the head of a pin. He pushed them into the cottage-cheese ceilings and onto the light pole in the parking lot. The things were about three millimeters across, total. He had to have paid a freaking fortune for them."

"So that's how he knew when she left, when she got home, when she was asleep. That's how he stayed out of sight."

The office nodded. "Sure looks like it."

"We didn't find lockpicks or a set of keys or anything like that, but with all the lockpick technologies on the market, he didn't exactly have to struggle to find a way in. His only risks were in getting caught, and his little listening post made sure that wasn't going to happen."

"We're going to need to get the uniforms and the black-and-whites out of here," Brig said. "Put plainclothes people down."

Agent Toeller said, "Actually, the FBI has jurisdiction on this one. The two murders in the school shooting take precedence over the current lesser crimes. Have your people clear the roadblock and get them out of the area. We'll have two agents in his listening post, two staying in the upstairs rooms in her place. We've also obtained clearance to use a snowbird's town house across the green. I'll be there with my partner. I want to keep the traffic down, let him think it's clear, so we'll have a couple of plainclothes guys outside."

"As persistent as he was in coming after her," Brig said, "I have to believe he isn't going to just give up and go away. He didn't spend the fortune that he's already spent to not get what he wanted. Keep some of my people on it, Toeller. You may need the extra manpower."

The churning in Phoebe's stomach agreed with Brig.

But she was safe from Michael. The FBI had the case. They knew where Michael had been and where he was going to try to be. What he was driving. What he looked like. How he'd gotten to her the first times. They were watching over her.

She wanted to believe she was safe.

But she couldn't.

Not until Michael was behind bars. He'd been planning this. He'd been preparing contingency plans. She knew he had. She knew *him*. Michael *loved* contingency plans. Which meant she had to be careful. She had to keep her eyes and ears open. And she had to do whatever she could to help put him behind bars.

"What do I need to do to help you?" she asked.

Brig started to say something, but Toeller held up a hand. "You can help us best by going back to your place. Do whatever you would be doing right now, act like this is a normal night. If Schaeffer put in four bugs, he may have a fifth that we haven't found yet. He may have some sort of listening device. He may have a remote set on his phone taps that will let him connect from a distance. We don't know, but we do know that if he thinks you're alone and all the excitement is over, he may come back. He may make an attempt to come after you."

"I don't want her to do that," Alan said. "I don't want her to be the bait."

"We have the area covered. We're not going to miss him, Dr. MacKerrie, and we're not going to let him slip by us."

Alan said, "I'd feel better if I could stay with her."

"I'd feel better, too," Phoebe agreed.

Toeller shook his head. "He's less likely to be lured into coming after her if you're with her. And we want to get this man as quickly as possible, before he hurts someone else."

Brig was frowning. "I'll clear all my people out of the way," he said. He looked at Toeller, and Phoebe saw some wariness in his eyes. "You've got it under control, right?"

"We've got it," Toeller said.

Brig turned to the uniformed officer. "Tell them the FBI has claimed jurisdiction and we're clearing off," he said. The cop didn't like it, and Phoebe could see that Brig didn't like it. Brig turned back to her. "You'll be all right. Just stay inside, do what they tell you to do, and stay safe until they give you the all clear."

"I understand," she said. She would go home. Lock her doors. Sit at the phone and read tarot for strangers for a few hours, and maybe a little longer than that. And Michael would come after her, and the FBI would arrest him, and he would finally be charged with the murders of her two students and for the murder of his first fiancée. He would be behind bars.

By morning it would probably all be over.

chapter 23

Alan watched Brig walk Phoebe next door. He watched the police leaving, watched FBI agents disappearing behind doors and into cars. It's going to be okay, he told himself. She'll be fine. She has two FBI agents with her. She's safe. Michael may try to get her, but he isn't going to get past these people.

But he was uneasy.

Of course he was. She was this delicate little woman with a bad knee, and if the bastard got through to her, she wasn't likely to be able to fight him off a second time.

Michael Schaeffer wasn't going to get through to her. That was the part of this that Alan had to hang on to. The FBI *had* the bastard. They knew where he'd been hiding, and no doubt were backtracking him from his lease. They knew how he'd been doing the things to her that he'd been doing . . .

God! Alan just about couldn't even let himself consider that. Her ex-husband had actually been in the same room with her. While she was drugged and helpless. At least once. Maybe more than once. Chick had dragged Alan to Phoebe's front door not because Phoebe was having a nightmare but because that monster had been in there with her. He could have done anything to her right then. But he hadn't.

Michael liked pain, she'd told him. Fear. And he liked being the smartest, outwitting people, leaving them baffled and confused. He liked winning, showing off, making the other guys look like bumblers and fools.

Alan was scared for her. Still. Dammit. He needed to do something to keep his mind off of this. Off the waiting, because the waiting was going to be the hard part. With luck it would only be a couple of hours. If it was any more than that, it was going to be like living under siege.

He didn't want to think about that.

He called the hospital ER. He got one of the nurses. Had her give him to Morrie.

"How is it tonight?"

"Not bad so far," Morrie said. "You feeling any better?"

"Yeah. Phoebe's okay. My hand hurts like hell, but it'll heal. I'm keeping ice on it. But we have some bad things going on here. Can't talk yet, but I'll fill you in as soon as I can."

"The nurses were describing your hand-smashing barf fest. Sounded pretty impressive, dude."

"Not my finest moment. But I'll be okay."

"I feel better, then. So. You wanna get your ass back in here and cover your shift so I can go home?"

"No way. I have to stay here in case Phoebe needs me."

"Is this a good time to bring up the Pussy Pool? Do I have, like, money coming to me?"

"This is not a good time. I just wanted to make sure you weren't swamped, because I feel guilty as hell for dumping the night on you. But things could get bad here. And with the hand, I'm guessing I'll be out for a couple of days, maybe. Have to let the swelling go down and get the fingers working together again."

"With the horrible weather outside, it's going to be good in here," Morrie told him. "Barring storm-related disasters, we'll be sitting in an empty house all night. *Nobody* is coming out in the middle of this shit for a three-day cold."

"Good."

"Later, then, man."

The phone call had eased Alan's mind about one of his

worries. But either he was going to pace in the middle of his floor like a trapped tiger or he was going to find something to keep his hands and his mind busy. He wished he could be with Phoebe. He wished he could see her. Hold her. Touch her.

He'd been such a fool for thinking that she could be like Janet. There was never a woman alive who was less like Janet. Never a woman more warm, more passionate, more sweetly funny and mind-blowingly sexy.

But he couldn't belittle Phoebe by saying she was just about sex.

He could see her in his future. Every night. Every day. He could see them walking hand in hand when they were old—someplace cool and green. Someplace with rolling hills that rose up to embrace them. They would have a little house that backed onto a hill, and it would have wildflower meadows around it and beautiful big old trees that bent over the house like protective parents.

And the kids would visit. And the grandkids.

He stopped.

After Chick's death, he had sworn that he would never again have kids. That he would never again chance the heartbreak, the devastation, the loss of a whole world that having a child would make possible.

He had been afraid. He had been frozen.

And now he was looking into a fantasy future that included children and grandchildren, that would make possible loss on a scale he could not even begin to conceive.

No.

He had been *right* to swear off of having another family. Look at him—at this moment he was facing the possible loss of a woman he had only known a handful of days, and he was a frantic mess. He wasn't strong enough to face a future that included marriage. He wasn't strong enough to look at another baby and hold that baby in his arms and feel the life in her or him and know that at any instant that life could be ripped away, and with it whatever little pieces of himself he had managed to salvage from the wreckage of the last time.

He found his wallet, pulled out Chick's lucky stone, and held it in his hand for just a moment. It was comfort. It was his talisman. The painted forget-me-not was worn and faded, but it was enough. He'd had Chick, and she was enough. She would have to be enough.

That was what he'd do.

He'd get out his tape recorder and a tape. Dictate notes on the book. He hadn't worked on the book since the day Chick had shown up outside his office. He'd been too scattered. He would write, and he would tell the stories he remembered about her. Before they faded like the painted flower. He would put them down and rejoice in the true happiness he had once had. In the love that still lived in his heart.

Chick was enough. Had to be enough.

chapter 24

The FBI agents put Phoebe in between them walking over to her front door, and one went in and did a quick sweep of her place while the second kept her on the stoop—in the wind and the rain—long enough to make sure they didn't have any surprises waiting for them inside.

Then they got her inside. "This place is a defense nightmare," the first agent muttered to his partner. "*Two* sliding glass doors; only two windows, and both of those face the front; that damned skylight. And the people with the end units have second-story balconies that connect directly to the roof, so they could step from the balcony onto the roof and walk across the roof to any other unit in the building. The floor plan is all cut up, and the patio privacy fence shields both sliding glass doors from the sidewalk."

They both paused and stared off into space for an instant at exactly the same time, and Phoebe almost got spooked. "Copy that," one of them said, and Phoebe looked harder at them and finally saw the tiny earbud and wire each wore.

"Our team across the street says they have the best possible view of your patio," one of the agents said.

She ought to remember their names. They'd told her, but they'd done it right in the middle of her finding out she couldn't stay with Alan, that Alan couldn't come with her, and that to help the FBI capture Michael she was going to have to go back into her place and act as live bait. They were tall, they dressed the same, they had the same short haircuts and square-jawed all-American G-man looks that spoke of plenty of exercise and ferocious attention to detail.

They were clearly competent. Focused. They established their watch posts—one in the unused upstairs bedroom, which had the window and gave the only halfway decent view of the patio and traffic outside the town house, and one in the loft at the top of the stairs, which gave the best possible view of the front door, the ground-floor window, and the sliding glass door in the living room.

They couldn't see her room. But the only access to her room was the sliding glass door, and they'd already established that its new locks were good ones and that no one would be coming in that way with anything less than a sledgehammer. Which they would hear.

They spent a few minutes reassuring her. Two agents stationed in the town house next door waited for any chance that Michael would reappear there. Two agents in the place across the green had a clear view of the front of her house, while her two agents had the vulnerable spots on the inside covered. Men were stationed around the parking lot, watching for anyone using Michael's space or anyone coming to any of the town houses in her unit. Police were looking out for red Porsches driven by men who might match Michael's description.

"Just do what you would usually do at this time of night," Ralph told her. "He's not likely to try anything in the middle of this storm, anyway. So try to relax."

Phoebe thought about the cost of the new locks on her doors and about the fact that she'd gotten in almost no phone time for the last few days and didn't yet have the rent covered, either. She sat at the table and got out her cards and tried to ignore the storm screaming overhead—and the fact that she felt completely exposed sitting at her table.

The agents faded upstairs and assumed their posts.

She wasn't alone. But not being alone didn't seem to be helping her feel any better.

Her skin was crawling, and she couldn't bear to sit still. She had the awful feeling that she and the FBI and the local police were missing something. That Michael wasn't going to just walk into this trap. That he was going to avoid it and still get through to her.

She couldn't affect anything Michael might do. All she could do was help the FBI as they'd asked her to. And all they'd asked of her was that she do what she would normally do at this time of night.

Which was read cards.

She had half a hurricane pounding on her windows and whistling over her roof—and from what the agent said, it would be that way for at least the next three or four hours and maybe a lot longer, because the storm was large and moving slowly.

So she shuffled her Universal Waite deck and took a deep breath. Had to calm herself or she was going to give awful readings.

Took the Motherpeace deck next and shuffled. The cards were slippery. Lively. Some nights they just lay there, but right at that moment they seemed to be humming with energy.

She ran through four of the seven shuffles, and a card popped out of the deck and slid across the table, faceup.

The Three of Discs.

She frowned at it. The Three of Discs was usually a positive energy card—it meant "working together to accomplish something worthwhile." And she could have read it that way easily enough. To see it as her and the FBI and no doubt Brig and the police, all working together to put Michael behind bars.

But that wasn't the sort of energy she was getting from it. She wasn't getting anything positive, anything good.

She looked at the image on the card carefully. Three women, two of them on a ladder and one on the ground, all of them lugging adobe bricks to build a wall. Above them, three discs. The background was bright yellow, the atmosphere was cheerful.

But something was wrong.

Phoebe kept staring at the card, while the hairs on the back of her neck stood up and the air around her got colder and colder.

The wall. That was clear enough. That was her protection. Locks. Bars. The FBI agents upstairs. The people in the other town houses. Obvious.

Something about the picture was not right. Was bad. A warning. She'd looked at the damned card for years, and she knew it by heart. Yet now something about it was giving her the creeps. Icy air blew on the back of her neck, and she had a knot in her gut and the crawling suspicion that this was a warning. *And she wasn't getting it.*

And then she saw it.

Well, she'd seen it ten thousand times before, but the usual meaning of the card was friendly and upbeat, and in that context what she'd seen had been only decorative.

Not in this context.

There was a hole in the wall. A big one. A you-could-sling-a-galloping-herd-of-moose-through-this-hole kind of hole—built right into the wall. Built right into the structure. No one was looking at it, but all three women could see it. It made the wall worthless for defense.

And the cold and the card and her fear told her that this was her confirmation. Her validation. That there was something she and everyone else had missed. A hole in their wall. A breach in their defenses that was so big and so obvious they were looking right past it. Thinking it was supposed to be there.

You have to get out of here.

Phoebe couldn't be sure if that whisper was her thinking or if Chick was giving her a warning.

But either way, Phoebe believed it. She couldn't stay in the town house. Something was wrong. Horribly wrong.

She decided not to do any readings. Money for the locks, money for the rent—it would just have to wait. Her averages would take a hit, too, but this was big.

She couldn't just walk next door, though. The FBI had told her to stay put. That they had everything covered.

She made her way up the stairs, building the lie in her head that she was going to have to present. She wasn't a good liar, and she knew it, so she made the story she was going to tell as true as she could.

"I'm not feeling too well," she said, poking her head in the door. "I'm going to go on to bed. If you need anything from the kitchen, or . . . anything . . ."

"We'll be up here until nine in the morning," one of the two agents told her. "We'll be switching off then, and the day shift will keep you company."

"Can I bring you anything to drink? Or eat?"

"No, ma'am. We have that covered."

"Okay, then. I'll see you in the morning."

"Sleep well," he told her. "You're in good hands." He gave her a friendly smile. The other agent, listening on a headset, nodded acknowledgment in her direction but didn't look up. Phoebe made her way down the stairs, grabbing her backpack from the top of the kitchen table, where she'd dropped it.

She went into her bedroom and locked the door the way she did every night, and wedged the bar under it. Then she went into the bathroom and barred the bathroom door shut. She turned on the shower, because the sound carried pretty well through the pipes even with the storm banging and roaring around, and she wanted the two men upstairs to think they knew where she was. She went back into her bedroom and undid the locks on the sliding glass door, and then she went back to the bathroom. Stood in the shower fully dressed, with the water as cold as she could get it, to lower her external body temperature. She didn't know if anyone was using infrared goggles, and she didn't know if what she was doing would help her hide if they were. But she was trying to cover all the bases, and that was the only plan she could come up with. When her nail beds were purple and her teeth were chattering, she turned off the shower. Then she

slung her backpack over her shoulder, slipped outside
through the sliding glass door onto her patio, and got
slammed by Helene, knocked onto her ass before she could
brace herself.

She fell hard, but the wind blew her against the building,
so the agents upstairs shouldn't have seen her. And she was
below the privacy fence line, so she should still be out of
sight to the ones across the green.

She closed the sliding glass door. Locked the little key
lock, which was basically useless. But, she told herself, better than nothing.

She crawled the couple of feet from her bedroom sliding
glass door to the part of the privacy fence she shared with
Alan's patio. She jammed her backpack under the fence.
Then she flopped on her belly and scooted facedown
through grass and leaves and water and sandy mud.

The board privacy fence swayed in the wind, and she
thought for a moment that if she got stuck and the rain kept
coming down the way it was, she could easily drown in a
couple of inches of water. Trapped.

Phoebe usually loved storms. Their energy and power felt
magical to her, and in a way she had never been able to explain to anyone else, or even to herself, they comforted her.
This storm was different. This storm felt like poison, and she
wanted out of it as fast as she could get there. She broke free
of the privacy fence and kept low and slow all the way to
Alan's patio doors, the ones that went into his main room.

She pounded on the glass. Hard. And waited.

Nothing.

Pounded again.

Nothing.

Oh, come on, she thought. It's me. Answer your damned
door. Let me in.

chapter 25

Sounded like something on the patio had blown loose and was slamming into the sliding glass doors in the living room.

Alan frowned, turned the tape recorder off, and muttered, "The hell with this." He'd been an idiot to think he was going to get anything done anyway.

He hurried down the stairs, listening to the screaming storm outside and to that unending pounding. What was it? The gate? A tree limb blown down? Patio furniture?

He pulled back the verticals and tried to look outside, but the heavy tinting on the windows and all the rain made it impossible to see. So he turned off the inside light and turned on the porch light.

Phoebe was looking in at him for one instant, banging on the patio door with both fists. But when the light came on, she went belly down onto the patio and rolled right up against the house.

He turned off the light as fast as he could, opened the patio door. Instantly, horizontal rain soaked him and blew into the house.

He half dragged, half carried her inside. She felt like ice, even though the rain was blood-warm.

His phone started ringing almost immediately. Dripping wet, staring at the bedraggled Phoebe, he answered it.

"Agent Toeller here. You got a problem there?"

"No. Patio furniture hit the sliding glass door. I had to drag it inside before it broke the glass."

"All right. Saw you come out on the porch and look around. I was just checking."

"Thanks," Alan said, and hung up the phone, and turned to Phoebe.

"What the hell are you doing? Why are you out in this? Are you crazy? Do you have any idea how dangerous this is? What if Michael had been waiting on your patio to grab you? What if one of the agents saw you sneaking around and shot you or something? For that matter, what if the wind just blew you away?"

"I'm fine," she said. "Now. But something was wrong over there. I—" She stopped and looked down at herself, then said, "Oh, I'm sorry. Look at the mess I'm making on your carpet."

"The hell with the carpet. I hate beige anyway. What's wrong?"

"I just got this . . . warning. That I had to get out of there right then. That we had all missed something big. You and me and the police and the FBI. Like a hole in our defenses that was so obvious we didn't see it; we were all looking right past it," she said. "I think I heard Chick telling me to get out."

"You think?"

"It got cold in there. In my head, I heard this warning. 'You have to get out of here.' But I don't know if it was Chick or if it was just me. Me being panicked."

"Maybe the panic is because of the storm."

"Maybe. I thought I loved storms, but there's something vile about this one."

He looked at her and sighed. "And now the truth comes out. My beautiful Phoebe *is* a freak after all."

"You don't like storms?"

"They scare the piss out of me. Especially around here. I don't like water. I don't like high winds. I don't like thunder or lightning."

"I'm sorry. I just love the wildness of it all."

He hugged her close. "You're insane. But I think I like that about you. And I'm glad you're here. I was going crazy trying to keep my mind occupied, telling myself you were going to be fine, and worrying about you anyway."

She kissed him once, a gentle kiss on the cheek that wasn't sexual. And she said, "Thank you for worrying about me" in his ear just as something huge crashed outside, and he about jumped out of his skin.

"Tree down," he said. "Close." But it hadn't hit the house; he could tell. And the lights were still on.

Alan held Phoebe tighter, because he was glad not to be alone in the midst of this storm that was a hell of a lot worse than what he'd expected. He kissed her, because she was both strong and soft and he loved her, but he didn't dare tell her that yet—it was too soon, and now with the mess in her life almost over, they were going to have time. He could tell her when the time was right.

He kissed her again, and her hands slid under his shirt, and he started to peel her out of her soaked clothes.

She laughed and said, "Cut them off if you have to. I don't know if there's any other way I'm ever getting out of these jeans."

And, deftly, he showed her another way.

chapter 26

They came together like the storm. All frantic groping and rain-slicked skin and bodies that pounded and surged and thrust and collided. Phoebe buried him in her and drew from his warmth and his strength a still place inside of her that she filled with him. With images of him. With memories of this moment.

The cold that she'd felt in her town house—the cold that was both a warning and a promise of darkness yet to come—would not leave her, but she didn't tell Alan that. She had come to Alan thinking that as soon as she was out of her house, away from that massive breach that they had missed, she would feel better.

But when she touched Alan, the cold only got deeper, and she trembled not just with his touch but with a wordless, chilling premonition that this was their last time. That the breach remained, that they were going to fall, that they were still falling, that before the storm passed, death would touch them.

Phoebe could not tell Alan about her fear. She had no pictures for it except an image of a thrashing sea. And darkness. Endless, cold, lonely darkness, stretching into infinity.

So she clung to him. She would have had something that made sense if she'd been reading him, she thought. So she was, perhaps, getting pictures of her own future. Of her own end.

She could not find a path through her fear to anything good beyond. She was watching the end of a dream; she was moving in a moment of fantasy that would be shattered before her eyes—that would shatter her and shatter him—and all she could think of was that she was grateful, so grateful, for this moment, his touch, his passion. She knew how it felt to love someone worth loving. And if she did not know how it felt to be loved, she at least knew how it felt to be wanted and cared for. She knew what it was to be touched with hunger and yearning and desire, to be seen as someone worthwhile and good. She had been appreciated. She and Alan would not part as enemies, with him thinking that she had tried to trick him or use him. The last things they said to each other would be good, not bad.

She would be gone—someplace cold, someplace dark and horrible—but she would have this moment to light the darkness. No matter what came after this, she would have now to hang on to and to cherish.

She kissed him deeper, hungering for the salt and sweetness of his lips, the plunge of his tongue against hers. She arched against him as he took her standing, pressed against the back of the couch and then lifted up onto the couch with her legs wrapped around him.

Crashing thunder, and the stream of the wind, and her screams as he brought her over the edge.

And they were on the floor, and side by side, and he laid her on her back and draped both her legs over his left hip, and he moved into her again, and reached new places in her. She shuddered and bucked and clawed the carpet, lost in him, with the coldness inside her shoved into a corner and silenced by heat and hunger.

And they were up against the wall, and he was holding her tight, his uninjured hand stroking her breasts and her belly, and tangling in her wet hair.

And they were in the shower, with the hot water pounding on both of them, bringing the storm outside in with them, and she was crying because he was more than she could have hoped for and she loved him and this was all there was. The end. The end.

All her life she had been waiting for this man, for this moment, for this place and time, and this was all she got.

And as he came into her, as they sank into the huge garden tub while their indoor storm, like a warm rain, grew gradually cooler, she thought, *Thank you. If this is all there is—if I die before the sun comes up—this will get me through the rest of forever.*

chapter 27

Alan woke clean and dry, amazingly and magnificently sore, deliriously happy, to the sounds of the storm outside and his cell phone going off next to his right ear. He swore at anyone who would call him at this time of all times. And what time was it?

Five a.m.

They'd slept that long?

Well, they'd had a lot of exercise.

He fumbled the cell phone off the nightstand with his left hand and said, "Yeah," and even though he was irritated with the caller, he still answered with half a stupid grin on his face because Phoebe was right there next to him and he felt like the luckiest man on the planet.

"Disaster plan activated," Morrie said. Alan could hear Morrie's voice shaking, something he'd never heard before. "Get in here now. Loaded charter bus hit a tractor trailer on I-95, and cars dominoed into the wreck. Every ER in the county is going to get buried in just a couple minutes."

And Morrie hung up before Alan could even protest that he had a hand that was swollen to twice its normal size. Then Alan realized that a banged-up hand really didn't matter under such circumstances. They were going to need him anyway.

The call left him as awake as any bucket of ice would have.

"Phoebe," he said, shaking her shoulder. "Sweetheart. I have to get into the ER now. You need to go back to your place. I don't want you to stay here if the FBI thinks you're over there. I don't want anything bad to happen. Okay?"

She rolled over and looked up at him, and he hoped what he thought he saw in her eyes was real. Because it looked like the future to him.

And then her expression changed and she whispered, "Don't go. Please. I'm . . . cold inside, Alan."

He pulled her close, realizing that she was cold on the outside, too. "Phoebe, there was a bad wreck on 95; I'm going to be tied up there all day—it's going to be hell. I can't stay."

She nodded, staring into his eyes, and he felt her fear, felt the cold. Icy, horrible cold that burrowed out from the center of him, slowed his blood, made his arms and legs heavy, made him weak. He shouldn't go. Shouldn't.

But the hospital was dealing with a disaster, and the storm would have the choppers grounded, which meant every hospital would be keeping the major trauma cases that landed on it. And this was his job. His duty. People would live or die today because of him—because he was there or because he wasn't. He couldn't *not* be there. He watched Phoebe while he pulled on a spare set of clean scrubs he kept for such situations and shrugged into his lab coat. Tried to flex the fingers of his right hand, and then knew that whatever else he would be doing, he wasn't going to be sewing anyone up.

And he almost called in and tried to beg off, because he didn't want to leave Phoebe. Because something was wrong.

But he had to.

Chilled and scared, frozen from the inside out, he said, "Get dressed. Hurry, sweetheart. I've got to walk you home, and then I have to go in to work."

Phoebe just nodded.

While she pulled on clothes, Alan called the number Agent Toeller had given him. Toeller answered.

"Phoebe got scared last night and spent the night with me."

"She . . . WHAT! How?" Toeller sounded furious, but in a calm, cold way.

"I don't have time to explain. We have an emergency at the hospital, and I have to get in there. I just called to let you know what was going on before I walked her over to her place."

"Don't. Hang. Up," Toeller said. In the background Alan could hear Toeller snarling. Because Alan couldn't hear the responses, he guessed the men who had been assigned to watch over Phoebe were catching hell. Toeller was snarling at them to speak up, to stop mumbling, to explain to him just how the woman they had been assigned to protect had spent the night somewhere else.

Phoebe had on underwear and a shirt and was fighting her way into her jeans when Toeller came back on the phone. "They'll both have questions for her when she gets there. I expect her to stay put and answer them. They had a slow night, but this sort of thing could have compromised this operation. It can't happen again."

"I'll tell her," Alan said, and Toeller said, "No. I'll tell her. Let me talk to her."

Phoebe got the jeans zipped, and Alan said, "Toeller," and handed her the phone.

She was quiet for a moment, her face pale and her eyes huge. "I know that an operation of this sort is expensive, sir. I realize that . . . I'm sorry. It seemed the best thing to do at the time." She closed her eyes wearily, and Alan hugged her. "It won't happen again, sir."

She handed the phone back to Alan without a word and slipped her shoes on, skipping any socks. She yanked her hair back into a quick, loose ponytail without even bothering to brush it first. She looked impossibly sexy, and Alan hated having to leave her even for a minute.

"I'm ready, I guess," she said. But her brown eyes were enormous, and he could see the fear in them.

And he couldn't stay. "I promise we're going to get through this," he told her. "You and me. We're going to win this and come out the other side of it stronger and better."

"You promise?"

"I promise."

She nodded then. "All right. I'll hold you to that promise." She tried a brave smile, but it wasn't convincing. He hugged her, she grabbed her backpack, and he walked her next door, waited while she let herself in, listened while she locked the door behind her, and then trudged through the dark, clinging to the puddles cast by the streetlights, all the way around the building to the other side. He'd parked in a guest space to give his own space to the FBI. One lucky agent had spent the night concealed in the back of a car just like Alan's, waiting to grab Schaeffer on the off chance that he decided to use his own parking space.

Phoebe would be fine, Alan told himself. And he would get back to her as soon as he could.

She would be fine.

He got into his car and the cold inside him just got colder.

Phoebe stood with her nose pressed to the peephole of her door, watching Alan until he disappeared from view. Then she sagged against the door, cheek pressed to the cool metal. The end of everything slithered toward her. Alan was gone, and the darkness was coming to claim her. Death was so close she could feel its breath on her cheek.

And then Phoebe stood up straight, realizing slowly that something was wrong. The lights were off downstairs—the place was completely dark inside.

And not quite silent—she could hear radio chatter in little bursts from upstairs. But something about that chatter *felt* wrong.

And something smelled horrible. Like iron and . . .

Inside her backpack, a phone started ringing. She jumped from the noise, but also from the impossibility of it.

She didn't have a cell phone.

But it was ringing.

She fumbled with her backpack, lifting the front pocket, reaching for the Browning.

That was where she found the cell phone. Her handgun was gone.

Her belly started cramping, and a wordless dread seized her.

When had the gun gone? When had the phone appeared? She'd last seen it before she went to Alan's. Before she took the cold-water shower and sneaked out the sliding glass door.

Which meant that while she was in the shower, Michael had found a way to swap them.

Phoebe pulled out the phone. It had a lighted face, and she could see the button highlighted with the word TALK just above it on the screen.

She pushed the button indicated, wanting more than anything to throw the phone away.

But she had to know. She had to know what had happened to her gun. How it had vanished. And what Michael wanted. Because this had to be Michael.

"What?" she said, and was dismayed to hear the shaking in her voice.

Over the phone, she heard a horrifying scream, and then Michael's voice. "I have Alan," he said. "And if you want him to live through this, you're going to do exactly what I say. If you understand, say 'yes.'"

Inside her, something whispered and slithered and rattled. Coming closer. Death. She could feel Death's gaze, could feel the chill of his breath. He was staring at her, and staring at Alan.

She'd thought Alan would be at the hospital, that he would be safe. "Yes," she whispered.

"Very good. I can see you. Do you understand?"

"Yes."

"Good. You're going to turn on the lights in your front room, and you are not going to make a sound, because if you do, Alan is going to have very bad things happen to him very quickly. Understand?"

"I understand," she said. She reached to her right, felt the switches that turned on the lights.

And in the flash of first light, she saw red and red and more red. Jammed her fist into her mouth to keep from screaming, from saying anything. Froze, so that she did not flee the town house, because she did not doubt for a moment that Michael had Alan, or that he would do exactly what he said he would do. More of what he had already done.

On the side wall of her town house Michael had nailed two hands, cut off just above the wrists. In blood over the hands, he'd scrawled, "Guess Ben will keep his hands off you now."

The blood he'd scrawled it with, though, wasn't Ben's blood. Because the FBI agents who'd gone upstairs to keep an eye on things were downstairs. Dead in chairs. Bound, gagged. Sheet-white, with big needles jammed into their arms and necks, and tubes running from those needles into Phoebe's big metal salad bowls. And in the salad bowls, deep pools of darkening red. And paintbrushes.

Michael had spent a lot of time with her white walls.

WHORE and SLUT and BITCH and CUNT repeated endlessly, and in between, YOU'LL DIE, YOU'LL DIE, YOU'LL DIE, YOU'LL DIE.

Blood on the carpet, blood on the stairs, blood on the table, blood on the furniture. He'd taken his time. How had he given himself so much time? How had he caught the FBI agents off guard? Why didn't Toeller across the green know something was wrong?

Phoebe heard the radio crackle upstairs again. Heard Michael's voice in two places—in her ear and upstairs. "She's in. She's fine. Reed is talking to her now about this stunt. Over."

The sound of the radio died away. Phoebe stood there, considering what she was hearing. Michael had killed the agents. Somehow. And then he had to have set up some sort of relay so that he could check in with the FBI, pretending to be those agents. Toeller had no suspicion yet that his people were dead. Wouldn't until shift change, which was still hours away.

He couldn't actually be upstairs. Because he had Alan, and he couldn't have Alan and be upstairs. By the time anyone knew to look for Alan—or her—they would be dead.

In her ear, Michael said, "Go into your bedroom now."

Knees shaking, Phoebe walked in, and in her bedroom found pictures of her nailed to the wall. Above the photos, Michael had painted the words, ONCE UPON A TIME, PHOEBE SCHAEFFER WAS A BAD GIRL. He'd taken pictures of her when she was sleeping. No. Not sleeping, she realized, creeping closer, looking at them. He'd taken them after he'd drugged her. He had posed her. Obscenely. Over and over and over, while he took pictures of her. She could see Michael's hands on her, doing things to her. Sometimes he had knives with which he was pantomiming cutting her and maiming her. In most of the pictures, he had worse things than knives. He'd created a photo story—a story of torture and bondage and rape and more torture and eventual murder—and pinned the story on her wall.

Beneath the pictures, he'd painted, AND THEN ALL HER DREAMS CAME TRUE. THE END.

In some of the pictures she could see her eyes half opened, could see that she was trying to make sense of what was happening. In some of the pictures she was in bed, in others she was on the couch. She realized the photos of her on the couch in her bathrobe had been the "nightmare" she'd remembered in enough detail to recount to Alan when he'd heard her screaming and run to her rescue.

Phoebe leaned on the foot of her bed, too sick to stand under her own strength. All the nightmares had been real. Everything had been real.

But they had been just the beginning.

And then all of her dreams came true. The END.

"You like my story?" he asked.

And she dropped the phone and vomited all over her bed.

From the floor, she could hear Michael saying, "Pick up the phone, Phoebe."

Her stomach heaved, she retched, the smell of blood and urine and shit were everywhere, two dead men and parts of another waited back in the main room, stenches and more stenches filled the air, and Death had pinned her future to the wall in Polaroids. She wanted to fall apart. To die right there, quickly—get it over with before the future that Michael had documented for her with such sadistic patience came true.

But, "Pick up the phone right now," Michael said again, and then Alan screamed.

Phoebe, still retching, collapsed to the floor and clutched the phone. "Here," she said.

"You like my story?"

"No."

"Wrong answer," he said, and this time Alan screamed for a long time—a hellish, high-pitched wordless scream. "I haven't started cutting anything off of him yet, but don't give me any more wrong answers. You understand."

"Yes."

"You like my story?"

"Yes," Phoebe said through clenched jaws, while her stomach heaved, empty.

"Good. You remember I warned you—more than once—that if you ever left me, you would come back to me."

"Yes."

"You're going to come back to me now, Phoebe. All by yourself, and all alone. Because you love me, Phoebe. Don't you?"

All she could think of was Alan, in Michael's hands. Michael, who had knives, and tools far worse than knives. Alan, from whom Michael had not cut off anything. Yet.

"Yes," Phoebe said, with tears starting from her eyes.

"That was a little slow, darling. I'm not going to make him pay for your slowness this time. But you want to answer quickly and enthusiastically next time. And every time thereafter. Don't you?"

"Yes," she said instantly.

"Good girl." Michael took a deep breath. "The FBI doesn't know their boys in there are dead yet. *You* are not going to give any signs. Open your closet door."

Phoebe crawled to her feet, grabbed her backpack, and walked to the closet, dreading having to find whatever Michael had left in there. The rest of Ben Margolies? Or someone else? Or some*thing* else?

But the closet was . . . the closet.

She stood looking into it. She didn't see anything out of the ordinary.

"I'm . . . I'm looking," she said.

"Yeah. You've all been looking." Michael laughed.

The image of the Three of Discs flashed through her mind. The hole in their defenses was in there? The thing they had all been overlooking—it was in the closet?

But the closet was on the *back* wall of the town house. It was nowhere near the town house Michael had rented. The side wall the closet shared was with Alan's town house. Its back wall was the shared wall with the town house that mirrored hers on the opposite side of the building. She couldn't see any advantage in bugging the closet. She couldn't imagine what other use he might have made of it, or how it could constitute a massive security breach.

Phoebe stood, frozen, trying to find anything that might be that giant hole the Three of Discs had warned her about.

"Come on, Phoebe. Figure it out. Because I don't have a lot of patience, but I do have your fuck-buddy here, and if you take too long, I have a lot of interesting ways that I can relieve my boredom."

"You could tell me."

"But then I couldn't use your stupidity as an excuse to hurt him," Michael said in a tone that sounded completely *reasonable*. Phoebe hated that tone.

She started shoving things around, looking, but not knowing what she was looking for. Something that could be hidden in a closet. But everything in the closet was hers. The few boxes. The clothes hanging up. The clothes folded on the left shelf. There wasn't anything else in there—just the closet itself, which was a rectangular walk-in box with a bare lightbulb overhead, the two side shelves, the bare wall to the back—

Stop.

No.

Michael wouldn't have rented two town houses.

The FBI had only found out about one. They were watching only the one beside hers. If Michael had access to the town house behind hers as well, she didn't think they were set up to monitor anything he did. The back half of her building had its own parking lot. Its own sidewalks and Dumpster. Its own cozy green. The FBI was set up to watch her green. Her side of the building.

They were looking in the wrong place.

She moved towards the back wall, trembling.

"Took a lot of work to get that passage right," Michael said, as she reached out and pushed on the wall. It swung inward at her touch. "Helped a lot that you don't use the closet much. Most of my first month I spent building the passageway when you were out. You don't go out nearly often enough, by the way. I spent hours making it sound as solid as the rest of the structure, making sure that its bracing wouldn't give way when I wasn't using it. Doing finish work on the edges. Getting the paint right. Cleaning up traces of sawdust and concrete block dust on your floor. But I think most of that was unnecessary effort. Every single one of you looked at my door while you were in there, and not a single one of you thought to push on it. Well, I did have it barred and braced when I wasn't using it, so that wouldn't have done anything anyway. But it's the thought that counts, don't you think?"

The hole in their defensive wall had been a literal hole in her wall. Michael had given himself a door straight into her bedroom.

He had never needed to deal with her locks. Her bars. Her defenses. She'd been defending everything except the path he'd created for himself, and the only effect everything she'd done would have had would have been to keep help from reaching her.

He hadn't needed to worry about being observed when he went from parking lot to front door, because no one was *watching* his front door. They were all watching the false lookout post. The one they had probably only found when he was ready to have them find it.

Meanwhile, Michael had been able to go from her bedroom to her kitchen, unseen, while she read tarot cards a few feet away, her back to him, because she was facing her front door. Guarding that damned front door.

He had been able to drug her. Had been able to just walk in and watch her while she slept. Could have done anything to her at any time—but instead he'd just taken pictures. Because the most important part of this whole fantasy of his, she realized, was that she come back to him on her own. She had to be terrified, because that was what did it for him— her fear. But she had to be the one to go to him, because that was what he'd said she would do.

And Michael always had to be right.

And the hell of it was, she was going to do exactly what he wanted her to do. She was going to walk right into his hands, because Michael had Alan, and she could not abandon Alan to him.

Phoebe stared at that open hole and into the darkness beyond, terrified to take the next step. Michael was over there. Alan was over there.

"Come on through, Phoebe . . . and close the door behind you. We have a lot to accomplish yet."

She shivered. Stepped through the doorway into his closet, which was empty. Dark.

She did not close the door all the way. She hoped he wouldn't notice. If he did, he didn't say anything.

"Keep going," he told her.

She opened the door, stepped into a place no one had seen yet but her. The bedroom that mirrored hers. Into Death's antechamber. Michael had turned the room into a gallery of drawings. Charcoal, pencil, marker. Drawings of her that covered every inch of every wall, every inch of the ceiling except for the place where the light fixture poked through. He'd drawn right on the walls in places, favoring red and black marker. And in places he'd pinned big sheets of paper to the walls.

Michael wasn't much of an artist. And his artwork only had one theme: Phoebe's pain, humiliation, submission. In the first glance, before she averted her eyes, she saw herself in ropes, in chains, with hooks through her skin, dismembered—

"You're supposed to look, Phoebe. I did all this for you. Look at the drawings; tell me how much you like them."

Michael was watching her. She couldn't see him yet, but he saw her. And he had Alan. So Phoebe looked. Walked along the walls, stared up at the ceiling. Tried to turn her face toward all of the hideous pictures without actually seeing any of them. They were pictures of the inside of Michael's mind, every single one of them. They terrified her.

So she remembered Alan, focused on Alan. Remembered what she had to say to keep Alan safe and in one piece. "I like them."

"Good girl. So do I. You've looked long enough. Go into the bathroom."

Phoebe was trying hard to keep her breathing slow enough that she didn't pass out. She couldn't pass out—that would leave Alan with no one to help him. Her heart raced, her hands shook so badly she needed two tries to turn the knob.

Michael wasn't in the bathroom.

"Undress," Michael said.

Phoebe almost balked. But . . . Alan . . .

She put the backpack down. Undressed.

"Brush your teeth."

She did as she was told.

"Get the scissors out of the medicine cabinet."

She took them out.

"Cut your hair off."

"What?"

"Cut your hair off. Don't leave more than about an inch all over."

She started cutting, and the sink quickly filled with curling black strands as long as her arm. It took her a while—she could only think of lambs being sheared, and that made her hands shake worse.

But at last she finished.

"Into the shower. I want you clean and smelling nice when we renew our vows—none of *his* touch on you, no whiff of your puke. You understand."

"Yes."

She showered, and he directed her to dry off and leave her clothes on the floor. She picked up her backpack, and he directed her into the kitchen, and from there into the dining room. Michael wasn't there, either, and neither was Alan. But another man was. A doctor. He lay on the floor against one wall, blindfolded, his mouth taped over with duct tape, his arms and legs bound. He had on scrubs and a white lab coat with DR. BEACHAM-SMITH embroidered over the left breast pocket. Phoebe could see his chest rising and falling. Blood in his hair, drying on his forehead.

"Don't touch Morrie. He did me a favor, albeit only at gunpoint—so he gets to live."

Morrie. Alan's friend.

Oh, God. Michael's path to her had been wide and bloody.

"Walk over to *my* table," Michael said, and Phoebe, who had been staring at Morrie, willing him to wake up or do something to show her he would be all right, jumped.

On Michael's table, which was a cheap card table set up under the dining room chandelier, she found clothes. White leather panties. A leather bra. A huge round white pillow thing with elastic straps on it that she couldn't figure out until she suddenly realized that it was the sort of maternity padding models who weren't pregnant would use to model maternity wear. A blonde wig. A white dress. White ballerina flats.

"We're going to renew our vows today," Michael said in her ear. "For better or for worse, until death do us part. Doesn't that sound nice?"

"Yes," Phoebe said, staring at the clothes on the table.

"Put your wedding clothes on. And the pregnancy padding. And the wig."

Phoebe started dressing. She kept the phone resting on her left shoulder, holding it in place with her ear, while she put on the bra and the panties. With her hair gone, her head felt too light. Her balance was off.

"I'm making a home movie of our ceremony, sweetheart. I filmed the wedding guests over in your place last night. Had nice mood lighting for them. And today, I'm getting great pictures of the bride dressing. You know, white actually films very badly. But your outfit is going to be white for such a short time, I think I'll be able to tolerate the glare while it is. It's the anticipation of color that makes white so exciting, you know?"

"Yes," she said.

"You want to sound happy and loving when you say that, sweetheart. Because the adulterer I have here is going to be our witness for the first part of the ceremony. And we want to have enough of him left to sign all the papers." Michael chuckled.

Phoebe put the cell phone down, struggled into the maternity padding, slipped into the dress and the flats, pulled on the wig, straightened everything. The shakes had given way to a horrible heaviness—to fear so bad she almost couldn't get her arms and her legs to move.

Alan, she kept thinking. Alan. Do this for Alan. Maybe, maybe, you'll have a chance to save him. Do everything you can to give yourself that chance.

She picked up the phone. "All right."

"You look . . ." Michael laughed—a happy, open laugh. "You look like a white cow, actually. Oh, God. The camera adds a lot more than ten pounds." His laughter died away. "This next part is going to be risky for you and your friend. Don't make any mistakes. Walk to the end table beside the front door."

Phoebe passed a bank of monitors, herself on some of them, empty rooms on others, the inside of an empty car on one. One screen, though, riveted her. On it, she saw Michael wearing a microphone headset, dragging a struggling, tape-bound Alan through an odd oval door, shoving him to the floor of a very small room also filled with monitors, and then looking at the monitors.

Until that moment, some part of her had held out hope that Michael didn't really have Alan. That maybe the screams were taped. Or that he was hurting some stranger.

"And here we both are," Michael said, seeing her looking at him. "Let me get settled." He took a seat in a swivel chair bolted to the floor, turned around so that he was looking straight at her, and rested one cowboy-booted foot lightly on Alan's crotch. "See your doctor?"

Phoebe saw Alan. He lay on the floor, bruised and bloodied, still in his scrubs and lab coat, glaring at Michael. He wore metal halo headgear that pulled his tongue out and clamped it, stretched, beyond the line of his lips. Phoebe remembered that headgear from her marriage. And then, while she watched, helpless to intervene, Michael took two alligator-clip wires and connected them from a small black box on the floor to the clamp. Phoebe remembered that box, too. Her breathing got faster, and the room started getting light around the edges. Started fading.

No. She had to breathe slower. Had to stay in control. She had to be able to help Alan.

Then Michael flipped the switch and Alan screamed and writhed and Phoebe's whole body went rigid—Alan's pain colliding with her memories.

"Isn't that fun?" Michael asked, flipping the switch off.

"Don't hurt him!" Phoebe screamed.

Michael flipped the switch again and over Alan's word-less screams shouted, "Wrong answer, whore."

Phoebe couldn't think of the right answer. Alan was screaming, and his pain was her fault, all her fault, and all she could think to shout was, "Yes, Michael. Yes!"

"Yes, Michael," Michael repeated, flipping the switch off again. "I like the sound of that. Wait until you see what we're going to do to him once you get here."

Breathe slower. Stay in control. Don't be weak. Don't be helpless.

Phoebe had to find a way to save Alan. Somehow.

"To the table, Phoebe. Time's a-wasting. Chop-chop."

She limped to the table, her knee suddenly throbbing. She saw a tiny white beaded handbag, a key ring with two keys on it—a car key and a house key—what looked like a hear-ing aid, and a little plug of some sort.

"You're looking at the wireless earphone/mike for your cell phone. And with it, the connector. The connector plugs into the base of the phone, the earphone/mike slips into your ear. You'll wear the wig with the hair down so that, just in case one of those sharp-eyed Eagle Scouts has wandered to the other side of the building, he doesn't notice something amiss. Put the earphone on, and then plug in the connector."

Phoebe did as she was told.

"Put the cell phone into the handbag. Pick up the keys. And . . . Phoebe, leave your backpack right there. You al-ready know your gun isn't in it, right? I have that here with me."

She'd known the Browning was gone—had known it the second she realized the cell phone was ringing from inside the bag's holster pocket. But for the last two years that back-pack had never been farther away than arm's reach. When she let it slide to the floor, she realized how very completely she was in Michael's power.

She was helpless.

At every turn, he'd taken her control away from her.

And he seemed to be reading her thoughts, for he said, "I don't have any intention of having you turn the tables on me this time, dear. I spent nearly three months in a coma last time, thanks to you, and an incredible amount of time and pain recuperating and rehabilitating afterward. So this time I've made very sure that everything will go just the way I want it to. I've spared no expense."

Phoebe held the keys in her right hand. Swung the little beaded bag over her shoulder.

"Pull the plug on the monitors, Phoebe," he said. "It's right next to the door. Take the power strip with you when you leave. You're going to toss it into the Dumpster on your way past."

She did as she was told.

"All right. Out the door, remembering that you don't want anyone to notice you. At all." In her ear, Alan screamed briefly. "Because this can get so much worse. Walk to space four-fifteen. The car sitting there is a light brown sedan. You're going to get into it. And you're going to come home."

Phoebe took the next step of her descent into Michael's hell, into the hopeless darkness.

She told herself that she had to hang on for Alan. Had to keep looking for a crack in Michael's armor. Had to keep fighting until she had nothing left to fight with, because Alan had no one but her to keep Michael from him.

But hope was gone. Dead.

A blanket of black clouds and the drizzle that was the last passing of Helene brought forth the bleak day. But for Phoebe, all that remained was darkness.

chapter 28

Brig stood in the parking lot in the strip mall while the woman who had called in the crime scene wept and hiccuped and talked all at once. Which made the interview an exercise in frustration.

"He . . . he . . . he . . . said he'd be here early. He was going to do a . . . a body aura reading . . . for me. And . . . and . . . and then we were going to share . . . share . . . our . . . share our essences. . . ."

Brig considered that for a moment, did a quick mental translation from New Age Bullshit-ese to Guy on the Make, and got the picture. Yeah. A before-work quickie. Or, since she was here at seven in the morning and the place wouldn't have opened until ten, maybe not such a quickie.

Very smooth.

". . . So I got here . . . and his . . . his car . . . car was here, and I had the key he . . . key he . . . key he . . . key he . . ."

Record skipping a groove there, honey, Brig thought, curbing the urge to thump her once on the side of the head to see if he could unstick her.

"And the guy you were going to share essences with is . . . ?"

"Ben . . . Ben . . . Ben . . . Margolies."

For Brig, everything screeched to a halt. He'd been called to the strip mall for a homicide, and the responding uniform had shoved this bleached-blonde, fake-titted, gym-bunny bimbo in her spandex leotard in his face as the witness, and nobody had said *which* store in the strip mall was the problem. The crowd was in front of Hot Bodies Gym. And Brig had assumed the body was in the gym.

But the gym sat next to Moonstruck New Age Shoppe.

Which Brig had visited the day before, to talk to Ben Margolies Phoebe Rain. Hadn't been a particularly interesting talk.

But now Ben Margolies was dead?

Fuck.

Brig bolted past the chippie, leaving her protests to fade behind him in the drizzle and the grinding, steaming early-morning humidity. He zigged around the ambulance and the black-and-whites and the medical examiner's van that had blocked his view of the doors to both businesses, jumped the crime scene tape in front of Moonstruck with badge in hand, and skidded to a halt just inside the door. Where he found himself beside techs and the medical examiner, and face-to-face with Ben Margolies, taped to a chair, sitting cross-legged with his eyes open and the corners of his mouth taped into a weird smile. A placard around his neck read, SURPRISE. With a signature in the lower right-hand corner, forty-five-degree angle upward. Sign of an optimist, Brig thought, and shook his head. The signature said, "Best wishes, Michael Schaeffer."

Ben's arms ended halfway down the forearms in bloody, ragged stumps. The amputated hands were nowhere in sight.

"Hands?"

"Not on the premises," the ME said.

Brig fished out his wallet. Found the card that Toeller had given him the day before. Flipped it over, located the hand-written cell phone number on the back.

Called.

"Toeller."

"Detective Brig Hafferty. We met yesterday."

"Go ahead, Detective."

"I'm at a crime scene that I think is related to your case. Guy named Ben Margolies, was one of our suspects briefly."

"Right."

"Missing his hands, wearing a little note from Michael Schaeffer. Note says, 'Surprise.'"

"How do you know it's from Michael?"

"He signed it."

A whispered "Shit."

"Yeah. You want to have your guys check on Phoebe for me real quick? Maybe run next door and see if Alan's okay? This is—this is creepy."

"Yeah," Toeller said. "She was . . . *they* were fine at five. I saw both of them. The doctor got called into the hospital for a disaster. Prior to that, they spent the night together at his place."

"Thought she was going to stay at her place."

"She's just been full of surprises," Toeller said, sounding pissed.

Brig stared at the cell phone. She'd gotten by them? Hell. He listened to Toeller on the radio, trying to raise his guys. Getting nothing.

Ice formed in Brig's stomach, in his veins. To the techs he said, "I'll be back. I'm going to check on something I think is tied in to this case."

And in his ear Toeller said, "Not getting them. We were good half an hour ago when we did our last check-in."

But they weren't good anymore.

Surprise.

"I'm heading over now," Toeller said, sounding like he was running, and Brig, running, too, kept the phone jammed to his ear as he jumped into his car. Put it on speakerphone, slammed it into its cradle, put the siren and the lights on and drove like hell through the nearly empty streets.

He was halfway there when he heard Toeller kick the door in.

Heard the hoarse "Sweet Jesus" an instant later.

And shouting. And the sounds of running feet. Upstairs. Downstairs. Doors slamming.

"Oh, my God," from Toeller, and a second later, "That sick fuck."

People shouting to each other in the background—nothing calm, nothing orderly. Brig heard chaos.

And Toeller saying, "Phoebe Rain is nowhere on the premises."

And then someone yelling, "Found it!" and a pause, and the sound of running and heavy breathing, and then Toeller proved he knew how to swear.

"There's a door cut through the downstairs bedroom closet, on the *back* wall," he shouted as Brig pulled into the parking lot, screeched to a stop, and jumped from the car. In his ear Toeller said, "Not the west wall into the listening post we found. The fucking *north* wall into the town house *behind* hers! And . . . oh, holy hell, I think we just found the doctor who called MacKerrie to the disaster."

Which was the last thing Brig heard before he walked into the nightmare.

chapter 29

Just ten minutes earlier, Phoebe drove away in the almost-new sedan that Michael had left waiting for her in his parking space. She hadn't seen any agents in that section of the parking lot, and if they were there, they hadn't recognized her. She had pulled out of the space, had driven away from the development, and no one had raised an alarm.

Now she traveled east with the gray smear of dawn in front of her, with rain spattering and spitting on the windshield. Traffic was still light; it was too early for most people to be going to work. Helene was almost gone, but driving off the main thoroughfares through neighborhood after neighborhood, Phoebe could see a lot of damage.

Phoebe listened to the voice in her ear. She couldn't hear anything from Alan, and Michael had grown uncommunicative. He didn't say much more than "Take the next left. Take the next right."

Phoebe had no idea where he was taking her. Just that she was headed toward the beach. Dawn stayed either to her left or in front of her. So . . . south and east.

And then Michael said, "Pull into the parking lot coming up to your right," and she saw a building ahead and a sign that said BAHIA MAR.

And she saw boats.

And suddenly she knew why the doorway she'd seen on the screen where Michael was had been oval, and why the chair was bolted to the floor. And why the space looked so cramped.

Now she knew how Michael planned to have his fun with her—and with Alan—without anyone interfering.

The Bahia Mar was a marina—a big one, with huge yachts and a forest of sailboats and smaller boats all tight to their piers against the storm that was finally passing. The water looked rough to Phoebe—black and ugly.

And her premonition came back to her. Of going under that water, of not coming back up.

If she was lucky, that would be her fate. But Michael's photo story and all his drawings didn't leave much doubt about what her fate was really going to be.

Not much doubt at all.

chapter 30

Alan lay on the polished wooden floor of Michael's yacht, drooling from the tongue clamp, the duct tape around his wrists and ankles so tight he couldn't feel his hands or feet. Michael was guiding Phoebe to him, and Alan couldn't even move to help her.

Alan was hoping—praying—that Phoebe would suddenly exercise simple self-preservation instincts and run away.

He was going to die if she did. But he was going to die anyway. Michael had spent a little time telling him how. And what he was going to do to Phoebe when he had finished up with Alan.

But Phoebe kept coming. Alan tried thinking messages to her, telling her that she couldn't hope to win this time, that Michael had stacked the deck against her, that all she could do was save herself.

But if she was enough of a psychic to get those messages, she was ignoring them. She was coming to try to save him, he knew—but it was all for nothing. When she reached the yacht—when she came aboard and put herself in Michael's hands—it would be all over for both of them. Michael would sail out into the rough seas and go someplace where no one would ever find them, and then he would get everything he'd planned for.

Michael had been quite enthusiastic about those plans while Alan was lying in the backseat of his own car.

His own damned car.

Michael had been waiting for him, hidden down on the floorboard, in the shadows, in the back. Had tampered with the interior light so that it didn't come on when Alan put the key in the door lock or when he opened the door. And that was all it had taken.

Alan sat in the driver's seat, and before he could even fasten his seat belt, Michael wrapped a garrote around his throat, jammed the tongue-clip headgear in place, dragged Alan into the backseat, and shoved him to the floorboard. Wired the headgear with two alligator clips and the blinding speed of long practice.

Alan guessed the whole thing had taken less than sixty seconds. The bastard had been faster than a rodeo cowboy in a calf-roping contest, and just as grimly efficient.

And the instant that Alan was secured and helpless, Michael had called Phoebe.

And had driven Alan to a marina, all the while talking to her, telling her what to do, where to go. Alan had listened to Michael's side of the conversation, trying to form pictures of what was happening to Phoebe. It had been terrifying. And then Michael had cut the tape at Alan's ankles, frog-marched him through the first gray light of dawn onto a small, elegant yacht anchored in the churning water of the marina, and retaped his ankles. Hooked him back up to the shock box. And there they'd stayed, while Phoebe drove closer and closer. Alan would have done anything to stop Michael, but even if he could somehow have called for help, he had no idea where to tell help to come. Fort Lauderdale was the Venice of America—there were any number of big marinas in the area and countless small ones.

So he prayed. And he tried to reach her with his thoughts, because he didn't have anything else.

Don't come, he thought at her. Don't come here. Save yourself.

But he heard Michael tell Phoebe, "Now get out of the car. You're going to take a walk on the dock," and any hope he had that she would flee died.

She'd arrived. All Michael had to do was collect her.

chapter 31

"You're going to walk onto the farthest pier to your right," Michael told Phoebe. She looked into the gloom—the water rough, the rain still coming down in hard bursts, the wind gusting.

And she had an idea, though she didn't know if it was a good idea or a stupid one. Sitting in the parking lot, she held the cell phone in front of her. It had about a third of its battery life left.

But she was pretty sure Michael couldn't know that.

From the brief picture she'd seen on the monitor, the camera was behind her, aimed out the windshield. Michael would be able to see the back of her head and the traffic in front of her. A limited picture. If she was careful, it would be limited enough to work for her.

So Phoebe turned the ignition off when Michael told her to, but she left the key in the ignition, dangling from the column and pulled just far enough out that the key warning would not go off as she opened the door. When she opened it, wind gusted into the car cabin. She repositioned her body to block the steering column from view and kept her right hand out of sight.

And tapped the key back into the ignition.

The key alarm chimed.

With her finger hooked through the key ring, Phoebe quickly pulled it most of the way back out.

"What was that noise?" Michael shouted. Phoebe was having trouble hearing him because of all the wind. She hoped he was having the same problem.

Phoebe tapped the key back in, got the chime, and yanked it out again. "Cell phone battery . . . dying!" she yelled over the wind. The car's chime couldn't sound much like the cell phone's actual low-battery signal. But she hoped the wind would mask that.

"Cell phone . . . dying?"

"Yes . . . breaking up . . . no sig—" she shouted, easing her bad leg out of the car.

"FUCK!" he bellowed in her ear, and she turned off the phone.

She didn't know where Michael was. She got out of the car, which was pointed toward the marina. If she stayed behind it, she would be out of sight of the camera.

She looked left and right for any sort of help.

Saw no one.

Phoebe needed to call 911.

But she couldn't just stand there. Michael was coming. She could feel it, even if she couldn't yet see him.

She had only limited places to hide. She couldn't run, or even walk very fast. She couldn't crouch down, she couldn't crawl in the damned dress—the skirt fabric wouldn't protect her knee the way denim did.

So Michael was going to find her. But maybe she could get the police to come to the rescue first.

chapter 32

Michael ripped the headgear and the tongue clamp off of Alan so hard Alan thought the tip of his tongue might have gone with it. Michael cut the tape around his ankles, dragged Alan to his feet by wrapping an arm around his throat and yanking, and jammed the gun back into his ribs.

"If you puke on me, I'll make sure you drown in it," Michael told him, and hauled Alan, stumbling and gasping and partially suffocating, down a narrow corridor and into a small room.

Alan wished he hadn't seen what was in the room. A big butcher-block table occupied the center; manacles punctuated the four corners of that table. The walls were all covered with the sort of perforated fiberboard that men with garage workrooms use to keep their tools organized—and Michael had used the board, painted glossy white, for the same thing. He had categorized his tools, hung them up in sections, outlined every tool in neat red paint, hand-lettered the name of each tool beneath its space. A place for everything and everything in its place.

But only some of his tools had come from a hardware store. Most of the rest looked like Michael Schaeffer had mail-ordered toys from hell.

Bad things were going to happen in this room, Alan

thought, and then Michael shoved a reeking, wet rag up to
Alan's nose and mouth and let go of his neck so that Alan
instinctively gasped.

"Breathe deep, asshole," the bastard said.

And Alan had enough time to think . . . chloroform.

chapter 33

Phoebe got away from the car, working her way down a snaggletoothed row of parked vehicles and empty spaces until she reached an expensive—and large—van. She leaned against it on the street side.

The wind buffeted her, gusts of rain soaked her. And the cell phone didn't seem to be doing too well in this area. Or maybe in the bad weather. She could see the signal-strength line on the left that was supposed to go from the bottom of the screen to the top, but that at the moment only showed one little block.

It's what I have, she told herself. It'll have to do.

She dialed 911. A voice answered, and she shouted over the wind, "My name is Phoebe Rain! I'm at the Bahia Mar marina! My ex-husband, Michael Schaeffer, is trying to kill me. I don't have much time—you have to send help! And get Detective Brig Hafferty! He knows what's going on. Hurry!"

She couldn't hear what the woman was telling her, so she simply shouted the same information over again, hoping that more of it would get through.

"You have to stay on the line," she heard at one point.

Phoebe started to repeat the information again, and suddenly Michael was there, smiling at her.

"I'll take that now," he said, and held out his free hand. She gave Michael the cell phone, wondering where Alan was and if he was still alive. Michael pitched the cell phone into the churning water behind him.

Michael pointed down the dock.

"Walk beside me, sweetheart. We have a wedding to attend. And then our second honeymoon."

chapter 34

Alan opened his eyes. The bastard was gone.

Chloroform. He'd breathed in some of it, but he'd managed to block his airway with the back of his tongue before he took in too much. And Michael had been in a hurry—hadn't held the rag in place long enough to force him to take more breaths. Had failed to completely knock Alan out.

Somewhere outside the yacht, something had gone just a little wrong in Michael's meticulous plan, and Michael had been in a hurry to correct it.

He'd made one tiny mistake.

Had created one feeble chance for Alan to do something.

Alan took stock of his situation. He lay with his hands numb and bound, his good hand injured, the yacht heaving beneath him, in a chamber of horrors that if he didn't do something fast was going to be the last place he ever saw. And Michael was either on his way to get Phoebe or he already had her. Alan couldn't just lie there and die. He had to fight.

He had this one chance.

Alan looked around the walls. Michael had a collection of knives on one set of pegboards, and Alan rolled over until he was beneath them, then managed to get to his knees. His feet wouldn't hold him. He tried to stand, and fell. But on his knees he couldn't reach the knives.

He slammed the pegboard in frustration, and it bounced.

Right. No one made expensive luxury yachts with peg-board walls. Michael had added the pegboard, nailed to fur-ring strips of some sort. If Alan hit the board rhythmically, between the strips, he might be able to get one of the knives to bounce off. He might also be able to get one to drop point-down onto his head and punch a hole in his skull. But he was going to have to chance that.

Alan thumped the wall. One AND two AND three AND four, and the blades were all bouncing, but nothing was shaking loose.

Harder. ONE and TWO and THREE and . . .

A couple of blades bounced free at the same time. One hit the floor and stuck point down in the teak. The other sliced a line across Alan's left forearm that burned like white-hot hell, but he bit back his scream. If Michael was on the ship, Alan didn't dare alert him that the chloroform had worn off.

He grabbed the knife with the smaller handle with his mouth, jammed the point of it into one of the holes in the pegboard to keep it steady, and began sawing at the tape around his wrists.

He couldn't feel his hands. Managed to slice himself a couple of times on both hands, a fact he only discovered once the ropes fell away and blood ran back into his wrists and hands and fingers and started pouring out the holes he'd made in himself.

His hands screamed and burned as life came back to them. He pushed the left one against the pegboard wall, forcing his fingers to straighten until he was actually able to make them move by will and intent. The right one he could flex a little, but with the damage he'd done to himself the day before, it was going to be mostly useless. He fought to get his left hand working, and considered his desperate situation and cursed every second that fled. He staggered to the door of the torture chamber, trying to find his sea legs. Opened it.

Looked left and right. Right looked like it led deeper into

the ship. Not the way Alan wanted to go. Left, he thought, would take him back up the stairs and out onto the aft deck.

And from there, maybe he could get some idea of what he could do to save Phoebe.

He could, he thought, take a goddamned weapon with him for starters. The torture chamber was full of them.

He went back, fighting just to maintain his balance, and grabbed a knife that looked sharp enough to use for surgery.

And then, knife handle clamped between his teeth as if he were a pirate, he grabbed walls and doorways with his one working hand and made his way through the corridor. Still no sign of Michael, nor any sound of him. Good. Maybe Michael was having a hard time finding Phoebe. Maybe she'd gotten away. Maybe . . . just maybe . . . she'd shot the monster and this whole nightmare was over.

But Alan kept the knife, because he wasn't a big believer in miracles.

He reached the stairs at the end of the narrow passageway and went up them, still staggering, and poked his head carefully out of the hatch at the end, and looked around. He was in the middle of a sea of masts and riggings, of furled sails and polished teak and brass fittings beneath dark skies, beneath bursts of lashing rain. Hundreds of ships were moored around him, all of them cross-tied against the storm, all of them rocking and bucking against the battering chop of the bay.

Alan had never liked boats, never cared for the ocean, never dreamed of living a sailor's life. He didn't find anything in this place that resonated with him except for a deep desire to set Michael's fucking yacht on fire and watch it burn to the waterline and sink.

Simple wish, but not one he'd be able to carry out.

No sign of Michael. No sign of Phoebe. What was Alan supposed to do? In all directions he could see only yachts and sailboats. He couldn't wander randomly, hoping to find them and stop them. He didn't want to leave this damnable boat and have them get back to it while he was somewhere else. If he picked a direction and it was the wrong one, Michael could be gone forever, taking Phoebe with him, before Alan could correct the error.

Nor could he take Michael in a straight fight. Michael had a gun. But even if he didn't choose to use it, Alan was hurt, and Michael was not only unhurt, but he was bigger and in extraordinarily good shape. Michael had been putting a lot of effort into his physical therapy since waking up from his coma.

Alan could not let himself sink into despair, though despair was certainly the most tempting direction at the moment.

Then inspiration hit. Hit hard. Alan grinned a little, found the gangplank, and made his way onto the dock.

Michael had cross-tied the yacht between two finger piers to keep it from slamming around during the storm.

Alan ran to the first mooring and cast off the line. Then to the aft one on the same side. The boat and gangplank pulled away from the dock, suddenly loose in the rough water.

And still no sign of Phoebe or Michael.

God. What if Michael had lost his temper and just killed her as soon as he found her?

No. Alan couldn't let himself think that; Michael had been planning his sick reunion fantasy for nearly two years, and he had been obsessive in every detail so far. Nothing Michael had done made Alan think he would deviate an inch from the plan.

Unless someone changed it for him.

Which was where Alan came in.

Alan ran along the dock, around to the other finger pier, and cast the fore and aft moorings there loose as well.

The rough chop of the waves in the marina dragged Michael's yacht forward, out of its slip, into the open waterway.

"Rule change," Alan whispered, watching it go.

And then he realized that Michael would still be coming with Phoebe and that, thwarted in his first plan of taking her into his torture chamber to kill her, he was going to do something unpredictable.

Alan had to be in the right place to save Phoebe when he did.

But what was the right place? And how did Alan get there?

chapter 35

"Where's your gun, Michael? I can't believe you'd do this without a gun."

"I told you that you'd come back to me," Michael said, and his smile stung her. Memories—hellish memories—washed over Phoebe, and for an instant she felt like she *was* drowning. That vision she'd had of going into the sea had felt literal, but this was certainly a bitter foretaste of what was to come for her. "I have your friend in a very special stateroom on my yacht, and each thing that you do that I don't like is going to cost him first. Your phone call to the police is the very first thing I'll punish him for. But everything can always get worse, Phoebe. Always. So you're going to walk with me of your own free will. My beautiful little whore, how I have missed you. And only seeing you when you were sleeping and helpless left something to be desired." He laughed a little. "Awake and helpless is *so* much better."

Phoebe was going to go with him. That was the hell of it. He was going to tell her which way to walk, and she was going to walk beside him, or in front of him, or behind him, because he was right. She would not—could not—leave Alan alone with whatever Michael had planned for him while any chance of saving him remained.

She'd called the police. Maybe her 911 call had been enough. Maybe help was on the way. Maybe it would arrive before Michael could get her where he wanted her and do with her whatever it was that he had planned.

Maybe.

But her vision—of the darkness of the sea swallowing her, of the end of her life coming to claim her—suggested otherwise. Suggested that everything she had done had been futile. Every preparation she had ever made against Michael had been of the wrong sort, every step she had taken had been worthless.

She wanted to live. She wanted to be with Alan. God, she had never wanted anything more in her life than a simple future in which she could wake to see someone who cared for her smiling down at her, brushing her hair back from her face. Not someone. Alan. She knew she would want Alan when she was a hundred—that she would be happy with him. That she had been meant to be with him.

And that Fate had played a cruel trick on her. And on him. And that they were never going to have each other. They were going to share the day of their death, perhaps, but nothing more.

I love him, she swore at the uncaring, unseeing force that had made them so right for each other and given them to each other as a joke at the end of one long hell and the beginning of a short one. I love him and I want him, and I would do anything to have him.

Anything.

But if only one of us can survive this, let it be him.

"You're awfully quiet," Michael said, watching her. "I thought you'd be all full of threats and fury. I thought you would at least be screaming for help."

"I called the police," she said. "They're on the way."

He shrugged. "We aren't going to be here when they get here. Sorry about that. But I do have to credit you with good use of the only resource you had. You were always surprising that way."

"I'll see if I can't come up with a few more surprises for you," she said.

He laughed. "Ah. There you are. The Phoebe I knew. I thought you'd be showing up. Nice to see you again." He turned. "Follow me, dear heart. We're going back to my yacht, and I'm going to let you negotiate for your boyfriend's life."

"Right."

"Oh, I will. I always do what I say I'm going to do, don't I, Phoebe? Whereas you don't."

"How the hell do you figure that?"

"You promised to be my wife until death did us part."

"You promised to love and honor and cherish me."

"I do love you, Phoebe. I honor the bond between us—I have been faithful to that bond as no man ever has been before or ever will be again. And I will cherish these last few days that you and I will spend together."

"Days," Phoebe whispered, remembering Michael's hellish photo-essay on her wall. "Days?"

"I've done a lot of reading on how to keep people alive. Took EMT and paramedic courses. Had doctors teach me all sorts of interesting things. I can start IVs, do minor surgeries, make little repairs to keep your heart beating and your mind functioning. I think, considering the admittedly extreme nature of what I plan, I'll exceed your capacity to survive my art in just a few days. If I'm lucky you may last a week."

A week, she thought.

And Michael wouldn't honor any deals he made regarding Alan, either. Her only hope was that she would see some opportunity to kill Michael before he got her where she was going.

If the police didn't leap out and rescue her. But Michael wasn't even trying to hurry her along—he seemed perfectly content to move at the snail's pace dictated by her damaged knee. So he knew that the police couldn't reach the two of them in time.

Which meant his yacht was close.

She was going to have to do this on her own.

She could, perhaps, catch Michael off balance and knock him into the storm-tossed waters of the marina. He might be eaten by a shark when he fell in, or hit his head on one of the big concrete pillars that drove into the sea—maybe he would drown.

Or maybe he would at least stay down there long enough that she could reach Alan and save him.

Except she had no idea where Alan was.

God.

How was she supposed to survive this? She had nothing.

God, let there be a hungry shark down there waiting, she prayed, and did a little sideways dive and grabbed Michael's knees.

He *did* fall. He just didn't fall into the water.

"I was wondering how long it would take you to try that," he said, sitting up, yanking the wig off her head, grabbing her hair, pulling her face up so that she was forced to look at him. "Nicely done."

"You'd thought of that, and you let me . . ."

"I've thought of everything, Phoebe," he said. "I had a long time where I couldn't do much else *but* think. And you were all I thought of. Aren't you flattered? You should be."

"I want you to die," she said. "I want to be the one to kill you."

"You had your chance." He laughed. "Now it's my turn. C'mon. I don't want to be out here any longer. This is disgusting weather."

She spat in his face.

He slapped her so hard her ears rang, and she tasted blood in her mouth.

If I were one of those berserkers, she thought, I'd taste my own blood and work myself into a frenzy and charge him and rip him to pieces with my bare hands.

It made a pleasant fantasy for the half second she had before he grabbed her throat and yanked her to her feet.

"By the way," he said casually, "that little stunt just cost your whore-mongering friend one body part, no matter what sort of deal you and I work out. But because I love you, I'll let you pick the part." He yanked her forward and she stumbled. "And if you try any more little tricks, we'll do dismemberment on a geometric curve—your next stunt will cost him two body parts, the one after that four, the one after that sixteen . . . and after that, basically I'm stuck dicing him into tiny little cubes. So don't be stupid again, you cunt."

She couldn't let herself think about it. She couldn't let herself believe that Michael would reach his yacht and that she would be his helpless victim. She had to keep fighting, because not fighting was certain death for both of them.

But she had nothing. She had absolutely nothing else that she could do, nothing else that she could think of. Michael had his turf and his plans and his weapons and Alan, and she had the wind and the rain and the taste of her own blood and fear in her mouth.

Michael led her past a dozen multimillion-dollar yachts.

To an empty slip.

He stopped, his head whipping from side to side, his body suddenly rigid, as if no one less than God had slapped him upside the head with a frying pan, and he screamed, "Where the FUCK is my BOAT?"

He turned on her. "Where the fuck is my boat, you bitch? Where is it? Where is it?"

She stared at him. "How the *hell* would I know?"

He slapped her across the face again. "Don't use that kind of language with me, cunt. I *own* you. And don't LIE to me!"

chapter 36

Alan hung half in and half out of the rough water, knowing damned well that he was bleeding into it and knowing there were sharks below him, around him, moving nearer with every second, that were tasting his blood, coming to feast on him, with other monsters in their wake.

Blood in the water.

He clung to the side of the dock, to the tiny rungs, and he prayed that Michael and Phoebe would reach him before the sharks did. He was only going to get one chance, if he got even that, so he prayed that he'd picked the right spot. That he was where he needed to be. That Fate would smile on him and deliver the monster into his reach.

God, he prayed, I don't like to think that I'm in a position to call in chips, but if you're out there, you know I honored my part of the bargain. I did medicine, I've saved lives, haven't asked for much, and I kept my part of the bargain even when you took the most important person in my world away from me. You owe me. You owe me a lot. Let me save Phoebe. That's all I'm asking here. If I die afterward, fine. If I die during, fine, so long as Michael Schaeffer dies first. But I love her, and I didn't think I was ever going to be able to love anyone again. You owe me. One good shot. One good shot and the death of that monster. For her.

He knew uncounted ways to save a man's life. Had never

been able to understand how anyone could kill rather than save.

But he understood now, and he was surprised to discover how useful all his years of putting people back together had become now that he wanted to take one apart. Alan hung there and planned where he would hit Michael with the knife. Where he would drive it in. Presenting parts—he thought of those—if he was facing the bastard, he would have to hit there . . . and there. A side shot would give him two different targets, one on the left, one on the right. A back shot—with a knife and a back shot, Alan thought he could kill the monster well, and quickly. Didn't matter that he had to do it left-handed. Didn't matter what angle he got. He was going to make his shot work for him.

If he just got an angle.

Where the hell were they?

God was playing his cards pretty close to the vest; he didn't give Alan a sign, or an okay, and Alan hung just below the edge of the pier, with waves pounding him and dragging at him and sometimes submerging him for an instant. He was terrified that he was going to be pulled under the water. Terrified of things in the water.

I hate the fucking ocean, he thought.

A wave slammed over him, and he hung on, gasping when it passed, and then he heard Michael's voice over the wind and the rain, screaming, "Where the FUCK is my BOAT?"

Thank you, God, Alan said silently, and poked his head over the edge of the dock.

Michael stood there, his back to Alan, slapping the shit out of Phoebe and screaming at her, accusing her of doing something with his yacht. Beating on her because she was in reach.

Yeah. That fit.

Hang in, Phoebe, he thought, and launching himself out of the water, he took the few steps he needed to reach Michael at a dead run, and punched hard with the knife—in through soft tissue, up, around. Left-handed. His shot wasn't perfect. He'd entered too far left.

He heard Michael grunt.

Blood poured over Alan's hand, hot and sticky.

And then Michael turned, ripping the knife out of Alan's grip in the process, throwing Phoebe halfway down the dock away from the two of them. Onto her back. Michael smashed a fist into Alan's face, and Alan saw stars.

Alan had taken a good shot—but he hadn't severed Michael's spinal cord, hadn't sliced through the ascending aortic artery that ran just in front of it. He'd gotten bowels and maybe a chunk of kidney, but not enough to stop the fucker from hurting Phoebe, if that was what he chose to do.

Alan had half a second to consider possible next moves. And then he was looking down the muzzle of Michael's gun.

And behind him, Phoebe screamed, "You said you didn't have a gun."

Michael shouted, "No. I said I didn't need one." And to Alan he said. "That hurts, you pissant. That hurts enough that I don't think I'm even going to play with you anymore. I'm just going to blow your fucking head into the water while she watches. And then I'm going to take her, and go somewhere with her, and do all the things I was going to do in the first place. You won't get to watch. But all the things I'm going to do to her will make something nice for you to think about as your face goes squirting out the back of your skull."

chapter 37

Phoebe crawled to her feet, saw Alan down on one knee with a gun shoved in his face, saw Michael bleeding with a knife jammed into his back, and all the world seemed to slow to a crawl.

Seemed to freeze.

Got icy cold.

Phoebe shivered, and exhaled, and her breath plumed away from her in a long, thin stream.

Save my daddy, Chick whispered inside her head.

Cold flowed into her right knee, silencing the pain, and Phoebe stared at the knife in Michael's back, and Chick screamed, *Hurry.*

Phoebe did not stop to think. She lunged forward, and her knee held, and her hands wrapped around the knife handle.

In the weird, nightmarish slow motion of dreams, where terrible things unfold at an unstoppable crawl, Phoebe started pulling the knife out. She could see Michael's finger beginning to tighten on the trigger, even as his head started to turn toward her.

She focused on the left side of his back, the place where his heart should be, and with all the strength in her, shoved the blade in between Michael's ribs—and blood spurted against her hands.

But not enough.

Michael's right arm flopped, and the gun went off, not

against Alan's forehead, but lower, and a blood rose bloomed low and to the right on Alan's chest.

And Michael sagged, but fought the gun in his hand back against Alan, who was falling, and Phoebe twisted the knife.

The universe slowed to a molasses crawl.

The bright flood of hot blood as she yanked on the knife.

Michael's arm steadying, his grip on his own handgun solidifying.

His finger tightening on the trigger.

Phoebe yanking the knife out.

His finger tightening.

Her jamming the knife into the side of his neck, blood fountaining from his back, and then from his jugular.

The wobble in his hand, his arm, as the shock of the blood loss overran his adrenaline at last.

The flash from Michael's muzzle, the sound no more than a soft pop above the tearing wind and a sudden burst of slashing rain.

The splash of Michael's blood against Alan's face—Alan's sagging face.

Alan collapsed, and Michael dropped on top of him, and Phoebe dropped the knife and tried to catch Alan.

Felt her knee wrench.

Fell.

Pain—fast hot explosive agony—hatched and ripped and clawed newborn and ravenous into her right knee. Bad pain. Important pain. Doctor-save-me pain.

She screamed at it but kept going, dragged herself in a wounded-dog three-legged crawl to Alan, and rolled Michael partway off of him.

Michael flopped, facing her, and for a moment she froze, staring.

He was looking at her. Right at her, with a fixed stare that chilled her blood—and then she realized that he wasn't blinking. Wasn't breathing. He was, at last, dead.

"Come back from *that,* you fuck," she snarled, and turned her attention to Alan.

She shoved the dead weight of Michael the rest of the way off of Alan, struggling because she was hurt—more than she wanted to think about or face—and the pain in her knee was keeping her from getting good leverage. The air around her got still colder, colder than air *could* be. Inside her head, the child voice screaming, *Hurry! Hurry!*

Cold and terror sucked the breath out of Phoebe's lungs. Her hands trembled. She pulled Alan's shirt up, found two small holes in his chest. One on the left side, one lower and to the right. They looked so small. Little horrible dark holes with blood bubbling out of them, with black edges, powder burns tattooed into gray-white skin.

Alan's eyes were open, but he didn't seem to see her. He wasn't breathing—at least she couldn't see his chest rise or fall—and she screamed at him, "Don't you die on me!" She got to her hands and knees—oh, God, the pain—and worked Alan out from under Michael's body, dully aware of the awful fire in her knee. Of time passing. Her fingers sought for a pulse at Alan's neck, and her cheek felt for the movement of air from his nose and mouth, and she got nothing. Nothing.

The whisper inside her head was fading. Chick was fading, the icy cold was blowing away in the wind and the rain—as if Chick was wearing thin, or had grown tired. Or maybe as if she had given up.

But Chick had one last word for Phoebe.

Believe, she said. And she was gone, and the last of the cold vanished with her.

Phoebe didn't let herself look at the bullet wounds in Alan's chest, at the blood on his shirt and her hands; she didn't let herself think about how hopeless this was. She lifted his jaw to clear his airway and blew two deep breaths into his lungs, and felt his chest rise. And heard bubbling.

Bad sounds.

Don't leave me, she thought.

She found his sternum and, shaking, rested the heel of her left hand on it, and put her right hand atop her left hand. She interlaced her fingers, and lifted them so they didn't touch his chest. Balanced most of her weight on her good knee, because something awful was happening with the bad one, but she didn't have time for that. Not yet. Maybe not ever.

It had been a long time since she'd taken a CPR class, and she fought to recall everything all at once. She knew she had to keep her elbows straight, had to keep the heel of her left hand right on top of his sternum. She mustn't bounce. She could rip up his ribs or even tear holes in his heart if she did this wrong. She didn't dare do it wrong. But she couldn't let fear paralyze her. He wouldn't live without her.

Fifteen counts, she thought, and put the weight of her upper body into the first push. "One and two and three and four . . ." she counted out loud, doing one compression at each count.

Her life, lived in shadows, streamed in front of her eyes. The shadows of what might have been, endlessly replayed; of what might have been prevented, endlessly regretted; of who she might have become had she not chosen so badly, allowed foolish honor and pride to keep her from listening to her screaming instincts, if she had only . . .

Everyone had regrets, though. Everyone looked in the mirror one day and said, "If only I had . . ."

She'd taken her risk at last, had let herself find love and experience true happiness. Bittersweet though these days since she'd met Alan had been because they showed her how hollow she had let her life become. These few glorious days meant everything to her. She had, at last, truly lived.

Please, God, if you're up there, if you're paying any attention to this, don't let me screw this up. Let me do it right. I just found him. I've waited my whole life, and I just found him. Please don't let me lose him this way.

I love him. I never even dared tell him that, but I love him. Please give me the chance to tell him.

Fifteen compressions, two breaths, fifteen compressions, two breaths, check for a pulse, check for breathing, start over.

He promised me we were going to make it out of this. He promised me we were both going to make it out of this.

The silence of the night moved through her and around her.

"I love you," she told him, feeling for his pulse, praying for his breath, finding nothing. "You have to live. Because you promised me." She fought against tears, against the swelling in her throat, against her own ragged breathing that would interfere with what she had to do to—to breathe for him, to make his heart beat for him. To hang on for him.

Believe. She didn't know if she could believe. She didn't know if she had any belief left in her.

She had never felt so alone.

chapter 38

Alan knew Phoebe was trying to save him. He could hear her voice, could hear the tremor in each word as she counted compressions, knew he was lying on the dock in a pool of blood, beside a dead man. He knew there were holes in his chest—right side, left side, a lot of damage. His professional opinion was that he didn't have much of a chance.

He could feel the thin thread that tied him to his body, a tiny glowing lifeline. He could stay, he thought.

But a breeze blew behind him, fresh and sweet as Kentucky springtime, and the sound of the rain pattered on glass, and he turned away from the sad scene on the dock—the pretty dark-haired woman fighting off tears, fighting to save a life, the dead man, the dying man—and he found an open window, yellow-and-white gingham curtains blowing, and on the other side a sky heavy with clouds, air hazed with a sweeter, gentler rain. He walked to the window, hoping, praying.

If any more of these windows open, don't go through them, Phoebe had told him, and he remembered that. But he looked out the window, and Chick was on the other side, sitting on a tire swing they'd had in their backyard, spinning in low, lazy circles. When she saw him, she smiled and called, "Daddy!" and for the first time in so very long, he heard her beautiful voice.

He did not let himself think about what lay behind him,

even when he heard Phoebe's voice say, "I love you. An
you promised me." His little girl was out there in the rai
and he was going to be with her again.

He climbed through the window, and there was no dro
He was simply and easily on the other side, and the we
grass swished around his ankles and the breeze was fres
and pure, and Chick's smile was so bright and beautiful h
would never need to see the sun again.

She clambered out of the tire swing and came running t
him, arms held wide, and he dropped to his knees and em
braced her. She was taller, but not much taller, older but n
much older. Time had passed for her, but nowhere near a
quickly as it had passed for him.

He pulled her close and hugged her, buried his nose in he
hair, smelled her little-girl scent that was shampoo and sur
shine and flowers and lovely spring rain rolled all togethe
"God, I missed you," he said.

"I was always with you, Daddy," she told him. "A part c
me will always be with you. Always." She kissed his chee
and he felt the brush of her eyelashes against his skin, an
he felt her arms tighten around him—little thin arms aroun
his neck, little hands patting his back. The same hands tha
he had held when she was first learning to walk, and late
when they were crossing streets or hiking over roug
ground. They were hands he'd thought he would hold whe
she grew up and walked down the aisle to marry som
young man who would love her and cherish her.

That hadn't happened. But now he had won his way bac
to her. He had his little girl again.

"I missed you more than you could ever know," he saic
And he smiled at her, joyous, triumphant.

But she shook her head. "I do know. I watched. And
waited for you, Daddy, because I was afraid you woul
come here. But you can't stay here. And neither can I."

She seemed taller as she said that, and her voice seeme
less a little girl's voice.

"No," he said. "I just found you."

But she was stretching, growing taller, turning into a
oman before his eyes, and when she spoke, her voice was
woman's voice. "You have your whole life ahead of you,
id I'm dead, and you have to move on. You have to let go
f me now. You have to live; you have so much to live for.
ou have Phoebe. And babies waiting for you to be their fa-
er. A whole future back there."

She pulled away, a woman with his daughter's face, tall
id beautiful and confident as he had always dreamed she
ould be. "I love you, Daddy," she said. "I will always love
ou. But I'm done now. I did what I came to do. We had as
ng as we had—as long we were supposed to have. You and
. . . we chose this before I was born, and before you were
orn. I had to leave you back when Mamma was so terrible
that I could be with you today. Right here, right now. To
ve you the secret you've been waiting for your whole life.
had to be here when you needed me, to tell you to go back.
nd this was the only way we could do that."

"I'll always need you." He looked at her, pleading with
s eyes for his child suddenly grown to womanhood to tell
m what he wanted to hear.

Instead she said, "You have to hurry, Daddy. Phoebe
eds you. You were meant for each other. For here, for
w, for forever. But if you don't hurry, it will be too late."

The pain was there again—the pain that had swallowed
m the day Chick died and that had never gone away. He'd
ft his little girl in a white box on a green hill, and the only
ing in the world he'd wanted to do was crawl in there with
r and let the earth fall down on top of him. And now he
d her back. He was holding her hands and looking into her
es and she was warm and real and alive, and she was
ling him that he had to leave her behind again. He didn't
ink he could do it.

She seemed to know what he was thinking, because she
iped the tears from his cheeks and smiled at him—the
nile that had wrenched his heart a dozen times a day from
e very first time he saw it. "It'll be okay, Daddy. I prom-

ise. I'll be waiting when you get back. When you're *su*
posed to be here. Hand me my lucky stone. Let it go, let r
go with it. If you let it go, it will free us both."

She kissed his cheek, and he believed her—that s'
would be there, that she wasn't lost. But letting go was
hard.

Still, he dug into his pocket, into his wallet, and pulled o
her lucky stone, the stone that had been his solid link
her—that had been with her the day she died and that h
been with him every day since.

She had survived. They were eternal, the two of them. F
ther and daughter, and eternity would still be there when
was supposed to return. He could let go of the stone. I
could set her free, and himself as well.

He handed her the stone, and she smiled. "Thank yo
she said. "Go, and live the life you were meant to live."

She shimmered away into the rain, a rainbow vanishi
while its promise lingered.

Alan started back into the darkness and the pain of li
carrying that promise as he had carried the pebble in his w
let—holding it in a safe place in his heart where nothi
could take it away.

chapter 39

walkie-talkie somewhere in the distance. A voice shouted,
"Ten thirty-three at Dock F, Bahia Mar. Out on the finger
[pi]ers, multiple victims, CPR in progress on one, dispatch
[ex]tra rescue units and backup."

Phoebe heard running. Behind the footsteps, sirens in the
[di]stance ripped through the night, getting closer, closer—
[an]d it should have been the sweetest sound she had ever
[he]ard. It should have been.

Believe, Phoebe told herself. But Alan wasn't breathing,
[hi]s heart wasn't beating.

Believe.

Chick's voice in her memory—the little girl's sudden
[co]nfidence. *Believe.* She'd been sure Phoebe could save her
[fa]ther.

Phoebe stopped CPR again, rested her fingers against
[Al]an's throat, and almost yanked her hand away at the deli-
[ca]te flutter under her fingertips.

"Alan," she whispered. The pulse was really there, getting
[st]ronger beneath her fingertips. She rested her cheek an inch
[ab]ove his face, but no breath moved. She lifted his jaw and
[m]ade sure she had a clear airway, and exhaled, willing him
[to] hang on. Her fingertips found the pulse at his throat, and
[sh]e closed her eyes and just breathed, and let the reassuring
[pr]esence of his beating heart carry her on.

"I'm with you," she told him, and breathed. Slow, deep

breaths. And between the breaths, "I'm with you. Stay wi
me. I love you."

And then strangers were with her. Cops. The good gu
had arrived at last.

"Alan has a . . . pulse again," she managed to tell the
between breaths. "He isn't breathing. And . . . I hurt n
knee. . . . A little. . . . It was hurting pretty bad. . . . Not
bad now, but . . . I feel kind of . . . funny. . . . They have
save him."

Sirens dopplered louder and then died to silence, and r
flected lights in red and blue and white danced across t
white ships, the black sea, the gray sky. Phoebe heard cla
tering metal behind her, stretchers being unfolded.

Feet running. And Brig, beside her, muttering, "Oh, Jes
look at this."

And between breaths she whispered to Alan, "I lo
you. . . . I love you. . . . I love you," and prayed that l
would hear her.

"Hurry up!" Brig yelled, and Phoebe heard answerir
shouts, but what they said she would never know. Sl
breathed for Alan, and someone put a big box beside her ar
opened it, and someone else said, "I have a pulse here
thready and fast. Let's get some Ringer's started, wide ope
two lines, and pressure dressings on those chest woun
and see if we can find the exit wounds."

She looked up at them—at the faces of strangers dete
mined to save Alan. And Brig, looking grim and fierce ar
scared all at the same time. She turned, thinking that sl
would tell him what had happened, thinking that it was
funny that everyone seemed to be running towards h
through a graying tunnel.

And she tried to get to her feet, and the last thing sl
heard was, "Grab her, she's going down!"

chapter 40

Alan lay in the darkness for a long time—it seemed like forever. Pain hazed his vision, slammed him with every movement of his chest. Something was breathing for him, and it hurt. He wanted it to stop.

He could remember things. Impossible things. The ghostly dreams of a dying man. They hadn't meant anything, had they? Had they been real? Had any of it been real?

He'd thought at first that Chick had come back to him. He'd thought that his future held some promise.

But the darkness went on, and on, and on, and with it the pain, and he waited for voices that should have been there—and for one voice in particular that had been the reason he thought he'd come back from death. That voice never came.

Maybe I'm still dead, he thought. Maybe this is hell.

But it was a hell with familiar sounds. Nurses titrating drips, rattling carts, turning off beeping monitors, talking to each other as if they alone existed in this dark little universe of pain.

Sometimes they would talk to him, but it was always in that awful we-don't-think-you-can-hear-us-but-we're-doing-this-anyway voice that made him think he was a lost cause.

Then he realized he could see light, and after a while he could make out shapes, and the fact that he had his eyes open generated a lot of excitement. But not from the right people. Only from nurses. And doctors, but not doctors he knew. Not anyone he knew.

Where was he? *When* was he?

And he remembered with sudden horror his attempt to kill a man on a dock, but in the haze that surrounded him, he couldn't remember much else. He was a doctor, though. Doctors weren't supposed to be murdering big men out in the middle of . . .

Storms.

He tried to focus on the storm, because there was something there that was helping this come back to him—storms and boats and knives.

"Up his morphine—he's thrashing again and he's going to rip all those tubes out and if he does he'll bleed out before we can do a goddamn thing."

That made sense in a disconnected way. He might have said such a thing once.

He faded back into darkness.

When he woke again, the pain was sharp and focused, and he was breathing on his own.

His throat hurt like hell. His mouth was dry and tasted like weasels had being partying and raising their young in there for a year or two. His chest blazed in agony, accompanied by the symphony of fire that was his back.

"Hey," he tried to yell, and it came out as a strangled cough.

He was in an ICU. In a bed with side rails. One of those rails would have a nurse call button somewhere on it—but he could hear frantic noises somewhere down the corridor: people crying and being shooed from the room, nurses moving heavy equipment, the whump of defibrillator paddles.

Code going on, he thought, and realized he was going to be by himself until that was over.

He remembered everything, though. The drugged haze they'd been keeping him in had bled away, replaced by the sort of pain that would snap a corpse to attention.

He knew a lot of what had been going on around him;

much more than he would have expected to know. He remembered being shot. He remembered Phoebe doing CPR on him, telling him over and over that she loved him, begging him to live, reminding him that he had promised her they would get through the hell of Michael and his evil. He remembered Chick, though he couldn't be sure that was a real memory. He wanted it to be. It had been so sad, but at the same time so full of hope.

But Phoebe hadn't been in to see him. Not once. Some part of his mind had been listening for her, had been holding on desperately to the last things he'd heard her say to him. "I love you . . . I love you . . . I love you . . ." Because he had wanted so much to believe it.

She hadn't been to see him.

Neither had Brig.

Neither had Morrie.

He could vaguely remember his mother's voice. His father's. His brothers'.

He was grateful for those memories—but he wanted to know what had happened, and only Brig and Morrie and Phoebe could tell him that.

He wanted to know if Chick had been right. If he had a future.

He wanted to know if that last encounter with Chick had been real—and that he knew he could never know, but he was getting the feeling that it had been the wishful thoughts of a dying brain.

He wanted so much.

"Call it," he heard a doctor say. "Nothing else we can do here."

Down the hall the code had ended—badly.

People moved into the halls again—heavy steps—some of the nurses, checking down the rooms. The doctor, chart in hand.

One of the nurses poked her head in his room, and he croaked, "Hey!" and still sounded like the voice from the grave in some horror film.

"Hey!" she answered. "You're awake."

She came in, started poking and prodding him, checking dressings, making him breathe, swabbing out his mouth, giving him little sips of ice because she said technically he was still NPO but maybe she would be able to get that order changed so that he could have some clear liquids as soon as his doctor had a chance to come in to see him.

He had a hard time getting a word in edgewise, or getting her to understand it when she finally stopped for breath.

"How . . . long?"

"You've been here for four days. You were in surgery once for the . . ." She paused, looking worried. "Do you remember what happened?"

"Yes. Gunshot."

She looked relieved. She was too young—when did they start putting twelve-year-olds in uniform and turning them loose in the ICU on unsuspecting patients? "Yes. That's right. You were in surgery for fourteen hours for the gunshot wounds. You've been on a ventilator for two days following that, on a morphine drip and some other things so that we could keep you in twilight sleep while you stabilized. We weaned you off as quickly as we could—you have done remarkably well, by the way. And here you are."

"I . . . hurt."

"Yeah. You're going to. You've had ribs stretched and cracked and everything put back together. You might as well have had elephants dancing the mambo on your chest, with everything your doctors did to get you put back in one piece and working again. I'll let Dr. Fletcher give you all the details." She smiled at him, a smile far too cheerful, and said, "But you're going to pull through."

"Can you . . . bring me . . . my wallet?" he asked her. Because part of the dying dream had been about the wallet. About the stone. Chick's translucent white lucky stone, which would have been a perfect skipping stone, Chick's stone, with its faded blue forget-me-not painted on one side.

He'd seen that stone in his last dream of her. He remembered handing it to her. Promising her that he would let it go. Let *her* go.

But that had been in a dream.

The nurse said, "As soon as I let Dr. Fletcher know that you're back with us." She bounced off. He almost expected her to skip.

Alan wanted to hold the stone. He could look at it and try to find the truth of the dream, if there was any truth in the stone's smooth surfaces. Maybe he should give it up in real life the way he had when Chick had asked him for it.

His mother came in while he was lying there thinking. She looked tired. Worn. He'd never actually seen her look so old. And he thought, That's my fault. I did this to her.

But she smiled at him. "Your brothers are out in the waiting room, and so is your father. They'll be in soon, but when the nurse told me you were awake, I claimed first visit by myself."

"I'm glad you're here."

"I can say the same thing. I know a lot of what happened, Alan—the *what*. The *how*. But I don't know *why*. I have tried to understand how you ended up being on that dock with those two people. I understand that you're a hero—that you are the reason that woman is alive right now. But . . . why you?"

He wanted to say, "I don't know." He wanted to say that he had done a foolish thing, that he had been in the wrong place at the wrong time, that nothing that had happened meant anything more than just him on a dock in the rain because he was That Kind of Guy. Because That Kind of Guy wouldn't have his heart broken when, after all the hell was over, the heroine never called him back.

But he clearly wasn't That Kind of Guy, because he opened his mouth and said, "I was in love with her, Mom. I would have done anything for her. Would have died for her."

His mother smiled. Actually smiled. "Really? In love? I'd so hoped . . ."

"Don't hope. Phoebe hasn't been here since this happened. I've heard everyone's voices, even when I couldn't answer. And she hasn't been here."

His mother stared at him. "Of course she . . . Wait. You haven't heard . . . Well, no—I don't suppose anyone *has* told you." She took a deep breath, and her face went bleak.

Alan shivered, that goose-on-the-grave feeling that sent his pulse skittering. "Told me what?"

"Phoebe couldn't have come here. She almost died saving your life. Something happened to one of her legs, and she ignored it, kept doing CPR on you until help arrived, and she nearly bled to death. She's still in serious condition over at your hospital right now."

His hospital. "Where am I, then?"

"Mount Sinai. Northridge didn't have the specialists they had to use to put you back together."

He digested that for a moment. He was glad there'd been specialists who could do what had to be done—but he wasn't thrilled to know it had been such a big deal.

"How's Phoebe now?"

"Well . . . they were going to amputate her leg because it would have been less expensive and apparently she doesn't have any money. But we told your hospital that we would cover any costs that you couldn't—to save her leg if they could. We figured she'd saved your life. We owed her that much. We didn't know about the two of you." And his mother smiled again. "You're really in love with her? I'm so happy. I thought after Janet and Chick . . ." And she faltered, tears in her eyes. "I didn't think you would ever find anyone again."

"I don't know that I have, Mom. I've never told her how I feel about her. I can't swear that she feels about me the way I feel about her. I *think* she does. But, it . . . wasn't something we talked about."

Somewhere else in the unit, Alan heard a flurry of activity: hurrying of feet, voices speaking low and fast and urgent, the movement of heavy equipment, the ward secretary going from room to room, closing doors and asking visitors to leave.

"They have another code, Mom," he said. "You'd better go."

She kissed him. And smiled. And said, "Believe, Alan."

And then she was gone, leaving him to consider all the things he might possibly believe in.

chapter 41

Phoebe stared out the window of her hospital room at the bleak, hard sunlight, the weary palm trees, the unending traffic. Too hot, too flat, too bleached, she thought. She was waiting for Brig, who'd said he would come by to take her home, since she didn't have anyone else. He said he'd found a place for her to stay—at least temporarily—since she couldn't go back to the place where she'd been.

Brig was running late. More than an hour late last time she checked. Not that it mattered.

Discharge day had rolled around at last, and she should have been glad. She had her leg. It hurt, but it was better than it had been, and it would keep getting better with continued physical therapy.

A pin had slipped loose and punctured an artery that day on the dock. She'd been sure she was going to lose her leg. But her orthopedic surgeon had put in an artificial joint for her that used fixative. And no pins. And told her that she would get to keep her leg after all.

She had a long way to go, but she was sure she would get there.

"What's wrong?"

Phoebe jumped a bit. Brig was quieter than a big man ought to be. She turned away from the window. "I'm just blue," she said. "Nothing important."

He said, "Sorry I'm late. But I have to thank you."

"For what?"

"I investigated that lead you gave me."

"Lead?"

"The one about the missing girl, and the diary. And the lockers."

Phoebe hadn't thought about that since she'd done the reading for Alan. Her mind had been on other things. "What did you find?"

"I found my missing girl." Nothing in his stance suggested that his news was any happier than her reading would have led her to believe. "Her father killed her. He'd been molesting her for some time, but she was getting older. And she had a younger sister. When he started looking at her sister, she threatened to tell, and in fact wrote down what had been happening in a school journal. She figured her father wouldn't read it, because it was where she kept her homework. She was wrong."

"What about the lockers?"

"There is a very exclusive private gym in Coral Springs that her father belonged to. I had another case there once. They have these tony brushed-aluminum lockers—never saw anything like them anywhere else. Big things. What was left of his kid after he burned her to ash was in his. And my partner just located her journal in the bastard's safe at work, which seals the whole deal for us. Wanted a couple of souvenirs, I guess. He gave us motive, method, and body. We've got the guy."

"I'm sorry it didn't turn out any happier," Phoebe said. "It would have been nice if I'd been wrong about her being dead."

Brig said, "Neither you nor I could have saved her. By the time she was reported missing, she was already dead. But her sister has a chance now, and she wouldn't have if we hadn't found out what happened to our victim." He paused. "Your nurse been in to do all that paperwork with you?"

"Yes. She said I'm just waiting on some prescription, and then I can go home."

"You really do look down."

"I am, I guess. I kept hoping we'd at least be able to stop by and see Alan, but his brother said he still isn't up to visitors." She sighed. "I don't belong in this place."

"I'll go get a wheelchair for you, then, and we'll get you out of here."

Phoebe hadn't been talking about the hospital when she said that, but she didn't correct Brig. He'd been very kind the whole time she'd been in the hospital. So why make him feel like nothing he could do would help her?

She turned back to the window. She wanted to be far away from Fort Lauderdale, but she didn't have anywhere to go or any way to get there. She had been in the hospital for twelve days—three times as long, the nurses told her, as someone who'd had a knee replacement usually needed. But Phoebe had come in with complications—nearly bleeding out, nearly losing her leg. The nurses assured her that considering everything she'd had to contend with, she was doing great.

But she'd spent twelve days not working. During her hospital stay she hadn't logged on once. She hadn't kept up her time in the days before her last encounter with Michael, either. Which meant she had destroyed her priority ranking with Psychic Sisters. She also hadn't made rent, hadn't covered the cost of those locks in her bank account. Hadn't pulled in enough to pay electric, or water, or phone.

Not that she could have gone home if she'd had the money, because her home was a crime scene and it was going to be months before anyone could live there. Phoebe never wanted to walk through those doors again.

Brig said he'd found her a temporary place where she could stay for free for a while. That helped. But what was she going to do long term? She didn't know.

And she didn't know how her situation with her life would affect her relationship with Alan.

Alan had moved out of ICU a few days earlier, and she had been able to talk to him by phone a couple of times. He said he was doing pretty well for a guy who'd been ripped from stem to stern. She told him about how her leg was doing and thanked him along with his family for covering her bills. She kept the conversations light—he didn't need her worries when he was fighting so hard to get better.

He hadn't been strong enough to talk for long, either, and she could always hear people in and out of his room, which made it impossible for them to talk about anything that really mattered.

Alan *had* mentioned that he had some important things to tell her when they were both out of the hospital—he said that they weren't the sort of things one said on the phone.

She had wanted so much to tell him that she loved him. To say it when he could hear her. When he could tell her how he felt, too.

She knew she loved him. She hoped he felt the same way about her.

But she didn't *know* how he felt. And the waiting, and the uncertainty mixed with the absolute bewilderment she felt facing her own future were almost more than she could take.

Behind her, the rattle of a wheelchair, and a thud as it bumped into the heavy hospital door. Brig moved quietly enough on his own, but Phoebe didn't think he sounded like he knew how to drive a wheelchair.

"Hey. You ready to get out of here?"

And it wasn't Brig behind her. Her heart thudded, and suddenly the air in the room was so thin she almost couldn't breathe.

She turned, not daring to hope for anything good from this, praying that she wouldn't show too much of what she felt in her face. "Alan," she whispered. "Your brother told me you were too weak to have visitors."

He looked thinner. He looked pale. But he was standing up, even if he did look suspiciously like he was leaning on the wheelchair to do it. He was smiling at her. He was alive.

And he was there. He grinned. "He lied. I told him to. I wanted to surprise you."

"I'm surprised."

"Can you stand to be in this room for a few more minutes?" he asked. "I wanted to talk to you as soon as I could. Brig has promised to keep everyone else out of here until I yell for him. I'm not sure when we'll have any time alone again for . . . well, quite a while. And this really shouldn't wait."

She nodded, and swallowed hard, and carefully made her way to the hard hospital bed. She sat on the edge of it.

He sat on the bed, too, but not right beside her. Not touching her.

"I died out there on the dock," he said.

"I know."

"I found that window again. The one you said I shouldn't go through. The one where Chick . . . where she was waiting for me. She was waiting to tell me good-bye. Things happened while I was there that I can't explain."

Phoebe thought about Chick begging her to save Alan, and the disappearing pain in her leg right before she ran for the knife.

Alan pulled a wallet that had seen better days out of his pocket. "In the place where she and I met, Chick asked me to give her back her lucky stone. To let go of her, so that she could move on to whatever was waiting for her, and so that I could move on with my life."

He opened the wallet, and Phoebe could see the dent where the lucky stone had been. But the stone wasn't there anymore.

"It was gone when they brought me to the hospital. The admitting nurse wrote down the contents of the wallet, and she swears there was not a stone in there when I was admitted." He looked down at his hands, at the worn leather in them, and he sighed. "I can think of a dozen logical explanations for how that stone came to not be in the wallet." He took a deep, unsteady breath, and looked up into her eyes. "And I don't believe a one of them. I think Chick took her stone back. And moved on. That she's safe and well somewhere. That she is always going to be safe. And well. I know it doesn't make sense. But I believe it."

"Something happened to me while we were out there, too. I don't have an explanation for it, either. Not one. And so far nobody has asked me about it, so I haven't had to say anything."

"What happened?"

She told him about Chick's voice. About her knee. About that last single message: *Believe.*

He nodded. "She was there. She was there for both of us, because . . ." He fell silent for a moment. "She told me something about the future. My future. And how it's supposed to be. But she made some . . . some assumptions. And despite everything that's happened, *I* can't just make those assumptions." He cleared his throat, and her heart skipped a beat. "I have to ask. I have to know," he said.

Phoebe nodded, her mouth dry.

"I love you, Phoebe. And . . . I have to know if you love me."

"I love you," she whispered.

He let out a short breath, and she saw his shoulders relax. "Then I can get through the rest of this. I know we haven't known each other long, but we've already had our 'for worse.' We made it through that. And I love you more now than I did before. But I want to have you for better, too. I don't want to spend a single day of my life not seeing you, not holding you, not touching you. I don't ever want to be away from you again."

Phoebe was trying hard to hear him over the roaring in her ears. Trying to believe what he was saying.

And then he said, "You may not be ready to marry me yet, Phoebe. You may not be ready to trust anyone that much again. But I want you to know that I'll wait. I'll wait as long as it takes, I'll wait forever if that's how long you need to make up your mind. But I want to be with you every day while I'm waiting." He very carefully dropped down on one knee and looked into her eyes. "I love you," he said. "I have never loved anyone the way I love you, and I never will again. Be with me. Be with me in whatever way you'll have me. Come with me and love me, and I promise if you say you don't want to marry me and you don't want me to ask you, I'll never ask you again."

He pulled something out of his back pocket. "But . . . just this once, let me ask." He opened a black velvet box and held a ring up to Phoebe. And Alan said, "Marry me, Phoebe. For now and forever."

Stillness hung between them. Unimaginable risks loomed before them, chasms of uncertainty sprawled between them. There were a million things Phoebe would never know about Alan, and every one of them was a risk. That someday, somehow, he could hurt her.

And yet, inside her heart, Chick's final admonition still echoed.

Believe.

Phoebe looked into Alan's eyes and whispered, "Yes."

Alan pulled her close and held her carefully.

"Why didn't you want to wait until we were out of here to ask me?"

"Because my whole family is outside those doors waiting for us. And my friend Morrie, too—finding a snack machine, I think—but he wants to meet you as soon as we can get by his place." Alan rubbed his forehead. "You and I are going to be lucky to get another moment alone before . . . well . . . tonight, now, I guess, but I wasn't sure if I could talk you into coming home with me."

"Do you want me to? Right away, I mean? Are you ready for me to . . . be there?"

"Phoebe, I've been waiting for you my whole life, though I didn't know it. I've been waiting even longer than that, I think. And I want the rest of forever to start right now."

They delayed the wedding until everyone who mattered to them could be there: Brig to give her away, Morrie as Alan's best man, Toeller from the FBI as guest of honor.

They held a quiet service, celebrating those who were there, but remembering the price of their happiness. The price of their love.

Alan found them a place in western Kentucky, and after the wedding the two of them traded the noise and over-crowding and endless heat of South Florida for seasons and green hills and small-town life. A family of their own if they were lucky. Time with Alan's family and their friends and the families they would eventually have if fortune didn't favor Alan and Phoebe with babies of their own.

Phoebe walked down the aisle with Brig and stood with Alan before the minister. Took Alan's hand. Said her vows. And sent a prayer of thanks to Chick, who had reached be-yond death to give Alan and her the gift of each other. Who had given them her love and helped them find their own.

Love, Phoebe thought, was stronger than evil, and stronger than death. Love could move the stars in the heav-ens, or a single pebble in a man's wallet.

She squeezed Alan's hand and felt him squeeze back.

Love, real love, lived forever.

For her. For him. Until the end of time.

Holly Lisle has been writing professionally since 1991 and has published more than twenty novels to date. You may find out more about her at www.hollylisle.com.

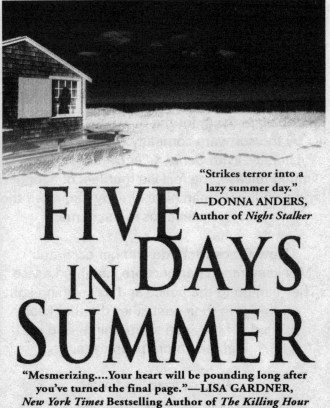

"Strikes terror into a
lazy summer day."
—DONNA ANDERS,
Author of *Night Stalker*

FIVE DAYS IN SUMMER

"Mesmerizing....Your heart will be pounding long after
you've turned the final page."—LISA GARDNER,
New York Times Bestselling Author of *The Killing Hour*

KATE PEPPER

0-451-41140-4

Monkeewrench

by P.J. TRACY

"FAST, FRESH, FUNNY, AND OUTRAGEOUSLY
SUSPENSFUL...THE DEBUT THRILLER OF THE YEAR."
—HARLAN COBEN

People are dying for the new computer game
by the software company Monkeewrench.
Literally. With *Serial Killer Detective* out in
limited release, the real-life murders of a jogger
and a young woman have already mimicked the
first two scenarios in the game.

Now Grace McBride and her eccentric
Monkeewrench partners are caught in a vise.
They can go to the police and risk shining light
on things in their pasts they'd rather keep
buried. Or they can say nothing—and let
eighteen more people die.

"A KILLER READ." —*PEOPLE*

0-451-21157-X

**Available wherever books are sold or at
www.penguin.com**